Fr... ...e Hampshire/Sussex border, at a time when her parents were just settling down from their life on the road. Her mother was descended from generations of fairground travellers and her father came from a circus family. The first person in her family ever to have a full education, Frances attended Chichester, Petersfield and Slough grammar schools before reading History at the University of London and then training as a teacher at Sussex University. Frances Brown is married and lives in Malvern, Worcs.

Dancing on the Rainbow

Frances Brown

HEADLINE

First published in 1991
by HEADLINE BOOK PUBLISHING PLC

First published in paperback in 1991
by HEADLINE BOOK PUBLISHING PLC

10 9 8 7 6 5 4 3 2 1

ISBN 0 7472 3691 7

Typeset in 10/11¼ pt Times
by Colset Private Limited, Singapore

Printed and bound by
HarperCollins Manufacturing, Glasgow

HEADLINE BOOK PUBLISHING PLC
Headline House
79 Great Titchfield Street
London W1P 7FN

For Foronda

Chapter One
1865

'No, no, *no*! You are not to carry on polishing,' the housekeeper screeched at her. 'Your job is just to start the shine, Mirella. How many times do I have to tell you?'

Mirella slapped the spoon down on the pile to her right without answering. But her expression must have provoked Mrs Newbolt into continuing with her harangue.

'Right, well let me say it again . . .' That voice! Fussy as a jay's. Mirella gritted her teeth to prevent herself saying something that would immediately be dubbed "saucy" and earn her a further rebuke. But really, the stupidity of it all! 'Mary puts the polish on. Ellen takes it off. You, Mirella Granger, will start to give the shine, but then it's for Millie to bring up full lustre. Got it now, Missie?'

Mirella nodded her head, wanting only to bring the tirade to an end and sink back into her own reverie.

An "honour", that's how her mother had described this chance to work in the royal household at Windsor, but then she wasn't the one who had to black the grates, whiten the doorsteps and scrub the floors. Sadie seemed interested only in having her elder daughter off her hands.

Mirella bit her lip. Why, why did she always feel so wretched when she thought about her mother? Because she knew she was such a disappointment to

1

her. She loved Sadie and wanted more than anything else to please her, but no matter how hard she tried, she always seemed to let her down. Still, this job should change all that – which is why she had set her heart on making such a success of it.

Sadie's obvious delight when her daughter was taken on at the castle made Mirella realise that here was her opportunity to impress her mother and show what she could do, and she had immediately resolved to be the very best scullery-maid there ever was, work so hard she could not fail to gain advancement, become a parlour-maid perhaps. Sadie would really like that: her daughter a parlour-maid at the palace. Mirella could almost hear her boasting of it to the neighbours.

Mirella sighed as she picked up another lacklustre spoon and urged herself to stop daydreaming and concentrate on her work. The trouble was, she could not stop her thoughts drifting away from these sorts of tasks because she found them so boring. And was it surprising? A healthy thirteen year old, used to spending most of her time out of doors, and here she was, trapped for hours on end in dank, smelly rooms surrounded by empty-headed girls doing menial chores. But what made it worse was that she had only been here a few weeks and had already fallen foul of the housekeeper, Mrs Newbolt, who seemed to be especially on the lookout to find fault with anything she did.

She looked at the woman now, in her white apron and dimity grey dress, officious clutch of keys hooked at her waist. She could hardly suppress a giggle, for Mrs Newbolt looked so much like Mrs Punchinello – what with her long pointed nose and the high colour on her cheek bones, heightened with rouge for some reason that Mirella found hard to imagine. And then those four front teeth snaring her lower lip as if it were some poor fleshy creature caught in a trap, and the

2

fact that her steel spectacles magnified her glassy grey eyes and gave her an expression of constant irritability. But most of all, it was the presence of the little bow of red ribbon worn on her white cap to distinguish it from those worn by the lower servants that reminded Mirella of the whining puppet.

'Put polish on, take polish off, burnish, then shine. *That's* how we clean the silver, Missie. But if you've got a better way, I'm standing here – we're *all* standing here – ready to listen to it,' she said with the sort of exaggerated patience that caused the other girls to titter at Mirella's expense.

This is how it was all the time. Stupid, petty little routines to be learnt and followed. Mirella's whole spirit rebelled against them.

She rubbed away at the bowl of a soup spoon, thinking: Gracious, don't I look awful upside-down? All nose and chin. Ah, that's better! (Rubbing on the convex side now, slowly so that she had time to examine her face.) Was it so obvious . . . ?

'Child, you look like a gypsy,' Mrs Newbolt had said when handing out her uniform on that first day. 'Is it true what they say, that your mother has dark blood?'

Well, how was she supposed to answer that? Say honestly: 'Yes, Ma'am. Both my mother and father travelled the fairs before Father settled down to his gamekeeper's job, and I probably get my dark looks from my mother's family who were true Romany.' No. Without hesitation she had in fact said: 'Oh no, Ma'am. I get my black hair and brown eyes from my grandmother on my father's side. She lives in a big house in Aldershot. Everyone says I take after her.' Which was true, if not quite the point.

'Come on, girl. Stop day-dreaming. We've forks to do next, and you're holding us all up.'

Mirella groaned. She had acquired an irrational hatred of forks since discovering they were the subject

3

of another of Mrs Newbolt's petty routines. It was not sufficient to rub all their accessible surfaces. You had to reach – and be seen to reach – all down the inner sides of the prongs as well, which meant screwing your cloth into a tight little finger and threading it through each pair of prongs in turn.

She winced when she recalled the day she had discovered her "quick way" and was just demonstrating to the other girls how all you had to do was stab the cloth and then rub all the prongs' surfaces simultaneously, when Mrs Newbolt spotted what she was doing and exploded in wrath.

'Mirella Granger, take back that pile and clean every fork again properly! And if you can't obey a simple instruction and carry out a straightforward task then you'd better return to your hovel and spend the rest of your life feeding pigs – which seems to be the level of your intelligence.'

The girls giggled. Mrs Newbolt had looked round at them approvingly, then reinforced her stricture with a sharp clip of Mirella's ear – which seemed to burn as she remembered the incident. So now she twisted her cloth and poked it through each prong in turn, rubbing the sides up and down and then the handle, starting to burnish – only starting, mind – being careful not to trespass on Millie's job, which was to bring up the full lustre.

She stifled a yawn. Whatever happened, she didn't want to get into trouble at the moment in case it jeopardised this afternoon's treat. Wombell's Menagerie was in town. Yesterday it had appeared by royal command in the Castle Quadrangle and all the more important members of the household had attended. Today there was to be a performance in the town and Mirella had arranged to meet her father and younger sister Cassie there. It was weeks since she had last seen them, and she missed her sister more than she had imagined possible – which was not altogether

4

surprising since they had been boon companions for as long as she could remember, she and Cassie.

'Oh no! Not the cruets this week as well.' One of the maids had just entered the room with a tray full of silver vessels. Mirella groaned and picked up another clean cloth with which to do battle.

If she had only known this was what it meant to "grow up", she wouldn't have so easily relinquished the days when she'd roamed through Windsor Park collecting berries, picking flowers, climbing trees. Of course, she and Cassie had done their stint in the house, but that hadn't taken all their time. When Mirella thought back to that period of her life which had ended only five weeks ago when, on her thirteenth birthday, she'd come to work up at the castle, it was the days spent outside helping her father train the dogs, check the coney-warrens and mix the chick-feed that she recalled most vividly. These sort of things had made up her childhood – these, and just messing around together with Cassie.

'Come on, Cassie, I dare you!' The two of them had been standing under the plum tree in their favourite part of the garden, engaged in one of their favourite pastimes: "acrobatics". The sun was hot on their hair, and the grass and bracken flattened just around them into a kind of nest. They were hidden from the rest of the world in general, and the pestering attention of their younger brothers – still more or less babies – in particular. Mirella must have been about ten years old and Cassie eight. They had done handstands, somersaults, and dropping down backwards into a crab, and then Mirella attempted a new trick.

Readjusting her dress which was already hitched up around her waist into baggy breeches, she climbed on to the brick wall surrounding the vegetable patch.

'Look, Cassie! Watch me – carefully – 'cos I'm gonner do something different this time.'

Hands and arms outstretched, her bare feet stepped

out and explored the top of the narrow wall for a toe-hold while her body swayed, threatening to topple. Balance regained, she stepped again – making the whole procedure look highly precarious. After ten or twelve paces, she came to a halt and announced: 'There! That's what rope-dancers do.'

Fair-haired Cassie looked unimpressed. 'I thought they walked along ropes,' she objected, 'not walls.'

'Well, yes – but this isn't as easy as it looks,' Mirella had muttered, 'and anyway, I haven't finished yet. This next bit's even more dangerous. Watch!'

She stood quite still, sizing up the gap between the wall and the plum tree. Then leapt through the air, flinging out her hands to catch on to a specific branch and swing there – to and fro, to and fro – free as a bird, before dropping gracefully (she thought) to the ground.

'You try it, Cassie. First walking along the wall, then leaping on to the branch, and then you have to swing as high as you can. Go on, you do it – while I watch.'

There had been a little show of reluctance, brought to an end by Mirella's challenge: 'I dare you.' Whereupon Cassie had scrambled up, tottered her way along the wall, stood sizing up the gap, and then just continued to stand there.

'Go on, jump like I did. It's easy. Just jump. You'll feel like a bird flying. It's lovely.'

Cassie wobbled and leapt – and fell, screaming to let the world know she had hurt herself badly. And then lay there on the grass, clutching her arm.

'Oh, Rella, Rella, it hurts,' she moaned. 'It's hurting. Oh!'

Mirella was terrified and didn't know what to do. Her first instinct was to run back to the cottage and fetch Sadie. But then, making a great effort to stay calm and act as she thought their mother would in the

6

circumstances, she tried to comfort Cassie and help her back to her feet.

'My God, what's happened now?' Sadie cried, as Cassie came stumbling through the door still clutching her arm and sobbing. Wiping her wet hands down her pinny, she lifted Cassie up and carried her to the settle. 'What have you done to yourself, my love? Show Mummy.'

'She fell off the wall,' Mirella explained.

'I didn't. I was jer-jumping,' Cassie sobbed. 'You made me jer-jump, Rella, and I cer-couldn't, 'cos I'm not big enough yet. And that's why I fell. You shershouldn't have made me.'

'There, there, my love,' Sadie had soothed. 'Don't fret. Mummy will make it better.'

'There you are, Cassie, I told you it wasn't that bad,' Mirella murmured, trying to add her own reassurance.

To her horror, Sadie took her words the wrong way and rounded on her, eyes blazing.

'Trust you to make light of it, my girl, but you're not the one who's been hurt, are you? How many times have I told you not to lead Cassie into mischief? You're old enough to know better than get up to such tricks.'

'But we were only playing. Cassie didn't have to . . .' Mirella started to say in self-defence.

'Shut up! I don't want to hear. I've got my hands full enough as it is without you always causing trouble.'

'But I don't *always* cause trouble. What else have I done wrong?'

Instead of answering, Sadie simply shoved a strand of hair back under the ugly cap she wore when doing housework and glared, her gold earrings swinging in token of her fury. Mirella thought it best not to say any more, and watched as Sadie regained her composure and began to utter soft words of comfort to

Cassie. But the expression Mirella had glimpsed on her mother's face continued to haunt her to this day, because it contained such hostility. And she couldn't think what she had ever done to deserve it.

'No, no, *no*! Not into a *shine*, Missie. Just the polish off. Are you dim-witted, or are you deliberately defying me?'

She jumped, suddenly aware of the silver salver which shone in lustrous accusation in her hands. She'd overshot the mark again.

'Right, Missie,' Mrs Newbolt's voice hissed between gritted teeth, 'since you cannot work in collaboration with others, and are determined to render superfluous the rest of my staff, you can do the rest completely by yourself.'

Whereupon she signalled the other girls to quit what they were doing and left Mirella to survey the trolley piled with uncleaned assorted tableware.

'All that – you will clean stage by stage by yourself this afternoon. And I shall come in regularly to check that you are doing it properly. You understand me, Mirella Granger?'

'Yes, Ma'am.' Her voice signalled defeat and she felt like crying. Was crying inside. Not with pain so much as rage. It was not just that she would be deprived of a treat – there was no chance now that she would be able to meet up with her father and Cassie at Wombell's – no, most of all she raged at what was being done to her. Something was being throttled inside her. She felt it. She was being smothered, squashed, strangled. Like some half-naked little bird dropped from its nest – splut! And where moments before she had been stretching her wings in anticipation of flight, now it was all she could do to edge out of the way of heavy clodhopping boots intent on stamping the life-breath out of her.

One by one the other girls left, until she was alone,

occupying the high stool where Mary had been sitting. She gazed around at the shelves stacked with platters, goblets, tankards, bottles, flagons, objects and things whose purpose she could only guess – all of which seemed further to oppress her spirits.

She picked up an ornate finger-bowl, the first in the pile left for her to put polish on, and started to smear the paste into its crevices. When all its former brightness had been dulled, she put it to one side to await the moment when, having gone through this process with all the other objects, she would climb to the next stool, and take the polish off them all. And then . . . and then . . .

Hell, why should she? Who was there on this earth who could make her do anything she didn't want to do?

All these objects in this ugly basement room were like jailers but they couldn't, shouldn't, force her to stay here in their prison if she didn't want to . . .

Furiously she started to take the polish off the base of the bowl, bringing up the shine – all in one go – and simply for the pleasure of conferring with her own reflection. The face mirrored back was pale and set. A thin face whose thinness was accentuated by the large floppy white mobcap that kept her black curls right off her face. Except for the ones that always managed to escape round her left ear. And why shouldn't they?

She pulled the cap off her head, letting her long hair tumble round her shoulders, for she had decided. She was going to keep her appointment with Cassie and her father. She'd only be away a couple of hours. Plenty of time to clean the rotten old silver when she got back.

But what would she say to Mrs Newbolt who would know she had gone missing? Mirella had no idea, and at this moment she did not care.

*   *   *

9

Hundreds of people were milling round in the streets of Windsor in their smocks and steaming cape-coats. It was late October, the air was damp and cold, harbouring a yellow-grey mist from the river and sharp animal smells. Although only mid-afternoon, it was already dark, the fog blurring the outlines of buildings and people.

There were plenty of horses, but no cows, pigs or sheep in the fair this year because of the dreadful cattle plague sweeping the country. Their absence gave Mirella cause to wonder whether the wild beasts of the show were at risk, but surely not, otherwise they would have come under the Mayor's ban as well. No, it was just something to do with animals which had cloven feet, she remembered. It wouldn't affect elephants or lions and tigers. Which was just as well, for it was the latter she was really interested in – or, to be more exact, their trainer.

She recalled the picture on the placards posted through the town – the handsome dark face with its long pointed mustachios and neatly trimmed beard – looking more like some Arabian prince than her own Uncle Tom.

Although she had kept a curb on her tongue in the scullery so that the other servants had no idea of the kinship, The Great Kazan was in fact her father's younger brother, but any resemblance to the daredevil hero on the posters stopped at the artificially darkened whiskers on his face. She, Mirella, thought of him as a rather plump, unimposing figure of a man, but one nevertheless with a twinkle in his eye as he teased her and Cassie. Not that she and her sister saw him often. He travelled with Wombell's all over the kingdom and had recently returned from a long tour of Ireland. Now he was here for a few days in Windsor and their father had promised the girls a visit to the show.

'Rella, Rella! Here! We're over here.' It was Cassie

10

calling and, pushing her worries to the back of her mind, Mirella ran to join her father and sister by the entrance to the Menagerie tent.

'Hello, Pa,' she said, glancing round, 'you didn't manage to persuade Mama to come then?'

'No, my love,' Johnny said, stopping to kiss her, 'you know how funny she is about travelling shows. Reminds her too much of the old days, she says, and she's still busy trying to put all that behind her.'

'Oh, yes, of course,' Mirella sighed, trying to hide her disappointment that Sadie had not taken this opportunity to come into town, if only to see how she was getting on. She was sure her mother would have made more effort if it had been Cassie and not she who had just left home. But then there had always been a stronger bond between Sadie and her younger daughter despite the fact that, as Johnny so often remarked, it was Mirella who resembled Sadie more closely in looks and temperament. 'Can we go straight in, then?' Mirella asked, clutching Cassie's arm.

There was no need for payment, her father simply whispered something in the ear of the attendant and all three of them were waved in – pushing their way through the damp grey canvas.

It was dark inside the tent until her eyes grew accustomed to the fitful flaring of the naphtha lights placed in front of the line of cages along one side.

'You two girls go and stand next to the lion cage. There aren't many people there yet, but once the show starts everyone will be crowding round and you won't see anything if you're stuck at the back. I'm just going to have a word with Tom to let him know we're here.' So saying, her father pushed his way through another canvas door with matter-of-fact unconcern, as if going into the backroom of a shop.

'Do you like working at the Castle, Rella?' Cassie asked.

11

'I don't want to talk about it,' Mirella quickly interrupted her. 'Not now. Oh, look! Look at him, isn't he
magnificent?' She gazed at the beast in a separate
compartment of the lion cage. Above him a placard
read: "Royal Bengal Tiger". As if further to impress
(or was it to show resentment at her ignorant staring?)
he hurled himself forward, snarling, his front paws
rattling the bars.

'Goodness, I wouldn't like to enter his cage,'
Mirella remarked.

Around them people had begun to gather, and they
found themselves being shoved closer to the part of
the cage labelled "Performing Lions".

'It's about to start,' someone was murmuring.
'Can you see all right? Oooh! That fella looks just like
our tabby at home. 'Course, they've all had their teeth
pulled out, and most of their claws as well, so they
can't do any real harm.'

'Nark it, Bob. That bloody brute's got a set of
gnashers I wouldn't fancy chewing anything of mine.'
The lads laughed coarsely.

'Drugged, that's what they say. Laudanum sprinkled on the food,' a woman was confiding to her
friend.

'Yes, I've heard that as well. So the tamer's in no
real danger.'

'Mind you, there was one poor chap set upon and
mauled to bits in the show a few years back, and I've
heard of someone else who lost an arm.'

'Shush! Something's happening. I think the show's
about to start.'

'Goodness, that can't be Uncle Tom, can it?'
breathed Cassie.

A hush settled over the crowd as a green baize cur-
tain was drawn back to reveal a figure inside the cage.
He looked to be a young man – quite boyish – which
reminded Mirella that her uncle was in fact less than
ten years older than herself, her own father being

second eldest in a family of five whose ages were wide-spread.

She felt like waving and calling out his name but checked the impulse, realising that she had a part to play in his charade, that it was within her power to alert the crowd to the fact that this was her homely, often rather sheepish, Uncle Tom under the grease-paint of The Great Kazan.

Or was it?

Looking at him again, she was no longer so sure. This was someone quite different. Taller, thinner, dashingly elegant in his exotic costume. No, this couldn't be her Uncle Tom. This man was foreign. Indian, maybe, or Persian or Turkish. His hair was short, framing his face in flat curls which also swept round the base of his neck and flicked up stiffly round his ears. His main costume was a buff-coloured tunic edged in red and with a studded red belt, but he also wore high red leather boots tapering up over his knees, emphasising the curve of his calf-muscles. His bare arms made him look extremely vulnerable.

Mirella found herself staring at his face, realising that despite the highly coloured complexion this was indeed Uncle Tom. And yet he was also a stranger whom she'd never met before. At one and the same time this man was familiar and strange, and it was nothing to do with the costume or grease paint but an inner transformation. Concentration on what he was doing, complete and utter, had transformed him.

His face was set in a mask; a smile, not fixed but playing permanently on his lips while his eyes remained sharp with intent.

There was something hypnotic in this disparity. A mouth permanently curved in the performer's smile but eyes serious and wary, whose concentration never wavered. While he was performing he was something much greater than himself. He was an artiste, and as such invulnerable. She envied him that.

13

Then Mirella stopped thinking and just watched, mesmerised, as the big lion prowled round the cage. Suddenly Kazan stamped his foot but the action seemed to annoy the beast who, instead of going on to perform the expected trick, roared and reared up on to its hind legs until it stood resting its front paws menacingly on the trainer's shoulders. The crowd gasped. Kazan was clearly startled and stood there for a long moment, shocked and apparently unsure how to proceed. The crowd held its breath. How would the lion react? Was it about to snap at the trainer's face? Mirella could hardly bear to look. Cassie grabbed her arm.

'Oh, Rella, will he be all right?'

Then Kazan, having made up his mind, snapped into action. With a desperate effort he thrust the huge animal backwards, falling to the floor on top of it and rolling over and over in what looked like deadly combat until the lion lay quite still as if dead.

The crowd, afraid to clap lest it rouse the beast to its former murderous fury, breathed out a sigh and turned to each other to register their relief (or disappointment).

But then, when Kazan got to his feet and placed his boot on the lion's body, the crowd erupted into cheers, which hardly diminished even after the beast crept miserably back to its corner.

'Oh, Rella, thank God Uncle's safe again,' whispered Cassie, but Mirella ignored her, watching speechless as Kazan let two more animals into the cage and put them through a series of tricks that involved standing on tubs and leaping through hoops, and eventually, after shooing the newcomers out, finished his act by commanding the biggest lion to lie down, obedient as a dog, and to open its massive mouth while he, Kazan, placed his unprotected head between the animal's jaws. And, quite submissive now, the lion let him do so.

14

Mirella was astonished. It was only minutes since the performance had finished. She could still hear the clapping, cheering and whistling of the crowd in her ears. Still in a daze she had followed Cassie out of the tent and round to the back where her uncle's caravan was parked, and climbed up the steps not knowing what to expect. And there he was, The Great Kazan, lifting a kettle from his stove and wetting the tea as if he hadn't just thrilled dozens and dozens of people who even now were praising his courage to the skies. And what was more, The Great Kazan was chatting to her own father in an ordinary voice about ordinary things, just as if he hadn't just escaped literally from the jaws of death.

'Do both you girls want a cup?' he asked as they entered. Mirella, overcome by shyness, dumbly nodded her head. 'Well, what did you think of my big cats?' he went on.

'They're wonderful,' said Cassie, 'especially the smallest one. I liked her best. Do they ever have kittens . . . I mean, baby cubs, Uncle Tom?'

He laughed. 'Not those, my pet. They're all males. But we do breed cubs here in the Menagerie.'

'Have you got any at the moment?'

'No, I'm afraid not, but I'll try to arrange for some to be born here next time we come. How would that suit you, Ma'am?'

Mirella was surprised to find herself growing jealous as Uncle Tom continued to pay attention to Cassie, teasing and joking with her, until he had her giggling contentedly.

She wanted to enter the conversation herself, say something clever to impress this uncle who had grown into such a stranger since she had last seen him, but the words wouldn't come and the longer she stood there the more awkward she felt.

'Well, Mirella,' he said, noticing her at last, 'draw

yourself up a seat, my love. There's no charge for sitting down up here. My! You've grown since I last saw you. Quite the little lady now, aren't you? And too proud, I'll warrant, to acknowledge an old trouper like me for an uncle?'

His joking made her feel even more gauche and tongue-tied.

'Oh, no. I thought your act was marvellous,' she said. 'But weren't you frightened when that huge lion jumped up at you like he did?'

Kazan laughed. 'I'd have been a damn sight more worried if he hadn't.'

'Why?'

'Because that would have meant I hadn't trained him properly,' he explained.

'You mean that was all part of the act? Just a trick to make people think you were being attacked?' Now she felt foolish.

'Of course,' he said. 'If old Caesar had really meant business, I wouldn't be here to tell the tale, I can assure you. But I've got him trained all right and as long as I keep the signals strong, he's harmless as a puppy dog.'

'Is it easy to train lions then, Uncle Tom?' Mirella asked the question, not out of real interest but to mask her confusion. She was wondering how she could have allowed herself to be so duped.

'Not easy exactly. You have to be very patient and learn from the animals themselves what they are capable of doing.'

'I don't understand. How can an animal tell you what it can do?'

'Well, some animals are natural balancers. You see that by the way they walk up a plank or a ramp. Whereas others, even though they're the same breed, just aren't suited to balancing tricks so you teach them something different.'

'Which do you think are the most dangerous,

16

Tom,' her father asked, 'lions or tigers? Or is it bears?'

Having poured himself out a pint-sized mug of tea, Tom lowered himself into an armchair before answering.

'Danger doesn't necessarily go with breed, you know, Johnny. I maintain there's two dangerous types of beast: those who are so clever they want to be "boss animal" even over the trainer, and the opposite category – those who are so stupid or nervy that they can't get hold of what you're trying to teach 'em.'

His eyes narrowed as if he was remembering some previous encounter and Mirella felt a pang of sympathy for the poor stupid beast which had had the misfortune to earn her uncle's displeasure in the past.

'Have you ever been really frightened, Uncle – when you've been in the cage with the lions?' she asked.

'No. But if I was frightened, I'd never show it. You know why?'

'Because the audience wouldn't like it?' suggested Cassie.

Tom smiled down at her where she was sitting on a low stool at his feet. 'No, love. I'd never show fear because that's what upsets a nervous animal most. Once he scents fear in the cage, he'll go for it and tear it apart. Can't help himself.'

Mirella shuddered.

'Yes,' her uncle continued, 'the vital things for every trainer to remember are never to show fear and never to frighten the animals.'

'But I thought that's what you did all the time when you kept cracking your whip at them,' objected Cassie.

Tom stretched out his hand and stroked her long mane of hair.

'No, my love. The whip was directing them, that's all. An animal will always turn to face anything that

17

moves. So, if I lay my whiplash on the ground just behind the lion's back, he'll turn that way. I can use that trick to manoeuvre him into any position I like.'

'Oh.' Cassie looked relieved. 'I thought you were really frightening them.'

'No, I'd never do that, Cassie,' he said, still stroking her hair. 'A frightened animal will never make a good performer. I know that well enough.'

The scene before her set itself in Mirella's memory like a photogravure. Her easy-going father was sitting smoking his pipe and starting to exchange with Tom news of the rest of their family. They talked briefly about Phoebe, their sister, who was travelling with her husband's show in the Devon area. Then there was their younger brother, Joey, the same age as Mirella herself and still living at home with their mother in Aldershot. But Mirella took little notice of what they were saying. She was too busy looking around her uncle's wagon.

The small space was kept very tidy, everything in its own place. The mantelpiece contained one or two ornaments reflected in the mirror above it – figures of a bear-trainer and a pair of haughty pink dogs, each carrying a limp rabbit dead in its mouth. Gruesome, she thought, looking away to the chest of drawers next to the stove which held a silver-framed photograph of grandmother.

Such a sweet face stared out of the frame, not exactly beautiful but strong and serene and full of character. Just how she had looked when Mirella last saw her about six months ago when, at the start of summer, she had accompanied her father on a visit.

Her grandmother was not very tall. Her hair was dark and her figure, despite her age (she was in fact not yet sixty, but that appeared ancient to Mirella), was still youthful – as were her voice and gestures. There was a vitality in her movements and thoughts that continually surprised. And yet by all accounts her life had not been easy.

Examining the photograph again, Mirella thought that she could see suffering scarcely veiled in the dark eyes. Was this connected with her own grandfather's sudden death? she wondered. Or was it to do with some earlier tragedy once hinted at by her mother who had immediately been shushed by her father with the words: 'No, Sadie. Don't say any more. It's best the chavvies never know.'

'Well, what time *do* you have to get back?' Her father was obviously repeating something he'd asked before.

'Me?' Mirella jumped, suddenly aware that she was being spoken to. 'Get back where?'

The two men laughed.

'That's my girl, still dreamy as ever. Does Her Majesty work you so hard that you fall asleep as soon as you come away from her, or is it so exciting at the Castle that you collapse with boredom anywhere else?' her uncle teased.

Memories of the day came flooding back: the scene in the scullery and the row undoubtedly awaiting her return. She felt like blurting it all out there and then and begging her father for help, but she didn't. Pride prevented her from admitting what a mess she was in and what a miserable failure she was making of her first job. Instead she forced a smile, got up from her chair and calmly announced: 'I'd better be going now in fact, Father. I don't want to be late. No, you and Cassie stay. I'm sure you've got a lot to talk to Uncle Tom about.'

'Right. Well, be a good girl then, Mirella, and remember your mother will be expecting to see you back home on your next day off.'

Uncle Tom came down the steps and pressed a florin into her hand as he kissed her cheek to say goodbye.

'Oh, dordy, sorry about that,' he murmured, rubbing away the greasepaint smear his lips had left.

'Fact is, I've got another performance in about half-an-hour so there was no point in getting cleaned up betweenwhiles.'

As she started to walk back to the Castle she thought of his going into that cage again, seeing him as the transformed Great Kazan, Lion-tamer, and wished with all her might that she had some other self she could change into at will.

She pictured herself entering the wild beast cage. She was dressed in a shimmering spangled tunic, wore red leather boots on her feet and in her hand clasped a long whiplash – not to beat anyone with, but just to show who was in command. And one of the beasts padded slowly towards her, opened its huge mouth and roared. But she was not afraid. She knew exactly what to do. Just raise the whip and lay it on the ground behind to make the beast turn its fury away from her.

Only this beast did not turn, but stood tense, snarling, and ready to spring, and she felt quite helpless as she looked into its face and recognised the features of Mrs Newbolt.

Chapter Two

Dragging her feet up the hill, several times Mirella paused to wonder what she should do. Go back home, perhaps, and face her mother with the news that she had packed in her job? No, that was unthinkable. On the other hand, she didn't know whether she could stand another moment of those hellish chores.

Oh God, why had she done it? Suddenly the great adventure had soured and she would have given anything to turn back the clock and find herself sitting safely in the scullery cleaning silver all afternoon.

But no matter how confused her thoughts, her feet seemed to know where they were going and directed her back to what she now regarded as the scene of her crime. She no longer felt any kind of bravado, only terror at the thought of facing Mrs Newbolt.

She walked under the stone archway and made for a door which stood hooked open. As if in some sort of nightmare she glided down a dark passageway, passing no one. Ahead of her was another door leading to the butler's pantry and this one was closed.

It was not too late to turn and run. After all, if she decided to quit her position and run home, there was little anyone could do about it.

Except that there would be an almighty row, of course. Her father would be furious, and as for her mother . . . Oh dear, that was the part she dreaded most – Sadie's angry face when she heard the news.

'Oh, Mirella, how could you let us down like this after all we've done to give you a good start in life? Your father and me never had it easy, you know. The things we've gone without so's we could buy you some schooling and bring you up like a lady. And I've never begrudged any of it because I never thought I'd see the day when you'd throw all the sacrifices I've made back in my face.'

Mirella winced as she pictured that face – the mouth tight-lipped, the weary brown eyes so full of disappointment. And in that moment she could not blame Sadie for not liking her. In fact, if she gave in now and crawled home, she would deem herself unworthy of her mother's love.

Still, thank goodness, it was not too late. There was time to make amends. Eat humble pie, apologise to Mrs Newbolt, and resume her campaign to be the perfect scullery-maid so that one day her mother would feel justly proud of her. That's what she must do. It wouldn't be easy, but for Sadie's sake she would try.

And then her hand was on the door and she was opening it and sidling into the butler's pantry.

Everything stood still.

Before, with her hand still resting on the handle, she had been aware of voices chattering, pans clattering, people going about their business on the other side of the door. But as she walked into their midst everything stopped. She stood in the sudden hush, dazzled and exposed by the lamplight's glare.

The silence, shrivelling her spirit and swelling her misery, seemed to last forever. She was aware of everyone – Mary, Millie, Ellen, a couple of other housemaids, a coachman, one of the errand boys and Mrs Newbolt – looking at her. She half expected them all suddenly to pounce and tear her to pieces. But no one moved.

She realised that because she had stepped out of

line, they didn't know how to react to her, even appeared frightened of what she might say or do next. It was odd, but she began to feel sorry for causing them embarrassment and instinctively spoke to put them at their ease.

'Hello, I'm back,' she said. She did not mean to sound nonchalant, just wanted to restore a more comfortable atmosphere, but she knew immediately that her tone was all wrong.

Mrs Newbolt's face tightened and her lips quivered as if needing to rehearse what she was about to say.

Surprisingly, what eventually came out was not a scream or a shout but a thin whisper: 'Fetch your things and go, Missie.'

Such a simple command, but for a moment Mirella was unable to take in the words and went on standing there, her mind a blank.

'I said, "Fetch your things and go", Mirella Granger. I am throwing you out.' The words were spluttered now, as if the housekeeper was too enraged to express herself freely.

'But can I just . . . ?' Mirella started to say something, anything, to soften the harshness of the atmosphere all around her.

'No. It's too late to apologise now. You're not fit to stay here amongst decent people. I knew it the moment I clapped eyes on you. You're trouble, Mirella Granger, and you'll always be trouble.'

Now the storm had broken the woman began ranting and shouting the most outrageous things, while Mirella stood transfixed, listening – and aware that others too were listening – to all sorts of crazy allegations against herself and her family. Spiteful things that had not a shred of truth in them. Most of the insults swept over her head but "stepped up little gypsy slut" – those were the words which pierced her.

She waited for Mrs Newbolt to pause. Then she took two steps towards her, looked her in the eyes and

23

heard her own voice say majestically: 'You have no
right to speak to me like that.'

Mrs Newbolt's face turned purple.

'No right?' she screeched. 'Don't you stand there
and tell me in front of my staff what I have the right to
do. I told you to get *out*!'

Mirella continued calmly: 'It's all right, I'm going.
I certainly don't want to stay here and work as a
skivvy like you all my life.'

Her words hung in the air for just a moment before
the housekeeper went berserk.

Mirella had no time to defend herself, let alone
fight back. Mrs Newbolt seized a broom and slammed
it against the side of her head. She registered a shooting pain behind her eyes, and put her hand up to feel.
Another blow caught her arm. Then her back. Then
her head again. She could hear a voice screeching:
'Hold her down. Hold her down, you girls. She
deserves this!' Then she keeled over on to the floor,
felt someone dragging her arms away from her body
and blows hammering down on her back and legs. She
screamed: 'Help! Help! Oh, stop her somebody.'
Then she simply howled with the pain until she sank
into oblivion.

'Hush, hush, Rella. Come on, it's all right now. She
won't touch you again.' It was Millie's voice, heard
through the moaning that she gradually realised was
coming from herself.

She was hurting all over, badly; especially her back.
And she couldn't move.

'What's happened?' she asked. It was dark and all
she knew was that her body felt as if it had been prised
apart, smashed, and then reassembled in a way that
no longer quite fitted together. She felt so ill that even
the memory of the row and the beating had no power
to disturb her. All she could do was lie there in the
attic bedroom where they had deposited her, and wait

24

for the days and nights to effect some sort of healing.

During all the time she was there, Mrs Newbolt never once came near. Instead, the other housemaids – particularly Millie and Ellen – took it in turns to bring her food and rub arnica into her bruises.

Her first thought was to ask someone to send word to her father to come and fetch her home, but the girls persuaded her to wait until she felt better.

'No sense in upsetting your folks by letting them see you in this state,' they said. And then Cook began to send up tit-bits from the kitchen, and the girls went out of their way to comfort and reassure her.

'Mrs Newbolt knows she went too far,' Millie said. 'She was really frit-scared when she saw what she'd done to you, so if you just play your cards right and don't cross her again, I reckon she'll let bygones be bygones.'

'You might as well, Rella,' agreed Ellen, ' 'cos, if you leave here with a bad name, you won't get another place in Windsor.'

Mirella had a suspicion that they were merely carrying out orders by saying these things to her – that Mrs Newbolt, for whatever reason, was no longer so keen for her to go. Maybe she was genuinely sorry for the way she had attacked Mirella. More likely she wanted to avoid the sort of scandal that would inevitably ensue if Johnny Granger ever got to hear how his child had been thrashed.

Nevertheless, as her wounds healed, Mirella decided that she herself had done nothing to be proud of and resolved to act less impulsively from now on – and to give the Castle kitchens another chance – at least until she could plan some other future for herself.

So the incident gradually blew over.

The first day she crept downstairs to eat breakfast with the other servants, Mrs Newbolt completely ignored her. Orders to go and make a start on blacking the fire-grates were issued to her through

Millie who thenceforth became Mirella's personal overseer and intermediary, relaying all instructions which had previously emanated from the housekeeper. No one spoke openly about the new arrangements. No one ever referred to the terrible beating that she had endured.

The changed situation did not make Mirella's lot any easier to bear. True she was relieved of the burden of Mrs Newbolt's constant fault-finding. Somehow, when Millie told her to do something, she did not feel the immediate instinctive urge to resist. It was as if Millie was interested only in the job being done, whereas Mrs Newbolt seemed to threaten Mirella's inner integrity – as if the housekeeper had been out to break her spirit, to tame her, make her perform tricks at the flick of a whip or click of a tongue.

However, despite the fact that she never spoke directly to Mirella, the housekeeper still made her presence felt. Her malice poisoned the atmosphere. By throwing black looks of pure hatred in Mirella's direction and exuding cold loathing, slowly she brought the girl's spirits low. She inflicted isolation on her, not by saying anything directly but simply by making it clear that she would make life difficult for any girl who was friendly to Mirella Granger. In this way, Mirella soon became an outcast, frozen off from any normal contact with her erstwhile companions.

She tried to convince herself that she did not mind. Stupid creatures, let them play their silly games, and see if I care, she thought. Anyway, I expect they'll soon move on and start picking on someone else, but I shan't lick that old harpy's boots like the other girls – no matter how nice she is to me by then. I'll remember this and see through her tricks. In fact, I shall make a point of siding with the next scapegoat just to show I'm not afraid of her bullying.

As weeks went by, however, Mirella remained at the bottom of the pecking order. She grew accustomed to living and working in a frosty void, unable to reach across to those who at best ignored and at worse used her as the butt of their evil spite. As the ''game'' progressed, even her name was stripped like some protective garment off her back and she suffered the indignity of never being addressed directly, only being referred to as ''the girl''.

'The floor must be scrubbed this morning,' Mrs Newbolt would announce, before muttering: 'Get the girl to do it' – as one might say 'Put the cat out!' or 'Feed the dog!'

In time Millie picked up her cue and ordered her about in similar fashion.

'Here, girl, fetch a mop and clean these flags. And make sure you do it properly.'

The ''game'' evolved so slowly, so insistently, that Mirella's spirit was ground down almost imperceptibly – day by day – by the ignominious routine. If there had been an argument, another open row, she would have stood up for herself, refusing to be downtrodden. She would have changed things or stormed out of the situation. As it was, she grew quieter, more passive and withdrawn, gradually losing her appetite for life.

Pride kept her from acknowledging her misery.

'Mirella, are you sure you're eating well enough?' her mother asked on one visit home. 'You've gone so much thinner. Why, this skirt's practically falling off you.' She tugged at the waistband, bunching the spare material into her hand. 'We'll have to take it in if we can't plump you up again.'

Feeling tears misting her eyes, Mirella quickly changed the subject, but her mother refused to be so easily put off.

'They do give you enough to eat at the Castle, don't they, Mirella?'

'Of course, Ma, but I run around a lot, you know. That's why I don't get fat.'

27

'And things are all right, Mirella? You'd tell us if anything was upsetting you, wouldn't you?'

'Of course I would,' she lied, knowing that Sadie was the last person she would confide in, the last person to understand why she had such difficulty fitting in with the sort of people she seemed doomed to work with.

'Well, I don't know. You just aren't looking as bright as you used to, and your dad and I worry about you. But if you say you're feeling all right . . .'

'There's nothing wrong with me, I tell you. I just wish you'd stop fussing.'

At Christmas time there was usually a gathering of the Granger clan and this year they met together in the home of Johnny's mother at Aldershot. Mirella was not allowed to take time off so she learned what she had missed from Cassie afterwards.

'You should've been there, Rella. We had such good fun. The Captain was in great form, really amusing.'

They always referred to their step-grandfather as "the Captain". In fact, everyone called him that, possibly as a sign of respect, for it had caused amazement when Liddy had married the retired army officer just three years after the death of her first husband, Jem. The amazement being caused not by the widow's decision to remarry – after all, she was only in her early forties and still comely in appearance – but by the fact that she had captured the heart of such a gentleman. All her adult life had been spent in gypsy wagons travelling from fair to fair, making and selling lace, occasionally hawking bits of gimcrackery. Yet to see her in her present setting you would never guess she came from this background. Still, nothing about her should really have surprised, because she was altogether unconventional – although, being Mirella's grandmother, the curious contradictions in her character were taken for granted and regarded simply as the way Granny was and how Granny did things.

Mirella listened as Cassie bubbled on about delicacies concocted from unusual herbs cultivated in Grandmother's garden – herbs were her speciality – like woodruff jelly and her delicious punch drink. Mirella was more interested to hear about the concert that the Captain had organised. Star performer had been Joey, their youngest uncle – although Mirella found it difficult to take someone her own age seriously as an "uncle". He had played his violin.

'He's good, you know, Rella. Although I didn't like all the serious stuff the Captain made him start with, whatever Joey plays you can't help enjoying it.'

'Yes, I'd like to hear him.'

'Well, you've had your chance for a while. He's off to study under some great violinist – a foreigner, I think. Anyway, Joey's gone abroad somewhere for at least a year to learn how to play good enough to give big concerts. It was all arranged by the Captain.'

Mirella was genuinely pleased. She loved Joey, but had always felt sorry for him. They had played together a lot as chavvies but, having had the misfortune to be born with a cleft palate, he'd had a difficult time and, without his music, it was hard to imagine how he would have made his way in the world.

'I wish I could play a musical instrument or do something really well,' she said wistfully.

'Yes. It would be nice, wouldn't it? Mind, you can dance pretty well, Rella. Better than me.'

Mirella recalled how all the family used to take it in turns to do the traditional gypsy step-dances when they met for a party, and to sing of course.

'Did you dance at Christmas?'

'Yes. That's the good thing about having Joey there. Once he'd finished all the serious stuff, he changed over to dance tunes. We were all sitting in the Conservatory – with a stove alight so it was very warm – and we had a good old sing-song and dancing. I think everyone enjoyed themselves – except of course everyone said it was such a pity you weren't there, and I really missed you, Rella. Nothing's as much fun when we're not doing it together.'

Mirella squeezed Cassie's hand, and the younger girl continued: 'Which is why I can hardly wait for my birthday so's I can come and join you at the Castle.'

With Cassie's blue eyes sparkling in anticipation, there was no way Mirella could confide her unhappiness.

Chapter Three

May 1867

It looks as if the circus is about to take to the road, and about time too, Mirella thought resentfully as she paused in her task of whitening the stone step. She stood up for a moment to stretch her spine, arching her neck backwards and twisting slightly so that she could savour the warm sun on her face.

The clock was just striking ten of the forenoon and as usual she had already been hard at work for five hours. She had cleared out yesterday's ashes from the grates, laid and lit fires, and placed kettles on stoves to boil. She had carried about a dozen cans of hot water to the upper servants' quarters for them to wash in before breakfast. Then she had gone outside to clean handles and other brass fixings on all the doors and for the last hour had been engaged in whitening the steps around the courtyard.

Once she stood up, she could see over on the other side of the castle green the royal entourage collecting itself together for the great journey. Eight black carriages were drawn up in a row.

'Whoa there! Steady, old girl,' the lead coachman's voice echoed across as he struggled to check his impatient horses.

And small wonder they're champing at the bit, thought Mirella, they've been kept standing there in the Quad for nigh on two hours, poor devils.

Although she had not watched what was going on,

Mirella had heard the clamour and clangour as grooms, ladies-in-waiting, physicians, dogs, trunks, hat-boxes, rugs and unmentionable appurtenances were loaded into the carriages. Then, about an hour ago, all this activity had gradually subsided and a hush settled over the retinue as they waited for the last and most important personage to emerge and take her place at the head of the procession. Occasionally, as Mirella lugged her bucket and brushes from one door-step to the next, she peered over towards the Quad-rangle to see whether the entourage had started to move yet, but no, horses were still stamping and snorting, carriages creaking, those passengers already assembled sitting like statues in anticipation, all atten-tion fixed on the door through which in her own good time Her Majesty would eventually emerge.

Normally in the month of May Queen Victoria would have been setting off for her annual Scottish jaunt and the paraphernalia now assembled in the Quad would have seemed justifiable, but this year there was such a furore over Reform that Her Majesty had allowed herself to be persuaded to postpone her visit to Balmoral in favour of a short stay at Cliveden. And, as some indication of the confidence she placed in Cliveden's domestic arrangements, Her Majesty had included only three doctors in her entourage and was taking only ninety-one persons from her own household to help out. Much as she hated the chores she was doing, Mirella was glad not to have been included, for among the number already sent on ahead was Mrs Newbolt.

The removal of her presence was like the lifting of a dark cloud as far as Mirella was concerned. She had been left in the particular charge of Millie, but immediate attempts to kindle more warmth into their relationship were met with little more than sniffs of acknowledgement, making it clear that, although Mrs Newbolt might be gone, there would be no relaxation of her regime as far as Mirella was concerned. She was still out of favour.

A stir, like a murmured sigh of relief, rustled across the castle green as the dumpy little widow woman, heavily veiled, eventually made her appearance and was helped up into her carriage. It was as if everyone had suddenly been recalled to life. A door slammed, whips cracked, wheels creaked and the coaches rolled forward towards the main gate.

Mirella was left with a couple more steps to whiten before returning to Millie for her next instructions, but for a moment she stood watching the procession wind past the saluting guards standing rigidly to attention, sweep out on to the road, swoop down the High Street. All that – ninety-one people, not counting the staff at Cliveden already trembling with expectation; the carriages, horses, ponies, dogs, equipment, baggage – all that for the benefit of one person who had never had to whiten a doorstep in her life! Mirella raged with indignation. It wasn't that she felt antipathy towards the Queen, God bless her if she could manage to live like this (and He surely did), but Mirella did resent having to whiten steps for others to make filthy, to haul up water for others to wash themselves in, to clean silver for others to sully without any thought for the poor devil doing the work.

I'm a drudge, she thought, before correcting herself. No, I work as a drudge, that's all. I refuse to *be* a drudge. I refuse to put up with all this for the rest of my life. Yet, let's face it, what else can I do except put up with it?

She had had such hopes when she first came to the castle. She'd been keen to get on, to impress, to earn advancement. She had worked hard and willingly, because she saw herself making her way upwards. Why it had all gone so badly wrong, she did not understand, but supposed she had to accept at least part of the blame. After all, Millie and Ellen had come

33

along the same path and look at them. Parlour-maids now. They'd worked their way up.

Standing there in the sunshine, she suddenly laughed aloud. Two or three years of doing this sort of thing – and doing it well, mind. Toadying to the housekeeper, minding her manners, being the perfect drudge, and she too might aspire to such lofty heights and become – a parlourmaid.

'I won't!' Suddenly she wasn't laughing any more but biting her lip. Throwing down the brush, she kicked the galvanised bucket, spilling the dirty grey water and sending it runnelling down the hill. 'I won't! I won't!' she muttered.

'Hey, girl! What d'yer think you're up to?' Ellen's head poked through an upstairs window. 'Just because Mrs Newbolt's away, don't think you can take liberties with me, 'cos I'll not put up with your tricks no more than her.'

Mirella felt her brows sinking low over her eyes, dimming her vision, darkening her thoughts. It wasn't Ellen's words so much as the tone which infuriated her.

Stifling her annoyance, she mumbled, 'They've all gone. I watched them go.'

'Well, you shouldn't have. It's nothing to do with you who comes and goes. You've got work to get on with and, like I said, don't go thinking you can slack just because Mrs Newbolt ain't around. I've got orders not to take an ounce of sauce from you, my girl, so you'd better watch it, OK?'

Mirella peered up at the fussy little flushed face. Despite evidence to the contrary in the form of ginger corkscrew curls, she was convinced there was nothing behind the parlour-maid's face except kapok, that what she was looking at was a large white stuffed mobcap fronted by a circle of pasteboard on which rusty freckles, eyes, nose and mouth had been painted with just sufficient skill to give the likeness of a human being. No use trying to communicate with that, so she simply added tonelessly, 'I've finished the steps.'

'Who says you've finished?' Ellen asked.

'But I have. I've done them all now, honestly. This is the last one.'

'But have you done them properly, that's what I want to know? Wait there while Millie and me come down to inspect, 'cos if they haven't been done well enough, I'm afraid you'll just have to do them all over again.'

Then she heard the whispering going on just behind Ellen and recognised Millie's giggling and realised they were having a game with her. She was so relieved. The atmosphere was lightening at last. Well, she liked a joke as well as the next person, so she would pretend not to notice anything was afoot, play along with them and show she was a good sport.

Ellen, straightening her cap and trying to look sniffy, came out of the hall door, followed by a demure Millie, and the pair of them examined the step.

'Call that white? That's grey, not white, Missie, and I want it white. Let it dry and, while you're waiting, start at the beginning and do them all again 'cos they're all grey. See the colour of my apron? That's white and that's how I want all them steps to look. So, down on your knees again and apply that blanco till they're the colour of my apron. And, remember, you haven't finished until I say so. Understood?'

Just a game to them, Mirella was convinced of it. She intercepted the glance from Ellen to Millie, her smirk and raised eyebrow, but how was she supposed to continue the scene if the only part they had assigned to her was that of victim and this was a role she declined to play?

'Right, Ma'am. Your wish is my command,' she said, smartly upending the bucket and scattering its contents in one long cascade of chalky grey sludge that splodged over all the newly-whitened steps.

'Jeeze, what are you doing? Stop it. Have you taken leave of your senses?' Ellen's face had turned as white as her highest aspiration and she was looking all about her as if terrified lest someone catch sight of this shocking exhibition and blame her for the incident.

'Mirella, for goodness' sake, clear it up quickly before someone sees.' Millie, equally agitated, was pleading rather than making a demand.

'Well, you'd better help me then,' Mirella announced, aware that her unpredictable behaviour had somehow put her in charge of the game and filing this fact away for future reference.

Millie and Ellen both rushed away to fetch mops to clear up the mess and together they finished off the job without asking Mirella to lift another finger.

Lunch was always eaten in the kitchen at half-past noon, a dull affair albeit a welcome chance to sit down, if not exactly be at ease when under the baleful gaze of Mrs Newbolt. In her absence, however, the mood was happier and Mirella sat in her place at the foot of the table and reached out for the bread actually feeling hungry for the first time in weeks.

'What, no chutney terday, ladies?' mumbled the groom, a florid man of about forty, already tucking into his fodder.

'Sorry, Mr Taylor. We forgot to put it out. It's in the dresser. Fetch it . . .' Ellen stopped in mid-sentence, swivelled round in her chair and glanced nervously at Mirella before moderating her tone, '. . . will you, please, Rella?'

'Of course,' she said, sliding off her chair and skipping over to the massive dresser with its shelves of shining covers, dishes and plates. Opening the cupboard underneath, she selected the required jar and brought it back to the table.

As usual Millie and Ellen and Cook were verbally ranging over the contents of their respective wardrobes, each dwelling on the finer points of their own Sunday bonnet, finding fault with the way one of the nursery-maids did her hair, and carping, in her absence, about Mary's latest choice of head-gear.

'Fancy choosing something that shade of green to go with a cherry-coloured coat, I ask you!'

They did not include Mirella in their conversation and she made no attempt to join in. Enough that they called her by her proper name and no longer treated her with such obvious contempt. She sat in silence broken only by a few desultory replies to Mr Taylor's remarks that the weather was unconscionably warm for the time of year and he wouldn't be amazed if a storm was threatening.

After lunch she did all the washing-up by herself and then set to work cleaning out one of the dark pantry-cupboards on the lower ground floor, scrubbing the shelves ready for the new stocks of preserves that would be made in a few weeks' time. By her own reckoning she worked hard – despite the sultry heat – completing the task well before supper.

'Millie, I've finished the pantry. Will you come and inspect and say what you'd like me to do next?'

Millie gave an awkward glance towards Ellen as if to ask, should she humour the girl or tell her straightway that she couldn't possibly have finished the job that quickly and still have done it properly?

Ellen raised her ginger eyebrows and said, 'We'd better both come and inspect it, Mirella. You know how fussy Cook is about all the shelves being spotless before they're filled.'

So the three of them traipsed down to the pantry. Ellen ran her finger along the shelves, above and underneath, scrutinising the corners of the ceiling and floor for any trace of dust or cobweb before, with what sounded like disappointment, declaring that Mirella had made a reasonable job of cleaning it out.

'Must admit, I thought it 'ud take you a deal longer. Still, now you've finished, we'll have to find something else to occupy you for the rest of the day, so come along with us and you can help with the linen.' She did not sound pleased and Millie did not look it. It was obvious the two young women regarded her presence as a blight on their companionable conversation so, to help them out, Mirella offered a suggestion.

'If it's all the same to you, Ellen, I'd like to go down into town to post a letter to my parents. I could ask Cook if she wants any errands while I'm at it, and I'll be back in time to help with dinner. Is that all right?'

Unused to being put on the spot and having to make a decision about such important matters as someone having extra time off, Ellen looked flabbergasted.

'Is there anything you or Millie would like from the shops?' Mirella asked.

'No,' Ellen muttered. 'I don't want anything, and in any case I'm not sure . . .'

'Oh, fair enough. But it's really no trouble, so if you think of anything while I go and ask Cook, just call me.' She left to go out without permission having been exactly given or refused.

Away from them at last! She slipped out of the postern gate, down through the kitchen garden and under the arch, avoiding the town, making her way to the river.

She felt an overwhelming need to escape from the castle and its occupants – Millie, Ellen, Cook, the grooms – all of them and their silly chatter. And more than that, she felt she had to escape from the grey stone structure of the castle itself – its heavy darkness oppressed her, weighed down her spirit. The town had suggested itself as an excuse to get out for half an hour, but once through the gate and out of the castle grounds her feet had shunned streets and people and of their own accord brought her here to the river.

She sniffed in the comforting marshy smells of mud and water all round her, each step she took releasing the scent of mint and rushes into the air. She loved the plush dampness of it all, lovely green, plashy, tapering rushes to be pushed through and smooth white swans with their superior snake-heads hissing to distract attention from their scruffy cygnets. And the dapper little dabchicks disappearing into the reeds. But most of all the free-rolling river. She let her gaze float with it. She wanted to float, to flow free, like the river. She was restless. Surely it was not natural to stay in one place, confined within walls. It certainly did not feel right.

Warm sun today. None of the usual inimical yellow mist shrouding the river bank, but warm green vapours. Water eddying round the roots of the willows, a line of stumpy pollarded willows near the water's edge, their leaves spear-shaped and some of them pimpled with reddish-brown blisters. She amused herself with collecting these and then climbed up into the branches of a tree.

A perfect nest. Cosy. She must bring Cassie here. Perhaps not – it was so good to have a quiet, secret place of her own. To think thoughts and dream her dreams.

She felt snug in her bower. The wood white and soft. She pulled out a chunk from the heart of the tree where it was so old and dry it broke off in dry, spongy hunks, clean as if washed and dried in the sun. There was something very satisfying in clasping it in her hand, like holding the stuff and fibre of life. She squeezed and crumbled it into tiny pieces. Like bread or white breast of chicken. She dreamed about how it would be to live in this nest in a willow tree if the world became so harsh that she couldn't stand it any more. She would come here, climb into this tree and live off its friendly white meat. She would drink from the river – and even make her own rush-lights when darkness fell.

She gazed down at the water swirling into the creek, brown where it lifted the mud under the tree's roots. She did not fancy drinking that, but further up, where the bank was a little higher, she would lie full length and cup the clear water to her lips, or crane her neck down to the edge and sup.

If the world grew too harsh, this is where she would come. She knew she could not really eat the willow "meat" nor make rushlights without tallow. Of course she realised that. But it did not matter. It was the peace and the solitude, and the tree supporting her above the earth while the river continued to move beneath. If ever she became really desperate things could be resolved here, she felt. This was her hiding place, her sanctuary. And no, she wouldn't bring even Cassie here. Not at first, anyway.

Cassie was due to start work at the Castle a week after Mrs Newbolt's return. That was something to look forward to, so life really did seem to be picking up. The trouble was there was Mrs Newbolt's return to cope with first and Mirella wondered whether the housekeeper's attitude to her would have improved with absence. She would do her best not to provoke trouble and hope the storm clouds had passed, especially as she seemed at last to have won some sort of respect from the other girls. This might stand her in good stead with Mrs Newbolt, who would see she was not a complete nuisance and troublemaker.

The tree rocked. Not the dry old solid heart, but the withies and branches sprouting all around. A wind had got up. She felt a breeze on her face, not cool or refreshing but warm rather. She heard the thunder's first grumble from away in the distance and knew she ought to be getting back. She had lost count of time, musing here in the heart of her willow, and there was still her letter to post, the excuse for coming out in the first place. But it was so hard to tear herself away and she lingered to watch the evanescent pink horizon turn slowly lavender as the sky snuggled down behind its blanket of cloud, leaving the fields and the town and the castle to grow increasingly gloomy and drab.

Now the thunder had moved closer, cracking and splitting the heavens into flickering fragments. A fissure of silver light slit the sky, followed by more cracking and crunching, culminating in a crash and another flash. She flinched as a loud bang, like something slapping against her shoulder blades, jolted the breath from her body. As she raised her eyes to see if the world had collapsed, she felt the first wet drops on her face. The sky, leaden now, let loose a torrent of rain, thrashing hard against the earth.

She knew she ought to be getting back, but the rain was so wild, rattling against the rushes, flailing the leaves, lashing into the river. She would be drenched if she set off now. Besides, sitting here with one knee humped up, the other stretched to give secure foothold against a lower branch, she was absorbed and happy. Watching the river lapping up the downpour, listening to the rain splattering through the branches, gazing at a leaf funnelling water invisibly to a point where it swelled into a shiny blister and continued to swell and swell into a crystal droplet before suddenly dripping away and being replaced immediately by another. She waited, watching minutely, trying to catch the moment when the drop became itself and fell, but always it took her by surprise and was there and falling before she captured it.

The storm had worn itself out before she eventually scrambled down from her perch and started to make her way back through a weary drizzle. She had been away a good deal longer than she had planned, and even now she could not take the short cut back because of the letter she had to post. Never mind, she would work extra hard this evening to make up for lost time. Millie and Ellen would understand, especially as she had proved to them how well she worked when she put her heart into it and was left alone to get on with the task. In any case, even if Ellen did reprimand her, it was worth it – to have found an hour of happiness. She was happy, licking the rain from her lips, raising her head to let the wet slick back her hair until it was plastered in damp curls round her face.

'It's all right, Ellen, she's back,' Mirella heard Millie call as soon as she pushed open the kitchen door.

'Where the hell have you been?' A demented Ellen came rushing up, her face swollen and grubby with tear stains. 'Why? Why are you playing me up like this? I've never done anything to hurt you. Don't you realise you could lose me my job? Mrs Newbolt left me in charge and if anything goes wrong while she's away, it's me she'll blame and yet you're doing your blind best to wreck things for me. Why? That's what I want to know.'

'I'm sorry. I only went for a walk and stayed out a bit longer than I meant. I didn't mean any harm.'

'You told me you were just going down to post a letter, and that was nearly three hours ago. Where have you been? Who have you been with all this time? That's what I want to know.'

'No one. I just went for a walk like I told you.'

'I wasn't born yesterday, dearie,' she muttered with no tinge of endearment, 'so don't give me all that malarkey. You've been down at the barracks, haven't you? Making eyes at some soldier boy. Oh, you ought to be ashamed of yourself.'

Mirella was astonished. Why on earth should anyone suppose she would want to go near the soldiers? She didn't even know any of them.

'I haven't been near the barracks, Ellen. Why do you think I have?'

'Look, I told you, dearie, don't act the innocent with me. Mrs Newbolt warned me what to expect and

I've had enough of your antics. So, either you tell me straight what you've been up to, or I make a full report of your behaviour as soon as she gets back.'

'I went for a walk. Nothing else. Just a walk. And it rained and I kept under shelter until it eased off. Then I came back,' she repeated in a monotone.

'You're lying,' Ellen snapped.

'I am not.' Mirella began to feel angry, but she tried to keep control of her temper. 'I know I'm late. I've said I'm sorry. I'll do some extra work this evening to make up.'

'You can't make up for the way you behave – don't you understand that? You just have to do as you're told at the time, not wheedle your way out of corners afterwards. The fact is I can't trust you. The moment you're out of sight, you're in trouble. God knows what gets into you, but if Mrs Newbolt thought I'd let you go near them barracks . . .'

'I haven't been near the barracks,' Mirella said wearily.

'Hmmm,' Ellen sniffed.

Millie introduced a more conciliatory note. 'Well, whether you have or not, we'll say no more about it for the moment, but just you bear in mind how worried poor Ellen has been with you running off like that. And all the kitchen staff – Cook and one of the footmen and Mr Taylor – they were all asked if they'd seen you, so don't be surprised if word gets back that you've done something amiss.'

'Don't worry about it,' Mirella found herself saying airily. 'Trouble's my middle name, didn't you realise? And frankly, I don't care if the Queen herself gets to hear that I went for a walk.'

Her listeners gasped with horror, encouraging her to continue: 'And what is more, if I feel like it, I shall take another walk.'

'Why, you cheeky . . .'

'Ellen, don't say anything more,' Millie cautioned,

throwing her a warning glance, shaking her head and shutting her eyes. 'Leave it be. It's best, believe me. I'll tell you why later,' she whispered.

Ellen took heed of Millie's advice and Mirella considered she had escaped lightly. She even felt grateful to Millie, until she overheard the muttered exchange which took place in the scullery after the two young women left the kitchen.

'Why did you tell me to stop? She needs a good ticking-off,' Ellen was saying.

'I know that, but ticking off's no good when you're dealing with someone who's touched.'

'What do you mean?'

'I mean I think that girl's deranged. You know, touched. Up here.' Mirella, in the act of carrying in the dishes, caught sight of Millie tapping her index finger against her forehead. 'She'll end her days being locked away in a bedlam, you mark my words.'

'What makes you say that?' Ellen asked.

'The way she looked the other morning when she threw that bucket of blanco over the step. There was a crazy glint in her eye and I said to myself there and then, that girl is mad and ought to be locked up before she does anyone harm.'

Mirella smiled to herself, but the smile died on her lips when she suddenly wondered whether Millie could be right. She certainly seemed to cause trouble. Not just with Mrs Newbolt and her own family, but with everyone. Other people seemed to toe the line without difficulty, but not she. She was always the misfit. Why was that? Maybe Millie was right. Perhaps she was a bit crazy.

Chapter Four

"Queer in the attic" – that's what the other girls were saying about her. At least she supposed they were referring to her. In the passage outside her room, she definitely heard Millie (or was it Ellen?) whisper the words on her way to bed, and who else would they have been talking about?

Again the following day, when she was detailed to help Cook prepare vegetables for dinner, she saw Ellen's look of alarm as she strode over to the knife-block to select a sharp blade. Idiot! she thought. And immediately assuming a devilish expression, took up the long stiletto used for boning meat and brandished it in the face of some imaginary foe.

'Put that down!' Ellen shrieked, rushing over and snatching it from her hand. Then, in the sort of tense and controlled voice you might use to calm a child having a tantrum, or a dangerous lunatic, she said: 'Now, Mirella, take this *little* knife. That's all you need to scrape the carrots, dear.' Mirella took it, pulling a face as she did so, just for the fun of seeing Ellen's startled reaction again.

It was from such trivial beginnings that the new game developed. No longer did the other members of the household put her at the end of the pecking-order and make her the butt of their jokes as they had done while Mrs Newbolt had charge of the situation. Now they avoided any conflict, remaining studiously polite and inoffensive in their dealings with her. Careful not to tread over the invisible line that might provoke her into one of her "crazy" fits. And Mirella observed the situation develop with glee. After all, she had the whip hand of the situation, able to make the girls, even Cook and Mr Taylor, twist and turn any way she wanted. All she had to do was act "crazy" for a brief second and watch them all panic.

Wielding this power over them gave Mirella a sense of exaltation, although it was not very long before this was accompanied by a sense of isolation, gnawing away at her insides, eating her up. On the outside she adopted an increasingly carefree, brash manner. But inside, loneliness gnawed at her. Such unhappiness was tolerable only while she had the whip hand. What would happen now that Mrs Newbolt had returned, she did not care to imagine. Still, her loneliness was bound to end once Cassie joined forces with her. She could face all the world as her adversary, so long as she had Cassie for an ally at her side.

She wondered whether she should warn her sister about the strange regimen that prevailed, but decided against this, partly because she could not bring herself to spoil Cassie's pleasurable anticipation, and partly because she felt ashamed. She would have liked to have paraded herself before her younger sister's eyes in a more favourable light.

She did not know how much Mrs Newbolt had been told about her misconduct, but was sure she must have heard something. On the surface nothing had changed since the housekeeper's return. Whenever Mirella was in direct line of vision, Mrs Newbolt acted as if she simply was not there. However, as if by second sight, Mirella was aware of the scrutiny she came under when her back was turned, could feel the cold stare of the pebble eyes assessing and judging her every move. And she was frightened.

If only the woman would call her to question, say something, even tell her to pack her bags and go. That would be a relief. Far better than this cold inquisitorial stare that tried to catch her in an offguard moment and detect the thing that proved she, Mirella Granger, was bad – or mad.

Cassie was brought up to the castle by their mother one Monday morning, looking so sweet in her new cap and apron, Mirella could hardly resist hugging her. She was even paler than usual, clearly a bit in awe of her new situation, but her eyes, blue and starry, betrayed how excited she was too. There was no time for Mirella to exchange more than a few words with her mother.

'Now, Mirella, your dad and me are relying on you to look after Cassie,' Sadie said, crop-full as usual with concern for her younger daughter but without a crumb of thought to spare for Mirella. 'Remember, she's never been away from home before, and it's up to you to keep an eye out and make sure she don't get too home-sick, d'yer hear me?'

'Yes, Ma, but . . .'

'No "buts", Mirella.' Her mother was unusually irritable this morning, unable to disguise how painful it was to part with her sweet-natured Cassie. 'I know you've already got your life nicely sorted out here,' she added with a hint of bitterness in her tone, 'got your own friends and everything around you, but Cassie isn't so independent as you and she'll need a bit of shepherding at first. So don't you go being selfish and leave her on her own, will you?'

As if she would! Mirella suppressed an angry rejoinder in an effort to avoid one of the old confrontations which had so often wrecked all harmony at home for them both. But she felt desolate because in her ears everything her mother said sounded like

47

an accusation, and she could not understand why Sadie felt this need to get at her all the time.

'Of course I won't, Ma. I've really been looking forward to Cassie coming and I'll look after her, I promise,' she said, smiling and doing her best to reassure Sadie, but failing to detect any sign of softening in her attitude.

Instead of smiling in response, her mother bit into her lip then muttered, 'It's not easy, you know, losing one girl after another. Especially as it leaves me with both hands full looking after your brothers on my own. Still, I know I should be grateful that you two are being given such a good start in life – more than I ever had, or could have dreamt of, I can tell you – so I won't grumble.'

She pulled her plaid shawl more securely round her dainty shoulders and turned away to greet Mrs Newbolt, who at that moment rustled into the lobby where they had been standing talking. Mirella instinctively tensed, ready to spring to her mother's aid if Mrs Newbolt should say anything untoward or offensive.

It was odd that she felt so protective, not just towards Cassie but also to her mother. She didn't really understand why. Her mother, it seemed to her, was two quite separate people. One, the lively, bright-eyed, fussy provider who entertained all the family with her vivid dancing and singing at Christmas time. The other, this rather dowdy little woman doing her best to appear inconspicuous and fit in with gorgio society, talking in a false, forced way that made all the words come out wrong and sound silly. She was so desperate to make a success of the life she and Johnny had chosen when they gave up their gypsy ways and settled down, and she tried to do this by carefully watching her neighbours and imitating all she saw and heard, levelling herself down, holding herself in, smoothing away all her sharp corners so that she could slot in with them.

Into what bracket would Mrs Newbolt thrust her? Mirella wondered, quite expecting the housekeeper to treat her mother with disdain, even rudeness, and ready to intervene if this proved so. Instead, to her astonishment, Mrs Newbolt wasn't merely polite, she was almost unctuous in her greeting.

'Good morning, Ma'am,' she twittered. 'How good of you to arrive so early. And is this the young lady who is coming to join my staff? Cassie, is it?'

Cassie dropped a slight curtsey, at the same time blushing to the roots of her fair hair and stammering, 'Yes'm.'

Mirella winced, feeling an irrational sense of betrayal in seeing her sister make this obeisance to her enemy, and yet realising that her reaction was stupid for she had given her family no clue of the situation between herself and Mrs Newbolt. In any case it struck her that Mrs Newbolt might even be smiling warmly on Cassie as a way of healing the breach with herself and that the gesture augured well for the future. It would be wonderful if this was the case. Buoyed by such a hope, she turned to the housekeeper with a smile on her face, ready to make amends for the past.

'Oh, Mirella, you've left the kitchen without finishing your chores properly again, and Cook's complaining that she's been left single-handed.'

Mirella stared in astonishment. The accusation was so unfair. She had asked Cook if she could come out and greet her mother. Not only had that permission been cheerfully granted, but she had finished the washing-up meticulously before leaving the scullery. And why was Mrs Newbolt speaking in that funny way? she wondered. Mirella had got used to hearing herself addressed in a tone that was cold and insulting, but now the housekeeper had affected a weary, long-suffering whine – guaranteed to win sympathy.

Seeing her mother's disappointed expression, she

49

opened her mouth to justify herself: 'But I did finish my chores and Cook said . . .'

Mrs Newbolt heaved a sigh, shutting her eyes as if in despair of ever being able to cope with this exceptionally awkward girl, and then said quietly and with apparently infinite patience: 'I know you will have your excuses. You always do, Mirella, but I'm asking you to return to your duties. Go now, please. I'm sure your mother will agree that, nice as it is for you to skip off whenever you fancy, it is necessary for you to show other people some consideration. At some point you will have to learn a bit more discipline.' She breathed out heavily, shaking her head sadly.

Mirella felt furious at being out-manouevred by her enemy and placed in such a shabby light in front of those she loved. She wanted to explain the situation to her mother, make her realise she wasn't work-shy (a vice Sadie held in highest contempt), but now was not the moment. If she stayed and tried to explain, there might be a scene and this would ruin poor Cassie's first day. No, far better to let Cassie start starry-eyed. Disillusionment would come soon enough, but at least she would have someone here to protect her against the worst abuses of Mrs Newbolt's regime – that Mirella solemnly vowed, as she smiled goodbye and returned to the kitchen.

A glance back revealed a puzzled-looking Cassie, and Mrs Newbolt in agitated conversation with their mother. It was almost more than Mirella could bear to think her mother's mind was being poisoned against her, without her being there to defend herself. Still, at least she would soon have a chance to explain to Cassie. And once her sister had experienced Mrs Newbolt in her true colours, she would understand how Mirella had come to cross swords with the old dragon.

*　　*　　*

All morning she had been looking out for her sister, but failed to catch a glimpse of her.

I just hope that old battle-axe hasn't started bullying her already, she fumed. She'll have me to reckon with if she has.

As time passed and she still had not managed to see Cassie, Mirella grew more and more anxious. It was not until midday that she caught sight of her and realised that her fears had probably been ill-founded, for Cassie was already seated at the table in the kitchen where all the servants took their lunch, and was chatting away happily to Ellen.

Mirella went up to ask how her morning had gone. Unfortunately there was no empty seat at Cassie's end of the table. Ellen and Millie had her sandwiched in between them and failed to make room for Mirella despite the fact that they must have noticed her disappointment. Still, at least Cassie was glad to see her and would have scrambled out of her seat to join Mirella lower down the table had not Ellen's restraining arm grabbed her skirt and pulled her down into her place again.

'You just sit where you are, Cassie, and finish your food. You can talk to your sister some other time.'

'Oh, but I just want to tell her . . .' Cassie murmured.

'Not now, dear. You get on and enjoy your meal. Your sister can wait.'

The words were harmless enough. It was the tone that was so insulting. Ellen had curled her lip as she said "sister", as if the word stank in her nostrils. Mirella felt herself put down again, humiliated in front of Cassie. Then, when the meal was over and she was still prevented from exchanging more than a cursory few words with Cassie, she began to realise there was some plot to keep them apart; that Mrs Newbolt had instructed her minions to prevent

Mirella and Cassie from enjoying each other's company. But why even so warped a mind as Mrs Newbolt's should decide to do this was beyond her.

'Cassie, Cassie,' she whispered, but it was not until she raised her voice that she managed to attract the other's attention and bring her scurrying down from the top of the staircase in a way that sent her candle-flame flaring. 'Where are you going?'

'To bed. I thought everyone had to turn in at this time. Mrs Newbolt told me . . .'

Mirella cut her short.

'Yes, yes. I know you're going to bed, but where are you sleeping? I thought you'd be coming into the dormer attic with me and Millie. There's plenty of room for another person.'

'Oh, Mirella! I hoped I'd be sleeping with you too, but Mrs Newbolt's put me in with Ellen and Meg instead. I think it's because Ellen's in charge of me for the moment, showing me 'xactly what to do and how I'm s'posed to do it. But I'm getting on all right, I think.'

'They're not working you too hard, are they? Or being unkind?'

Cassie's blue eyes opened wide.

'Oh no. They're really nice, all of them. Much nicer than I expected. And all I've done today is follow the others around and watch what they're doing. Oh, yes, and I helped Mrs Newbolt cut some flowers from the garden and then she took me with her when she went into the royal apartments and that was ever so interesting.'

So that was where Cassie had been all afternoon while Mirella had been scouring the floors and furniture in the basement. No wonder she had not seen her. Still, it was good that Cassie had enjoyed her first day in the castle. Nothing untoward had happened to her, and maybe tomorrow, or the next day, when there was less need for Ellen or Mrs Newbolt to keep such strict vigilance over their protegée, there would be more opportunity for her and Cassie to get together and share the sort of companionship they were used to at home.

Cassie was still prattling on about some magnificent looking-glasses she had seen in the royal apartments when Ellen's voice suddenly summoned her to bed. Not wishing to get her into trouble, Mirella kissed her on the forehead and bade her goodnight before making her way to her own bedroom in the upper garret.

She was able to snatch a few words with Cassie next morning before breakfast, but much to her annoyance again the table had been arranged in a way that prevented them from sitting near each other. But Cassie appeared happy and if, as some curious offshoot of her own situation, her sister's position in the castle kitchens was made more secure, then Mirella was glad. And so, while making the most of every opportunity to snatch a few words with her – on the stairs, at the beginning or ending of meal-times, nodding and signalling to her across a room – Mirella resigned herself for the most part to continuing in her loneliness, and life settled down to a fairly tranquil, if not exactly comfortable, routine.

'Rella, why don't you make more effort to be friendly with the other girls?'

Caught on the defensive by her younger sister, Mirella reacted sullenly: 'Why should I?'

'Because they're quite nice – Millie and Ellen – and it's more fun working with friends beside you all day. I mean, you can have a laugh about things. But you don't. You seem to be always on your own and so much more serious than you used to be at home. I think you'd be happier if you made more friends.'

It was like seeing Cassie swept into another world, tamed and domesticated. Not only submitting to all the rules, but co-operating, accepting them gladly as if they were what her spirit craved. But not she, Mirella. She would never submit, she thought bitterly, trying not to dwell on Cassie's disloyalty and her own sense of betrayal.

She brooded about the difference between her and her sister, recognising that there was something wild in herself that raged against the world and the way things were. Well, not against all the world exactly. Not against birds and creatures and trees and sky. These were all right. You knew where you were with wild things. But people, even her own family, were treacherous. She resolved never to trust people.

It was Thursday afternoon and all the scullery-maids were gathering in the basement for another cutlery cleaning session. The only good thing about it was that cleaning cutlery afforded Mirella a rare opportunity to sit down in her working day, but this was small compensation for having to perch on a stool for hours on end in a rank, stupefying atmosphere, alongside empty-headed Millie, listening to her chattering away to the other girls. Mirella was so bored she would actually have preferred to scrub floors, scour tables, do anything that allowed her to stretch her limbs, especially if it could be done out of doors, on her own or with Cassie.

'Cassie, come and sit with me and I'll show you what to do,' she called, as she caught sight of her sister who had just come into the scullery and was standing looking rather lost as the rest of the girls took their places round the long bench and selected their cloths.

Cassie scrambled up on to the high stool next to her, muttering: 'But I know how to clean silver, Rella. I used to do it with you at home, remember?'

'Of course. But we do it a bit differently here,' Mirella explained. 'We each have a different part of the job to do – working as a team, you see. For example, I'll probably be taking the polish off and if you sit here, you'll be putting on the shine. And then someone else next to you will give it the final polish.'

'Coo, what a performance,' said Cassie, picking up a cloth, as Mrs Newbolt wheeled in the first trolley of silver objects.

'Yes, but it's important,' Mirella continued, trying to help her sister avoid the pitfalls that she herself had slipped into, 'and what you must remember is just keep to your own job and don't . . .'

'Cassie Granger!' Mrs Newbolt's screech caused poor Cassie to jump and nearly topple off her stool. 'What do you think you're doing sitting there?' Her question was accompanied by a look of such malevolence that even Mirella quaked to see it.

'I . . . I . . . just sat here next to Rella,' Cassie stuttered.

'Well, you don't sit there,' Mrs Newbolt hissed.

'I'm sorry. I didn't know. Rella just said . . .'

'I can imagine what Mirella just said, but Mirella is not in charge of this household. I am. And you will not listen to her; you will listen to me. Do I make myself clear, Cassie Granger?'

'Ye-es. I'm sorry, Mrs Newbolt. I di-didn't think,' Cassie whimpered, hastily sliding down from the stool and walking a couple of steps away from Mirella, who all this time had been sitting clenching her fingernails into her palms and holding back her urge to rush in and defend her sister.

'All right, all right, Cassie.' Mrs Newbolt had calmed down, and in an obvious effort to sound sweeter, assumed an embarrassingly mellifluous tone. 'But don't let this sort of thing happen again, will you, dear?'

'No. No, I won't, Mrs Newbolt,' Cassie, wide-eyed and on the brink of tears, blurted out. 'I'm sorry.'

Oh, Cassie, don't! Don't demean yourself. Don't

keep saying sorry when you haven't done anything wrong. Mirella longed to say the words out loud, but by dint of great effort kept a still tongue in her head, aware that any remark from her would exacerbate the situation and make Cassie feel worse. So she kept quiet while inwardly raging, and watched as Mrs Newbolt gestured to Cassie to take a seat next to herself at the top of the table.

The other girls who had been watching and listening to the exchange in silence now slowly started to chatter amongst themselves as they got on with their work. No one, however, spoke a word to Mirella. So, preoccupying herself with her dreams as she had become so accustomed to doing of late, she picked up her cloth and started to remove polish from a selection of cutlery passed to her from Ellen sitting on her left.

Scarcely able to hear the tick of the big wallclock through the chatter and clatter, Mirella occasionally took a peep at its face just to make sure that time was still passing. She also could not resist the temptation to steal a glance at Cassie, now busily engaged in putting the final shine on a pile of dish covers being passed to her from the line of workers on the other side of the table. Whenever their eyes met, Mirella smiled encouragement and was happy to see that Cassie felt able to grin back at her, seemingly recovered from her agitation.

Mirella had finished the spoons and forks and just started on a pile of napkin rings. Her hands were working methodically to remove the polish, leaving her thoughts to range through woods and along river banks. But her preoccupation was brought to a rude conclusion by someone's hand gripping her right arm. Without looking up to see who it was, she instinctively twisted and jerked her body to shake off her assailant, only to find herself hauled abruptly down from her high stool in such a rough fashion that she toppled backwards and fell sprawling on the floor.

'Get up! Get up, you stupid child, and follow me. I want to talk to you.'

It was Mrs Newbolt who had grabbed her and was now issuing this command, while the other girls – apart from Cassie – were convulsed with laughter at the sight of Mirella sprawled on the floor rubbing her bruised elbow, trying to make sense of what had just happened. One moment she had been working hard, her mind – it was true – not completely on the task in hand, but still she had been doing her job as well as she knew how; the next moment someone had unceremoniously pounced on her and sent her crashing to the ground. And she didn't know why.

'Get up. Get up, you sly little minx, and stop shamming.'

'Shamming what?' Mirella asked, scrambling up but still rubbing her bruises.

'Shamming that you're hurt,' Mrs Newbolt bellowed. 'Trying to get people's sympathy, that's what you're doing; trying to distract their attention from what you've done. Well, it won't work. I've caught you out and you won't slip off the hook this time.'

'Caught me out doing what?' Mirella was completely baffled.

'I've told you. Don't try to act the innocent with me. It just won't work, Missie. I know what you've been up to and I'm asking you to turn your pockets out now – in front of witnesses – to show what's in them.'

'In my pockets?' Mirella was even more mystified.

'Yes. Stop wasting time. Millie,' Mrs Newbolt turned to the senior maid, 'if she won't do it, just take hold of her apron, will you, and put your hands in her pockets and show us what you find.'

Mirella instinctively wanted to stop the other girl

taking such liberties, but she managed to stifle any resistance and stand impassively while the charade was played out. Slowly Millie went through both her pockets and then with something like a conjuror's flourish pulled out a handkerchief which she shook and held up by one corner for all to see. Mirella was about to snatch it back when the sight of Mrs Newbolt's thwarted expression made her forget her own anger and want to laugh instead.

'Not that, Millie. There's something else. I'm sure there is. Here, let me look,' Mrs Newbolt said, giving vent to her frustration. And then, before she fully realised what was happening, Mirella was spun round and suffered the indignity of having the housekeeper search the pockets of her apron and her dress and then roughly prod her fat fingers all over her clothing, trying to find whatever it was she was looking for.

'Stop it! How dare you touch me like this?' she screamed.

'Where have you put it, then? Fetch out that spoon and then there'll be no need for me to search you.'

'What spoon? What are you talking about?'

'That silver teaspoon you were cleaning just now. The one that never reached the end of the line because you pinched it. The one you've got hidden somewhere. I know because I've counted the spoons and there's one missing and there's no one else but you who'd pull a trick like this.' Her face was ugly with emotion, her eyes bulging behind her round glasses, the tip of her nose quivering with rage. In the face of such frenzy, Mirella grew suddenly calm.

'You mean you think I took a silver spoon? You're accusing me of stealing a spoon?' She spat the words out, so distasteful did she find the very idea.

'You did. You know you did. You must have taken it.' Mrs Newbolt's tone was faltering slightly. 'I counted them all at that end of the table,' she pointed to where the first maid was sitting ready to smear the paste on to the silver – 'and, I repeat, one of them did not arrive at the end of the line. I've been suspecting something like this and now I've caught you at it, Missie, and you'd better just hand over your ill-gotten gains. Come on, where is it?'

'I don't know. I certainly haven't got your rotten old spoon and I object to being called a thief.' Even as Mirella said the words, she caught sight of Cassie, ashen-faced and trembling, and felt doubly enraged. She had been branded a thief, and this stigma would be removed only when she had received an outright apology from her accuser. She would not let the matter rest until she had obtained such an apology, but for the moment there was still the matter of this wretched spoon and its whereabouts. Had it in fact gone missing or was the whole incident a figment of Mrs Newbolt's imagination, or even deliberately contrived by her to bring disgrace on Mirella?

'Mrs Newbolt,' Ellen's voice sounded thin and tremulous, 'it's not this spoon you're looking for, is it?' She held out a glass mustard jar with its newly polished silver cap holding in place a tiny silver spoon so that the only part visible was the very top of its handle. Mrs Newbolt seized it, took off the lid, removed the spoon and put it on the little pile of exactly similar spoons at the end of the table.

'Yes, that's it,' she snapped, 'but it shouldn't have been put in the jar. I've told you that before, Ellen. The things must all stay together in their own piles so that they can be accounted for. Right, well, back to work, the rest of you. And, as for you, Missie . . .' She turned to Mirella who supposed she was now going to receive some sort of apology for the unjust accusation ' . . . all I can say is that you've been lucky this time. But, remember, I'll be watching you, so don't think you'd ever get away with it if you did try filching something here.' Then turning back to Ellen, she said in a whisper loud enough for all to hear, 'You know what I mean, don't you, Ellen? You can never be too careful with thieving gypos around.'

Mirella winced and looked at her sister. Whereas, just the moment before when the spoon had been found, Cassie's face had shone with delight, now it was puckered with pain. Seeing this, Mirella exploded in fury.

'How dare you say that! You're crazy, Mrs Newbolt, stark crazy, and my sister and I won't stay here a minute longer to hear your lunatic ravings. We're leaving. Ready, Cassie? Let's fetch our things.'

'Oh, no, Mirella. Not me. This is nothing to do with me,' poor Cassie moaned.

'That's right, my dear.' Mrs Newbolt strode over to Cassie and threw her arms around the girl's shoulders. 'Don't you take any notice of her. If anyone's crazy round here, it's her.'

'No, Mrs Newbolt,' Mirella spoke slowly and quietly. 'I'm not crazy, but I've put up with enough of your spite. You accused me of being a thief just now, and you were found to be wrong. Well, I want an apology, please.'

'Apology? I don't apologise to the likes of you,' Mrs Newbolt screeched, her face turning blue and her hands beginning to tremble.

'No? Well, I'll not stay here to be abused any longer. I'm stepping outside for some fresh air, unless you want to search my pockets again first?'

Mrs Newbolt was looking round now, as if in search of a broom or some such weapon, and with the same expression on her face that had presaged her previous assault.

'Go out of that door, my girl,' she screamed, 'and I swear you'll never come back in again.'

'For once, Mrs Newbolt, I heartily agree with you. So, best of luck with your skivvying,' she beamed a wide smile at the assembled kitchen staff, 'and I bid you all good afternoon.' When she skipped through the door, she knew that this time there could be no going back.

Chapter Five

'Never, no matter what. I'll never go back to that place,' she was still muttering half an hour later, hugging her knees and sitting in the heart of her special willow tree. 'So what now, then? Crawl home to Ma and Pa, I s'pose, and tell them what's happened.'

She cringed. She knew what their reaction would be. That it was all her fault. That she had been too hoity-toity and not worked hard enough. Already she could hear her mother's voice whining: ''After all your father and I did to get that place for you, and you chuck it up just like that. All those special clothes I made up for you. All the expense to get you kitted out. And poor little Cassie – what effect will your waywardness have on her future, do you think? But then, you never do stop to think, do you, Mirella? That's the cause of all the trouble.''

But it wasn't true. She did worry about others. And it was Cassie's fate that was haunting her now. Left alone in that dreadful place to fend for herself, how could she possibly cope? Mirella pictured Cassie as she last saw her, tear-stained and trembling, but being comforted – yes, that was the unpalatable truth – clasped to the bosom of Mrs Newbolt. And when she thought about it, far from needing her protection, Cassie stood to gain more from Mirella's absence. Once she was out of the way, Cassie would be free to cultivate her own friendships and probably flourish under the housekeeper's wing.

Aware for the first time how tense she was and that her chest was hurting from the strain of holding in her breath for so long, Mirella let out a long, slow sigh. Why do I always get myself into this sort of trouble? I don't do anything bad but somehow I manage to set everyone against me – all the girls, and Cook, and old Newbolt. And now Cassie's involved as well and I'm dragging her down with me. It's not fair for her to be shackled to a sister who makes life so difficult all the time. She'd be better off – everyone would be better off without me.

This thought was accompanied by a feeling of such desolation that tears began to course down her cheeks. I didn't want things to turn out like this. It's just that bloody woman poisoning people's minds against me, never giving me a chance to make good. I hate her, I hate her, I hate her! Tears continued to roll down her face, tears which she made no attempt to brush away. She sniffed. If I cry hard enough, she thought, my tears will turn this tree into a proper weeping willow. The thought pleased her – her tears taking the place of rain drops pattering through the branches, sliding along the leaves until they swelled at each tip and dripped into the river and were carried down to the sea, turning it into an ocean of sorrow.

She shivered. She was wearing only her indoor clothes when she fled, having decided against the risk of rushing up to her room and grabbing a coat and a few belongings. Then one of the first things she had done whilst running through the gardens was to cast aside her cap and apron.

No, there was certainly no going back, so she must make up her mind what to do next. Going home was the obvious choice, despite the storm that would break over her head. And then? Well, she would look for another position and make herself useful to her mother in the meantime. Now she felt more dejected than ever. "Making herself useful" would not mean helping her father to check the game covers or patrol the woods. It would mean helping to look after her little brothers, doing the washing, the ironing, the baking; being confined day in and day out in that pokey little cottage, listening to her mother's barbed homilies. "Well, Mirella, you had your chance . . ."

No, she couldn't bear the thought of going home. And she couldn't go back to her job. And she had no money, no friends, no future.

She stared into the eddying water and down into its muddy depths, allowing her imagination to sweep her along past banks and paths and cottages until she drifted at last into the ocean and there was no more point in worrying about what people thought or how they persecuted her.

They'll be sorry then when they realise what they've done, she thought angrily, and they'll want to make it up to me, but it will be too late. The thought was accompanied by a vision of her body drifting face down in the tide at the ocean's edge, and the vision was so sad that she cried again, sobbing out loud: 'But it will be too late then.' And she was horror-struck because, by picturing it so vividly, she seemed to have made the event actually happen. But how will poor Cassie feel when they tell her they've found my body? And Ma and Pa, of course? They'll all blame themselves and I shan't be able to tell them it isn't their fault, that all I want to do – all I've ever wanted to do – is escape and live as I please. I don't want to upset anyone, but I've just got to find my own way in life.

Once more she found her attention focusing on the surface of the water, on the play of light and shade as breezes shook the tree's branches. The light scattering and shattering and then shaking together again into a living form that, even as she stared, took on a woman's apparel – floating full skirts that swirled this way and that in a flowing spiral. Slow and stately swirlings that sent the embroidered skirt billowing out to reveal shoes with silver buckles that sparkled with each step.

It was the buckles that made Mirella remember. Those buckles had decorated Grandmother Liddy's shoes when she had danced all those years ago.

Mirella couldn't have been much more than six years old at the time, but the occasion had etched itself into her memory because she had never seen Grandmother Liddy dance before and, if the reaction of the grown-ups was anything to go by, neither had they. There was something so special in the way Liddy danced that Mirella, young as she was, had felt like cheering and would have done so had she not noticed, on looking up at her father, that he was shaking his head and had tears in his eyes.

Was it wrong for her grandmother to be dancing, Mirella wondered, or was it something else that was upsetting her father so much? She racked her brains, trying to bring the episode to mind so that she could understand what had been happening that day.

There were lots of people around, that much she remembered; and Joey playing his fiddle, and Aunt Phoebe, all dressed up in a splendid costume and wearing bright ribbons in her hair, standing next to Uncle Joby in a circle. Of course! It all came back now. It must have been a party held to celebrate Aunt Phoebe's marriage to Uncle Joby. Yet, despite the gaiety, there had been an undertow of sadness, because Grandpa wasn't there to see his daughter being wed. Mirella's mother had often alluded to that dreadful year when typhoid had carried off Granpa Granger, and poor Liddy was left alone to cope with yet another tragedy in her life.

It was odd that Mirella had been so unaware of this family drama while it was happening. Try as she might, she could summon up only the dimmest recollection of Grandpa Granger. In fact, the only thing from that time she remembered at all clearly was seeing Liddy dance.

Her grandmother swirling in an embroidered skirt and richly coloured shawl had seemed to be dancing life itself that day, assenting to the music with her whole being, and smiling as she did so. Mirella remembered that smile now and pictured it shimmering up at her from the face in the river, and as the reflection continued to smile and dance across the water, her spirit had no choice but to smile and dance too.

All right, Grandma. Don't you worry. I shall dance too. Somewhere, somehow, you'll see me dance just like you managed to dance, despite the sadness in your heart. All I need is to find my own music, and I certainly didn't hear it playing in Windsor Castle kitchens!

She raised her head to listen as somewhere in the town a clock chimed. Three o'clock. She must make up her mind what to do. She peered back into the water, but the dancing form had faded and she couldn't conjure it back again no matter how she tried.

Grandma . . . She'd understand and not keep lecturing me about how wayward I am, but would it be fair to burden her with my troubles after all she's been through? Besides, how do I get to Aldershot from here? I might be able to take a train or carrier cart if I could borrow money from someone like . . . Of course, that's the answer – Uncle Tom. I'm sure he'd lend me my fare, and he's not too far away at the moment.

An announcement that the Menagerie was open on Maidenhead Moor for the week had appeared in the *Windsor and County Express* with The Great Kazan receiving special mention as their chief attraction. It was a long walk along the river bank, but if she set off straight away she could reach Maidenhead before dark and ask Uncle Tom's help.

She glanced back to the river, half expecting to see her grandmother's face appear and nod approval, but the water eddying around the roots of the willow was empty of reflection. Without delay she slithered down from the tree, pushed her curls out of her eyes, dusted down her dress and twisted her black stockings in a vain attempt to hide the ladder she had snagged in them whilst climbing up – and then she set out. As she walked she hummed a tune that seemed completely new to her. It was only later that she realised that the tune echoing through her head was the dance music that Joey had played on her aunt Phoebe's wedding day.

Her relief at arriving in Moor Meadow and seeing the tent and all the beast wagons drawn up in a circle turned to doubt and apprehension when it came to presenting herself before Uncle Tom. How on earth would she start to explain things to him? Suddenly she felt that he was a complete stranger to her, this uncle who travelled the roads and tamed lions and tigers and bears, and lived a life so far removed from anything she had ever experienced. Here he was on his own ground and she was about to burst in on him without knowing how he would react. It had been a mistake to come. She had no right to trouble him. She must go away and think of something else. All these thoughts did nothing to stop her mounting the steps in front of his yellow wagon and knocking on the door. After all, she was here now. She was tired and it was getting dark and . . .

'Why, God love us, it's Mirella! What are you doing here?'

She was startled to see that the man who opened the door had a face all orange and rouged, with unnatural-looking black eyebrows.

'Hello, Uncle Tom. I . . . I just wanted to see you about something.'

'Well, this is a surprise. Is Johnny with you, or the rest of the family?' he asked, peering over her shoulder.

'No, it's just me. I'm on my own,' she explained awkwardly, as if it was a crime to venture here without a chaperone.

'Come along in then, and don't mind the mess. You've caught me in the middle of getting ready for the seven o'clock. But there's just time for a cup of tea before that, I reckon, so sit yourself down and tell me all about it,' he said, regarding her with an expression that bespoke amusement, or bemusement; she could not be sure which.

'Tell you all about what?' It was a silly question, but she felt the need to play for time.

'Come on, Mirella, tell me why you're here – on your own – and looking as if you've walked a million miles through hell and high water and not found Sunday.' His gaze was taking in her filthy shoes and torn stockings and mud-spattered dress, and she felt like some bedraggled blackbird brought in by a cat. 'Did you come to see the show, or were you just passing?' he added, while she remained staring at the floor lost for words.

'No. No, I wasn't just passing,' she said.

There was another silence while Tom checked that there was enough water in the kettle and moved it over to the centre of the stove. When she next spoke, the words came out in a rush: 'In fact, Uncle Tom, I came specially to see you. I've walked all the way from Windsor and I've come because . . . well, I hope you won't take offence, but I was wondering if you could lend me some money.'

'Sure I can, Mirella. Do you want it in gold or will a banker's draft be more convenient?'

'No, you don't understand. I'm being serious,

Uncle Tom. I've got myself into trouble and . . .'

His face dropped.

'Does your father know?'

'No. And I don't want to tell him yet. I want to have a go at sorting something out for myself first.'

'Something like what?'

'Well, a job for a start. You see, I can't be a scullery-maid any more. If you only knew what . . .'

'Whoa, Mirella, not so fast. Let me understand exactly what's happened. You say you've got yourself into trouble and you don't want to go home to your Ma and Pa. But that's silly talk. They'll have to know sooner or later, won't they?'

'Yes, but it's going to be such an awful shock to them.'

'You can say that again! Your poor mother, she's the one I feel sorry for. And it will be a blow for our Johnny when he hears, there's no denying that. Still, what's done is done. I'm sure you're not the first little wench to get herself into trouble, and I don't suppose for a minute you'll be the last.'

Mirella was surprised at the degree of concern her uncle was showing. She ought to be grateful, she supposed, that he took her situation so seriously, but at the same time she could not help feeling that he was making unnecessarily heavy weather of it all.

'The thing is, Uncle Tom,' she said in an effort to reassure him, 'I'm not sorry about what's happened because at least it means I've had done with that awful job.'

He clapped his hand on his forehead in a gesture of despair and muttered through clenched teeth, 'Oh, if only it were that simple, Mirella, but think what it means to your poor mother and father . . .'

At that moment his expostulation was cut short by the sound of two sharp whistle blasts from outside.

'That means ten minutes to go,' he explained, dragging off his shirt and replacing it with a mustard-coloured tunic. Then, opening a closet door, he stood behind it to tug off his breeches and put on some tights. Finally, he stood before her first on one leg and then the other while he pulled on his red gladiatorial boots.

'Look, I've got to go now, but you just sit up here quietly until after the show, and we'll talk about this properly then, all right?'

'Can't I come and watch?'

'No, it's probably better for you to sit there and rest for a while. The crowd can be a bit rough, and it won't do for you to get elbowed or shoved.'

'Oh, come off it, Uncle Tom. I'm not that delicate or refined, and crowds don't bother me.'

'Hmm,' he grunted, fumbling with the top of a small silver flask. 'Well, that's as may be. I don't know much about these things, but I'm sure you ought to be a bit careful in your condition, despite all your bravado.'

There was no time for further discussion, because within a few seconds Tom had gulped down a mouthful of whatever was in the flask, muttered 'Ah, that's it!' and gone through the door, leaving Mirella alone once more with her thoughts.

What a strange fellow her uncle was, and what an odd turn of phrase he used. Worried lest she should be jostled by the crowd – that was quite sweet, really. Still, he was probably thinking of other things, his mind already set on his forthcoming ordeal. It had been bad timing to call on him just before his performance, and she only hoped her conversation had done nothing to distract him. After all, he needed all his wits about him once he entered that cage.

She shuddered. How could he bear to do it – day after day – risking his life like that? When she thought of her uncle confronting his lions it made her own problems seem petty and his reaction all the more surprising. She had not expected a lion-tamer

71

to view running away from a job as quite such a catastrophe.

"See the Conquering Hero Comes" was being played by the brass band and she could hear a muffled roar of cheers and clapping coming from the Menagerie. If she had not felt so weary after her walk she would have risked Tom's displeasure and sneaked a glimpse at his performance. After all, who knew when she would have another chance, and she did love the excitement of being in that tent and standing surrounded on all sides by cages of snarling lions and slinky tigers, serpents and monkeys, kangaroos, wombats, eagles and cockatoos; sniffing in the sharp smells of sweat and dung and dank, damp straw; awed by the wraiths of smoke and shadows leaping from the naphtha flares.

Now, however, was not the time for such diversions. She had to decide what to do if Tom refused to lend her money and persisted with this idea that she should return home. Would he force her to go back? No, not once she had a chance to explain how she felt and how, in any case, she would only run away again if her parents arranged for her to go back into service.

It seemed hours before "See the Conquering Hero Comes" proclaimed that the hero, having concluded his act, was now in fact making his triumphant departure. And then almost immediately Tom was back in the wagon with her, his painted face streaky with sweat. He threw himself down on to a sidelocker seat, legs outstretched, eyes shut, and emitted a long sigh.

'That's better,' he said, perking up again. 'Now then, young lady, let's talk about your situation properly. It's too late to do anything about getting you home tonight, but that's no problem. You can have my bed and I'll kip down in the tent. But tomorrow, come first light, I shall be taking you back where you belong.'

'No, Uncle Tom. I'm not going home, no matter what you say.'

'Look, Mirella, I know how you feel but you haven't got any choice. There's no one else in a position to help you.'

'I don't need much help. Just enough money to tide me over until I find another job, and then I can stand on my own two feet. That's what I want.'

'Brave words, my love, but you don't know what you're talking about. OK, I know our Johnny's going to cut up rough when he hears, but give him enough time and he'll come round. If there's one thing you can be sure of, it's that he won't turn a girl of his on to the street, no matter what she's done. And that's important because, let's face it, Mirella, when the babby comes, you're going to need all the help you can get, and it's only your own Ma and Pa who . . .'

She couldn't help it, she had to laugh.

'Oh, Uncle Tom, you don't . . . you can't think that . . . oh, no! That's the funniest thing I've ever heard.' She realised that he had been sitting there labouring under the misapprehension that she, Mirella, was with child. What on earth had put such a preposterous idea into his head she couldn't imagine. But it wasn't only that which made her laugh, it was her uncle's face as his expression changed from solemn concern to doubt and then utter perplexity. 'Oh, you couldn't really think that I was going to have a baby, Uncle Tom! You don't think I'm that sort of a girl, do you?'

'No, of course not. But, look here, you said you'd got yourself into trouble so what else was I to think?' He sounded so aggrieved, she felt it incumbent on her now to explain as fully yet simply as possible what had prompted her to run away. He listened to her story without interrupting until nearly the end, when he asked: 'So why have you come to me? Did you think you might find work in the Menagerie?'

'No, I thought of you because . . . Wait a minute, what do you mean "work in the Menagerie"? Could I do that?' Travelling around the countryside, working with the show, she had never considered that as a possibility. The idea certainly appealed. 'I mean, do you need anyone to feed the animals and clean out their cages and things?'

'No, that's a man's job. We wouldn't have a girl do that. I was just kidding really, thinking you might have come here with some romantic notion of being a parader.'

'What's a parader?'

'It's what the word says: someone who parades out in front of the show to attract a crowd. Surely you know what I mean? You've seen them often enough.'

'Of course. I just didn't realise they were what you called paraders. You mean all those clowns and tumblers and girls who dance and sing? But they're so clever. I could never stand up on a platform in front of everyone and do that kind of thing.'

'Well, it's not difficult if you've got the right temperament, but I don't think it's the sort of thing your father would want you to do.'

'Why not? What's so wrong about it?'

'Nothing. There's nothing wrong with being a parade girl. Even the Guv'nor's missus and his daughter do it for this outfit, and between them they put on one of the best shows on the tober. But it means travelling, you see, and this sort of life doesn't appeal to your mother and father. That's why they gave it up years ago. The first of our lot to become a house-dweller, Johnny was, because he couldn't abide the travelling life. Mind you, I think it was mostly your mother's influence. She thought they'd better themselves by settling down.'

'And did they?'

'Yes, by their own reckoning, I s'pose. But there again, show a cur another cur and he's bound to say it's a greyhound.' He slapped his thighs, chuckling at his own joke. She liked him so much better in this lighter mood.

'Does that mean you'd never live in a house even if given the chance?' she asked.

'Me, in a house? No, that would never do. I was born on the road and you'd never catch me settling down and becoming gorgiefied. Travelling's in my blood, you see.'

'Well, it's in my blood too. On both sides, remember. Maybe that's what stops me settling to an ordinary job and makes me so restless.'

'That's right. With Scampe and Lee on your mother's side, and Granger blood from your father, you can expect two itchy feet, my girl,' he grinned.

'So, tell me more about this parading business. Do you think there's any chance of Mr Wombell taking me on if I tell him I can sing and dance a bit, and that I'm willing to work hard at whatever else he wants me to do?'

'Hold on, Mirella, for goodness' sake. Like I said, you've got to have the right sort of personality to be a parader; not be afraid to make an exhibition of yourself. There's no room for shrinking violets on a show platform.'

'Yes, I realise that, and I take back what I said earlier on. I think I could do it given a chance, so will you speak to Mr Wombell for me? Please, Uncle Tom, it's what I really want to do.'

'By Jove, Mirella, you're impetuous, aren't you? We can't sort things out just like that. Take it easy and think things out a bit more,' he said, reaching for some wadding and starting to wipe the colouring from his face. 'What sort of future would there be for you in such a life? A young girl can't live on the road on her own. Where would you sleep, how would you manage?'

'The same as everyone else – in a wagon, in a tent

. . . I don't care. It's what I want to do.'

'But you're not used to all the rough and tumble of travelling. It's a hard life. Besides, our Johnny would never agree to it.' Tom had rubbed off most of his greasepaint now and retreated behind the closet door to take off his costume and put on everyday clothes. He carried on talking, enlarging on all the difficulties, the stamina needed to cope with the journeys and mishaps. 'On a travelling show everyone has to pull their weight: men, women and children. You can't afford to be ill unless you're nearly dead. In a crisis it's all hands to the pump, and there's always a crisis. Rarely a day passes when one of the animals isn't whelping or falling sick, or a big cat escapes and mauls a fellow to death.

'And the tiredness, Mirella! You might think you know what tiredness is, but you can have no idea until you've travelled all night in pelting rain and arrived at some poverty-stricken little town and have to open up and sing and dance to earn your next crust of bread. Because, remember this, the show always comes first. In a Menagerie that means animals take precedence. They're the attraction, and they have to eat even if you have to starve yourself to feed them. And there have been times I've done just that, I don't mind telling you.'

Mirella sat smiling as she listened. Though Tom's words were clearly designed to leave her in no doubt that the idea of her joining the show was utterly absurd, they had the opposite effect.

'So when can I start? Will you ask Mr Wombell tonight for me?' she coaxed. 'And then I can start practising in the morning, and get a costume ready, and send a letter off to Pa, telling him what I'm doing, and let Cassie know, and . . .'

'Hang on, hang on. If you're really that sure, I'll have a word with the Guv'nor in the morning. I know he's been looking for another girl, because he talked about placing an ad in the *Era* (that's our trade paper, you know), but he didn't go ahead because he was scared of getting stuck with some useless hussy. Of course, he might think the same about you, so don't build your hopes too high.'

Chapter Six

The first week was the worst. Even in the Castle garret she'd had a bed to call her own, but not when travelling with the Menagerie, where for the sake of propriety it was arranged she should sleep in the Guv'nor's wagon and share a bunk with his daughter, Lily. Nevertheless the arrangement worked, partly because Lily proved to be pretty amiable and, more importantly, because Mirella was able to stow her stuff in Tom's wagon which she quickly came to regard as home.

Frank Wombell (usually referred to as the 'Guv'nor') had not needed much persuasion when Tom asked him to take Mirella on as a parader.

'She's a good-looking gal,' he'd said, after looking her up and down, 'and as long as she can sing and throw her legs around a bit, she should do all right. But I don't want any shennanigans, Tom. Handling the crowd and keeping them in good spirits, that's what it's all about. If there's any larking about on the side, she goes immediately, understood?'

'Naturally. But I've told you, Frank, Mirella's been well brought up and she's not that kind of girl.'

'Right, well, I'll take your word for it. And providing you're prepared to accept full responsibility, and she makes herself useful, she can start as soon as she likes, with full board and all found. And, hmm . . . as for money, well, we'll have to see how she shapes up before we decide anything on that front, OK?'

By "shaping up", Frank Wombell meant that, in order to stay with his outfit, Mirella would have to show that she had it in her to be a real "trouper" and the main arena for this was on the platform, so that first afternoon when she took her place in line with Lily and her mother she knew that she had to learn quickly or be thrown out.

Tom had not been quite right when he said the animals were the show. Of course they were the essence of the Menagerie, but in a fairground where the act took its stand amongst a whole galaxy of brilliant entertainments, it could not rely merely on its collection of animals to bring in customers. It had to offer, or seem to offer, drama, excitement and thrills not available in any other show. In the form of "The Great Kazan's Dance with Death in the Lions' Den", Wombell's Menagerie could undoubtedly offer thrills, but the timing of these performances posed a problem. The Great Kazan could not, even with the best will or most aggressive spirit in the world, keep on fighting his lions all through the day and a good part of the night. Neither was it worth putting on his performance just for the sake of three or four people who'd paid their twopence to watch. The problem was, how to get folk to stand around long enough for a decent-sized audience to collect.

Well, for a start, there was the permanent notice proclaiming that the Wombell's show was "JUST ABOUT TO COMMENCE". Then there had to be specific moments when the attention of the crowd was focused on Wombell's to the exclusion of all else, a moment when the Menagerie went into action. Never mind the Fattest Woman in the World, the Thinnest Man, the Pig-faced Lady or the Pipe-Smoking Oyster – when Wombell's Parade started there would be a stir and then a wave passing through the crowd like the backwash from some large ship. People would start to move in one direction, massing, pushing against each other, jockeying for position, desperate to get a better view; the urge to join such a throng irresistible.

The murmur would pass from onlooker to onlooker: 'It's Wombell's Parade. Wombell's is just opening up. Come on, you'd better hurry or you'll miss it.'

That was Wombell's one great chance. Fluff it and they would have lost credibility not just with this crowd, but with all their neighbours and friends waiting to hear what was worth seeing in the fair this year. But seize that moment, turn it to the good, woo the people, entice and excite them, get them to laugh, get them to cry, get them to want more – and then stop the Parade and open the doors for the inside performance of The Great Kazan, and even though this part had to be paid for, who would be able to resist the surge up those steps and into the Menagerie?

Mirella's part in the Parade was at first confined to singing and dancing and looking pretty. With this in mind she was dressed in one of Lily's parade frocks with the excess material nipped in down the sideseams of the bodice and at the waist. It was in the popular new short style, worn quite a few inches above her ankle, with the skirt of white gauzy muslin very full and wafting out over layers and layers of saffron and pale yellow silk petticoats. The neckline was cut low, modesty being suggested if not served by a loose lace fichu crossed at the front with its ends taken back under her arms and tied behind, while a sash of saffron silk completed the ensemble. To keep her curls from falling in her eyes, and also to lend her extra height, the front of her black hair was drawn up into a top-knot entwined with a spray of orange flowers, whilst the rest of her long tresses were left flowing freely over her shoulders.

'My, what a difference!' Tom had muttered when

81

he caught sight of her in her new get-up. But though she waited for him to say more, he simply stood screwing up his eyes and scrutinising her appearance as if trying to find fault.

'Well, what do you think?' she asked.

'Like I said, that clobber certainly makes a difference.'

'But do you like it? Do I look all right?'

'Oh, yes. You'll do,' was all he said.

Still, the costume made her feel good and she was quite confident when she took her place alongside Lily and her mother behind the showfront; even excited to be standing there waiting for the brass band to strike up with the overture to *Zampa* and the curtains to be pulled apart.

Earlier that day in rehearsal she had been shown how to kick up her legs and dance in line with Mrs Wombell, a thin, weary-looking woman, not the type you would associate with the stage – or with Lily. For Lily Wombell at eighteen was full of herself. She was chubby and had curly auburn hair, blue eyes, and a bubbling little voice which every so often frothed over into giggles. She, Tom announced, was a real trouper, someone whom Mirella should watch and imitate if she wanted to learn how to be a really good parader. So Mirella had got Lily to teach her how to dance, and what gestures to make as she sang "Walking in the Zoo" and "Shan't I Be Glad When Sandy Comes Home", and everything had gone fine.

How could she have known that it would feel so different when she found herself in front of an audience?

The music was playing. In front of her a mob of bonnets, mantillas, top hats, flat hats and shakoes bobbed on a sea of upturned faces, and she was overwhelmed by the fact, which she should have realised before, that anyone standing on a stage is *looked* at. Well, of course she had known this, but

82

what she had not bargained for was how it felt to be looked at. And now she was feeling it and being quite overwhelmed.

There was a huge guffaw from the crowd and someone even started to clap. She was dimly aware how stupid she must look, standing there gawping at the audience whilst the band played and Lily and her mother strutted and sang, but she couldn't think how to get out of her fright, couldn't remember what she had to do or say, didn't in that moment know what on earth she was doing there in front of all those people. And she turned and ran off the stage, vowing never again to expose herself to such humiliation.

Lily laughed about it afterwards.

'You silly goose, Mirella! There's nothing to be afraid of out there. The lads might hoot or catcall a bit, but you mustn't take any notice of that. Just get on and do your stuff, and they'll love you for it. Especially with your looks, you could soon get them eating out of your hands. It's just a matter of letting yourself go and enjoying the fun.'

'Oh, Lily, I don't think I'll ever be able to bear all those eyes on me. Didn't it make you nervous, when you first started?'

'No, not me. I was performing almost as soon as I was out of my cradle. Ask Dad, he'll tell you. He's had me doing somersaults, stride splits and flip-flaps on the stage for as long as I can remember.'

'So it's easy for you. You don't know what it's like to be nervous.'

'That's true. All I can say is that you've got to find a way of getting over it, or do something else for a living. Dad won't tolerate a bad performer for long, I can tell you that.'

Lily's matter-of-fact tone of voice carried no malice. That was what Mirella liked about her. Lily was uncomplicated enough to know who she was and what she wanted from life. Whilst she would probably never put herself out on your behalf, you could rest assured that she would not undermine you either, because she was too busy pursuing her own affairs – and these were all of the heart; Lily's heart. The only tiresome thing was that she did tend to burble on at inordinate length about her latest conquest and expect you to be equally enthralled. And it was particularly difficult for Mirella to take her seriously when the object of Lily's passion at the moment was the Menagerie's lion-tamer. Mirella could not imagine how anyone could seriously be enamoured of her uncle Tom.

It didn't occur to her then that if it hadn't been for the fact that he was her uncle, Lily might have been less enthusiastic about her joining the show. As it was, the Guv'nor's daughter made full use of Mirella's natural intimacy with Tom to bombard her with questions about his thoughts and feelings, and gave her trivial messages for him and then quizzed her on exactly how he reacted when these were delivered. The game was wearisome but harmless enough. At least, so it seemed.

Even now, despite Mirella's despair after making such a mess of her first appearance on the show, Lily quickly moved away from the subject and asked her to ask Tom what he thought about the way she'd handled the serpent just now.

'The thing is,' she confided, 'I used to be terrified of snakes. Couldn't bring myself to go anywhere near them. It was only when Tom brought one and stood holding it close to me so's I could touch it and gradually get used to it, that I got over my fear and agreed to do the snake charming act on stage. And, do you know? Tom says the snakes don't take to everyone, but they seem to like me and that's why I'm so good at it. He calls me his little charmer. And he doesn't only mean with the snakes,' she giggled.

The last person Mirella wanted to see just now was

Tom, and yet she also had an instinctive feeling that he, if anyone, would understand what had gone so badly wrong this afternoon and help her to put it right. So she went to his wagon, made a cup of tea, and settled down to wait for him to finish his act.

'Hello, I was hoping you'd be here,' he said, as soon as he came in the door. 'How are you feeling?'

'Terrible. Oh, Tom, I made such a fool of myself! And I let you down. I'm sorry. I knew the song and everything. Lily taught me exactly what to do, but when the moment came I funked it. I don't know why. I just couldn't do anything. My mind went blank.'

'That's good.' He was stirring his mug of tea and smiling at her in a much more friendly way than she had expected.

'No, it's not good. I've let you down, and Mr Wombell and everyone, and I feel like crawling away into a hole and dying somewhere.' She tried to assume the air of tragedy required by such feelings but found it impossible to keep it up in the presence of his satirical smile. 'Why are you smiling like that? You know I let you down. And what do you mean, "that's good"? How can it be good when I made such a fool of myself right at the beginning of the show?'

'I'm smiling because you take yourself so serious and yet you look so funny when you're upset. And I say it's good because that sort of thing only ever happens to you once – stagefright, I mean – and now it's happened to you, and you've got it over with, it won't happen again, I promise you.'

'How can you be so sure? I mean, how do you know that I'm not a shrinking violet that will, well . . . keep getting shrunk?'

He threw back his head, laughing and keeping his eyes fixed on her so that she couldn't help joining in.

'Oh, Mirella, you'll do! I just know it. You're going to be great on the platform. Because you'll never forget what it felt like today to let an audience down. That's the vital lesson to learn. And when you go on that stage again and find out what it feels like to please them, you'll never let them down again. And you *will* please them. You have that power, believe me.' She was aware of Tom's pale blue eyes staring into hers in a way that vaguely disturbed yet excited her, and she noticed for the first time how prominent his eyes were – and how very still. She did not altogether believe what he said, but vowed she would give the next performance all she had and not relax her concentration for an instant as she danced on to that stage.

This was why the signal for the next parade found her already lurking backstage, going over in her mind all her movements and words, even figuring out what expression to fix on her face for her entrance.

'Relax, Mirella. Don't look so glum,' Lily chided her. 'Remember, it's only a bit of fun. Let yourself enjoy it.'

The band struck up the overture to *Zampa*. Immediately it finished, the dancing girls went on – Mrs Wombell in a striking red costume, Lily in pink and Mirella in her orangey-white – and together they sang "Walking in the Zoo" with some cheeky winks and gestures that had the men in the crowd whistling and roaring. At the end of the routine a fellow in the audience took off his hat and whooped. And when Mirella smiled his way and saw the expression of happy delight in his eyes, her heart warmed. Old enough to be her grandfather, he stood there communicating his enjoyment, and she knew that he was her public. And so was the plump woman standing next to him, clutching her bag and hanging on to the arm of a younger woman who was saying something and smiling. And the little lads mucking around at the front of the crowd, they were her public too. And she knew she was not letting them down, that she was in fact pleasing them. She knew she could carry on pleasing them and would always do so from now on – because being able to please people in this way made her so happy.

Once she had experienced this realisation, she was able to relax and enjoy the rest of the parade.

The Guv'nor stepped forward and in stentorian voice started his spiel about the "never, in this part of the world, seen before" wonders of his menagerie – the Bengal tigers, the Abyssinian lions, the African elephant – these wonderful beasts provided more than just entertainment, they were an education; his establishment was a dome of science in which the public could explore for themselves the evidence of Mr Darwin's theories . . .

In the midst of all this solemnity, just as Mr Wombell was getting carried away by his own oratory, the clown known as Bingo threw a somersault from backstage that landed him on the front, and began to strut behind Mr Wombell aping his every move. The crowd howled with laughter. Then, whenever Mr Wombell suddenly twisted round in an attempt to discover the cause of all this hilarity, Bingo turned at exactly the same moment so that he was always hidden behind Mr Wombell's back. Soon half the crowd were roaring to alert Mr Wombell, whilst the other half cheered Bingo on. And then in came another clown with a blackened face to do a boot dance which Bingo joined in too, until a big black dog bounded in and took hold of the seat of his trousers, whereupon he had to scramble on to a perch high above the stage from which his voice squeaked: 'Everyone's afraid of the dog but me.'

And then it was time for Lily to appear again, this time in jester's costume and with a gigantic serpent coiling about her body. There was another song and dance routine then finally, amid a fanfare of trumpets, The Great Kazan appeared and stood in silent majesty while Mr Wombell adumbrated the daring tricks and dangerous act he was about to perform in the lions' den – 'Tricks only once before attempted in this country and that was by the great Van Amburgh, himself; the very same tricks, ladies and gentlemen, as resulted in the death of that previously peerless performer, and let us all pray heaven we don't experience a similar tragedy here today. Roll up, roll up!'

Then came a bugle fanfare, with more than a hint of the "Last Post" in its tone. The Great Kazan grimly turned and left the platform, signalling that for the moment the outside show of Wombell's was over, but that the paybox was open and those able and willing to pay tribute in coin of the realm could now flood inside to see even greater drama and excitement.

Some time in mid-August, after she had been travelling with the Menagerie for about nine weeks, Mirella stayed up late to prepare Tom some supper to sustain him through what threatened to be a very long night. Caesar, one of his best lions, had fallen sick.

'Pneumonia, I'm pretty sure of it,' Tom muttered, piling up straw round the poor animal's heaving body as it lay in its cage. 'Oh, that's good of you to fetch me some grub, Mirella. But I can't touch it just yet. I've got to move fast if I'm to save poor Caesar.'

'What can you do?'

'Apply a poultice for a start. There's a little packet of powdered mustard seed lying in the corner of my top locker – the one by the door – could you run and fetch it for me, love? And a jar of vinegar and a lump of horse-radish as well.'

It did not take her long to find these ingredients, but she lingered for a while in the tent, watching him stir the mustard and vinegar together and then scrape some horse-radish into the mixture.

'Why are you adding that?' she asked.

'To make it stronger,' he explained before rubbing

it through Caesar's thick fur well into his chest and round his sides.

In the midst of the task, Tom stood up, groaning and stretching his back.

'You look tired,' she said to him. 'Can't you rest for a moment and take something to eat?' A coke fire had been lit close to Caesar's cage to help the beast sweat, and this was keeping Tom's pipkin of broth hot.

'No, I won't stop now. It's essential to get this mustard well caked into a plaster, isn't it, boy?' he murmured into the lion's ear. 'I can't really stop till I've finished.'

'Will you let me take over for a minute, then?'

'What, have you rubbing Caesar? Would you dare come and touch a lion like that?'

'Yes, I'm not scared of old Caesar. We're friends, aren't we, boy?' She came up to the cage and peered at him through the bars.

'Come on, then. Walk in here quietly and keep your movements slow and calm whatever happens. Remember that. Keep calm and alert and never for an instant turn your back on him, understand? You may be friends, but you can never trust a big cat. You stay on your guard all the time. Have you got that, Mirella?'

'Yes. Don't worry. I won't do anything stupid.'

The heat from the coke fire was almost overpowering once she entered the cage, and she felt the sweat trickle down her face. But she was not afraid. How could anyone be afraid of a poor beast lying down on the floor grunting and whickering with pain? Besides, she had complete faith in Tom. He wouldn't let her put herself at risk.

As soon as she put out her hand to touch Caesar, he turned his great head, his jaws gaping wide to show a mouth full of teeth like a spiked guillotine.

'Don't flinch,' Tom warned her. 'You must never let him think you're afraid.'

89

'Well, I'm not – very . . .' she whispered, putting out her hand to pat the lion. 'Come on, Caesar, I'm your friend and I won't hurt you.'

The lion growled and opened its jaws again, but not so wide this time. Mirella felt confident enough to scoop up some paste and start rubbing it in, making the dun-coloured fur even more sticky and matted.

'Do you know, Lily has been brought up with jungle cats all her life, yet you wouldn't catch her coming near one like this.' Tom's words gave Mirella a thrill of pride. 'In fact, I tried to persuade her to join my act once. Got a really good routine worked out, but she wouldn't do it.'

'I'm surprised to hear that. I would have thought she'd have jumped at the chance to work with you.'

'Oh, she wanted to work with me, right enough. It was the big cats that put her off. And the Guv'nor. It was obvious he wasn't keen, so I didn't push the matter.'

In the darkness around the edge of the tent, some beast was prowling up and down whilst from another cage came the sound of an animal's coughing grunt. The candles grouped together to shed maximum light on Caesar's den guttered and spluttered, causing the shadows to lengthen and dance. Tom fetched his broth, but never took his eyes off what was happening in the cage, and as soon as he had eaten, returned to Mirella's side to take over again. Eventually he finished the job off by littering Caesar with straw until the lion was practically covered.

'All I can do now is wait,' he said, slumping down on the floor.

'Will you stay up all night with him?' Mirella asked.

'Quite likely,' he sighed. 'I shall have to make sure he doesn't get too parched.'

'Well, I'll stay up for a while to keep you company

then,' she announced, settling down next to him after pouring him a drink.

'Shouldn't you be cutting along to your bed before the Guv'nor gets the wrong idea?'

'No, it's all right. He knows where I am. I told him I was bringing you out some supper.'

'Good. Well, I have to say it, you're a great help on the show, Mirella. And the Guv'nor's well pleased. He told me so himself.'

She felt her face flush with pleasure. 'I like working with the Menagerie, Tom, and I just thank my lucky stars I'm not still slaving away in some rotten kitchen. I owe my escape to you. But how did you get involved in this business in the first place? Did your father teach you how to train lions and tigers?'

'No. Dad was a prize-fighter in his younger days and then, when he gave that up, he went in for fairground amusements. We had a nice set of dobbies and a sideshow when he died, but it was hard trying to run them almost single-handed. You see, there was only me able to do the work really, because our Joey was still a sprat and Ma couldn't manage anything heavy. So we decided to get rid of the roundabout and try to manage with the sideshow and a bit of hawking. We just about made a living but there was no future in it so, when Mr Wombell offered me a chance of a job, I seized it with both hands.'

'But how did he know that you were any good as a lion-tamer?'

'He didn't. He just knew I had what they call "a way with animals". Everyone on the fairground knew that, because I used to doctor their horses if they were sick. So Mr Wombell took me on as a keeper, not a trainer. It was some time before I was able to work my way up from there.'

'And are you completely happy being a lion-tamer and doing what you're doing now?'

He startled her by grabbing her arm as he answered.

'You've fallen into the same trap as everyone else,' he said. 'You referred to me as a "lion-tamer". But I'm not that, nor is anyone else, no matter what the posters say. The man hasn't been born who could tame one of the big cats. All he can hope to do is train it. Preferably "gentle" it first, and then train it. But whatever methods he uses, he'll never succeed in taming a wild nature and it's the height of folly to think otherwise.'

'Yes, I understand what you mean,' Mirella spoke lightly, 'and I accept that you should be called a trainer, not a tamer, but that still leaves the question – are you happy doing what you're doing?'

'Happy enough,' he replied moodily. 'This job's fine in the summer months when we're travelling around, but not so good in the winter when Mr Wombell retreats to his farm and hibernates for about four months.'

'I hadn't thought about that. What do we do then, Tom?'

'Well, I usually go with him to look after the animals and use the time for practising, but as for you, you'll have to make your own plans, I'm afraid. Take another job or spend the time at home and then decide if you want to come back next season.'

'Oh.' Her world suddenly collapsed and she sat miserably trying to build something acceptable in its place. All this would come to an end in a couple of months time and she would have to return to the tawdry world of cleaning, clearing, and cooking – what a prospect!

'Unless,' said Tom, as if reading her thoughts, 'you'd fancy getting involved in the act I tried to interest Lily in and taking it round the halls with me? If we tried it out, and you could manage it all right, I'm sure I could get bookings for us and we could finish up earning a tidy little packet over the winter season. Would you fancy doing that?'

'Of course I would! I can't think of anything I'd like better. What would I have to do?' she asked, hardly stopping to think about how her parents might react, hoping that by the time they heard what she was up to, it would be too late to stop her.

Chapter Seven

Tom's idea was that Mirella should take the part of the Rajah's daughter in an act which he dubbed "The Condemned Preserved", and they sat together excitedly discussing this.

'What I'd do is this – choose three or four really fierce-looking lions and drag their cage on to the stage, right? Then you and I and one other bloke would play out this little drama which I've got worked out in my head. It's about an Indian boy who dares to fall in love with the Rajah's daughter. For that the Rajah condemns him to be torn to death by lions.'

'Ugh! And you'll play the Indian boy, I suppose?'

'You've hit it,' Tom said. 'I can get one of the keepers to dress up and act the Rajah. That's an easy part. And you, Mirella, will make a perfect Rajah's daughter.'

Yes, she could see it. Wearing a bright silk sari and with her long black hair loose, she would dance across the stage. She could have some jewellery that glittered and shone in the light . . . Yes, she liked the idea.

'So how does the drama end?' she asked.

'Well, the boy – that's me – is cast into the lions' den, but in the confusion the Rajah's daughter – that's you – follows him and seems to be in great danger of being torn apart herself.'

'Yes, yes. I can see that,' Mirella murmured, not quite so enamoured by this part of the story.

'And there's the poor distraught father left standing on stage, crying: "My child! Who will save my child?" And of course yours truly quells the savage lions and restores the darling daughter to the Rajah who is now prepared to receive the valiant rescuer as his son-in-law. What do you think?'

'Hmm. It sounds good,' Mirella agreed, not prepared to admit to any twinge of doubt she might have about the daughter's role. 'But what about the lions? I mean, this lot belong to Mr Wombell, don't they? Where will you get yours for the winter?'

'No problem. The Guv'nor will agree to lease this lot to me which will work out well from every point of view. It would take me too long to train another lot of beasts, and it saves the Guv'nor's feeding bill. Lions eat anything between eight and fifteen pounds of horseflesh a day, you know, so it makes sense for them to be earning their keep through the winter.'

'And what about Caesar? Will you take him?'

'I'm not sure,' Tom said, glancing anxiously towards the cage. 'First he's got to get over this little lot, and that's gonner take a few weeks. But I'm hoping.'

Mirella was summoning up courage to question Tom about what exactly the Rajah's daughter was supposed to do once she had entered the lions' cage, but their discussion was interrupted at that moment by Lily.

'Oh, there you are, Mirella. Dad said you'd be over here. What are you doing?'

'*She's* been helping me put a mustard plaster on Caesar's chest,' Tom said, laying great emphasis on the word "she" as if to point up the fact that no one else was prepared to help him in this way.

'What? You went into that cage with that savage animal? You must be mad.'

Mirella laughed. 'You couldn't exactly call Caesar a savage animal at the moment. It's as much as he can do to draw breath, let alone attack somebody, poor devil.'

'Hmm! Fat lot you know about lions,' Lily snarled, tossing her head. 'I know a bit more and I wouldn't trust one, not even if it was dead and skinned and I was wearing it as a coat.' She was looking challengingly at Tom as she spat this out.

'My dear, you don't need to wear a lion's skin to be mistaken for a cat.'

Tom, I wish you wouldn't do that, Mirella thought, for she had discovered that Lily, despite her giggles, had no sense of humour. Moreover, it was obvious that she was still smitten with Tom and regarded any response from him as deadly serious. Yet (and this Mirella couldn't understand) far from being nice to him, just lately Lily had gone out of her way to provoke. And, what was worse, Tom was always saying things deliberately designed to annoy Lily. Their bickering made Mirella feel like banging their heads together. Instead, she tried to stay aloof from their quarrels.

Changing the subject now, she scrambled to her feet and announced: 'I'm off to bed, Tom. I do hope Caesar's better in the morning.'

Before she could go, however, Tom had seized hold of her hand and with unusual warmth thanked her for all her help.

'I didn't do much,' she muttered, uncomfortably aware of the effect that his display of gratitude was having on Lily.

'Nonsense,' he said, continuing to cling to her. 'You'll have made Caesar a friend for life by what you did tonight. And that,' he darted a brief glance at Lily before slightly lowering his voice, 'could make a big difference when you join me in the act.'

It was almost as if he was deliberately playing her and Lily against each other, but Mirella refused to put such an uncharitable interpretation on her uncle's remark. It must be that he did not understand how little it took to make Lily jealous.

He let go her hand and she left, but before she was out of earshot she heard the sounds of Tom's and Lily's voices, the latter shrill with anger.

'So you tell me your version of this little act you and Tom are cooking up between you,' Lily whispered later that night after crawling into bed alongside Mirella and humping more than half the blankets over to her side. 'Tom says you're keen to help him work the lions.' Her tone was petulant, as if she blamed Mirella for trying to steal a march on her in some way.

'It's not quite like that,' Mirella said, and went on to explain how the suggestion had arisen from her need to find some way of earning a living in the winter months.

'If that's true,' replied Lily, still sounding very sulky, 'I would have thought you could find something less stupid than taking part in Tom's act. You know he's already asked me, don't you? I refused, of course.'

'Yes, he told me.'

'Bet he never told you why, though.'

'He said it was because your father wasn't keen,' Mirella said tactfully, deciding not to repeat Tom's jibe about Lily being afraid of the big cats.

'Well of course he wasn't keen!' Lily whispered back. 'And nor would you be, if you'd seen your sister ripped apart by a tiger.'

Mirella's stomach clenched and she felt suddenly cold and sick. She tried to persuade herself that Lily was inventing the story just to frighten her.

'It happened to my aunt Helen,' Lily's voice went on insistently, 'and my father was there and saw it. She wasn't much older than me. People called her "The Lion Queen" and she used to do an act in the Menagerie where she went into a cage of lions and

98

tigers and put them through their paces. Then in the middle of a show at Chatham, or it may have been at Greenwich – I'm not sure now, but Dad will tell you – for some unknown reason a tiger turned on her and mauled her so badly she died within minutes of being dragged out of the cage. And people said it was a mercy she did die, because if she'd survived, well, her injuries were . . . It's no good, it's just too horrible to talk about.'

Mirella agreed and wished Lily had not already said so much. For the rest of the night she lay awake, because every time she closed her eyes she saw a vision of Caesar, not lying weak and prone but turning his great head to snarl, and opening huge jaws to reveal those spiky fangs.

Next morning, when she sought out Tom, she found him sitting on a tub in Caesar's cage, talking to the animal.

'Yes, we're over the worse now, old boy. All we must do is take it easy for a week or two and we'll have you back to normal.'

'Is he really getting better?' she asked.

'Yep. He's over the crisis.'

'And have you been up all night with him?' Her question was prompted by the tiredness in his voice. Also, now that she turned away from the sick animal to peer at Tom, she could see how grey and hollow-eyed he looked.

'Yes, but it wasn't too bad. I brought down a blanket and catnapped on the straw for a couple of hours.'

'So shouldn't you go and get some proper sleep now? You've got a couple of performances this afternoon, remember.'

'No, I'm all right. And it's important to keep to my usual routine with the animals. My control over them depends on that. Which is a lesson you'll have to learn if you're to work with them too.' He touched her arm to gain her full attention. 'You're still keen on doing "The Condemned Preserved" act with me, aren't you, Mirella?'

There was a brief moment of silence.

'I . . . I think so,' she said, with as much conviction as she could muster.

His eyes narrowed and she felt the grip on her arm tighten. 'So what's made you have second thoughts?'

'Nothing really. No, that's not true. I think I'm a bit frightened of your lions.'

'Ah,' his tone softened, 'well, there's no need to be, Mirella. You remember how well you got on with Caesar last night? You've got the right touch, else I wouldn't ask you to do the act with me.'

'Are you trying to tell me that lions aren't dangerous? What about that chap – Van Amburgh, wasn't it? – who the Guv'nor always mentions in his spiel? Didn't he get torn apart doing just what you do?'

Tom laughed. 'Van Amburgh? Van Humbug, more like! You ought to know better than to be taken in by the Guv'nor's spiel.'

'Wasn't he a real man, then?'

'Oh, yes, he was real all right. Used to appear at Astley's. A Dutchman, I think, but lived in America. He was the first to bring a lion-taming act over to this country and became a great favourite with the Queen. But as for being killed – well, it became something of a joke in the end. You see, it started off as a publicity stunt. Something to get his name in the newspapers. According to them he was "killed" at least half a dozen times, usually by having his head bitten off by a tiger, but none of that prevented his actually dying safe in his bed about a year ago.'

'I see.' Mirella felt greatly relieved. 'And the story about the Guv'nor's sister being attacked by a tiger – is there any truth in that?'

'Who told you that?' She was startled by the sudden

100

sharpness of his tone. 'Did the Guv'nor say something? Because if he did it would only be because . . .'

'No. It wasn't the Guv'nor. It was something Lily said.'

'So that little minx is trying to cause trouble, is she? You needn't take any notice of her. She's just jealous of you, that's all.'

And I know whose fault that is, Mirella thought, before saying aloud: 'Then isn't it true that her aunt was The Lion Queen, and that she got killed doing her act?'

'Yes,' Tom declared, 'she was and she did, but she brought it on herself. She tormented the poor animals by constantly flicking at their eyes with her riding whip.'

'And they turned on her?'

'Naturally. But I can honestly say I've never known an animal turn like that on its trainer unless it's previously been ill-used.'

She found his words reassuring.

'So you think that as long as I'm kind to your lions, I won't be in any danger?'

'There's a bit more to it than that, Mirella. There's lots of ground rules to learn before you start working with big cats, and the first and most important is the need to be patient. We shan't be able to rush our preparations, that's why you've got to make up your mind pretty soon. But just remember, when you're trying to decide, that it's me, your uncle, in charge of the act, and rest assured that I'm not likely to do anything that would ever put your life in danger, OK?'

After that she entertained no more doubts, and in the weeks that followed Tom worked out the details of the act and introduced her to the mysteries of animal-training. Every morning she accompanied him into the cages and sat quietly, without touching the lions in any way, until they became completely accustomed to her presence.

'Now, remember this, Mirella,' he cautioned her, 'it's not your physical presence that they're likely to be disturbed by, so much as your state of mind. If you enter this cage feeling upset or with your nerves all jangled, the lions will pick it up immediately and you'll be in trouble.'

'You mean they can read my mind?' she asked incredulously.

'In a way, yes. They may not know *what* you're thinking, but they know *how* you're thinking. And if you're in any kind of panic, your own fear will be communicated and unsettle them to the extent that they'll be likely to turn on you. That's the bad side of it, but the positive side is that if you, Mirella, can gain control over your own mind, then you can control the beasts. Few people realise that it's possible to achieve that sort of power.'

She found herself gazing at Tom, awestruck. This was a totally new concept to her. Control over her own mind? Didn't she have this already? Didn't everyone?

As if reading her thoughts, he went on: 'Most people let their minds run riot all the time under the illusion that because you can't see a thought, it does no harm to think whatever comes into your head. So, they could enter a lions' cage, do all the right things, everything that they've observed me doing in fact, but they'd be lucky to get out again alive.'

'Why?'

'Because the lions would pick up their inner fears and defensiveness and be bound to attack them. Lions can't help but attack anyone who's scared or falls down in front of them.'

'Even Caesar? Would dear old Caesar behave like that?'

'I'm afraid so. Even the most tractable cats can "go bad" – which is why their trainer must always be several moves ahead of them, ready to deal with anything

102

out of the ordinary. Lions depend on routine and often the tiniest unfamiliar object can upset them. A dog or a house cat coming too close, the whiff of heavy oil, a sudden thunderclap – all these things can unsettle the animals and lead to accidents. It's up to the trainer to be on the alert and stay calm and in control.'

'Phew, that sounds a tall order!'

He smiled reassuringly. 'Don't worry. We've plenty of time, so we can take it very steady. All I want you to do to start with is come with me into their cages every morning and just sit quietly – do some sewing, if you like – and keep your mind calm but alert to everything that's going on around you. Do you think you can manage that?'

'I don't know,' she said, 'but I'm certainly willing to try.'

Things went well. She spent about half an hour or so in the lions' cage every day after that. The animals got used to her, and she got used to them. Moreover, as she grew more aware of the individual characters, habitual movements and mannerisms of the animals, she began to notice how her mood, if not her thoughts, did seem to influence their behaviour and concluded there was truth in what Tom said.

For instance, in retrospect she knew she should not have entered the cage while still feeling upset by some remark made by Lily. Not that there wasn't every good reason for her to feel upset, mind.

'I don't know how you can stand that man being all over you like he is,' Lily sneered. 'Everyone in the outfit's talking about it, you know, and they all agree it's disgusting.'

'What do you mean? Who on earth are you talking about?' Mirella asked.

'You and Tom, of course. Proper pair of lovebirds you seem to be.'

'Don't be ridiculous, Lily. Tom's my uncle.' She assumed Lily had forgotten that obvious fact, but no,

Lily refused to accept that such a close blood tie necessarily ruled out any romantic attraction.

'I know several cases of cousins getting married,' she insisted. 'In fact, it's almost a tradition in my family. And it's a fact that Tom and me were getting on fine before you came along, then he suddenly changed. Besides, like I said, anyone can see he's smitten just by the way he looks at you. Personally I think you're very wrong to encourage him like you do.'

Mirella was still seething with indignation when half an hour later she entered the Menagerie tent. She said nothing to Tom as she fetched her chair and basket of mending before joining him in the cage. Then, keeping her tone level, she muttered her usual greetings to the three lions, Caesar, Hanno and Trajan, sat herself down, careful not to make any jerky or sudden movement, and took up the first of the stockings that she intended to darn.

How dare she slander me like that? she thought, as she dug her needle into the cotton. Spreading a pack of lies about me and Tom. Well, it will have to stop.

From the corner of her eye she noticed Trajan's tail twitch and start to sway side to side. 'Good boy,' she murmured, 'good boy, Trajan. Good boy.' He growled, dipping his head, and ambled off to a corner.

She lowered her sewing into her lap and gently turned to observe the other two lions. She found that their heads were slightly swaying and, with their attention fixed on her, they were uttering soft snarls. 'All right, Hanno. All right, Caesar. I know I've been neglecting you, but it's all right now. You can both take it easy. There's nothing wrong,' she crooned. Their signs of displeasure subsided and they also ambled away.

'Good work, Mirella,' Tom said, keeping his tone very even. 'I was about to intervene but hoped you'd spot it first. But learn your lesson from that little scene and, whatever personal problems you might have, always leave them outside the cage.'

She took his advice, devising for herself a little ritual in which she cast aside her worries and stilled her mind before tackling anything hazardous or nerve-racking. The result of this was that on stage and when she was working with the animals she was able to rise above any mental conflict. But at other times she remained vulnerable as ever and could not control her rage whenever she recalled Lily's despicable accusation. For, stupid as it undoubtedly was, it had ruined her relationship with Tom. Now, when they met to go through another rehearsal of "The Condemned Preserved", or discussed costumes or possible bookings, she was on her guard and constantly trying to avoid any situation which could possibly be misinterpreted.

Tom, observant as always, noticed something was wrong and demanded to know what was up. Her inability to explain only served to widen the rift between them. Soon it became impossible for them even to speak to each other without the conversation degenerating into some kind of clash.

'Tom, you know what you're always saying about the need to be absolutely alert and in control of your thoughts when you go into the lions' cage? Well, why do you take a swig of the bottle before your performance?' She had not intended to put him on the spot. It was a genuine question asked because she was puzzled, and so the violence of his reaction really shocked her.

'Come on, out with it! What are you trying to say, Mirella? That I have to drink in order to get Dutch courage before I face my lions? Well, you're wrong. I don't drink that much.'

'I know you don't, Tom. I just happened to notice that you always down a mouthful beforehand and I wondered why, that's all.'

'Well, for your information it's just a sensible precaution I take.'

Ah, she thought, so that's it. Tom's got his little rituals too. 'Do you do it to calm your thoughts then?' she asked.

'No. I don't need to calm my thoughts. I do it to cover up any slightest taint of fear on my breath. Sometimes a man can carry fear in him without realising it, and that's what I have to guard against. But that's not to say that I'm in any sense nervous,' he concluded sharply.

Mirella was not altogether satisfied with this explanation, but his tone made her reluctant to press the point.

As days grew shorter, travelling became more difficult. Now when the Menagerie left one tober early in the morning to journey to the next, it was often still so dark that a road-torcher had to ride ahead to beacon the way. It rained a lot that autumn, too, so that carts and wagons churned the country roads into quagmires. Everyone was called upon to help chock the wheels as the loads lumbered up hills, or cling to the backs of the beast-wagons in an effort to restrain their accelerating passage downwards again. It was exhausting and dirty work, but Mirella found it exhilarating. She also loved the parading, and the social life which built up as she began to get to know fellow travellers.

The Menagerie was in the habit of visiting two completely different types of tober. Sometimes Mr Wombell's advance agent would arrange for them to pull on to a common or piece of waste ground in a town or village where on their own they would provide the only form of public entertainment. In such a place the attractions of a Menagerie could be counted upon to draw the people in, so unaccustomed were they to having such a wonder on their doorstep and so desperate to take advantage of any break in their daily grind. Even dour schoolmasters were prevailed upon to give their pupils time off to visit an "Exhibition which combines Scientific Instruction with Moral Amusement" – if the posters could be believed. But because there was a limit to how many performances could profitably be bestowed on a small population, such places tended to receive no more than brief one- or two-night stands, and a succession of these meant a lot of arduous travelling.

Much as she enjoyed bringing laughter and delight to some poor benighted local audience, for Mirella there was nothing more exciting than the huge gathering of shows and entertainments that made up the charter fairs such as St Giles's at Oxford. The Great Western Railway Company laid on special excursion trains for the benefit of folk from nearby towns and the surrounding countryside and, held as St Giles's was after Harvest Home, thousands of agricultural labourers and their families, all dressed in their best, came in to enjoy the fun.

Among the big shows there were several travelling theatres, one offering a programme which included a performance of *Richard III*, a comic song, a couple of dances, a charivari of clowns and a grand "tableau" – all of which took no more than twenty minutes! Then there were circus artistes, performing monkeys and mice, panoramic views, and portrait-taking booths guaranteeing likenesses at the cost of a penny each. There were peepshows supplying "only correct views" of the Abyssinian campaign, or of the Murder in the Red Barn. And in the unlikely event of anyone still being ignorant of the details of this crime, a jaunty little lad stood outside the latter and kept up a continuous patter, exhorting people to "Walk up and you will see true to life pictures depicting the death of Maria at the hands of the villain, Corder. And also you will see historically accurate pictures of how the ghost of Maria appeared at her mother's bedside on three successive nights, this leading to the discovery of the body and the arrest of Corder at Evenly Grove House, Brent Ford, which is a distance of seven miles from London.''

It was all daft, but Mirella loved it and, when not working, she spent her time sauntering under the avenue of elms inspecting the stalls of toys and gingerbread and twisted mint humbugs, sniffing up the odours of frying sausages and fish, and gazing curiously at the glass pavilion, erected just beyond the church, where beautifully dressed young people were dancing very differently from the way her own folk danced at family gatherings: they were dancing together in couples.

Mr Wombell disapproved of this sort of exhibitionism, but that did not deter Lily. Although even she drew the line when it came to dancing with ''flatties'', as fairground people called non-travellers, she prevailed upon several young showmen to escort her into the dancing ring.

Mirella, on the other hand, had until today declined any invitations to tread the light fantastic with a young man. But this morning, when Harry, a young actor on the booth next to the Menagerie, had pestered her to dance with him later, she had half agreed. Now, looking at the girls being whirled around to the music by their partners, she felt excited at the prospect. Tom's outburst when she went back to his wagon took her completely by surprise.

'What's this I hear from Lily about you arranging to dance in the ring with some ne'er-do-well from that acting booth?'

'What do you mean? There's nothing wrong with it, surely? Nearly all the girls who come to the fair like to dance.'

'But you're not ''all the girls'', and I thought you'd have more self-respect.'

'Oh, come off it, Tom. They're only dancing in the

ring together. I can't see what you find so objectionable in that.'

'Look, Mirella, I think you ought to get one thing
straight. We're showmen and we don't come to fairs
for our own health or pleasure. We're here to work
for our living, and there should be no time to go
gallivanting. Besides, those dance pavilions are fre-
quented by gals no better than they should be,
flaunting themselves and cavorting with young men
before they're even plighted, tempting them to take
liberties.' His words left Mirella feeling guilty, but at
the same time angry that she should be made to feel
this way when she had done nothing wrong.

'But we can't be working all the time,' she
remonstrated. 'Besides, what about Lily? She goes
dancing with different fellows and no one stops her.'

'Never mind what Lily does. You're not Lily. And
just because that little hussy acts . . . well, like she
does, it doesn't mean you have to copy her. Don't you
see, you're different from all that? You're my Mirella
and you're above that sort of thing.'

He seized her hand and twisted her round so that
she could not avoid his gaze. His eyes were pleading
with her not to let him down – and yet she was not
sure what he wanted from her. Could it be that he was
afraid that she might allow herself to be distracted
from the new enterprise and give up on "The Condemned Preserved" before it even got off the ground?

That might explain this curious reaction. Arrangements had been made with Mr Wombell and various
halls had been booked, so it would be disastrous if she
backed out now, too late for him to train a replacement. And apart from that, they worked so well
together, she and Tom, and the act was coming on
splendidly. But then why should he think that her
having just one dance would jeopardise their future?
Surely he knew her better than that. Still, if that's how
he felt, then she'd better humour him, and tell him that

she wouldn't dance in the ring if he was so against it.

'Good girl,' he said, squeezing her hand. 'You see, apart from anything else, I'm responsible for your welfare and I've got to keep thinking about what your mother would say if she found out you were misbehaving.'

That remark almost prompted her to renew the argument, but there was no time. A crowd had already gathered, waiting for the lions to be fed, and as usual Mirella accompanied Tom into the Menagerie tent to help him deal with what was every bit as much of an exhibition as his regular "lion-taming" performances. She had still not completely conquered her fear of these big cats – but then, as Lily pointed out, who could feel at ease with a beast that stood half as high as a horse and weighed about a quarter of a ton? Still, she was beginning to understand their nature better and learning to interpret their movements – the flash of an eye, twitch of a tail, the lie of the wrinkle about the jaw, and whether they were more or less restless than usual.

The more she learned, the more respect she had for the lions, and the more she pitied them. You're the ones who're the 'Condemned Preserved', she thought. Condemned to a life of captivity and preserved to amuse your captors. And there's nothing I can do about it, because you're here now, snatched away from your lovely green open spaces and your freedom to roam. It tears my heart to see you all locked up in this tiny cage and not be able to do something about it. I would change things if I could, but I can't. All I can do is cherish your dignity but at least I'll always do that, I promise.

Looking at them now it was hard to imagine that the animals needed any such patronage from her. Tom, in his normal workaday clothes and unrecognisable as The Great Kazan, had entered their cage, such a puny figure when confronting four massive

110

lions who were pacing round him, snarling, clearly roused by the smell of meat. She hated this moment, just before their food was brought in, and breathed a sigh of relief when Bingo, also anonymous without his clown costume on, at last came lugging in the tub.

The tent was packed with people who kept shuffling further and further forward to get a better view until the front row had their noses pressed up against the bars as if they too would participate in the feast. Trajan was now growling and lifting one of his front paws at Tom and clawing the air. The crowd gasped and shuffled back a pace.

The lions had not been fed the day before because, for the sake of their digestion, they were fasted every seventh day. This was why they were particularly fractious.

Come on, get on with it, Bingo, Mirella silently implored. As if he heard, Bingo dipped his hand into the tub, produced a chunk of bloody meat and passed it to Tom. After that, the two men worked quickly, with Tom flinging the chunks of raw flesh one piece after another into what became a tumultuous, leaping, snarling, roaring tangle of lions. The noise was deafening as one after the other launched itself six or seven feet into the air to snatch a piece of meat before it fell within the reach of another.

Outside under the glass pavilion couples were dancing to silvery music, but Mirella was barred from taking part in that unseemly activity. She was expected to be content with the world of the Menagerie, a world which at the moment under its grey canvas seemed so drained of natural colour that even the parrots and cockatoos appeared drab. And she found her stomach turning against the spectacle of these poor beasts being made to scrabble and fight against each other in an unreal struggle to win titbits from the hands of their lord and master.

111

Chapter Eight

Letters from home were few and far between because Mirella rarely knew her whereabouts well enough in advance to enable her to get a letter to her parents and still leave them enough time to reply. However, when the Menagerie was travelling towards a big annual fair held on a fixed date, such as Chichester Sloe Fair on October 20th, things were different. She had been delighted to find two letters waiting for her there poste restante. The first she opened was from her father.

Because of the travelling life Johnny had led in his youth, his education had not progressed far beyond what he had gleaned at his mother's knee. Mirella knew that writing was an effort for her father, and so his brief letter was especially welcome.

My dear Mirella,
Just a line to hope that you are well as I am pleased to say it leaves all well this end.
Your mother sends you her love and tells me to say your sister Cassie is doing very well and it is not too late if you change your mind and want to have a nice job, as she knows of a lady in the town who is looking for a good girl which you might suit.
Your brothers are well, apart from Benjie still having the ear-ache what with the cold winds at

present and he not always speshal about keeping his wool hat over his ears. But Albie helps me in the woods as good as a grown man now and never mind him not being eight yet. They say hes a chip off the block, and I think there right.

I hope your finding the fairground life not to hard as I know its not easy but there again if its what suits then you make the most of it, dont you? Give Tom my regards and make sure you do not be a trouble to him as I think he has been very good to look after you the way he has done. I think it is a good idea you helping him with his new act over the winter so long as you take great care and do what he says as I know he will not let you do dangerous things. And dont forget to keep on writing as your mother and me worry if we go to long without hearing news from you.

Well my love, I must close now and look forward to one day soon when you travel closer to us and I will come and see you for myself and maybe bring your mother and brothers to see you to. Look after yourself and never be feared to come home here where you are always sure of a welcome from

your everloving
Father

Dear Pa. His letter told her little that she did not already know, more particularly that her mother was still upset with her for running away and did not consider that parading with a travelling fair was anything like an acceptable alternative to doing a proper day's work as a scullery-maid! Well, every communication had conveyed that same message in some shape or other, and Mirella had to accept that her mother would probably never be happy about anything she chose to do in life.

Her father, on the other hand, was different. He

had driven over to see her as soon as he received word that she was with Tom. He had been angry, of course, but had listened to her reasons for quitting her employment and agreed that, in the circumstances, he would have done the same.

'The only thing that grieved me was the fact that you didn't immediately come back home. Of course I know how difficult things are between you and your ma. The pair of you have never found it easy together and you don't have to look far to find the cause – you're too much alike to get on with one another – but that wouldn't have stopped Sadie welcoming you back. No matter what went on in that place, between us we might have been able to put it right.'

So far she had refrained from going into detail about the beating she had received. Now she was tempted to tell him everything, but fear of ruining Cassie's chances – and thus further upsetting her mother – prevented her, and she dwelt instead on her wish to get right away from Windsor and see the world a bit, stressing that this was the reason she did not want to return home.

At first her father had found that hard to accept.

'If you was a lad, I could see it, Mirella. I felt the same need to be independent meself at your age. But it don't seem right to have a girl gallivanting round the country on her own.'

After a while, though, he relented and said he would support her decision to stay with the Menagerie on one condition: she must put herself under his brother's tutelage and allow herself to be guided in all things by Tom. She had readily agreed and felt satisfied that she had kept to her side of the bargain.

Skimming back over the contents of his letter, she re-read the last paragraph. Oh, yes, it would be good to see the family again, and even better if they could come and see her performing in the new act. She would love to see the look on her mother's face as she,

115

Mirella, walked into the lions' den. And Cassie – it would be lovely if Cassie could come as well, if she was not too busy. And surely she must be very busy, for what else could excuse the fact that she had not yet written one word in reply to Mirella's last three letters?

A glance at the other envelope in her hand confirmed that it was from Grandma Liddy, not Cassie, for she recognised the writing. Liddy often wrote to her and her letters were the kind Mirella liked to take away to some quiet corner and read slowly, savouring every word. If she was honest, she did not always find the news they contained of much interest, but it was how her grandmother said things that never failed in some mysterious way to make her feel better.

She took the letter now to the far side of the field, away from the showfolk and fairground bustle, and sat on a fallen tree trunk to read.

My dear Mirella,
I thank you for your last letter with all its most welcome news about the stage show you are planning with Tom. I am very proud to think my granddaughter is standing so well on her own two feet and making her way in the world. And although from my own experience I realise it can't be easy for you, yet I am confident that you will succeed if you put your heart into what you are doing.
Here life continues quietly, especially in the absence of Joey and his fiddle. I told you in my last, I think, how Joey had been fortunate enough to be taken under the wing of Herr Pollitzer, a wonderful violinist and teacher. Now, to our great delight, he has been accepted as a member of a regular orchestra based at Crystal Palace. He has found good lodgings nearby in Sydenham and so, although I miss him rather dreadfully, I am glad that, like you,

116

Mirella, he is proceeding positively on his chosen path in life.

Of course, Captain Cresswall is the one who deserves most credit for giving my son this chance, as I should never have been able to afford the costs of proper tuition. And in regard to the Captain, I am happy to report that he is well and . . .

Mirella raised her head and thought for a moment. Crystal Palace? Surely Tom had recently mentioned Crystal Palace as one of the amusement halls where they were booked to appear in "The Condemned Preserved" this winter. Fancy Joey being there, playing in an orchestra. That would please Tom, because he was fond of his kid brother. It was something she would look forward to as well, because she and Joey, being much the same age, had always got on well together and would have lots to talk about now.

Anxious to go and share the news with Tom, she read the rest of Liddy's letter more quickly. The usual bit about Captain Cresswall's health and more instances of his kindness to her . . . She had received a visit from a scholar writing a book about gypsies who seemed to think her some sort of expert on the subject . . . Her herb garden was coming along beautifully . . . She would like to hear from Mirella, but not to worry if she couldn't find time to write, as Liddy knew full well how busy life on the road could be. That's why she wasn't surprised not to hear very frequently from Tom, and so would Mirella please give him her love and assure him that everything at home was going along very nicely?

Yes, her grandmother's letter had worked its usual magic and Mirella felt stronger and happier for having read it. It was important to her that Liddy approved of what she was doing.

'Tom! I've got a letter from Gran,' she called from the steps of his wagon. 'Tom?' At the top of the steps she paused to knock before grasping the lower door handle. Before she had pushed it open, the top half of the door opened inwards a few inches and Tom was asking irritably, 'Yes? What do you want, Mirella? I'm busy at the moment. Can't it wait?'

'Of course. It's nothing important. Just a letter from Gran. I'll tell you about it later.'

'Yes. Do that, will you?'

She turned away quickly, feeling uncomfortable. She had never seen Tom look so embarrassed before. Could it be that he's unwell? she thought. Then she heard someone giggling inside the wagon and realised that he wasn't alone.

That sounds like Lily's voice, she thought. I wonder what they're up to that's so private? I must say, I don't understand the way they go on. One moment they're the best of pals, the next they're each other's worst enemies, and now it seems they're friendly with each other again. Oh, well, if it sweetens Lily towards me a bit, I shall be glad.

After that she gave the matter no more thought.

From Chichester the Menagerie journeyed east to Arundel and then north to Petworth where it arrived in the middle of November in time for that town's annual Winter Fair. Here Tom and Mirella were due to make their last appearance with Wombell's before separating from the Menagerie and travelling with just two beast wagons up to the Agricultural Hall in Islington to start their own tour of engagements.

They found Petworth packed as they pulled into the Market Place and, although people were complaining that the cattle ban meant that hardly any stock had been brought in for sale on Hamper's Common, this did not seem to dampen their enthusiasm for the Pleasure Fair. The only annoying thing was that Wombell's found themselves stuck with a position on the tober dead opposite their keenest rival – Ringer's Waxworks – who had just taken delivery of the most magnificent showfront. From the moment the fair opened, crowds stood before it admiring all the beautiful gilt carving, crowds such as to rejoice any showman's heart – if only he were seeing their faces and not their backs! Mr Wombell lacked this privilege.

'It's no good starting yet,' he growled, as Mirella, Lily and the others assembled behind the curtains ready to launch into their Parade. 'Look at Ringer's. They've got the crowd and they're gonner hold on to it unless I can think of something.'

'Shouldn't we just make a start anyway, Dad, and hope they turn once they hear what's going on?' Lily suggested.

Mr Wombell shook his head. 'No,' he said slowly, 'that still leaves them dummies with the advantage. I've got a better idea.'

He disappeared for a few minutes and they heard him crawling about under the parade floor. 'Right!' he called, pushing up the trap door which was set in the middle of the stage. 'All of you be ready to start the instant I give the signal.'

Mirella was at a complete loss about what was happening, until Mrs Wombell whispered, 'It's all right, he's done this before and it worked like magic. Watch what comes out of the trap.'

She watched, but all she could see was a flimsy wraith of white muslin, misty and indistinct, dancing at the end of a long fishing rod which was similarly shrouded. The "wraith" floated out high above the heads of the crowd surrounding Ringer's, paused, and then fluttered down in front of their eyes. Such a simple trick but, as Mrs Wombell said, it worked beautifully. With one accord, the crowd turned to see where the strange thing had come from and at that same moment Mr Wombell's voice bellowed: 'NOW' and the Menagerie's paraders went into action. The spectators' attention once hooked, they flooded into the Menagerie for the rest of the afternoon. In fact, so successful was the ruse that for safety's sake, and to facilitate a continual healthy flow, Frank Wombell had to resort to another.

He nailed up a previously prepared placard decorated with an arrow and a message in nice lettering which read: "THIS WAY TO THE EGRESS". All it needed then was for one of the animal keepers to move through the dense crowd, murmuring, 'Make sure you don't miss the egress,' for there to be a surge of folk pushing their way out of the tent and leaving room for more customers.

It was well after midnight before the showmen shut up shop and the last revellers straggled away from the ground. As usual, Mirella helped Mrs Wombell make cocoa for all the company and then, carrying two steaming mugs, pushed her way into the Menagerie tent in search of Tom.

'Are you all right? There's nothing wrong, is there?' she asked when she came upon him staring glumly into Caesar's cage. He still had his greasepaint on, but under the colour his face looked strange, the skin puckered into an angry fold around his jaw as if he was assessing some damage he had just discovered.

'No,' he snapped. 'There's nothing the matter with me, why do you ask?'

'You look a bit annoyed, that's all.'

'Has Lily said anything to you?' he muttered.

'No. She's already gone to bed. Why? What could she have said?' She was casting her mind back over the last twenty-four hours, trying to recall whether Lily had in fact said anything that would account for Tom's mood, but as far as Mirella could recall the girl had not mentioned him. In fact, she hadn't really talked about anything all day long apart from the virtues of her latest swain, and since this was a paean very oft repeated, Mirella had taken little notice beyond registering the fact that this time Lily had chosen a sweetheart from within the bosom of her own family.

Mirella had met Max Wombell on a couple of occasions and been struck by the strong resemblance he bore to the Guv'nor, his uncle Frank, except that he was so much younger of course. Max's father, being the elder of two sons, had inherited the circus which had hived off from the original Menagerie founded by old Mr Wombell and had gone on to make a considerable fortune from this legacy. Ever since the birth of Max and Lily in the same year, their two fathers had joked that one day marriage might unite their offspring and thus enable the family to put the grandest show in the kingdom on the road.

'I don't suppose there are many so obviously destined as me and Max,' Lily had boasted today. 'Look, he's just sent me a photograph of himself taken on the back of one of the ring-horses. Isn't he handsome?'

'Yes,' Mirella had said, 'I don't think I've seen a finer looking stallion – or is it a mare he's riding? I can't quite see from this.' Whereupon Lily had snatched back her photograph and finally taken the hint to shut up about her suitor.

Smiling now at the incident, Mirella supposed it was just the sort of pleasantry that might cheer up Tom and proceeded to tell him about it. He interrupted her long before she reached the punch line.

'That's right, you laugh at me as well,' he said bitterly. 'It's my own fault. I should have known better. Everyone knows what she's like.'

'Who?'

'Lily, of course. You've heard she's getting married to that fancy cousin of hers, haven't you?'

Mirella laughed. 'Getting married? Has it got that far with this one? Well, that's something, I suppose. After all, she can't drag them all to the altar steps, can she?'

'What the hell do you mean by that?'

His tone was sharp to the point of menace and so she modified what she was about to say, puzzled by his irascibility.

'Let me put it this way, Tom: Lily can be rather flirtatious, but I don't think she means much by it. It's just her way of amusing herself. She likes the drama.'

He grabbed her arm, making her spill half the contents of her mug. 'What has she told you about me?'

'Nothing. I mean, I know she likes you and thinks . . . oh, wait a minute, are you trying to say that you've been getting sweet on Lily?' Tom taking Lily seriously? Mirella would have dismissed that as some kind of joke had not the look on his face told otherwise.

'All right, I know it's stupid, and I don't want to talk about it, but I'll get my own back on that little trollop, you'll see.' Despite his protestations, he couldn't stop himself talking about it, and in the course of the next half hour, Mirella gleaned something of what had been going on.

Tom, according to him, had never really been interested in Lily – well, not seriously – but the girl had pestered him ever since he joined the show, and eventually he'd weakened. What man wouldn't when something like that kept offering itself on a plate? You see, it wasn't just Lily. It was the fact that he had his way to make in the world, and there were harder paths to prosperity than marrying the Guv'nor's daughter. And, as far as he was concerned, that was the understanding between him and Lily, although they had agreed to play things very discreetly until the right moment came to approach her father. Then, tonight, after his last performance of the season, the Guv'nor had sought him out and sorted him out good and proper. Warned him off any further dalliance with Lily. Informed him that, as far as he was concerned, his daughter's future was settled. She would be marrying her cousin Max, and he was not prepared to see that situation compromised in any way. So if Tom had other ideas, he'd better take his money and go now without expecting to come back to the Menagerie next spring.

'Oh, Tom,' Mirella tried to console him, 'don't take it so much to heart. I don't think she's worth it, honestly.'

'I know she's not bloody well worth it,' he spluttered, 'and I'm not grieving about losing her. It's my future prospects with this show that've gone up the spout. Do you think I can face coming back here next year with this behind me? No, that little trollop has put the kibosh on that.'

Mirella watched him as he stomped off to his wagon, probably to seek consolation in a bottle. She was amazed at this new side of Tom that had been revealed.

The man whose dominion over himself enabled him to outface lions and tigers had allowed someone as silly as Lily to upset him. Here was The Great Kazan who boasted that he could control his own mind and reactions, but where his emotions were concerned, he wasn't so much in control as he pretended. She felt a flutter of fear when she recalled the spite she had seen in his eyes when he talked about Lily, and knew she'd never again have the same faith in him as before.

But at least she was not stuck in a cage with him, like the poor wretched lions. She was free to come and go as she liked. And in future, she would think for herself a lot more and make up her own mind about things. (She had not forgotten the dancing pavilion.)

On the other hand – and this was the surprising thing – since Tom had shown himself to be vulnerable and imperfect and so much more human, she found herself liking him more. Besides, she was grateful to him and wanted him to succeed. He had put so much effort into their new act. People who had seen them rehearsing said it was good and she was determined that no trivial upset over Lily was going to ruin their prospects now. So, the first thing she would do was try to restrain him when it came to the booze. After all, there was no reason why people who had only paid to see "The Condemned Preserved", should be treated to the spectacle of The Condemned being eaten!

Chapter Nine

Royal Agricultural Hall, Islington.
Grand
CHRISTMAS FETE
1867–8
will open for the season
MONDAY, DECEMBER 23rd
with the greatest combination of
ATTRACTIVE EXHIBITIONS
Ever brought under one roof – INCLUDING
A Menagerie, Circus, Royal Moving Waxwork,
Star Marionette Exhibition, Ghost Show,
Performing Dogs & Monkeys,
Steam Circus, Aquarium,
The Great Kazan in THE CONDEMNED PRESERVED
Performance every two hours.
And all the Fun & Frolic of a Country Fair.
A GRAND BAZAAR & GIGANTIC XMAS TREE.
Accommodation for 80,000 people, wet or dry.
. . . . .
Doors open on Boxing Day and during the following
week at 10 a.m. till 11 p.m.
Thirteen Hours Amusement
ADMISSION SIXPENCE!

Mirella read the poster again, this time letting her eyes
rest on just two lines:
The Great Kazan in THE CONDEMNED PRESERVED
Performance every two hours

It was almost as exciting as seeing her own name there in print. Especially when she considered that as many as eighty thousand people might be in the Hall in any one day and want to see their show. Mind you, there was so much competition, they would have to work hard to keep attracting the crowd.

The Aggie, as locals affectionately called this building, had been built just five years ago by the Smithfield Society to house its annual cattle show. It was a gigantic structure covering no less than three acres, with the main hall nearly four hundred feet long and over half as wide, covered in by a magnificent iron-and-glass roof. Every year the Aggie played host to a grand Christmas Fair which lasted for six weeks and offered a variety of entertainment unrivalled anywhere in the kingdom. This year Mirella Granger was star of one of its shows and she was enthralled by the place, the people, and the occasion.

Yesterday, the Fair's first day, it was chaotic and Mirella too busy to look about her. Today being Christmas Eve, although the place was still crowded, a calmer mood prevailed, and she took advantage of a lull between performances to wander up to one of the side galleries and survey the hall.

In the centre stood the gigantic Christmas tree laden with toys and surrounded by gingerbread stalls, tables piled high with fruit and nuts, "penny dip" lotteries, and other nick-nacks. But it was the tree which commanded her attention by the way it simply stood there in its majesty and stillness amidst a world which whistled, screeched, screamed and squealed all around it.

Next in pride of place stood the latest wonder of the age, the steam circus – a merry-go-round not pushed into motion by men or pulled around by a pony, but actually powered by steam. All day long crowds of people stood staring in amazement at the contraption, huddling back when it suddenly roared and snorted steam or blew its shrill whistle, cheering all those courageous enough to climb on the backs of the bright steeds and allow themselves to be whisked around at such breath-taking speed.

She would certainly have a go on that herself as soon as she had a chance, Mirella decided, before glancing around to take in the rest of the Bazaar, the Aquarium, the Marionettes, the Exhibition with the great painting outside showing monkeys dressed as jockeys riding on dogs in a hurdle race, and then a large theatrical booth with a stage in front on which Pantaloon, Harlequin and Columbine were going through their familiar antics prior to the performance within. There was a queue in front of the Phantoscope waiting to see Professor Pepper's famous ghost illusion. And then there was the Waxworks which she had decided to give a miss to after seeing their bilious-looking statues being unpacked before the Fair opened.

One end of the Aggie was entirely given over to a real circus (as opposed to the steam merry-go-round variety) and almost everything in the hall stopped when its performances started, because there was no way anyone else could compete with the magnificent spectacle of "St George and the Dragon" as presented by the Sanger Company. And that reminded her: she must make sure Albie got a good view when he came up on Saturday.

She was really looking forward to seeing her family again despite the fact that her mother wouldn't be there, Sadie having decided she couldn't risk exposing Benjie to London's smoke and fog. At least that's what she said, but Mirella suspected her of using this as an excuse to cover the fact that she simply did not want to come, wanted no more to do with her ne'er-do-well daughter.

Oh, Mother, why won't you ever give me a chance

127

to show I'm not so bad as you think? thought Mirella, sighing and biting her lip to deflect the pain she felt. Still, at least Cassie would be coming, she reminded herself. Cassie, her father, and Albie – she pictured their faces as they looked round at all the wonders of the Aggie. And she imagined their reactions as they witnessed the daring part she played as the Rajah's daughter being rescued from the lions' den . . .

Just at that moment she caught sight of her "rescuer". Tom had his face blackened by burnt cork and was wearing sandals and a loose robe to cover the flimsy sarong he considered suitable for his role as Indian boy. From the way he was scanning the crowd, she guessed he was looking for her, afraid maybe that she would stay away too long and not allow sufficient time to prepare properly for their next performance.

Thank goodness he seemed to have got over that nonsense about Lily, and was full of plans for developing their act and, instead of going back to the Menagerie, trying to negotiate a contract with a travelling circus for the next summer season.

'That's why it's vital we shine here, Mirella. You never know who might be watching the show, you see. Georgie Sanger, for instance. I've had a word with him already and he's definitely interested. And the beauty of it is, he's got his own beasts I could work with, if I don't manage to buy Caesar and the others off old Wombell.'

'George Sanger?' she'd queried. 'Was that the dapper little man with the goatee beard I saw you talking to this morning? Does he own the outfit who are doing the "George and Dragon" spectacle, then?'

'Yes, together with his brother. But he's the real boss, and if I can get him interested in our act, we'll really be in the big time, you and me.'

'Did you tell him we're going on to the Crystal Palace as soon as we've finished here?' she asked.

'Yes, and that impressed him, so I'm pretty sure

he'll be in to look us over. If he likes what he sees, I'll do a deal with him.'

'But how could we make our act work in a circus? If the audience are sitting all round the tent, half of them won't be able to see what's going on, surely?'

'Simple,' he had explained, 'instead of using a cage with a solid back like it's got now, we get one made with bars on all sides and then everyone will be able to see, no matter where they're sitting.'

As Tom caught sight of her now, she waved to him before turning her back on the swings, shooting-saloons, and aunt sallies that were set out along the galleries, and making her way down to rejoin him in the main body of the hall.

'Shouldn't you get yourself ready for the perform-ance?' he bellowed to make himself heard above the musical organs and whistles and bells and firing guns and smashing bottles that accompanied all the laugh-ter and screams from the minute the Fair opened to the time it closed.

'Just going,' she mouthed back at him.

Her father, brother and sister arrived as planned on the following Saturday. They had travelled up by train from Windsor and were going to stay overnight with Tom and Mirella before journeying back the fol-lowing day.

'After all,' Johnny announced as he hugged and kissed her, 'I don't get much chance to see my eldest child and I want to hear everything she's been getting up to.' He was affecting a mood of gaiety, but Mirella was quick to pick up some underlying anxiety in his tone. She looked immediately towards Cassie for some clue to its cause but the change in her sister's face and demeanour did nothing at all to reassure her. Cassie had gone thin and pale and her eyes were ringed by dark shadows. Mirella, suddenly fright-ened, wanted to blurt out: 'What's the matter? Is it

Mother? Is it Benjie? What's happened to make you look like this?' but restrained herself and kept up a cheerful banter until such time as she could be alone with Cassie and find out what was wrong.

When discussing their accommodation before setting out on their winter tour, Tom and Mirella had decided that Mirella should take over the bed in the living wagon whilst Tom slept in the front compartment of one of the beast wagons. This arrangement worked particularly well at the Aggie, where the showfolk camped in a commodious outbuilding, drawing up their wagons in orderly lines but leaving enough of a gap between the rows for tables and chairs and cooking paraphernalia to be set out. After the Fair shut each night groups of people gathered in these spaces to eat their supper, discuss the day's happenings, and generally enjoy each other's company.

'You're lucky to be given time off so soon after Christmas,' Mirella commented, as Cassie left the others chatting round the fire-drum and followed her up into the wagon where they were both going to sleep. 'Are you still enjoying yourself working at the Castle?'

'Hasn't Dad told you? I'm not there any more. I left. I couldn't stand it, Mirella. Oh, you've no idea what that awful woman did . . .' Mirella listened, astonished, to the sorry tale that she herself might have told just a few months since. Poor Cassie, it seemed, had fallen prey to the same systematic bullying and victimisation at the hands of the housekeeper as her sister before her.

'But I don't understand,' she interrupted, 'Mrs Newbolt seemed to like you. Why should she turn like that?'

'I don't know,' Cassie sniffed, her eyes welling over with tears. 'She was all right at first. I thought you were making excuses for yourself when you said how nasty she was. Then, when it was obvious you weren't

130

coming back to the Castle, she changed and began to pick on me for no reason at all. And I was working as hard as I could! I did everything I could think of to please her and make her like me again, but she said such mean things about me in front of the other girls. Like how fed up she was with having dirty little gypsy girls in her kitchen. And then Millie asked me about you one day, and I said you were really happy travelling with Wombell's. And Millie must have repeated that to Mrs Newbolt, because she really tore me off a strip then, saying she didn't want to hear your name mentioned ever again in her kitchen and if I thought you were so happy travelling the roads like a common gypsy, why didn't I go and join you, instead of making the other girls think you'd done something clever by running off the way you did.'

'Ooh, I just wish I could stick her in a cage with Caesar and Trajan, they'd soon sort her out,' Mirella muttered. She was pleased to see Cassie smile at that idea. 'Still, you've escaped from her clutches and that's the main thing. So what are you going to do now? Are you looking for another post?'

Cassie shuddered. 'No. I can't bear the thought of going back into service, and Ma says she's pleased to have me at home for a while so I'm gonner stay and help her. There's plenty to keep me busy and I'm happier at home.'

'Why don't you do what I'm doing? Join a travelling show? I could ask Tom. Why, you might even be able to join us . . .'

Cassie interrupted her. 'No, not me, Mirella. I couldn't do that. I'm too shy. Besides, I feel happier being at home, now I know what people can be like outside.'

But she did not look happy, Mirella thought, cursing that spiteful Newbolt woman again.

'Don't you get lonely, sleeping up here by

yourself?' Cassie asked, pushing back the bedshutter and prodding the mattress.

'No, I love living in this wagon. You see, there are so many people about during the day time, it's nice being able to come up here and climb into my own little world at night.'

'But they're so strange, those people out there. And some of them dress peculiar and talk funny. Don't you find them scary?'

Mirella was puzzled for a moment, and then it occurred to her what Cassie meant. The midgets and freaks whose appearance was so bizarre against the background of their particular show, simply melted into the rest of the community after closing time, and because she knew so many of them individually Mirella tended to forget there was anything odd about them. There were also some foreign-looking people amongst the showfolk – Spaniards and Italians, one or two black men from Africa, and some Jewish Londoners. And everyone, whether foreign or not, referred to non-showfolk disparagingly as "jossers" or "flatties" and peppered their talk with fairground slang.

'No, Cassie. They're not frightening once you get to know them. It's like living in one huge family,' Mirella said, realising for the first time how fond she had grown of all these people, how in fact she felt far more at home here than ever she had done in her actual family, maybe because there was no one here to keep criticising her and making her feel inadequate all the time; they accepted her for what she was. 'You'd be surprised how friendly everyone is and we really enjoy each other's company, especially when the flatties go home and we just sit and talk round the fire. And if anyone's in trouble – like a little girl from one of the circus families taken ill with measles last week – then everyone rallies round and helps out.'

'I still don't think I could live like this,' Cassie

murmured, 'and as for risking my neck going into a lions' den several times a day like you, well, I just don't know how you dare.'

'It's a lot easier than outfacing old Newbolt, I can tell you that,' Mirella laughed.

Before changing into their nightgowns, they went outside again to bid their father and uncle goodnight, and found them sitting sprawled in a circle with several circus men who were passing round a two-handled pot of ale and telling jokes which had the company slapping their thighs with laughter.

'Off to bed now, my maids?' Johnny beamed.

'Yes, Pa. I've got to be fresh and alert for the lions tomorrow.' The remark was not barbed, but as soon as the words left her lips, Mirella realised that Tom would take it as aimed at him, for he was sensitive on the subject of his drinking habits. In an effort to forestall any reaction that might spoil the mood of the moment, she smiled reassurance in his direction, only to find that the gesture was intercepted and returned by a complete stranger. Overcome by embarrassment, she found her smile freezing into a grimace which was then imitated by the stranger in such a comical way that she laughed out loud.

'Yes, I think you'd better call it a day, Mirella,' Tom's voice cut in, 'and let's hope there are enough hours left on the clock for you to sleep off your muzzy-head.'

She stared at him, but before she could think of a suitable reply, out of the corner of her eye she caught sight of the stranger's expression changing again. This time his face became so doleful that her attention was irresistibly drawn back to him just in time to receive a small smile. He did not say anything, but later, when closing her eyes for sleep, she remembered his smile and his eyes – dark brown eyes flecked with amber, full of life and intelligence and, yes, complicity. He had looked at her, not as a stranger would

look, but as someone who knew her – intimately –
already.

'You, yes. Of course, it's you. I recognised you at
once,' his dark eyes seemed to be saying. But that
was stupid when she knew they had never met before
today. What gave him the right to look at her like
that? she asked herself, finding his familiarity faintly
alarming. And she was not sure she *liked* being looked
at like that, she decided, trying unsuccessfully to dismiss him from her thoughts.

'Tom, who was that man you and Pa were talking to
last night?' she asked the next morning after Johnny
and her brother and sister had left.

'Which one? The big ginger-haired chap or the
smaller one who's dark and foreign-looking?'

'Yes, him. The smaller one,' Mirella said, noticing
and taking stock of the young man sitting on a stool in
the midst of the circus wagons, apparently writing or
sketching. He was a couple of inches taller than Tom,
she had noticed when they were standing side by side
last night, and about the same age, but thinner and
more wiry. He had short black wavy hair, a dark silky
moustache, and yes, Tom was right, there was something about his appearance or manner that was
undeniably foreign.

'That's Levic. He's with Sanger's at the moment.'

'What does he do?'

'What does he do?' Tom repeated. 'What *doesn't*
he do! Do you mean you've never heard of Levic? He
caused a sensation back in the summer, doing a trapeze act out over Morecambe Bay, hanging from a
swing slung under a hydrogen balloon.'

'He's a trapeze artiste like Leotard, then?' Mirella
asked, looking with renewed interest at the young
man.

'No, not really. I think that was just a piece of
derring-do to win some wager. He doesn't specialise

134

in trapeze work. He's an equestrian and an acrobat and a juggler, and I've seen him turn a somersault on a tight rope as well. But I suppose what he's best known for is his clowning. Oh, you must have heard of Levic the Clown. He's famous.'

'No, I haven't. But then, we didn't talk about circuses at home much, unless they happened to come to Windsor, of course.'

Tom shrugged. 'Well, there you go. Levic spends most of his time travelling on the continent with circuses like Renz and Franconi's, so you wouldn't expect to see him in Windsor, unless it was by royal command.'

'What nationality is he then?'

'I don't know. You'd think English by the way he talks, but there's a bit of an accent there. Polish, possibly. Or Russian. But let's go and ask him if you're so interested.'

'No, he's obviously busy,' she said, feeling suddenly shy.

'Oh, he won't mind me interrupting him,' Tom insisted, taking hold of her arm and dragging her across to meet the famous clown. 'Levic, my friend, do you mind telling me something? Mirella here was asking me what country you come from and I'm blowed if I know.'

As she feared, he looked irritated by the interruption and she felt angry at Tom for being so ill-mannered.

'I'm sorry,' she muttered, 'I didn't mean to be rude and I can see you're busy.'

'Not at all,' he murmured, scrambling to his feet and inclining his head in a slight bow as he addressed her. 'I am honoured that you take such interest in my antecedents.' He pronounced his words with slow, musical preciseness.

'No, it's not that. We were just talking and . . .' Mirella was overcome by confusion, unsure whether

135

the man's politeness was sincere or mocking, and instead of coming to her assistance, Tom stood by in silence seeming to enjoy her discomfiture.

'Many people ask this question,' Levic's slow deliberate voice came to her rescue. 'That I am not English, this is obvious, so what part of the world, they say, is responsible for this strange fellow? I will tell you, Mrs Granger, I was born in Hungary but left my native land at a tender age after my father was killed in political troubles there. I came then to this country and was brought up here to consider it my home, in so far as I wish any place to be a home. You understand?'

When he smiled, his brown eyes shone with warmth, or was it mockery? Though still unsure which, she found herself smiling back at him as if greeting an old friend.

'And Tom tells me you are performing in the circus here at the moment,' she said.

'He *is* the circus here at the moment,' his ginger-haired colleague interrupted.

'Apart from St George and the Dragon, and the chariots and the horses, and the lions and tigers and elephants and camels, not forgetting the princess, of course, and the tumblers and high rope walker, this is true,' Levic agreed modestly. 'But you must come and see the spectacle for yourself, Mrs Granger, if you have not already done so. I think you would enjoy our little show.'

'Oh, yes. I've been wanting to see it, but it's been so crowded up to now and I've been waiting for a quieter moment.'

'In the gallery, yes, it is very full of people every performance, but in the comfortable sofa lounge, there you may sit and watch at ease. So, with your husband's permission, I shall give you two lounge tickets which you may use at any time to see the show.'

'Oh, I wasn't trying to hint,' Mirella began to say at

136

the same time as Tom cut in with: 'Well, that's very nice of you, Levic. And let me return the favour by inviting you in to see our little show. Not that it's in the same league as Sanger's, of course, but I feel confident you won't find it a complete waste of time.'

'I shall be delighted,' Levic said, acknowledging Tom with a slight inclination of his head before turning back to Mirella. 'So you will now have no excuse not to have seen Levic and laughed at him. And I shall take the first opportunity to see – what is it?—"The Condemned Maiden"? Which I am sure, with your presence in it, I shall enjoy.'

'Not if she stays "condemned", I trust,' Mirella said. 'For my sake, it's meant to be "The Condemned Preserved".'

'And indeed I'm glad that is so. My mistake is a bad one. It could have proved fatal.' His remark was accompanied by a sardonic smile.

'Don't worry. Your other mistake was not so terrible. You seem to think I'm Tom's wife, but I'm not. I'm only his niece.'

'Only his niece?' His eyes widened and he repeated the words slowly as if they were difficult to comprehend. 'But somehow I was given the impression . . .' He glanced questioningly at Tom who stared blandly back at him. 'You are Tom's niece, so you are then Miss Granger perhaps?' he continued, seeming to collect his thoughts again.

'That's right. Miss Granger, perhaps. But Mirella, certainly.'

'Mirella,' he repeated. 'This is a beautiful name and it suits you.'

Feeling the colour rushing to her face, she was almost relieved when Tom announced they must go because they had work to get on with.

'You must watch yourself with chaps like him,' he muttered as they walked back to their own wagon. 'All that oily charm, but it doesn't mean anything.

137

Levic's just a philanderer on the lookout for another conquest. You saw it yourself, didn't you? As soon as he got to realise you weren't attached, he started taking liberties. Couldn't resist it, because that's the way they treat women in their country. But when I see them trying it on over here, it makes me sick.'

'That's funny, I didn't find him at all objectionable. In fact, I rather like him. And what on earth did you say that led him to think you and I were married?'

'I didn't say anything of the sort. He just picked up the idea from seeing us together, I suppose, and to be frank I didn't go out of my way to set him right because it's no bad thing for folks to have that idea when we're on the road. It makes you less vulnerable.'

She thought about that for a moment.

'I understand what you mean, Tom, but I don't agree with you, so please put people right if they get the wrong idea in future, will you?'

'You don't agree with me!' he snarled. 'What the hell do you know about anything? Little Miss Hoity-toity, don't you get on your high horse with me! If I see you fluttering your eyelashes at fellows, I shall pack you back to your father faster than you can say "Kazan", got me?' He had seized her arm as he was saying this and held it in a painfully tight grip.

'Let go of me,' she hissed. 'You're hurting.'

He did let her go, but not before squeezing her arm once more and saying: 'All right, but don't you start playing games with me, Mirella. I'm responsible for you, remember, and you'll do exactly what I say.'

She shook herself, wondering what she had done to provoke such a storm from a seemingly clear sky. Instinctively she glanced back at the circus wagons where Levic still stood staring towards them. Fortunately, he could not have heard any of Tom's words, but she felt ashamed to think what he would make of such an undignified scene.

Later in the day Levic brought the promised

complimentary tickets over to Tom who had sufficiently recovered from his ill temper to suggest they
take early advantage of them.

'I think we can make their last performance if we
call it a day after our seven o'clock turn, and then
afterwards I'm going to take you in a cab down the
City Road for a bite to eat at the Eagle Tavern. Would
you like that?'

She agreed with as much good grace as she could
muster, wanting the atmosphere to be sweet between
them again whilst at the same time still disturbed by
Tom's sudden outburst of that morning. The animals
too seemed to pick up the increased tension. Hanno
was all right, but Trajan was in an awkward mood,
and there was a moment during the performance
when even old Caesar began to turn nasty. Tom saw
the danger and brought them to heel in a showy way
that had the crowd cheering louder than usual, so the
episode passed off all right. However, Mirella was
aware that there was something different in Tom's
manner, that he was not in complete control, and her
worst fears were realised when she smelt the drink on
his breath as he finally "rescued" her and carried her
out of the cage.

Anxiety about Tom – his irascibility and drinking
bouts – dominated her thoughts that evening. This
was a pity, because in other circumstances she would
have thoroughly enjoyed her visit to the circus. As it
was, the only time she forgot her worries was when
Levic appeared.

Having met him in ordinary life, she was particularly interested to see how he would look in his professional guise and sat anxiously awaiting his first
entrance until her attention was caught by an
immaculately dressed individual, clad in a baggy-
sleeved, turquoise satin costume, who came
sauntering into the ring and simply stood there,

pigeon-toed and with his knees together, staring at the audience. It was hilarious. The audience howled with laughter, and Mirella joined in. Slowly the clown turned and looked in her direction, causing her laughter to falter and become a gasp of astonishment. It was Levic! And she had failed to recognise him despite the fact that she had been watching out for him and he used hardly any clown make-up beyond the traditional white face and exaggerated eyebrows.

Fascinated, she gazed while he fished around in his pocket to produce an oyster on a half-shell which he proceeded to serenade. His face contorted with pain as he sang of the sufferings endured by "A Crustacean Crossed in Love". Then, eventually reaching the end of his sad tale, he raised the object of his devotion on the palm of his hand and tipped it down his throat.

After that he slipped away almost invisibly and when he next appeared it was in enormous sagging trousers as a country bumpkin trying desperately to mount a horse. Of course he couldn't manage it and the crowd roared as he stumbled and fell off and tried again, only to finish up sitting back to front facing the animal's tail. Once, however, he reached the stage where like a butterfly he shed the rough clothes to reveal his own splendid costume underneath, he revealed that he was an expert horseman as well as a clown and gave a remarkable exhibition of bareback riding.

She was amazed at his versatility and realised that his friend had not been exaggerating when he listed Levic's skills. Effortlessly he slid in and out of the ring, binding all the other acts together, bantering with the ring-master and the audience, lampooning famous people and topical events, juggling with words as easily as with plates and bottles and spoons, reciting and tumbling and wire-walking. Never vaunting his skills as the other artistes did, but seeming to discover his talents as he went along by always taking on whatever life had to offer.

After watching Levic, the grand finale – the much advertised drama of St George and the Dragon – proved to be something of an anti-climax. It was spectacular enough with all the chariots spinning round the ring, and the lions and elephants and other exotic beasts lending their helpful presence to the saint who was for some reason played by a girl, dressed up in armour and riding a white steed. But it lacked the poignancy of the clown who all evening long, refusing to be worsted, had kept battling on against the buffetings of fate. His predicament struck much nearer home.

'He's really good, isn't he?' Mirella exclaimed, as she and Tom jostled their way through the crowd leaving the Aggie.

'Who?'

'Levic, of course. I think it's amazing the way he juggled those plates, and balancing on that rope, and somersaulting off the back of his horse while it was still galloping, and I had no idea he could be so funny!'

'Yes, he's clever. But a lot of it's show. He acts the fool first, gets the jossers on his side, and then whatever he manages to do next looks better than it really is.'

'I don't think that's fair. I mean, when you think of all the different things he does, you wouldn't expect him to shine at everything, and yet whatever he did seemed to turn out first-rate to me.'

'Oh well, then, he must be the genius you seem to think he is,' Tom sneered. 'Now correct me if I'm wrong, but I didn't see him put his head into a lion's mouth or do anything else really dangerous. If you think about it, you could see most of his act at any penny gaff. The only difference is that Levic's made a name for himself by putting a hotch-potch of things

141

together in a way that's useful for a circus.'

Mirella could not understand why Tom's tone was so derogatory. It seemed obvious to her that Levic was a great artiste and she wondered if perhaps Tom was jealous of this fact. If so, it was pointless prolonging the discussion. Instead, she sought to please him by expressing her excitement at the thought that their own act, "The Condemned Preserved", might soon be billed on Sanger's posters.

'Yes,' he agreed, 'that's what we've got to cling to, you and me, Mirella. Forget everyone else and concentrate on our own success. Because you and me, we're going to climb high, I promise, and once we've made it to the top, then let old Wombell remember the days when we were just starting out and not considered good enough for the likes of his family!'

Chapter Ten

Crystal Palace . . . The name conjured up visions of light, some fairy palace carved from ice, hung with gossamer and lit by chandeliers. There would be music in the palace, and dancing. When Mirella closed her eyes, she could hear the music and see the shadowy figures, the gentlemen waltzing with their ladies in white, swirling them in and out of the rainbow rooms.

The reality was different, of course. More massive and monumental, but in its own way no less impressive as it rose up, tier upon tier of iron girder and glass. It was amazing to think that this enormous structure had, just a year before Mirella's birth, started life in Hyde Park, been dismantled section by section, transported to this site south of London, and then built up again as if it were no more than a canvas tent.

'You'd never think anyone could move a huge place like this around the country, would you, Joey?' Mirella said, as her youngest uncle greeted her on the terrace.

'No, but I'm glad they did. It makes a wonderful setting for our concerts.' At first she had to listen carefully to catch the sense of his nasal intonation, but after a few minutes she forgot his impediment and had no trouble understanding what he said.

'So you're still scraping away on that old fiddle,'

she teased, 'and, according to Grandma, you've actually found someone willing to pay you to make all that horrible noise.'

He gave her a lop-sided smile. 'Yes. I've been lucky. My teacher recommended me to Herr Manns. He's taken me into his orchestra and we give weekly concerts here. In fact, there's a really good one coming up next Saturday when we're playing a Beethoven symphony and a Fantasia composed by my teacher, Herr Pollitzer, and some Gounod and Verdi. I'm hoping Ma and the Captain will be coming up to hear it, so if I get you and Tom tickets as well, do you think you'd both come? I know Ma would like that.'

'Grandma is coming up to the Crystal Palace for your concert on Saturday? But that's wonderful news, Joey. I haven't seen her for ages, and she'll be able to see "The Condemned Preserved" as well, because we're scheduled to do a couple of performances in the afternoon. And then we can all come and hear you play. That sounds like my idea of a perfect day.'

Tom was not quite so enthusiastic.

'I shall be pleased to see Ma, of course. And the Captain. I always get on well with him. But as for sitting through one of those concerts, that's definitely not my idea of fun. It's not like you imagine, no dancing or proper sing-song like we had in the Eagle. These concerts are more like going to church, with a lot of stuffed shirts sawing and screeching away for hours on end while the audience sits dead still and only cheer at the end to show how glad they are the torment's over.'

'Well, I want to go because I've never been to a serious concert before. Besides, I think Joey and Grandma will feel let down if we're not there.'

'All right, then. I suppose I'd better come as well. But don't say I didn't warn you when you find yourself dying of boredom halfway through.'

Tom's remarks failed to diminish her excitement as their first Saturday at Crystal Palace approached. They had set up their living-quarters in the ruined north transept which had formerly housed the Egyptian Court before it was gutted by fire last year. Their arrangements were similar to those at the Agricultural Hall with Tom sleeping in his usual compartment attached to the beast-wagon and Mirella using the caravan. Because it had been decided that Liddy and the Captain would take tea with them before the evening concert, Mirella spent most of her spare time polishing the mirrors, brass stove-rail, the candle brackets, and anything else that would take a shine. She also bought new china cups, baked some queen cakes and Richmond biscuits, and worked herself into a state wondering if she had done enough to impress her grandmother.

'Look, take it easy, Mirella. My mother's been used to living on the road herself, remember, and she doesn't expect to be entertained like royalty,' Tom protested, when she started rubbing at the bottom of the tea-kettle in an effort to erase all trace of former use.

'But you know how spotless her kitchen is and I don't want her to think I'm letting the side down.'

'She won't think that, not if she remembers her last visit to me – that was when I was still with Wombell's and we opened in Aldershot's Manor Park – this place was a pig-sty then compared with how it is now. I wasn't used to coping on my own, you see, and I was afraid Ma would have a fit when she saw it, but she didn't pass any comment.'

'Will she definitely be in the audience for our show?'

'I think so. She never missed a chance of coming in to see my lion-taming, and I'm sure she won't want to miss the new act, especially as you're in it.'

145

Peering from behind the curtains before going on stage in her role as the Rajah's daughter, Mirella gazed all around at the rows of spectators, trying to pick out her grandmother's face. Failing to find it, she decided there must have been some bad delay on the journey. She was acutely disappointed. She had been so looking forward to seeing her grandmother in the audience, hearing her comments after the show, and knowing she would take back a good report to Sadie. Again her hopes had been dashed, but once the performance started all else was forgotten until the final applause.

She arrived back at the caravan ahead of Tom, who had to supervise the removal of the lions' cage from the main hall before coming off duty, and had just changed out of her sari when there was a tap on the door. She opened it on a small woman, dressed in a full, blue velvet dress, cape and matching bonnet. 'Gran! I'm so glad you've managed to get here at last,' she exclaimed, opening wide the door to allow Liddy and the Captain to come in.

'I wouldn't have missed seeing that performance for the world, Mirella – even though I had my eyes shut half the time you were in the cage. Everyone near us was muttering about how clever and daring the act was, weren't they, Philip?'

'So you *were* in the audience? I was looking out for you both, but didn't see you.'

'We were there all right,' the Captain said, shaking her formally by the hand before sinking down on to one of the side seats, breathing heavily. He seemed thinner than ever, if that was possible, the skin on his face almost as white as his beard and side whiskers. Together he and her grandmother made an incongruous pair, for despite the fact that there was little more than a dozen years between them, Liddy at fifty could easily have passed as the Captain's daughter.

146

'Have you seen Joey yet?' Mirella asked.

'Yes, he was here to meet us when we arrived, but had to dash off almost immediately for last-minute rehearsals. We don't expect to see him again until after the concert. Then he'll take us back to his landlady who has kindly offered to accommodate us overnight so we don't have to start our trek back until tomorrow. Joey has got it all very well organised.'

'Yes,' Mirella agreed, 'he's been very helpful to me since I've been here, showing me round and making me feel at home.'

'Yes, he would do that. But he's actually been inside this building long before it came to this part of the world, you know,' Liddy said, sitting herself down in the only armed chair and loosing her bonnet strings.

'Do you mean Joey visited the Crystal Palace while it was still in Hyde Park?' Mirella said slowly, trying to work out how such a thing was possible.

'Yes, but he wouldn't remember anything about it. It was a few months before he was born,' Liddy said, smiling and for a moment seeming to drift away in thought. 'Your grandfather and I took some of the children to see the Great Exhibition – not Johnny, he'd already left home by that time – but Jemmy and Phoebe and Tom – they were all there – and we stood outside queuing in the pouring rain, but . . . it was such a good day,' she finished abruptly, as if afraid of becoming trapped in memories of the past.

'I'm glad you've told me that, but it's funny Tom never said anything. He would have remembered, wouldn't he?'

'Yes, if he wanted to, but he's not one to dwell on the past. I think he likes to put all his energy into forging the future. Talking of which, where are you and he planning to take "The Condemned Preserved" next?'

Mirella was just explaining that she was not sure what they would be doing after their six week contract expired with the Crystal Palace in mid-March when

Tom arrived and took over the conversation while she prepared tea.

Later, in the crowded concert hall, she sat between Tom and her grandmother, staring up at the gilded pipes of the Handel organ and the hundreds of gas lights until the orchestra filed in and took their places, Joey almost hidden in the back row of the fiddles. Amidst the applause which greeted the conductor as he arrived on the platform, she heard a sigh from Tom who was stretching out his legs and leaning back in his chair as if preparing for a long wait until life caught up with him again. Soon after that, the first instruments started up in a dreadful cacophony and she was appalled. Tom was right. This was going to be murder to listen to. She looked around, surprised to see everyone else sitting with polite attentiveness and hiding all signs of distress.

'Just warming up. They haven't started yet,' Liddy explained.

Next there was a pause in which Herr Manns held his baton aloft and glared at the players. Then the baton fell and the orchestra struck up with the overture to *Masaniello*, and soon Mirella forgot who she was and where she was and everything except that she was listening to music and loving what she heard.

After that first experience she tried never to miss a Saturday concert, enjoying them all despite the presence of Tom acting dog in the manger at her side. For despite her protests, he insisted on accompanying her everywhere as chaperone.

'Hey, Mirella, have you heard who's coming here the first Monday in March?'

She guessed by Tom's excitement that it must be either royalty or some big name in the show world.

'No. Who is it?'

'Blondin.'

'The rope walker, you mean,' she said, rather disappointed.

'Of course. What other Blondin is there? They say when he appeared here last time, more than two million people came to see him.'

'But why has the management booked him now at such short notice? Aren't they satisfied with what we're doing?' she asked, trying not to sound anxious.

'Don't worry, it's nothing directly to do with us. It's all part of some big charity event being organised to raise money for the Oxford Hall which burnt down last month, so there'll be lots of famous people taking part – Ethardo the spiral ascensionist, Madame Senyah on the trapeze, and Levic will almost certainly make an appearance.'

Now she was interested. It would be good to see a familiar face again. Apart from Joey and Tom, she had found few people to talk to at the Crystal Palace and, although she had never said much to Levic, for some reason she was excited at the prospect of seeing him again.

'Yes, they're gonner stretch a rope right across the top of the main nave,' Tom was saying, 'and Blondin will probably do all his usual tricks like walking across it blindfold and with baskets on his feet and pushing someone across in a wheelbarrow. You wait, Mirella, you're in for a real treat.'

The Crystal Palace was closed all day before the Oxford Hall Benefit to enable preparations to be made for the event. What Tom had said about Blondin's daring really struck home when Mirella stood watching a dozen or so men scrambling around in the dome of the great nave trying to secure a cable. She began to realise then what it might mean to walk one hundred and fifty feet above ground across that vast hollow space.

'I suppose they'll put up some sort of safety net, won't they, Tom?'

'Nope. Blondin refuses to use one.'

'Isn't that just foolhardy?'

'Maybe. But, unlike most of his competitors, he's never had a bad accident yet. In any case, a man who's crossed Niagara Falls on a high rope and with no safety net underneath must know what he's doing.'

She imagined what it would be like to step out above rocks and a foaming torrent of water, feeling the spray on her face, wind whistling about her ears, her body being buffeted, the elements conspiring to bring her down. She shivered.

'Why does he do it, Tom? Why does anyone choose to do such dangerous things?'

'Like sticking his head between a lion's jaws several times a day,' he said bitterly. 'I suppose Blondin's no different from me, Mirella: has to risk his life to make an honest crust.'

'Oh no.' She refused to believe it. 'There's got to be more to it than that. After all, there are easier ways of making a living.'

Tom laughed unpleasantly. 'You think you know it all, don't you? You get a job as a scullery-maid, but that's not good enough! So you come running to me and I find you something else to do, and it's all so easy it makes you think the world owes everyone a living. Well, it doesn't.'

'You sound very bitter, Tom.'

'Not without reason when you consider the life I've led.'

'I didn't know it had been that difficult.'

'No, well, it wouldn't have been if I'd copied your father and just upped and got out when it suited me. But no, I was the one who stayed and got lumbered when the others went.'

She felt uncomfortable listening to Tom carping about the family which she had been brought up to respect. On the other hand she was interested to know what it was that had left him so embittered so, as they turned away from the preparations in the nave and wandered back to their wagon for some tea, she did nothing to discourage his grumbling.

'Take the time when my dad ran out on us when I was a nipper, and soon after that my oldest brother went for a soldier, leaving me as main bread-winner for Ma and Joey. Can you imagine that? Me, just ten or eleven years old, shouldering the burden for three. Not that I didn't do it willingly, mind. I'd have laid down my life for my mother in those days, but I don't think she really appreciated it. She showed that when Father eventually turned up again and she had no more pride than to take him back as if nothing had happened. That stuck in my gullet, I can tell you. And then, when things were starting to get back to normal, Father died, which left me lumbered again.'

Tom's tone seemed to imply that his father had dropped down dead just to spite him. She had never before seen him in quite such a mood of self-pity.

'Still,' Mirella said brightly, 'you've made a success of your life, so you can afford to forget all those problems now.'

'Yes, I'm a great success all right,' Tom muttered, reaching up for the little silver flask and using it to lace his tea liberally.

'You've made yourself into The Great Kazan,' she ventured.

'Yes,' he agreed, 'and he's quite a boy, The Great Kazan, especially when he's rescuing the little Rajah's daughter, eh?'

She looked sharply at him. His voice was becoming slurred, confirming her suspicion that he had been imbibing more than the contents of the silver flask that morning. He must have more drink stowed away in the front of the beast wagon. Well, thank goodness there was no performance today. It certainly wasn't safe for him to go near the lions in this sort of mood.

'Tom,' she spoke very tentatively, 'you don't think you're drinking more than is good for you, do you?'

He laughed. 'Of course, I am, Tulip. It's my day off and I'm celebrating. Yesterday I put my head in the lion's mouth. Tomorrow I shall put my head in a lion's mouth. Today I'm just resting and having a good time. So don't nag me about it, Tulip.'

It wasn't only his drunkenness, it was the contempt in his voice when he spoke to her that made her so furious.

'I am not nagging and I am not called Tulip,' she snapped. 'My name is Mirella and, if you can't be polite, then I don't wish you to speak to me.'

'That's right, Tulip. Show a bit of spirit. I like a girl with spirit. That was the trouble with Lily, she never had any spirit. Caved in as soon as her old man spoke to her.'

'I'm not interested in Lily, I just hate you near me when you've been drinking.'

'No, you don't hate me near you, Mirella. You liked coming with me to a Music Hall and you like me taking you to those bloody concerts. You must admit I've shown you life since you came on the road with me.' His voice had sunk into a maudlin whine, and she was just beginning to feel sorry for him when he reached over, grabbed her arm, and dragged her off her chair until she was sprawled awkwardly in front of him.

'I'm right, aren't I?' he whispered. 'You like being with me, don't you?'

She felt sick. He had brought his face close to hers, and she could smell the drink on his breath as he nuzzled his nose up and down her cheek.

'Stop it!' she opened her mouth to say, but the words were smothered by his lips. He was kissing

152

her, this man who was her uncle; this man whom she had looked up to as a father; this man whom she now hated.

She wanted to hit him, but he had tight hold of her hands and she was helpless until, pulling her mouth back from his, she was able to sink her teeth into his face.

Chapter Eleven

'Mirella, Mirella! Come back. You don't understand. I can explain . . .' Tom's voice pursued her as she leapt down the steps, gathered up her skirts and ran. Glancing back, she saw that he had stumbled through the wagon door, slipped on the steps and fallen to the ground as he tried to follow her.

Dear God, don't let him up till I've got away, she begged, sobbing and starting to run again. Sobbing and running down empty corridors of statues and exhibits, with no idea of where she was running to, only that she had to get away from Tom. A door appeared and she flung herself against it, seizing the handle to wrench it open. Outside she could see the gardens, shrubs and fountains and open paths for her to run along . . . if only she could get this door open. She wrenched again at its handle, refusing to believe the door was locked. Outside the inaccessible paths mocked her.

She turned. She must escape, but how did you get out of this nightmare palace of glass? The main entrance, that would be open. At any moment she expected to hear Tom's footsteps pounding behind her. Choking back her sobs, she started to run again. She could hear voices ahead of her. There were people in the central transept, but she couldn't help that. She would have to pass through them if she was to reach the main door.

155

She rushed into the transept, stopped for a moment, gasping for breath and gazing wildly around to get her bearings.

'No. No!' She struggled to shake off the hand which had fallen on her arm. 'Let me go,' she moaned, hardly able to speak and wincing from a pain in her side.

'What's happened? What is wrong, Mirella?'

Now that she had been forced to a standstill, her lungs exploded in protest against the torture they had just endured, and left her panting and gulping for breath. It was no good. She couldn't run any further. She turned and faced her captor, already aware that it was not Tom but someone else whose voice she knew . . .

'That's right,' he was saying. 'Take it easy. Don't try to talk until you have your breath back.' The words were spoken slowly and carefully in a voice which was unmistakably Levic's.

'It's nothing. I . . . I just wanted to get outside,' she explained as soon as she was able to speak.

'To go outside? And without a coat in this weather?'

She was beginning to breathe more easily but could do nothing to stop the noisy gulping sobs that still shook her body. People all around – workmen and performers getting the hall ready for the next day – were gawking at her and turning to whisper to their neighbours.

'Come,' Levic said, 'it's too cold outside. Let's go together into the south transept. There you can sit down and recover yourself and maybe tell me what has upset you so.'

Conscious of having attracted too much attention, Mirella allowed him to lead her away.

'Now you must agree this is most civilised,' Levic commented, as they entered a hall labelled "Grecian Court" and found themselves wandering among the pillars of an ancient temple dedicated to Jupiter. She had never examined this part of the exhibition before, the room always seeming too crowded when she put her head through the door. To find herself in here now alone with Levic felt as strange and yet strangely familiar as if they were intruding on each other's dreamscape. He did not immediately pester her with questions, but allowed her to stand and stare and find comfort in the serene statues.

'That's Jupiter or Zeus,' he said, pointing. 'He reminds me always of Blondin. How beautifully poised he is, and that wavy hair and splendid beard – but my friend Blondin, he does not threaten us with a thunderbolt like the god, I am glad to say.'

'It's a lovely statue,' she said, calmer now. 'But how do you know he's got a thunderbolt in his hand when that bit's missing?'

'Ah, well, I know the story of Zeus, you see, and he is always armed and ready to throw his thunderbolts.'

'Why? Is he the god who punishes people?'

'No. Look at his face. He is a good god of light and he wishes us all to share the light, but that we cannot do if we are asleep. So he uses his thunderbolts to wake us up.'

Obediently she looked, but she couldn't really see what Levic meant. To her the face appeared unsmiling and grim.

'I think I'd rather stay asleep than be woken up by him,' she murmured.

'Yes, I know, but for us there is not the choice, I'm afraid. Zeus is all-powerful and if he decides you will wake, then you must wake even if it takes all three of his thunderbolts to shake you.'

'Three?'

'Yes, Zeus has three thunderbolts, but it is better to take warning from the first and not wait around for the third one to strike.'

'I can believe that,' she said, and gave an

involuntary shudder which caused Levic to peer at her anxiously.

'Now you are feeling more calm,' he smiled, 'perhaps you wish to share your troubles with me? As your friend, I wish to help.'

'No. It's all right, really. There's nothing anyone can do. I was just being silly.'

'That I cannot believe. The young lady who walks calmly among lions does not run amok in public unless something – or someone – has seriously upset her. Was it Tom?'

She felt confused. How had he guessed? Her expression must have revealed more than she intended. It was too late to deny what was clearly obvious, so she nodded her head.

'Did he strike you?'

The anger in Levic's voice startled her and she hastened to reassure him. 'Oh, no. He didn't hit me. He's never done that.'

'But he spoke sharply to you, threatened you perhaps?'

Now she swiftly gathered her thoughts together and decided not to tell anyone what had really happened.

'Yes, something like that. We had a row over something stupid, and I felt I had to run away before I lost my temper. But I shall be all right now. You've calmed me down.'

'You had a private row, and I don't wish to pry but . . . how do I say this to you? I came in and saw your act at the Agricultural Hall. It was good, Mirella, but – something is not quite right.' He paused, clearly searching for words.

'I was doing something wrong?'

'No, not you. It was Tom and the way he handled the animals.'

'Oh, he's really very good. He just tries to make it look as if he's not in proper control to make the act more exciting.'

'Yes, I know this. But I have been long in the circus and also have worked with animals, and when I look at an act and have this feeling, it worries me – especially when there are others at risk.'

'Who do you mean?'

'You, Mirella. I should not be saying so much if I weren't concerned about you.'

All this time she had been gazing fixedly at the statues. But now, as Levic spoke, he laid his hand on her arm, forcing her to look up and meet his eyes – brown, flecked with amber, she noticed again – and their expression put her in mind of Caesar when he was suffering from fever.

'You've no need to worry about me,' she said lightly. 'I'm never frightened of the lions.'

'That is the trouble. You should be, Mirella. Not frightened, but always on your guard. Lions are pack animals and it only needs one to turn.'

'I know. Tom taught me all that.' She hoped her voice did not betray too much impatience but, really, did this Levic think her such a fool? That was certainly not the impression she wanted him to have.

He sighed. 'And you have complete trust in Tom. Which of course is a good thing. And he is your uncle, so you respect him, and this is good.' Levic seemed to be thinking aloud. Waiting for him to say more clearly what was on his mind, she was disappointed when he concluded feebly: 'So why I have this feeling, I don't know. Maybe it is simply for myself I am worried.' With this thought, he shook himself out of his reverie and adopted a brisker tone of voice. 'But when you say you feel calmer now, does this mean you will be able to go home without fear? You are not frightened of Tom?'

'No, of course not,' she lied.

'Well, in that case, I have certainly spoken out of turn. Forgive me.' His remark was accompanied by that formal little nod of the head. 'I will add only that

I beg you to remember that you have a friend who, if ever you are in trouble, will reproach himself if you do not feel free to call on him for help.'

'Thank you, Levic,' she said, and smiled, wondering if his words contained anything beyond mere courtesy. Not that it mattered for she could not bring herself to confide in this young man who, despite his kindness and charm, was a stranger to her still.

'Ready to go back now?' he asked.

'Yes. Well, no,' she said, nervously. 'I mean, I don't have to go back immediately.'

'Good. Then let us both return to the central hall where there is someone I should like you to meet.'

As they left the Grecian Court, Mirella glanced back at the figure of Zeus standing poised with his invisible thunderbolt. She tried to convince herself that there were traces of a smile on his face, but the god stared grimly back at her.

'Halloo, Jean-Francois!' Levic called up to the gallery, where someone was kneeling in front of the Handel organ and inspecting the cable tied to one of the stair rails nearby. The man looked up, waved, and immediately came down to greet them.

In looks not unlike Levic – middling in height, and with dark waving hair and neatly trimmed moustache – he could easily have been taken for the younger man's father, a resemblance further enhanced when he started to speak in a strong foreign accent that Mirella did not immediately recognise as French.

'Jean-Francois,' Levic was saying, 'I wish you to meet one of our famous Lion Queens, Mademoiselle Mirella, she who enacts the part of the Rajah's daughter in the wild beast drama being presented here at the moment.'

'Enchanté, Mademoiselle. I must confess this drama is still for me a pleasure to look forward to.'

Mirella was about to protest that she was not really very well known, when Levic continued the

160

introductions by saying: 'And this is my good friend, Jean-Francois Gravelet, better known to the world as Blondin.'

'Blondin of Niagara?' she exclaimed.

'That's right,' he said, 'Blondin of Niagara and Crystal Palace. My fame I owe to the former, my fortune to the latter.'

'But I thought you were here to do a charity event,' Mirella said, puzzled.

'That is so, Mademoiselle. The remark is just my little plaisanterie for when I came 'ere in '62 the management was 'appy to pay me one hundred pounds for every time I walk along my rope – and so I stayed and walked my rope many times for them, you can be sure.'

She raised her eyes to look at the rope now wound round the great spiral staircases at each end of the huge enclosure and weighted down with sandbags to hold it steady.

'And you're going to walk up there tomorrow without any safety net?' she asked incredulously. 'How on earth do you keep your balance?'

'On earth it is no problem, Mademoiselle. But up there I need to keep my wits about me. And as for how I manage this, eh bien, I 'ope you will come and see for yourself.' Then, grinning at Levic, he added: 'Are you still 'appy to play your part, my friend?'

'Yes, you can count on me,' Levic said, before turning to Mirella and explaining. 'I promised to let this daredevil carry me across that flimsy thread tomorrow. We're going to combine our acts so that when, in the middle of my clowning, Blondin arrives and calls for some worthy person to volunteer to be his passenger on the tightrope, I am to be the sacrificial victim.'

Her face must have registered her horror.

'It's all right, Mademoiselle,' Blondin hastened to reassure her. 'I 'ave done this thing many, many times and for me it is no more than to cross the

161

boulevard and miss being knocked down by a hansom cab. I depend only on Levic here not being too fidgety when I carry him piggy-back, but I don't think he will be. You see, I threaten 'im. "You be a good, quiet passenger, my friend, or I shall simply put you down in the middle of the rope and leave you to find your own way back." '

Mirella joined in their laughter. The problem which had loomed so large in her life just an hour or so ago had now shrunk into insignificance. Here she was talking and joking with the world-renowned Hero of Niagara and with Levic the famous clown. They treated her not as an equal exactly but at least as a comrade, a member of their own select fellowship, and she basked in their acceptance.

And Tom? She would find a way of dealing with him. He had behaved very badly and it was up to her to make sure nothing of that kind ever happened again. The main thing was she did not feel frightened of him for she realised it wasn't Tom himself who was the problem, but Tom under the influence of drink. All she had to do was get him to accept that fact and cut down on his drinking, and then all their problems would be solved.

He was sitting on the steps of the wagon, his head in his hands, when she got home.

'So you've decided to come back at last,' he growled, looking up. 'And I suppose you went straight to our Joey to complain about me, so now my name's mud in the family?'

'Of course I didn't. I haven't seen Joey today.'

'Who did you tell then?'

'No one. It's not the sort of thing I'd want to talk to anyone about.'

He looked relieved.

'That's right. It's no one else's business, and I think we should agree to keep it that way.'

162

'But you were wrong when you . . . when you tried . . .' Mirella faltered.

'Yes, yes,' he said quickly. 'I admit I was out of order, but that was only because I'd had a bit to drink. It's not likely to happen again. Of that you can rest assured.'

'You mean you're going to stop drinking?'

He looked sharply at her.

'I mean I shan't step out of line again. As for anything else, that's none of your affair, and you'll oblige me by not going on as if I'm some kind of sot.'

She wanted to continue until Tom was left in no doubt about the way she felt. She wanted to tell him plainly that his drinking put the act and both their lives in danger. She held her tongue, not because she was scared of his reaction but because she felt sorry for him. He looked so dejected and miserable it would be like kicking a dog when it was down. Instead she chose to change the subject by telling him of her meeting with Levic and Blondin. Tom's response was quick.

'Blondin, you say? You've actually been speaking to Blondin? Did he say anything interesting? Had he heard of us, do you know? I'll take you to see his performance tomorrow, you'll enjoy that.'

She had seen the great hall in the Crystal Palace crowded for concerts, but that was nothing compared with how it looked on the day of the Oxford Benefit Gala. They were running special omnibuses and train services, and the place was packed. Not that Mirella was interested in how big the crowds were. For her the day was special because it provided an unusual opportunity to dress in her Sunday best and enjoy life as a mere spectator.

She sat next to Tom in a seat in the gallery and looked down on one performer after another, the elite of the entertainment world.

163

There was Signor Ethardo, the incredible spiral ascensionist who, balanced on a silver globe, proceeded to roll it up a steep, narrow plank, negotiating several twisty bends until he reached a height of about twelve feet and then, in a silence broken only by occasional gasps of disbelief, rolled it slowly down again, backwards.

Mirella was not terribly impressed by Madame Senyah. She had heard so much about the wonderful feats of Monsieur Leotard on his "Flying Trapeze" at the Alhambra that this swinging and somersaulting from one bar to another fell short of her expectations.

'Have you ever thought of having a go at that?' Tom asked, after the applause had finished. 'It wouldn't be a bad idea if you found another string to your bow. We could introduce it into the act in some way.'

'Are you suggesting that I do a trapeze act over the lion cage?' she joked.

'It's an idea,' he said, taking her seriously. 'We could take the top of the cage off and make your act look really daring.'

'No, I don't think so, Tom. If I do something else, I'd like to keep it quite separate from the lions, thank you.'

'Well, there's your singing and dancing, of course. They're always useful. But we can't keep on with "The Condemned Preserved" routine forever. Sooner or later we'll have to find some other gimmick.'

His words echoed in her mind until Levic entered the arena in his satin costume and stood motionless with that expression on his face which reduced everybody to fits of laughter. He then went through a routine similar to the one she had seen him perform at the Aggie, and now that she had got to know him better – well, that was not quite true. Now that she had had a longer talk with him – she was even more fascinated. Unlike so many other clowns, he wasn't

164

just doing stupid things and demanding, 'Look! Laugh at me, everyone, because I'm funny!' He was acting out the ridiculous little things which lurk hidden in everybody. And the beauty was, he presented them in such a way that you couldn't help loving both the frailties and the human nature which harboured them.

'Ah, now this is the moment I've been waiting for,' Tom muttered, as a fanfare announced the arrival of the Hero of Niagara and Blondin strutted in wearing a magnificent full-length purple cloak. For a few minutes he paraded round the arena, occasionally standing still and bowing to acknowledge the thunderous applause and then, just as it began to diminish, he swept off his cloak to reveal a chest plated with medals and marched majestically towards the staircase.

Levic meanwhile had faded away to the side. But now as the great man mounted the stairs, he reappeared and aped the stately parading, sweeping off his invisible cape to reveal a chest bulging but empty. Miming his intention of going off to search for medals, he left the arena.

All eyes were now on Blondin as he picked up his pole, carefully centred it, and with little more ado stepped on to the rope and walked nonchalantly its length and back. No sooner had the applause for this feat died away than he walked out on to the rope again, but this time stopped in the middle, sat down and stared around at the audience. He made it look so easy, but it was unnerving to feel as Mirella did that his gaze had fallen specifically on her. She guessed that he had the knack of making everyone feel like this, but she derived no comfort from the thought. Blondin was looking at her, throwing his challenge at her. He was saying, 'Here I am, putting my life on the line, and you think I would take this sort of risk simply to amuse you? Well, there's no point in my trying to convince you otherwise, because nothing I say would make sense to you who sit safely on the edges of life.'

And now he had put down his pole and left it balancing by itself across the rope and was leaning back until his body was stretched out full length. He was actually lying down on the rope! But he had not finished yet. His knees were coming up and he was curling into a ball. No, surely he couldn't be trying to . . . not on a rope! Before her eyes, Blondin had just turned a back somersault, picked up his pole again and walked back along the rope to where he started.

Mirella spontaneously jumped to her feet, clapping. Most of the audience was doing likewise. Surely no one else on earth – well, above the earth! – would dare to attempt such a feat? The applause thundered on until Blondin held up his hand and gestured for silence. He called out something but she couldn't catch what he was saying.

And then Levic appeared in the arena again with a saucepan lid and a bit of red ribbon proudly attached to his chest and it was obvious from his gestures that Blondin was shouting for someone to come and help him with his act and dear silly Levic was offering himself.

There were several near disasters on the stairs before he reached the great man and stood beside him at the end of the rope, a deal of pantomime as Blondin explained what they were about to attempt and Levic, now that he realised what he was in for, clearly not quite so keen and turning to the audience for advice. Should he let Blondin carry him on his back all the way across that high rope? He was so full of innocence and naivety, the children in the audience grew alarmed for his safety and screamed: 'No, Levic. Don't do it! Don't!'

Now Levic was being torn apart by his wish to

please both the audience and Blondin, but it was the latter's persuasion which eventually prevailed, and he allowed Blondin to hoist him up and carry him piggyback right out across the rope until they were suspended over the abyss.

Mirella could hardly bear to look. When she did, she was struck by Blondin's wrapt concentration as he slowly walked and kept his pole balanced.

'That's the secret of it,' Tom whispered, 'he looks straight ahead and keeps the pole level, and as long as he does that they can't fall off.'

Suddenly something was happening. It seemed that Levic had lost his nerve. There was an altercation between the two men and Levic was beginning to panic. For an instant Mirella was forced to shut her eyes. When she opened them, she couldn't believe what she was seeing. Blondin had shaken Levic off his back, dumped him in the middle of the rope and left him stranded there, one hundred and fifty feet above the ground with nothing to break his fall.

'Sit down!' Tom said, dragging at her arm, but she wanted to do something. She couldn't just sit there and watch while . . .

She sank back into her seat while Levic danced as carelessly off that rope as if it had been a footpath in the park.

She was bewildered. She had inspected that rope close up. It was little more than two inches in diameter and, despite being weighted down, it swayed with every slight movement made on it. And yet Blondin could walk along it and Levic had trained himself to walk along it. Was there anything these two men couldn't do? She sighed. She admired them both so much, but how could they ever be her friends when everything they did set them so far above common humanity? She smiled at the joke. And then, thinking aloud, said: 'I want to have a go at that too. I wonder how I can train myself to be a rope-dancer?'

Chapter Twelve

'Here, rub some of this on your shoes to stop them slipping.' Tom handed her a box of rosin and then walked across and tugged the rope to make sure the knots would hold.

At first he had not been too keen on her idea. 'Think of all the paraphernalia you'd need, poles and cables and things. Mind, if you were to concentrate on wire-walking, that wouldn't be so bad. It's those blooming great cable-ropes that weigh so heavy. Do you realise the one Blondin crossed Niagara on had to be over a thousand feet long? Well, I don't fancy carting a thing like that around the countryside.'

'Aren't you being a bit premature, Tom? I haven't managed to walk more than a dozen steps without falling off yet.'

'True, but you're getting better and I don't think it will take long for you to pick up the knack, especially if you listen to my advice.'

'I'm listening,' Mirella said, taking off her soft leather shoes one at a time to rub in the rosin.

'Right. Well, the main thing to remember is this: at the moment you're practising less than three feet off the ground, so now's the time to do your experimenting and make all your mistakes. Get to know yourself and your own sense of balance. Because that's what's important. Your own instinctive sense of balance. Never mind all the other tricks of the trade like keeping your eye on the end of the rope and keeping the pole exactly level once you start using one. What this job is all about is balance. And not just of your body. You gotter keep completely level-headed when you're on the rope, just like keeping control over your mind and feelings when working with the animals. Do you get me?'

She had to admit his words made sense, although she wished he wouldn't keep drumming them into her head day after day. For one thing, she found it irritating that Tom did not practise what he preached. For another, she did not want anything that anyone said to come between her and this new adventure. Give me enough rope and leave me to find my own way of walking along it, that's all I want, she thought.

For her the rope was an adventure, even though, as Tom kept reminding her, as yet it was only three feet above the earth.

It had not taken her long to master the art of walking along the narrow wooden pole that Tom first fixed up for her, but it was a very different story when he replaced this by a rope cable. Still, she refused to become disheartened and spent every spare moment of the day practising how to walk along it.

'Do you think I should start straight away using a pole to help me balance?' she asked Tom.

'No. You've got to find your feet first and never mind any fancy contraptions. Like I said, concentrate on your own inner balance all the time. This is a tight-rope – leastways I've tried to get it as tight as I could – and so that means you've got to keep your centre of gravity bang over the rope all the time if you don't want to fall off.'

'Well, that's obvious, isn't it?' she asked.

'Yes, I s'pose so, but what I'm trying to say is this: walking along a tightrope is very different from walking a slack rope. For that you'd use almost the opposite technique.'

170

'How do you mean?'

'Like I said. When you're walking the tightrope, you move in such a way as to keep your centre of gravity over the rope, but on the slack rope, you move the rope to bring it under your own centre of gravity.'

'I see. I hadn't thought of that. But in any case, I want to concentrate on the tightrope because, once I've mastered it, I want to walk really high up like Blondin and Levic did on Monday.'

'Hmm, well, there's no harm in hoping, but all we're aiming for at the moment is for you to be able to do a nice little ropewalking act as part of the Parade in front of the show in the summer. After that, if you want to develop it further, I might find a way to use a rope act in next winter's tour.'

She had put her shoes back on again and was climbing up on to the box which served as mounting-block for the rope.

'Do you suppose Blondin fell off as much as I do when he first started?' she asked.

'Yep, I'm sure he did. There's no other way to learn.'

'But he started very young. That must have been a help,' she said, remembering how she and Cassie used to walk along the tops of walls when they were little and how much easier such tricks had seemed then.

'How do you know he started young?'

'I asked him when I met him in the Hall last Sunday,' Mirella explained. 'He told me how when he was five years old, he saw some ropewalkers performing and thought he'd like to have a go, so he fetched a rope and tied it to a couple of chairs, and then got really upset when the whole thing collapsed under him as soon as he tried stepping on it.'

'How did he go on from there, then?'

'He tied his rope round a couple of trees and tried again.'

'Yes, that would work better.'

'Not at first, though. The poor little thing was only five, remember, and he couldn't even tie knots properly so the rope kept slipping undone until someone came by and saw what was happening. As luck would have it, the chap turned out to be a sailor who not only showed him how to tie knots but came back a little while later with a boat cable for him to try with.'

'Hmm, sounds as if Monsieur Blondin told you his bloomin' life story. You must have spent a long time chatting with him,' Tom muttered. 'I hope there were other people around. He might be famous, but that doesn't mean to say he wouldn't take it the wrong way if you was to be overfamiliar with him.'

She drew in a breath between clenched teeth. She hated it when Tom said this sort of thing. Still, now was her practice time and she mustn't let him put her off.

She closed her eyes and breathed out slowly. No turgid emotions. No anger. No doubt. Just the clear straight line of the rope and responding to its challenge.

Holding on to a bar attached to the wall behind her, she placed her right foot on to the start of the rope. Then still holding on, she pushed her left foot in front of it until she stood with both feet firmly set on the rope, feeling it as a line of force tugging her onwards. Slowly she let go of her handhold and simply stood. This was the moment. Now, when she could feel the forceful line of the rope warring with her own body's desire to stay here fixed immobile on this one balanced spot. Now, in this moment, she had to lay hold of her inner sense of balance and work only from that.

It wasn't easy. It demanded intense concentration. Yet this is what most attracted her to ropewalking. When she was stepping along the rope, nothing else mattered. It demanded relaxation yet complete concentration, total dedication. She could not afford to concern herself about anything else except meeting

172

the demands of this ever changing path under her feet, attuning herself to its every nuance of mood and movement, knowing that the penalty for inattention would be instant downfall.

She had started out on her odyssey again. Her right foot swung forwards, her body keeling over immediately to the left but quickly righting itself, wobbling and then righting itself again, while her outstretched hands flapped against the air like stunted wings.

No time to reconsider that step, already the next is being taken, and she wobbles again, listing this time to the right before retrieving her balance and taking another step forward towards her goal. And another step, swinging her body forward lightly and easily now, almost skipping along the friendly rope which clings to her feet as if they are a part of itself.

It's so easy when you know how. Anyone could . . .

An unsteady tilt to the right, an attempt to pull back. A moment of tottering from side to side in a vain attempt to steady, thinking, How do I stop myself wobbling? But it's already too late. The rope is unforgiving. Her arms flail wildly as she slips off and topples to the ground.

'Ouch! Damn rope, why can't you keep still?' She examined the graze on her knee before glowering at Tom and saying, 'It's no good. I'll never be able to do it properly.'

'No, I don't suppose you will if you let a little fall like that put you off,' he said laconically. Immediately she straightened up and struggled back on to the box ready to have another try. Soon she was feeling the rope under her feet again, challenging her.

This time! This time she would walk it to the end. This time she would give it her full attention. There would be no more lapses, no reason for the rope to snub her. For she was beginning at last to understand that its demands were as compelling as those of a god. She could turn her back on the rope and forget this whole enterprise, just as she had turned away from the statue of Zeus. But what she could not do was be half-hearted in its service. One moment of indifference and there she would be, floored again while the rope swung in contempt at her petty efforts to bring it under her own sway.

Why then did she want to do it? Why keep trying to walk along a rope that led nowhere and which, when it was slung higher, would present great peril? Mirella could not answer this question. She knew only that it had something to do with the exhilaration she felt when she managed to walk any distance along its stretch. While she was concentrating on keeping her balance, she felt more fully herself than at any other time. She knew that when she walked the high rope she would be living dangerously and that the price of failure would be death or disablement, yet she realised too that every time she walked the rope successfully she would be paying the price that purchased her life anew.

'Well, you've cracked it, Mirella. And now you've done it once without falling off, you should be able to manage it again. So, come on, straight back on to the rope and let's see you repeat that performance.' She had actually walked the whole rope from end to end. Tom was pleased with her. 'You know,' he was saying, 'you've really got a natural talent for this sort of thing. If you work hard, you could develop it into a nice little circus act.'

She did not need this kind of incentive. In the weeks that followed, perfecting her art became such an obsession with her that she practised whenever she could, breaking off only when she had to perform essential work connected with the beast show, and sleeping when she could neither practise nor work.

With Tom's help, she gradually raised the rope a foot at a time until it reached something like six feet off the ground – though not without some nasty falls, resulting in a badly sprained shoulder.

'Tom, I've been thinking, couldn't we rig up one of those rope and pulley devices like the trick riders use to take their weight if they slip off the horse – just until I'm a bit more expert at least?' she asked, applying camphorated oil to her shoulder. Tom had offered to help her rub it in, but she shrank away from his touch. Apart from the rescue scene in "The Condemned Preserved", she was careful to avoid all physical contact with him nowadays.

'No, like I said, forget any fancy contraptions. In the long run they don't help. They just stop you developing your own instinctive balance.'

'I was afraid you'd say that,' she sighed, looking up and wondering how high the rope would have to be strung before it became advisable to use a safety net.

As if reading her mind, he went on: 'It's like people who get used to having safety nets underneath them. They come more unstuck than artistes like Blondin. He puts trust only in himself and his own ability to do the thing right.'

'Yes, but even *he* must make mistakes sometimes surely? Or something beyond his control goes wrong. I mean, I can't believe that he's never taken a tumble in all his professional life. And yet, you're right, of course. He doesn't have a safety net when he performs, so he must consider he's beyond making any mistakes.'

'Nonsense! He's not that stupid. He's got his escape route well planned, believe me. But he doesn't advertise it to the jossers so, if he has to use it, it only serves to make his act more exciting.'

'What do you mean? What would he do, what *could* he do, if he suddenly lost his balance and felt himself falling?'

'Grab the rope, of course.'

'Yes, I realise that. But how would that help him? He wouldn't be able to hang on for long and, if his pole had dropped, he wouldn't be able to get his balance back even if he managed to stand upright again on the rope.'

'Correct, so he'd stay hanging from his hands and work his way across the rope.'

'What, a distance of a hundred feet or more?' Mirella said incredulously.

'No. Just as far as the nearest guy-rope and he'd slither down that. It works. He's got himself out of trouble several times that way and the beauty of it is, the public are treated to a spectacle more exciting than the original act, whereas if he was to drop into the safety net they'd feel cheated.'

'I see. So does that mean you're against safety-nets?'

'Yes, especially for your sort of act. I'll see about getting hold of a thick mattress to spread under the rope, but there's no need for a safety net because you won't be walking more than about a dozen feet up outside the show.'

'But I might like to go higher than that,' she mused.

'No, you won't,' Tom said firmly. 'There's no call for it. We're not training you to be a female Blondin. All we want you to do is a little spot of rope-dancing as an extra act in the show.'

'I see,' Mirella said, preparing herself to tackle the rope again, 'so you're trying to warn me against getting ideas above my station?' But Tom failed to appreciate her jest.

After leaving Crystal Palace they fulfilled a number of engagements at amusement halls in and around London, arriving at the Highbury Barn Gardens in Islington at the beginning of June, the same week as Blondin who had been engaged to perform here throughout the summer months. Mirella sat reading aloud to Tom a notice that had been placed in the *Era* newspaper.

' "Highbury Barn Gardens in conjunction with the Alexandra Theatre, sole Proprietor Mr E. Giovanelli, is proud to announce that BLONDIN this summer will do feats never before seen in England. BLONDIN will cook an omelette on the High Rope. BLONDIN will turn a somersault on the High Rope. BLONDIN will perform the Chair Trick, the most daring feat in the world. BLONDIN will take his Breakfast and Drink a Bottle of Champagne on the High Rope. BLONDIN amidst a great display of fireworks will trundle a wheelbarrow and present the Public with a souvenir from the High Rope. BLONDIN will walk the High Rope in a Sack and with Baskets on his feet. BLONDIN will appear as a gymnast on the High Rope. Admission one shilling." '

'Old Giovanelli didn't put in anything like that for us, note,' Tom grumbled. 'It's always the same. "To those that hath, give the bloody lot." I mean, Blondin's made his name, there's no need to keep going on about what he can and can't do, whereas a bit of extra publicity could really set us up at the moment.'

'Still,' Mirella said, 'if his name draws the people, that means better business for us.' She was trying to buck him up because she knew how riled he had been to read on another page of the newspaper a description of the "interesting showland wedding" of Max and Lily Wombell which had recently taken place in Southampton.

Now that she had gained a fair amount of expertise in tightrope walking herself, she watched Blondin's preparations with even greater fascination, noting how closely he inspected the rope before it was hauled up into place.

'Are you afraid it might be a bit too worn?' she asked.

'No, not at all. I had it this season new from Messrs Frost Brothers, and with them I am sure it is sent to me only after it has been most rigorously tested by steam-power. No, it is not the intrinsic strength of my rope I 'ave cause to worry about. Malheureusement – or sadly, I should say – it is the machinations of my rivals that I must fear.'

'Oh, surely not? I find it hard to believe anyone would stoop so low as to sabotage your rope.'

'I also, Mademoiselle, but I am afraid it 'as 'appened, so I must believe it.'

'Do you mean your rope actually broke while you were walking on it, and caused you to fall?'

'Fortunately not, else I should not be here to tell the tale, I fancy. No, I am 'appy to say that I discovered the mischief in time. It 'appened while I was performing in Asnières last summer. Some lunatic had sawn through my rope until only one fibre was left and it would certainly have given way should I 'ave put my weight on it. Eh bien, so now I am even more careful to examine every part of my equipment – me, moi-même – before I make my performance.' He turned and shouted to the waiting workmen, 'OK! You can 'aul it up now, if you please,' and the enormous rope stretching nearly three hundred feet, the length of the grass plot next to the Alexandra Theatre, was hoisted up and secured to two masts seventy feet high. Along this Blondin was due to give two performances every day, one late in the afternoon, the other after ten o'clock at night when he would walk in the limelight and conclude his act by letting off a huge number of fireworks.

Afraid of getting in the way, Mirella made an excuse to wander off and explore, pausing to take in the new white and gold entrance to the Barn with its ornate mirrors and chandeliers, the crystal dance platform and the advertisement for *No Thoroughfare At Highbury*, the burlesque playing at the Alexandra Theatre.

I wonder whether Tom would fancy seeing that tonight? she thought to herself. It might cheer him up.

Sometimes she wondered how long their partnership

could endure under the strain of Tom's ill humour. The trouble was, his moods were so unpredictable. For days on end he was fine, dealing with all the paperwork that went with their bookings, making plans for the future and joking with other showmen. And then from out of the blue came the thunderbolt and she found herself tossed around in the storm, more often than not completely at sea as to its cause. Such was the case now when she came back to the wagon and asked him about going to the theatre.

'*No Thoroughfare At Highbury*,' he mimicked. 'Well, the title couldn't be more appropriate, could it? You sure you're not going to shy away if I sit in the seat next to yours?'

'I don't know what you're talking about, Tom. I thought you might like to go and see the play, that's all. But if you don't want to come, that's all right. I shall just go on my own.'

'Don't you dare, Mirella! That's not the sort of entertainment a young lady could safely go to on her own. And let's not forget,' he went on, leering at her, 'that you are a young lady who must be protected from bad company – even, or I might say especially, that of your own uncle whom you treat as if he's not good enough to wipe the floor beneath your dainty feet with.'

'Oh, Tom, for goodness' sake don't start going on like that again or I shall quit.' She felt the sting of tears and fought to keep them back. Tom's onslaught had come as such a shock. She had come in full of the world's delights and quite unprepared for any unpleasantness. 'I can't take much more of your nastiness,' she said, trying to keep her voice calm.

'All right, all right. I'm out of turn again.' He groaned, shaking his head. 'I'm sorry, I'm sorry. I've no right to take things out on you, but I feel so . . . so . . . oh, you know what I mean. And all I'm asking for is a little bit of sympathy, that's not so wrong, is it? I mean, I'd do anything in the world for you, you know that, but you seem to begrudge me even the time of day. I know I've made my mistakes, but I'm not such a bad chap really. It's just that no one understands . . .'

He put out his hand and touched hers. His face was so full of misery and she felt so sorry for him, she wanted to cuddle him like she used to cuddle her little brothers when they had hurt themselves.

'Look, Tom,' she whispered, 'I do understand. It's just that I don't know how to cope with your bad moods.'

'I know,' he said, 'and I can't blame you. I know I'm a bastard when I'm down in the dumps, but you don't want to take anything I say that seriously.'

It's not what you say, it's what you might do that bothers me, she thought, but could not express this fear aloud. Instead she said, 'Well, if you'd give me some signal when you're feeling low, it would help. As it is, your moods catch me offguard. And what makes it worse is that then you always seem to turn against me, so that nothing I say or do is right.'

'I know, love,' he said, stroking her hand, 'but, like I say, it's not the real me reacting to you like that. It's just these demons get hold of me sometimes. It's them you hear talking. What you've got to understand, Mirella, is that you're my good angel. Without you to help me fight against them, I don't think I'd stand a chance.'

She shivered. She wanted to tug her hand away from his and dash out into the fresh air. Outside in the bright gardens the sun was glinting off the crystal dance platform and high overhead a rope was suspended way above this dark trap she felt herself slipping towards. She wanted to be on that rope which, in her mind's eye, stretched like a bridge from this dangerous world towards one of inner calm where the only thing that mattered was complete concentration

180

on her next step. Whilst walking that rope she would be her own mistress, her thoughts under control, her feelings safely beyond the turbulence caused by other people's demands. At the moment she had learnt only to walk just above people's heads, but what she longed to do was step out nearer the sky.

'Ah, well,' Tom was saying, 'nearly time to open up, so I'd better go and check on the beasts before getting changed. OK, Princess?' He let go of her hand and smiled at her with steady, clear blue eyes which left her feeling ashamed of entertaining such doubts about him. After all, no one was perfect and maybe she was at fault for expecting too much of people. Besides, Tom certainly had his finer points. He was generous, for example – only that morning urging her to take advantage of this longish stay in Islington to visit a dressmaker and order herself a new outfit for the warm weather. And he had been so helpful when she was first finding her feet in the show world, and just lately had encouraged her to develop her skill on the rope. Yes, she had a lot to be grateful to Tom for and, just so long as he was aware that he must not step out of line with her, then it behoved her to support him in any sort of difficulty he might have.

By the time it came to July, it was hot, so hot that Mirella was heartily glad of her lighter clothes and took great delight in wearing her new white muslin dress with its matching bonnet trimmed with corn and field flowers. She was also glad that the show had moved to the Royal Gardens at North Woolwich on the Thames where there were beautiful walks along the river front. Here she was able to enjoy the cool shade of the trees and what breeze there was coming off the water. Poor old Caesar, Hanno and Trajan, however, paced irritably up and down the cage twitching their tails, clearly distressed.

'It's odd, isn't it?' she remarked to Paddy, one of

181

the keepers. 'You'd think they'd be used to the heat and feel happier now the summer's come.'

'Well, yes. It's certainly hot where they come from, so it's not the heat that's bothering them. It's the sultriness. They gets very contrary when the weather's close. That's what I was warning Mister Granger about this morning. "You want to watch yourself a bit at the moment," I said, "especially with Caesar and Trajan." Hanno, bless him , is docile enough, but the other two, I have to say it, they're acting up a bit and there's nothing gonner settle them until a good thunderstorm comes to clear the air.'

'And what did Tom say?'

'You know Mister Granger,' Paddy sighed, shaking his head, 'he just shrugged his shoulders as if it was all the same to him if those beasts were docile or at point of kill. Still, that's his profession, isn't it? He knows best what he's dealing with, I dare say.'

'I suppose so,' she agreed, but when she emerged from the pavilion where the beast wagon was parked together with all the other trappings of their show, she looked anxiously up at the greenish sky in the hope that a storm was imminent.

The gardens were beginning to fill now, with people surging up from the landing pier in regular waves as the steamers berthed. The boats arrived every twenty minutes, bringing people clutching their special eight-penny tickets which included the return fare from Hungerford or London Bridge as well as admission to the gardens. And far more frequently – every few minutes, in fact – trains were arriving to debouch their passengers, all got up in their smartest togs for a day out. Mirella noticed that white was the season's fashionable colour and was glad she had taken the advice of the seamstress in Islington when it came to choosing material for her own new dress.

In the little time left to her before getting ready for the show, she wandered among the crowds, admiring the elegant dresses – what was that French word the dressmaker had used to describe the new look? "Watteau", that was it. She did not understand what it meant exactly, but even the sound of the word conveyed this picture of young women gliding by in their billowing gauzy dresses and straw bonnets or simple mantillas of voile or lace. A few unfortunates were still so far behind the times as to be bundling along in their old crinolines, but for the most part an almost audible sigh of relief could be heard from those who had discarded the clumsy contrivances.

After entering the gardens, most people seemed to make their way towards the swings and roundabouts and refreshment booths in the north field, or chose to saunter along the rose walk leading up to the pretty pavilion where an orchestra was playing. Mirella preferred to stroll along the pebbly embankment, where her gaze was soon drawn away from the crowds to fasten itself on the moving water of the Thames.

She had some serious thinking to do. The situation with Tom was becoming impossible. His drinking bouts were becoming more frequent and his moods were worse than ever so that she never knew from one moment to the next where she stood with him. It was no good him keep blaming his "demons". As far as she was concerned, it was becoming increasingly difficult to tell him and his "demons" apart, and she wanted to distance herself from both of them. If only there was someone she could talk to about it, that might help. But there was no one.

It was funny that her life was spent in the midst of crowds of people and yet they always remained strangers to her, or rather she was a stranger to them. Take now, for instance. She raised her eyes to observe the pleasure-seekers, strolling in the gardens, all in couples or little groups; hardly anyone like her, on their own.

I wish Cassie was here. I haven't seen her for an age, she thought. Maybe there'll be a chance for her to come up soon. Or, if I could screw up enough courage to face Mother, I could go back home for a visit. After the Abyssinian fête next week perhaps, there might be time for a little holiday.

She stared back into the water. What would taking a holiday solve, though? At the end of it she would still have to come back and face the same situation. Besides, going back home might be the very worst thing she could do. Once she started talking to Sadie about the way things were going, she might say too much and her mother would insist on her returning to live at home. Painful as her present situation was, it was preferable to going back to all those rows. For no matter how they tried, she was not convinced she and Sadie would get on any better now than they had before.

It had always been the same – for as long as she could remember. And it was no good her father muttering about them being so much alike. As far as she could see, they were complete opposites, she and her mother. Sadie was so strait-laced all the time, content to live a sort of half-life. Whereas she, Mirella, wanted to live life to the full and was impatient of any constraints. It would not be so bad if they could agree to differ. But no, Sadie always managed to make her feel guilty. As if it was a sin to feel the way she did, as if it was shameful to have such strong feelings.

No, she would not go home until she could look Sadie straight in the eye, knowing she had made some sort of success of her life. Because I will, she promised herself. One day I shall do something that will make the whole family proud of me, and then maybe Ma and I can start again and be good friends.

She had reached a particularly lovely part of the river bank where pinky-white hogweed and pale purple valerian were growing, reminding her of the meadow at Windsor. She remembered sitting in the branches of her willow and making the great decision that had changed her life. She had never regretted that decision. Well, perhaps it was time for her to make another one.

One thing was now clear. She didn't want to go on much longer with Tom like this. She refused to consider going back home as a possible alternative, so what else could she do? Whatever it was, she must retain her independence, on that she was determined.

And then it came to her. There was nothing to stop her making her own way in show business. She would be sixteen next month. Many girls her age were already wives and mothers, so surely she was not too young to take responsibility for her own life. How would she do it?

She would answer one of those advertisements in the *Era* newspaper, she decided, such as the one this week which read: ''Wanted, Lady Paraders, also Flying Trapeze or Rope-dancing Act. Long engagement to suitable people. State lowest terms and full particulars in first letter to Gander's Menagerie, Showground, Tottenham.''

Tom would be furious when he found out, of course. And no doubt her father would raise objections. But there would be no possibility of anyone stopping her, because she had made up her mind and that was that.

Chapter Thirteen

She felt so much better now that she knew what she was going to do. Marching back to the wagon in a new mood of determination, she paused only to marvel at the sky iridescent with pink, mauve and that strange tint of apple green. We're not going to get much of an audience this afternoon, she thought. No one in their senses would pay to sit in a stuffy pavilion in this heat.

As it happened, though, many people, perhaps drawn in by the prospect of shade, did part with their money and Mirella saw that the auditorium was fairly full when, just before the start of the show, she peeped from behind the curtains. Beside her on the screened platform it was so dark that she could barely make out the shapes of the lions in their cage, but she was aware of their fretfulness as they paced up and down waiting for the performance to begin.

'Caesar,' she whispered, 'good boy! Settle down now, Trajan. And Hanno, hush now! Good fellows.' Her voice seemed to have the desired calming effect and she waited confidently until the music signalled her and Paddy on the other side of the stage to pull open the curtains. Whereupon Tom, in the gladiatorial costume that went with his role of The Great Kazan, strode on to the stage and began the show by putting the lions through their paces, demonstrating how well he had them 'tamed'. In fact Tom appeared to find the beasts unusually difficult to handle, but as far as the audience was concerned that simply made the act more convincing and impressive. Only Mirella and Paddy were aware of the real tension under Kazan's haughty smile as he acknowledged each round of applause.

Next there came a short interval during which Tom changed into the sarong of the Indian boy and then he and Mirella took the stage in front of the curtains to enact the opening sequence of "The Condemned Preserved".

'Watch out for Trajan, he's in a funny mood,' Tom hissed in her ear, whilst Paddy as the angry Rajah was reciting the speech in which he sentences his daughter's impudent suitor to be thrown to the lions. There was no time to say more as they mimed the subsequent confusion – the Indian boy running wildly through the jungle as he tries to make his escape. He is recaptured and about to be bundled into the lions' den when the princess intervenes and in the ensuing struggle it is she and not the boy who is bundled into the savage lions' den.

Beyond the cage there was the platform, the crowded auditorium and the doors into the gardens, left wide open to admit as much fresh air as possible on this hot airless day. Somehow Mirella was acutely aware of all this, as if suddenly granted an overview of the pavilion as she entered the cage to be shut up with the lions until they had played out their terrible drama to the satisfaction of all these spectators. And for the first time since she had taken on this role, she felt wrong in the part, wrong to be doing what she was doing, wrong to allow herself to be shut in here for the entertainment of the public as if she had no more say over her destiny than these poor dumb animals. She felt wrong and she felt frightened.

No. Enough of these thoughts. She was here and now. This was Caesar, Trajan and Hanno; her friends and partners in the great work. 'Shush! Hush! Quiet now,' she was whispering to them. 'We've work to do. That's right. Quiet now.'

She was wearing her usual purple sari. It was vital always to wear exactly the same costume, as the slightest variation in clothing or props could upset the lions and ruin the act. Chaos lurked, waiting to rush through any chink in exact routine. As now, for instance. To the audience it looked as if Mirella had collapsed in helpless despair once she found herself trapped in the cage and left to her fate. She threw up her arms and beseeched heaven to come to her aid. She beat her breast. She lowered her head and wept and wailed. But all in strict sequence and carefully rehearsed style as she faced the lions and uttered gentle soothing sounds whilst miming frenzied despair. Every gesture was planned and had been added slowly, one by one, over weeks of patient rehearsal so that the lions were conditioned to know exactly what was coming and, far from being put out by this display of emotion, would have been thrown had any gesture or movement been omitted or come out of order.

Outside the cage Tom and Paddy were doing their bit – with the Rajah mirroring his daughter's despair and beseeching the heavens for help whilst the Indian boy, as yet unaware of what has befallen his loved one, was in mid-flight still intent on eluding his captors.

You could almost hear the hush and sense the indrawn breath of the audience as they sat waiting to see how the crisis would be resolved.

'That's right, good boy,' Mirella crooned as Trajan put up his front paw in mock aggression when she fluttered her sleeve in his direction.

There was no warning. The thunder crashed overhead as if the day of judgement had come. Crack! A second of silence and then a cannonade that threatened to split the roof.

Mirella felt herself jump at the first shock. What was happening? She instinctively raised her gaze to the skies. Out of the corner of her eye she saw Trajan drop to the floor and heard his deep growl. Instantly she recollected herself, where she was, what she was doing. Gave full attention to the lions: Hanno with his head swinging worriedly side to side; Caesar looking at her with a gleam of panic in his eyes. 'It's all right, it's all right, chaps,' she soothed, staring levelly at them before slowly turning her head to assess Trajan's state.

He lay snarling, crouched on his haunches, and his eyes flashed not panic but anger.

'All right, Trajan, all right,' she crooned at him. But it wasn't all right. He didn't rise to his feet and amble back to his normal position, but stayed there swishing his tail across the floor, head on one side, the growls seething up from his throat in mounting fury. And she, the object of that fury, standing there trying to think what to do, how to call him back to their former amity.

She was aware of Tom sliding into the cage even though she could not take her eyes off Trajan.

'Go behind me, slowly, and get out of the cage,' he rasped.

She did as she was told and had just reached the door when Trajan leapt. Twisting round and seeing Tom pinned by the animal against the bars, she screamed for Paddy. It wasn't necessary. He had already seized one of the sharp stakes kept ready for such emergencies and, whilst remaining outside the cage, was taking up position behind Tom's back from where he could use the weapon to push Trajan off. Meanwhile other men had run on to the stage with wattle hurdles which they shoved between the bars to keep the other two lions at bay.

'Tom, Tom!' She had fetched a stake too and was thrusting it into Trajan's shoulder, piercing his skin,

190

trying to force him to back off. Like a mad thing she lunged and jabbed. Anything, she would do anything, to get this ravening beast to leave Tom alone.

The struggle lasted only minutes, but it seemed to go on for hours.

For days and nights afterwards every time she closed her eyes for sleep she was back there, pressing herself against the cage, thrusting that stake into Trajan, trying to push him off Tom. But in her dreams all her endeavours were futile. As she pushed her stake deeper and deeper into Trajan's unresisting flesh, so the deeper he sank his fangs into Tom, chewing up his limbs, gnawing at his body as if it were no more than the usual blood-dripping chunk of meat daily fed to him. She woke screaming and then had to live through the actual experience immediately again in order to give it a more acceptable ending, remind herself that they had succeeded in driving Trajan off, Tom had managed to hobble out of the cage, he was going to live. He was still in the Infirmary and his arm had been badly mauled, but he had survived.

It was wonderful how people rallied round to give support when they heard of the calamity. There were visits, accompanied by gifts and reassurances, from most of the family. Her father and sister came up immediately and tried to persuade Mirella to go back home with them until Tom had recovered enough from his injuries for them to assess what the future held for him.

'You've got to face it, my love,' Johnny said, 'he might never be in a fit state to work again. And as for the lion act, I can't see him ever going back to that, not with a gammy arm. So you might as well come home with us now instead of hanging on here and dwelling on what's past.'

'No, I can't do that, Pa. I have to stay here and look after things until Tom comes out of hospital. Besides, I must stay close by so that I can visit him every day and help keep his spirits up. He saved my life, you know. It could easily have been me in that hospital bed now.' She turned her face away, hoping her father would not see the tears.

'I know it could. That's why I want you to come home for a while. You've had a nasty shock. You need to get right away from this place to give yourself a chance to get over it.'

'No. I won't leave Tom. Please don't mention it again.'

Her father refused to give up that easily and she had to restate her case several times and weep openly before she convinced him that it was useless to argue with her any further. Finally, his doubts about leaving her were only overcome when Cassie asked whether she might be allowed to stay and keep her sister company for a few weeks. He saw the sense in that idea and, when it was time to leave, seemed in a happier frame of mind as he bade them both farewell.

After waving him off, Mirella said, 'Cassie, I must go and see Paddy for a minute to make sure everything's all right with the lions. He's very capable but I like to make sure there are no problems.'

'Ugh! I don't know how you can bear to go near those brutes any more. Why don't you get rid of them, Rella? Sell them back to the Menagerie or pay someone to shoot them. I don't think Tom will ever want to clap eyes on them again.'

'No. It wouldn't be right to have them shot. It was only Trajan who turned savage, and that wasn't his fault. If anyone's to blame, it's me. I shouldn't have let that thunderclap shake my concentration and make me lose control.'

There, she had said it aloud now, the terrible thought which kept spinning round and round in her mind. It was her fault. She was the one to blame for the fact that Tom was now lying in a hospital bed in agony. To think of all those times when she had berated him for endangering her life by his drinking and then, when the moment arose, he had not hesitated to risk his own neck to save hers.

'Well, why don't you sell them then, get rid of them back to a Menagerie like I said?' Cassie insisted.

'No. Dad suggested that to Tom in the hospital and it really upset him, so we can't do that. Besides, the manager of these gardens has already taken it into his head to advertise them as a special attraction. You know, "Come and see the only true man-eaters in London. Your chance to witness the famous lions who attacked and savagely mauled their trainer." '

'I don't believe it! People wouldn't fall for a thing like that,' Cassie objected.

'You wouldn't think so, would you? But there's been a queue outside the pavilion all day. At least as many as came to watch "The Condemned Preserved". And, quite frankly, it's good to see the money coming in to pay Paddy's wages and give Tom something to live on while he's laid up.'

'I see. I hadn't thought of that. But you wouldn't go back to the lion act after what happened, would you, Rella? Ma and Pa are against it, you know. And Ma says . . .'

'I can imagine what Ma says and, to tell you the truth, I don't think I do want to carry on with the same sort of act, but there's something else I've a mind to try. Wait till I've had a word with Paddy and I'll show you.'

The practice tightrope which Tom had helped her put up was hanging coiled from one of its posts. Without explaining to Cassie what she was about, Mirella unwound the rope, securely fastened its end to another post and then, after making sure it would remain taut, put on her proper shoes and climbed up ready to step on to it.

'Good lord, Mirella, how on earth did you learn to do that?' Cassie asked when she had finished her little display.

'Tom's been training me because he thought it might make a useful side attraction in the show. But the thing is, if he isn't well enough to do much for a while, I thought perhaps I could get a job as a parader and rope-walker and keep us both until he gets his strength back.'

'Oh no, Rella. Not rope-walking. It's much too dangerous. The lions were bad enough, but think how you'd get hurt if you fell off a proper tightrope, because real artistes use something a lot higher than this, you know.'

'Of course I know, you idiot. I've watched Blondin walk across Crystal Palace at a height of a hundred and fifty feet.'

'Don't, Rella. You're making me feel ill just talking about it. Can't you be content with just singing and dancing? You do both those things well and they're not dangerous.'

'We'll wait and see,' Mirella said, changing back into her ordinary shoes. 'The main thing is I've got to get something worked out before Tom comes out of hospital, so that he doesn't start worrying himself to death about money.'

On the afternoon of Monday the thirteenth the Royal Gardens were overflowing with people come to enjoy the fête held to celebrate the safe return of Sir Robert Napier from Abyssinia. Besides all the usual attractions in the grounds, there was a huge hydrogen balloon and a gigantic picture representing the route taken by the British Army up to the heights of Magdala. Returning after a visit to Tom, Mirella and Cassie had difficulty pressing their way through the crowds. They had been back just long enough to remove their bonnets, kick off their shoes and flop down on to the lockers when there came a knock on the wagon door.

'Come in, if it's you, Paddy,' Mirella called out.

'And if it isn't, should I stay out?' a familiar voice replied.

'Who is it, Rella?' Cassie whispered whilst quickly slipping her shoes back on.

Instead of answering, Mirella went immediately to the door and opened it to see Levic standing on the steps, clutching a bunch of pale golden roses.

'Hello, Mirella,' he smiled. And she found herself smiling back into eyes that were dark brown and burnished like mahogany. 'I am glad to find you in, but please forgive me if this is an inconvenient time to call. I heard there had been an accident—' his face grew serious and he looked at her so intently she felt her cheeks flare '—that Tom was hurt and that you, yourself, had a narrow escape.'

'Oh, I'm all right, but Tom was hurt quite badly,' she faltered.

'This is what I heard and the reason for my visit,' he said in his precise manner. 'Please, a little token of my sympathy.' He handed her the roses. 'And I wish to talk with you about my plan, if you can spare me ten minutes.'

'Thank you, they're lovely,' she said, standing back so that he could come into the wagon. 'Look, Cassie, aren't these beautiful roses Levic has brought us? Oh, of course, you two don't know each other, do you? Levic, this is my sister, Cassie.'

'Hello, Cassie,' he said, greeting her with a formal bow. 'It is good to know our Mirella has someone here to help her at this difficult time. Are you staying long?'

Cassie explained and there followed a conversation in which Levic was brought up to date with Tom's injuries and progress towards recovery.

'It is a tragic matter when an artiste is maimed and his livelihood threatened in this way. We in the profession all feel this deeply. When one of us is hurt, all share the pain. I speak therefore not just for myself

195

when I say we shall do all that we can for Tom.'

'It doesn't look as if he'll ever be able to use his right arm again, but I can't see him quitting show business. He loves the life, and once he's got his strength back . . .' Mirella said, trying to sound cheerful.

'Yes, I'm sure things will work out for him. And to help them along a bit, his friends – hopefully with your approval – are proposing to hold a grand benefit with all the proceeds going to help Tom get on his feet again.'

'His friends?' she queried, casting her mind back over all Tom's acquaintances without conjuring up one whom she would have designated "friend".

'As I said,' Levic hastened to explain, 'everyone in our profession is a friend to a fellow artiste in trouble. Already some of the biggest names have consented to appear. My friend Blondin. Signor Ethardo, almost certainly. I shall lend my humble services, of course. And the proprietor has generously placed these Royal Gardens at our disposal for one day, so call me a Hungarian if we don't succeed in turning all this to good account for Tom.'

'Levic, I can see how much effort you've put in to this scheme already. For Tom's sake I really am most grateful, never mind how much money you raise.'

'Good, so you approve. Now I can get the full programme worked out and place the necessary advertisements in the press. Don't you worry, Mirella, soon the accident will be a memory, no more than a difficult corner which had to be turned by you and Tom to enable you both to see your future.'

He was looking into her eyes, as if searching for the answer to some question. His words echoed in her mind. A difficult corner which had to be turned to enable you to see your future. She wished she could believe that. Her vision of the future was hazier now than before the accident. Then she had been confidently making her selfish plans to desert Tom. Then she had seen her future clearly enough. That was the trouble. She felt so ashamed when she recalled that vision now. And as for the future, she could see nothing beyond her need to make it up to Tom in some way, even if she spent the rest of her life trying to do it.

'Come on, the day is too fine to stay indoors. I should like to invite you two young ladies to come and take tea with me in the park. Will you do me the honour?' Levic's words woke her up and she realised that she had been staring at him like a dinnilow since his last remark. In time she remembered her manners and politely tried to demur, but was glad when he brushed aside her objections by mentioning that it would also be a great help to him if she would take him on a guided tour of the gardens. 'We shall want to make the best of all the features on Tom's benefit day, you see. For instance, I'm thinking of a grand firework display to round things off and wondering whether the lake would be a suitable setting, or do you think they would look more spectacular on the river bank?'

'I don't know. I think you must go and have a look. Of course we'll come with you, won't we, Cassie?'

Her sister had other ideas. Whether she was feeling left out and afraid of making an awkward threesome, or whether her excuse of having to write a letter home could be taken at face value, Mirella lost no time in trying to decide. For herself, there was nothing she wished to do more than walk with Levic in the gardens. She had already begun slipping on her shoes. Now, having received Cassie's assurances that she would put the flowers in water straightaway, she picked up her bonnet and led the way out.

'No,' Levic said, 'I know what you're thinking and they didn't come from here.'

They had paused halfway along the rose walk to sniff in the sweet perfume.

'Are you sure? These lemon ones look awfully familiar.'

'True, but they are lemon, and for you I purchased nothing less than gold.' He took hold of her arm and tucked it through his, and they strolled on together – as she saw so many other young couples strolling together – quite ordinarily arm in arm. But she knew nobody else could be feeling like her. For it wasn't the heady scent of the roses or bright warmth of the sun, it was Levic's arm pressing against hers, feeling the hard strength of his bones and pulse of his blood, that filled her with such excitement that she wanted to sing out loud, or do a wild dance, or spin into the sky.

Without meaning to, she found herself suddenly squeezing Levic's arm to tell him how happy she felt to be out here in the park walking with him and he, in response, reached his other arm across and grasped her hand in his. He squeezed her fingers and, momentarily shutting her eyes, she felt giddy as his blood tingled and pulsed strongly against hers. Walking along together, that's all we're doing, she reminded herself, almost afraid of the way she was feeling now, this feeling of wanting to press closer and closer and closer to him.

In silence they sauntered on until he paused and broke the spell by murmuring, 'Mirella, what will you do once Tom comes out of hospital? I mean, you surely do not plan to carry on as before, do you?'

'No,' she said immediately, 'I'd already made up my mind to quit working with the lions.' She forbore to tell him why she had made that decision.

'So what are you thinking of doing instead?' he asked, forcing her to collect her thoughts which had been thrown into confusion by the feel of his body so close to hers.

'I'm not sure. Some parading, maybe, and I did think I might try . . .' unconsciously she lowered her voice as if fearful of confessing something so close to her heart '. . . to become a rope-dancer.' The words which cost her so much to say fluttered into the sunshine like frail butterflies and were lost among the flowers which Levic was leaning over to smell. He did not hear them.

'I ask you because,' he said, straightening up, 'I wondered whether you would like to join Sanger's troupe. They're always happy to take on pretty girls who can sing and dance and are used to the business, and although the pay would not be princely, they're a good outfit to travel with. Besides, I'm staying with them for the rest of the season and so I could make sure you're looked after.'

'Looked after? I'm not a child. I don't need to be looked after,' she protested.

'Of course you don't. I'm only teasing. But the offer is a serious one, and it would make me very happy if I could persuade you to come and join us.'

'Why?' She forced him to stop in the middle of the path. 'Why do you want me to join you?'

For answer he leant over and kissed her forehead, whispering, 'Because you ask questions like that. You don't play silly games with me. You speak what's in your mind and I love that.'

She thought for a moment. 'But that still doesn't answer my question. Why do you think it's a good idea for me to join Sanger's – if they'll accept me, that is?'

'Come, let's find a place near the river where we can sit in the shade and talk properly.'

She knew she was not looking her best. She hadn't been able to eat or sleep properly since the catastrophe and for a moment she was vain enough to regret that Levic was by her side and seeing her like this. Then a picture of Tom lying maimed in hospital gave cruel perspective to her vanity and she dismissed her appearance as a matter of no concern. It seemed as if

Levic was mocking her therefore when no sooner had they sat down on the grass under a plane tree than he murmured, 'You're beautiful, do you know that?'

'Yes! Those who like girls who look like ghouls, with dark circles round their eyes and skinny shanks, find me irresistible,' she laughed. 'And before you say any more, do you know what you are, Levic? You're what my grandmother calls an "ear-tickler", so I'm afraid your blandishments are wasted on me.'

'Oh, dear.' He pulled a series of tragic faces. 'A girl and her grandmother, that is a formidable combination! No wonder I find you such a challenge. Tell me about your grandmother.'

'What do you want to know?'

'Everything you choose to tell me.'

'Why?'

'So that I can begin to understand you.'

'And why do you want to understand me?'

'Because you are beautiful.'

'Well, to save this conversation going round in circles again, I'll tell you about my grandmother Liddy, because she really is a beautiful lady . . .' Partly to cover her embarrassment, partly because it was so pleasant sitting here on the grass beside Levic and just talking, she told him about her family and her own early life.

'So most of your people are travellers even if they aren't all showfolk? I'm glad about that. Travelling people are special. They haven't made so many compromises with life as other people have.'

'What sort of compromises, Levic?'

'Well, let me explain it this way. I believe there was a time when the whole of humanity spent their lives travelling the earth, wandering where the mood and the hunt for food took them. And then one day someone had the bright idea of settling down in one spot and putting a fence round animals and inventing ways to make the earth yield more than it naturally did, and in that moment mankind got greedy and weakened his own spirit. Anyway that is what I think, and so I'm all for the finders and spenders rather than the builders and keepers.'

'What do you mean by builders and keepers?'

'House-builders and house-keepers, or house-dwellers in general, I suppose. All those people who spend their lives accumulating things instead of doing things.'

Into her mind flashed a picture of the kitchens at Windsor, the shelves piled high with dishes, covers, cups, platters and pot-bellied salt cellars, and all the poor benighted girls whose lives were spent washing, cleaning and polishing all that clutter.

'But it's not really possible to live without things, is it?'

'Not completely, I grant you that. But we can try to make sure we don't encumber ourselves with too much baggage, don't you agree?'

'Yes, I do agree. I was brought up in a house, but I feel so much freer living in a wagon and moving round the country when we go to different fairs and enter-tainment halls. I wouldn't want to go back to a settled life. I'd feel like a wild bird stuck in a cage if I did.'

'Exactly. Wild birds, that's what we travelling showfolk are.'

'Birds of a feather, who flock together,' she mused.

'Yes. Who flock together, but who must always be able to fly free,' he insisted.

They wandered out of the gardens to take tea in a shop providing an excellent spread which included fresh shrimps and watercresses.

'I have enjoyed this afternoon, Mirella,' Levic murmured, pushing the teapot aside so that he could lean over the table. 'I hope you are going to allow me to take you out again very soon. Which reminds me, have you thought over my suggestion that you should come and join Sanger's?'

'Yes. Well, no. What I mean is, I can't really give you an answer until I've spoken to Tom about it.'

Her hand which was resting on the table was suddenly enclosed in his.

'Look, Mirella, who knows when Tom will be well enough to advise you properly. Besides, whatever he says, you've got to start making your own decisions about your future.'

'I know that. I'm not just trying to dodge the responsibility, but I've got to be very careful to include Tom in all my plans so that he doesn't feel deserted in any way. You understand that, don't you?'

His hand tightened on hers. 'Yes, I understand, but I don't necessarily agree. Feelings for others can become cages, if you're not careful.'

'Do you think it's wrong to have feelings for other people, then?' she asked incredulously.

'No, that's not what I said. But I do think it is wrong to let your feelings ensnare you, especially before you have known the joy of really flying free.'

That night before she went to sleep, she revelled in the memory of Levic's touch and tried to recall everything he had said. Some of his words excited her beyond imagining, made her feel as if she were flying towards the sun. Others left her feeling vaguely disturbed.

As soon as she got back to the wagon Cassie wanted to know all about how she had spent the afternoon with her handsome friend.

'He's got an interesting face, hasn't he?' she mused. 'I mean, I don't usually like whiskers on a man, but Levic's moustache is so soft and silky-looking, it gives him an air of distinction. And those deep brown eyes . . . ooh! Don't they just melt your heart away? I hope you appreciate what a sacrifice I made so that you could have him all to yourself. But if I'd realised it was going to be shrimps and watercresses, I might not have been so obliging,' she complained after Mirella had regaled her with details of the tea. And Cassie continued to bombard her with questions, all of which Mirella managed to answer without giving away any of the substance of her conversation with Levic. She also avoided mentioning that he had kissed her, under the trees near the river on their way home. He had held her close and pressed his lips gently to hers and then had whispered, 'I think I'm falling in love with you, Mirella.'

And now that she recalled the words, she understood this new feeling of warmth inside herself and knew that she had fallen in love with Levic.

Chapter Fourteen

Mirella's heart always sank when she approached the Infirmary, which was no more than a couple of miserable wards housed in a wing of the workhouse. Apart from its dismal surroundings, it possessed a frowsty smell which made her feel sick – a smell which she could never quite pin down, except that it seemed to be compounded of ether and beeswax and turpentine, old stewed cabbage and that disinfectant they sprinkled so liberally round the ward – chloride of lime, the nurse said it was.

'When is he coming out of this dreadful place?' Cassie asked as they were mounting the iron staircase on their way to visit Tom the next day.

'On Thursday. Gran and Joey are coming up to fetch him and take him back to the Captain's house to convalesce. He'll be much better off with Gran looking after him and, although he's a bit sarky about her herbs and potions, he's got more faith in her than in these quacks.'

'I should think so, too,' muttered Cassie from behind her perfumed pink gloves which she held before her face as if trying to arrive incognito. 'And how long do you think he'll be staying at the Captain's?'

'That depends on how fast he recovers and what he decides to do once he's better.'

'Do you mean he might decide to stay on with Gran indefinitely?'

'No, I don't think so,' Mirella said, remembering Tom's bitter memories of his former home life. 'He likes the Captain, but I don't think he feels all that comfortable in his presence. Besides, he's ambitious and values his independence too much to want to stay beholden for long.' Even while she was saying this, Mirella could not help thinking how much simpler it would be if the opposite proved to be the case and Tom found some niche for himself in Aldershot. She would still continue with her career, of course. She would start by going to Sanger's where, with help from Levic . . . and at this point her sensible planning dissolved into dreams from which it was hard to shake herself, even when she was standing next to the bedside and smiling her greeting at Tom.

'Hello, you're looking happy today,' he said, stretching out his good hand to lay hold of hers.

'That's because I've got Cassie here to cheer me up,' she fibbed, ushering her sister forward into the only chair provided.

'And because she's got some good news to tell you,' Cassie beamed. 'Go on, Rella, tell him about the benefit.'

'Yes, I think you're going to be really pleased about this, Tom,' she said, going on to explain what had been proposed but, whilst giving details of most of the events so far planned, leaving out the prominent part that Levic was playing in the arrangements.

Tom's immediate reaction was not encouraging.

'No. I don't want any charity, thank you.'

Mirella felt as deflated as a punctured Magdala balloon. She frowned at Cassie, trying to caution her not to waste her breath on some futile defence of charity. She knew Tom's views on this subject too well. No, there had to be another way of tackling him.

'Wait a minute, Tom, you've misunderstood,' she said, moving on to a different tack. 'The idea of the benefit isn't just to raise money for you because

206

you're in special need, or anything like that. It's being held in your honour, but not just for you. You see, I don't think you realise what a hero you've become, especially for the showfolk. They want to celebrate your heroism in some way that brings what you did to the notice of the public.'

'And how does that benefit anyone except me?' he asked.

'Well,' she said, thinking quickly, 'you know yourself what showmen are like – always desperate to promote a good image of themselves, especially with all this criticism of fairground rowdies at the moment, and people even suggesting that Parliament should do away with fairs altogether. So, quite frankly, the good publicity surrounding your benefit is coming as a godsend to them and they'd be devastated if it didn't come off.'

Tom didn't look convinced, but by chattering on she had given him time to get used to the notion and a justification for changing his mind. Far from putting up any more objections, he began to ask her to repeat who was going to be taking part.

'Blondin, you said. Has he actually promised to be there? And Ethardo? Gracious, that really is an honour. I've never known them turn out just for one person's benefit before. Mind you,' his face creased with agony as he used his left hand to rearrange his bandaged right arm on the covers, 'no benefit and no amount of money can ever compensate for this.'

'I know.' She closed her eyes. His face still raw and lacerated. His arm mangled and useless. And it was her fault. All her fault.

For a moment she couldn't think of anything to say and was grateful to Cassie for breaking into the conversation in an obvious attempt to brighten the atmosphere.

'Guess what, Mirella was taken out to tea yesterday by a handsome young fellow, weren't you, Mirella?

And he bought her shrimps and watercresses . . .'

'Someone took you out to tea, Mirella. Who was it?' Tom demanded, before Cassie could get any further.

'Oh, just Levic,' she answered lightly, hoping quickly to change the subject.

'Levic,' he spat the name out. 'What was he hanging round for? Did you go out with him alone? Why didn't you go with them?' he hissed at Cassie, as if blaming her for something.

'They asked me but I didn't want to go,' she stammered.

'Yes, I bet they asked you. Aagh!' His face contorted with pain as he moved too sharply.

'I only took Levic round the gardens to show him where Blondin's rope could be put up,' Mirella explained quickly. 'He'd been sent over to inspect the site because he's helping to organise the event.'

'Putting his rope up in the tea room, are you?' Tom growled, settling into a new position.

If he hadn't been so ill, she would have given him a tart reply. As it was, she found herself regretting yesterday. The last thing she wanted was to upset Tom at the moment, and yet that was exactly what she had done by going out with Levic. Well, it wouldn't happen again, she would make sure of that. Not while Tom was lying sick, his poor body mangled because of what he'd done to save her.

No matter what had happened between them previously, no matter what wrong feelings he might still harbour towards her – and sometimes Mirella wondered whether he loved or hated her – none of that was important now. The only thing that mattered was Tom and getting him well again.

When the day arrived for him to be taken down to Aldershot, Tom made an announcement. He had changed his mind about the lions. He had no intention of ever working an animal act again and would be glad if Paddy and Mirella would make suitable arrangements for selling the beasts.

'There you are, what did I tell you?' Cassie said after Tom had gone. 'I knew Uncle Tom wouldn't want to do his Great Kazan thing again.'

'Yes. Well, I'm heartily glad, I can tell you. Although I'm still fond of the cats, especially dear old Caesar, I can't go near that cage without remembering what happened to Tom.'

'So what will you do with them?'

'Sell them back to the Menagerie, I suppose. Paddy's already been in touch with Mr Wombell and he's agreeable. Even offered Paddy his old job back as keeper, so he'll be taking them down to Southampton the day after Tom's benefit.'

'Can't they go before?'

'They could, but the Manager of the gardens wants them here until the last moment because they're still such an attraction. He's already commissioned posters for the benefit announcing "Positively your Last Chance to see the Woolwich Man-eaters".'

'Ugh! Well, I shall be relieved when they've gone. Every time I hear a roar, I'm terrified in case they've got loose and are roaming around.'

'No, you mustn't get the wrong idea, Cassie. Those cats are always securely locked up and well looked after. Even the act shouldn't have been dangerous. It was just bad luck, that awful storm breaking out when it did. In fact the more you get to know about acts that seem dangerous, the more you realise they're under better control than they seem and there really aren't many bad accidents, so don't let yourself get nervous about things. I mean, you watch out for Blondin when he performs here next week. That will be an eye-opener for you.'

'Yes, it might be, if I could bear to watch him. A rope seventy feet high, you say? And he intends to walk along it blindfold. Well, it sounds awfully clever, but I'll be so scared he'll fall off I shan't enjoy it.'

'Oh, come on. Like I said, it's not as dangerous as it seems. He'll have his performance completely under control all the time. What you'll see him doing is . . .' and she went on to describe the basic technique of rope-walking and the sort of tricks Blondin would pull to make it look more hazardous than it really was.

As Mirella talked, she could see Cassie becoming more and more interested until she eventually interrupted with, 'Do you know, I was just thinking of those games we got up to when we were little – do you remember, Rella? – pretending we were acrobats and doing tightrope-walking along a wall. I wouldn't mind having a go on your rope, if I could start really low and you'd show me how. I don't think I'll be any good at it, mind.'

She was right. At first she could not take more than a couple of steps without falling off, but she seemed to find it fun and there was so little else to do in the couple of weeks leading up to the benefit that the two of them spent a lot of time messing around, practising rope-walking, Mirella showing Cassie the simple tumbling tricks and singing and dance routines she had picked up. And between whiles, sitting in the shade of the wagon or under one of the trees in the park, they talked about the future.

With Tom gone, Mirella had to work hard to convince the family that there was still good reason for her to stay on in Woolwich Gardens. Someone had to check the daily takings, pay Paddy, and generally keep an eye on things until the lions were dispatched to Wombells, she argued. However, what she was really pleading for was time to sort out her own plans.

She was quite clear what her first move should be. She would accept Levic's offer to use his influence to get her a job with Sanger's troupe. She wasn't too bothered about what she did so long as she could be independent and continue to practise her ropewalking. The fact that Levic would be in the same company was exciting but a little frightening.

'Why doesn't Uncle Tom like your friend Levic?' Cassie asked as they were sprawling on the grass after a strenuous bout of practising.

'How do you know he doesn't?'

'By the way he carried on when I mentioned you'd gone out to tea with him.'

'Oh, that was just Tom being over-protective. He likes to think of himself as a father guarding his innocent daughter from the wiles of wicked men. He means well enough.'

'But if he feels responsible for you because you're living with him and away from home, how do you think he'll react when he hears that you've gone off in his wagon to join this circus troupe?'

'Oh, I think he'll see the sense in it,' Mirella said with more confidence than she felt. 'I shan't mention Levic's part in the arrangements though, because that might bother him. Even though there's no reason why it should.'

'I wish I could come with you,' Cassie sighed. Backed by Mirella, she had tried to persuade their parents to let her stay on longer, but one daughter running wild was enough, Sadie had said, and insisted that she be ready to return home when Johnny came up to fetch her on the day of Tom's benefit.

'Still, I can see Ma's point of view in wanting you at home to help her,' Mirella said, trying to console her. 'For one thing you're so good with Albert and Benjie. And there again, you're only fourteen which is a bit young to be living this sort of life. Still, maybe they'll let you come for another few days once I've got more settled. And in the meantime we'll keep in touch with letters so you'll know where I am.'

Sanger's circus was at present pitched in Croydon

211

and she would join them there just before they packed up and travelled to Mitcham Fair. She had no idea where they were due to move to after that, her only concern being to make herself a useful member of the company and not be a cause of embarrassment to Levic.

Levic . . . the name had become her talisman. With it, she conjured him up every night so that his dark eyes might smile before hers and blot out the vision of Tom on the floor of the cage being ripped and torn. She listened over and over again to his voice whispering, "I think I'm falling in love with you, Mirella," until it muffled Trajan's roar and the sound of her own screaming terror. Then, "Levic, I love you," was the whispered spell which repeated itself until it invoked sleep.

The trouble was, it was so much easier to meet Levic in her dreams than in real life where her delight in his presence was alloyed with despair at such stark betrayal of Tom. The day before the benefit, for instance, when Levic had arrived at the door of the wagon, bearing more flowers for her, she could do nothing to disguise her joy at seeing him again. He reached out his hand for hers and they stood for moments smiling and looking at each other, neither of them wishing to add to the simple pleasure of just being together.

'Your little sister, has she gone home already?' he eventually asked, looking round the wagon.

'No. She's just slipped down to the shops to buy some ribbon. But what brings you here today?'

By way of answer, he kissed her forehead.

'I see,' she said. 'Then I am honoured, and shan't distract you by mentioning that your friend Blondin has also arrived and can at this moment be found putting up his rope near the lake.'

'Ah, it's funny you should mention his name. It did just occur to me that he might by chance be here today.'

'And you have an arrangement to see him?' she suggested.

'Yes, I confess it. But I did not bring him flowers.'

'Ah,' she sighed, taking the pale roses from him and sniffing their scent, 'then I shall refuse to be jealous – so long as you don't allow him to talk you into cavorting with him on the high rope tomorrow. Seriously, though, you're not planning to do that Crystal Palace act with him again, are you? I was so terrified you were going to fall last time.'

'There was no danger of that. But no, to set your mind at rest, I shall not be assisting the Chevalier on the rope tomorrow. Not from any reticence on my part, you understand. The exclusion order comes from on high. Blondin does not relish the competition. And I can see his point. I should not want Blondin to steal my thunder by clowning beside me in the ring.'

'Well, he's welcome to steal mine. Anyone is. I've had enough thunder to last me a lifetime.' She found herself instinctively glancing up.

'Amen to that,' Levic murmured, lifting his head and gazing heavenwards too. 'But do not worry. No more bolts from the blue. Your horizon is clear now, Mirella.'

'Is that a promise?'

'Yes, by Jove!'

'Ah, you speak for him personally, do you?'

'Not exactly, but we are very good friends.'

Leaving a note for Cassie, Mirella accompanied Levic out into the gardens in search of Blondin. They arrived at the lakeside to find the rope already in position, and Blondin contemplating the scene as if rehearsing in his mind the details of tomorrow's performance.

'Is everything all right, my friend?' Levic asked.

'Yes. I think the site is good. All I await now is the spectators, and with all the advertisements you have placed I 'ave no doubt they will come and make the day successful.' He turned and smiled at Mirella. 'In any case, we shall do our best, Mademoiselle.'

She was about to give him her thanks when there came a shout for Levic from the direction of the pavilion.

'OK, just coming,' he yelled back, before turning to Mirella and Blondin and explaining, 'It is the acrobats I got to replace Ethardo, because he is in Norwich. I must go and explain the programme to them. You two will please excuse me for a few minutes?'

'Bien sûr,' Blondin murmured, his eyes twinkling, 'and really, my friend, there is no need to 'urry back on our account. Mirella and I will do very nicely as company for each other, isn't that so, Mam'selle?'

'Yes, you can tell me about the tightrope,' Mirella suggested. 'There are several questions I'd love to ask you.'

He heaved an exaggerated sigh. 'Levic, my friend, you may depart with an easy mind knowing that we shall be talking about ropewalking. Eh bien, Mirella, so what is it you wish to know?' he asked more seriously, once Levic had gone.

'I wondered whether you ever train other people to do what you do?'

'Yes, I do. If it is clear they are born with talent, then I see it as my job to help them along the way, just as my teacher, Monsieur Charles Blondin, "put me on the right ropes", as he used to say.'

'Was he a relation of yours?'

'Because of the name, you mean? Ah, non. He was simply my teacher and a very great artiste and so I took on his name as – how do you say? – ah, oui, a tribute to him, a mark of gratitude for all that he taught me so well.'

'And now you yourself teach others? Would you be able to teach me?' she asked in a rush.

His eyebrows shot up. 'You? You wish to walk on the high rope? But you are a girl. I would never teach a girl to do this thing. No, no. That would be impossible.'

'Surely not. I've heard of other women doing it.

Like the one who crossed the Thames, for instance.'

'Ah yes. The "Female Blondin" they called her. And of course you are right. There were very many Female Blondins a few years ago, but not any more. So where are they all now, have you stopped to ask yourself that?' His voice sounded thin and angry.

'No. I didn't know there were a lot of them. I've only heard of the one who crossed the Thames. She's quite famous, although not nearly as well known as you, of course, Monsieur Blondin,' Mirella added hastily, wondering if she had upset him by referring to a competitor.

'Ah, yes. She was much celebrated for crossing the Thames on a high rope. People remember that. But what they don't remember is the time she fell off her rope, that same young woman. And they certainly don't celebrate the fact that she was left a cripple who is now unable to walk even the pavements without the support of crutches.'

'Oh, no. That's a terrible story.'

'Terrible, but true. It happened about six years ago at the Highbury Barn, and it was by no means the only disaster. After that there were many such tragedies. Which is why, when I ask you, "Where are all the Female Blondins today?" you have to say some were lucky enough to be crippled into retirement, and most of the others, they are dead.'

'Killed by falling from the rope?' Mirella had to put the question, even though she did not want to hear the answer.

'But yes. There have been too many such accidents. Fine young men and women plunging to their deaths. And do you know why? Because they were ignorant of the profession they were engaged in. They knew how to walk along a rope, yes. And they could perform tricks on the rope, yes. And having conquered the rope, they could treat it with disdain, or so they

215

thought. But in the end, it was the rope which betrayed them.'

'How?'

'By simply giving way under their feet.'

She gazed up at the huge cable hanging from its scaffold poles.

'But a rope that size couldn't just snap, and surely somebody about to walk on it would check to make sure there was no sign of fraying anywhere,' Mirella objected. 'Or do you mean they hadn't secured it properly at one of the ends and it came loose while the poor person was walking on it?'

'Yes, in one case certainly that is what happened. But you, Mademoiselle, if you will forgive me, show the same ignorance of the rope as led to all the other misfortunes. You make assumptions. But if they are the wrong assumptions and you act upon them, then . . . Pouf! You will find yourself toppled to the ground. Now, down here on terra firma this is not important. But up there' – he pointed up to the rope – 'act on a wrong assumption and you are finished.'

'And what are these wrong assumptions?'

'That you can spot where a rope is weak by looking at its surface. That the rope you walk on today is necessarily the same rope that you will walk upon tomorrow.' She must have looked as perplexed as she felt, for he added: 'You must realise, you see, that there are invisible factors which affect ropes, just as they affect animals and people. Take your thunder-storm, for instance. You walk one day on a brand new tested rope, no problem. But the next time you come to walk, there has been a storm with lightning and . . . Pouf! the rope has been injured. This is what led to the death of my friend, Carlo Valerio, at Cremorne.'

'And yet you still continue. None of these dreadful accidents have put you off.'

'Ah no, and nor will they. For me it is different. I have been walking the rope now for thirty-eight years and never met with a single accident worth recounting, but please note I take nothing for granted. I am more careful now than ever before to see that my rope is in perfect condition and perfectly secured. I myself take full responsibility for this. I delegate to no one.'

'But surely, all that you're saying goes to show how important it is for you to pass on all this experience, because if you trained others to follow exactly in your footsteps, there wouldn't be any accidents.'

'But I have trained others. There was a young American I helped last year who is now doing very well in his country. What I will not do is train a woman. That goes completely against nature.'

'Hers or yours?'

'Pouf!' He shrugged his shoulders. 'Hers, naturally. I know there is that old saying: "Maidens make the best funambulists", but the other side of the coin is that love inevitably destroys the sense of balance, and you must agree that in this respect a maiden is very susceptible.' His mood had changed. Now he was smiling mischievously, but she did not want to be sidetracked by his teasing.

'I don't agree with you. I know there are lots of girls who think of nothing but flirtation and love, but we're not all like that. Some of us are as serious about our profession as any man and I don't think it's right that you should try to stop us being successful.'

'Mon dieu, what have I said?' Blondin drew back in mock alarm at her vehemence. 'You misunderstand. I have no wish to hold women back in any way. On the contrary, I wish only to protect them.'

'From what?'

'From themselves, if necessary. But don't look so solemn, Mirella. There are many more openings for you in show business. You are pretty and, if you can do a little singing and dancing, that is all you need.

Leave the dangerous things to us menfolk. We are not pretty, so we are dispensable.'

Although she was disarmed by his manner, his words annoyed her. "A little singing and dancing" – what good was that to her? There was no challenge in doing a little bit of singing and dancing. She wanted to walk the high rope just as he did. Of course rope-walking was dangerous and many people had been killed doing it. Blondin was right to try to warn her off, but he had no chance of succeeding. He was too late. The rope had already seduced her.

It was a pity, though. She would like to have learnt more from Blondin. It was one thing to stand below, watching him, but altogether something else to be up there and . . . An idea suddenly occurred.

'Levic told me you're not using his services tomorrow, so does that mean you'll be carrying someone else across the rope?'

'Yes, if I can find a suitable volunteer in time. I was thinking of asking one of the acrobats to oblige.'

'What about me? Would I do?'

'You?' His head fell back as he laughed.

'What is so funny about the idea?'

'You, ma chère. You are so serious.'

'You'll let me do it, then?' she persisted.

'Why not? So long as you have a head for heights and stay absolutely calm, you'll be all right. But could you stay calm, that is the question?'

'I stayed calm enough in the lions' den.'

'Exactly so. That is what I was thinking. And on my rope, doing precisely what I tell you, you will be no worse off. So, as I say, providing you do not faint when you see the height, I am prepared to try with you. If nothing else, I am sure such experience will cure you once and for all of wishing to walk the rope.'

'Yes, you're probably right,' she agreed, smiling.

Without giving him time to have second thoughts, she rushed off to change her dress and fetch better shoes and soon managed to prove to his satisfaction that she had no fear of heights. After that it was just a matter of going over the details of how she should conduct herself on the rope. For propriety's sake it was decided that instead of Blondin carrying her on his back, he would repeat a variation on his act which he had used several times before. Dressed as a gardener, he would wheel a barrow filled with flowers across the rope and on his return trip Mirella would climb inside and, if she felt sufficiently confident, scatter the flowers above the heads of the crowd.

'Do you think you could manage that?' Blondin asked, apparently as excited with the idea as she was. 'Visually it will be most impressive. You in a pretty dress, and all the flowers fluttering down. The people will love it.'

Levic laughed when he first heard what they were proposing to do.

'No need for you to be afraid of competition now, my friend. With Mirella in your wheelbarrow, your act will be a push-over,' he joked.

'You don't mind my doing it, then?' she asked.

He hesitated, studying her face before giving an answer. 'Would it matter if I did?'

'Well, I wouldn't want to do anything to upset you.'

Still aware of his watchful eyes, she heard him say, 'If it matters so much to you what I or other people think, then do not do it. Go home and help your mother peel potatoes. That way you will upset no one.'

She was too busy the following day to feel nervous. She had to make sure that Paddy had been paid properly and that all the arrangements had been made for his journey with the lions back to Wombell's. And then there was the arrival of Johnny, come up to represent his brother and to take Cassie back home at the

219

end of the day. She warned them both that she would be leaving them after lunch in order to assist Blondin in the presentation of his act, but fortunately neither seemed to guess that this would mean accompanying him on to the rope.

The Royal Gardens were as crowded as on a Bank Holiday and, since most of the gate money was going to his benefit fund, this boded well for Tom. All around her she could hear the happy sounds of families picnicking under the trees, children's voices echoing across the lake, and somewhere in the distance a hurdy-gurdy churning out "Champagne Charlie Is My Name". She found herself humming the tune as she brushed past promenading couples – dark-suited young fellows, straight-backed like poles around which curled exotic beanflowers of girls, arms and waists entwined. She was happy and could tell that others were happy too.

Blondin, wrapped in a calf-length cape to cover his costume, greeted her as soon as she arrived at the foot of one of the masts supporting the rope.

'You have not lost your nerve then, ma petite? I was, you know, quite resigned to scattering my own flowers if you had thought better of your rash offer overnight.' He kissed her on both cheeks. 'But, as it is, I am very glad to see you. And I must say, your dress is just perfect for the part.'

She had put on her parading dress – the one with the saffron sash and full muslin skirts over layers of silk petticoats – and had drawn her hair into a topknot held by a wreath of the same kind of yellow marigolds that she was to strew into the crowd. All that remained was for her to practise climbing into the barrow and work out with Blondin the best position to sit in whilst he wheeled her across the rope.

It was two o'clock. Time to begin. The rope had acted like a magnet, a thin bar magnet, drawing to itself circles of people who now stood gazing up at it.

In a daze she watched Blondin going through his familiar routine: marching across the rope to the rousing strains of the "Sabre Dance"; running backwards, lying down, standing on his head. In the same daze she watched him take on the guise of a gardener, twisting string around the bottom of his corduroy trousers and tying a hessian apron about his waist. Balancing his long pole, he stepped out on to the rope, plodding up and down its length clearly searching for something. But what? Ah, now he was remembering where the lost object could be found, was making a beeline back to the platform and hauling it out from where it had been stowed under a tilt – his wheelbarrow, of course. Every gardener needed a wheelbarrow, even one whose flower borders sprouted seventy feet up in the clear air. However, what he didn't need was a long balancing pole, so this he now set aside in favour of clasping the handles of the barrow and wheeling it shakily along the rope.

'Oh! Oh, no!' the universal cry of terror rose as if from one throat as Blondin went through his usual trick of stumbling and pretending to fall. Even Mirella, who well knew what to expect, found herself gasping and then joining in the clapping as he regained the balance he had never lost. And then he was pointing to the flowers in his wheelbarrow and calling for a volunteer to help him distribute them, and she had to react quickly before any man or woman in the crowd took it into their head to answer the summons.

She was climbing the steps up and up towards the platform. Had the whole world really fallen silent all of a sudden? The whispering, the giggling, all the chattering and the sighs suddenly silenced? The round smoothness of the steel in her hands and under her feet and the feel of her body growing lighter, more biddable, less earthbound the higher she climbed. Higher and higher. All eyes on her but she herself free of all sensation of being watched by the crowd, because she had climbed out of their reach.

At this height the usually smiling Frenchman was cold and quite impersonal, just another figure on this bridge above the world. It did not matter, for at this height she was alone and had no desire to share her solitude. Stepping into the wheelbarrow now, carefully distributing her weight, finding her balance. Head raised, chin up, smiling, and the feeling that she was being spun along in a sun-chariot. She barely looked at him at all; was afraid to look, if she was honest. But she wasn't afraid to look down at the crowds, flat and two-dimensional beneath her, each individual person small and intact.

'The flowers! Throw them now!' Blondin hissed. 'But calmly, remember! Keep it calm!'

She had completely forgotten the flowers, but now as if in a dream she gathered up handfuls of blossoms and gently cast them down to the people.

'Bravo, ma petite. That was excellent,' Blondin beamed at her after the cheering was all finished and they had climbed down to earth again. ' "Mirella sans peur", that should be your name from now on.'

'Sans what?' she asked, still breathless.

'Without fear. I shall call you "Mirella without fear".'

'No, not without fear. The fear was there all right, but kept hidden.'

'I'm glad to hear it. The person who stands seventy feet above the ground and does not have fear, does not have sense either!'

'Mam'selle, this is yours? Something you have dropped, I think?'

Spinning round at the sound of his distinctive voice, she found Levic at her side proffering a long-stemmed marigold.

'No, I didn't drop it. I threw that one to you.'

'To me in particular?'

'Of course.'

'Then I must have been standing with many particular people, for they all caught one. Seriously, though, you did very well. Didn't she, Jean-Francois? I'm proud of you,' he said, kissing her hand. 'We'll make a proper trouper of you yet.'

Chapter Fifteen

It was an honour to be asked to take the part of Britannia in the Sanger street parade, Mirella was aware of that. It did not occur to her to say no, despite the fact that it meant being shackled to a lion all the way – the reason, of course, why she, with all her experience of working with big cats, had been asked to stand in for Mrs Sanger while she was sick.

She had been travelling with the circus along the south coast for three weeks now, loving every minute of it. Performing in the ring, sewing costumes, mucking in to help with the cooking and washing up – her life was certainly arduous. Except that all was not work but high adventure when Levic was nearby.

The company, having played to full houses at Arundel, were full of good humour when they arrived and built up here in the Sussex Club Cricket Ground in Hove and were now bustling around getting ready for the one o'clock parade. The tent – one of the largest on the road – like a gigantic red-striped mushroom with a gaily-painted showfront, squatted on the field waiting. It could seat more than two thousand people, and when they opened at big fairs, all that was needed to bring in the crowds was a platform parade like the one Mirella had taken part in at Wombell's. But on tobers like this, where they were the only attraction, something more was needed to drum up an audience – and this is where the street parade came in.

'Come on, let's get the bandwagon on the road!' Georgie Sanger was shouting. And from her high perch on the tableau Mirella smiled to see him standing, impatiently tapping his little malacca cane against his leg. Ignoring the heat of this August day he was dressed for the public eye as usual in his top hat and velvet-collared frockcoat, flower in lapel, silk handkerchief flowing from breast pocket and a thick gold chain and fob watch stretched across his front.

The last of the bandsmen was still scrambling aboard as their carriage clanked out of the field, looking gaudily magnificent with its carved angels, mermaids and tritons, gilded and glittering in the sunshine. Behind it followed a line of performers in their ring costumes, riding singly or in pairs. Then a mirrored tableau and a further line of riders. Next the red and gold beast wagons came rumbling into the line, another chariot, and then it was her turn in the Queen's Tableau, centrepiece of the whole parade.

Clasping her shield and trident, and wearing a Greek helmet on her head, Mirella had taken her place in good time on the top of the three-tiered wagon so that the lion, Nero, could be led up the ramp and quietly settle himself down by her right knee as companion piece for the "lamb" (which was actually a fully-grown ram) lying on her left. Levic had told her that George Sanger had got the idea for this tableau from a bishop's remark that there would be no peace in the world until someone succeeded in getting the lion to lie down with the lamb. Taking this as a direct challenge to himself to bring about the millennium, George selected a suitable lion cub and a lamb and reared them together in the same cage until they became friendly enough to be paraded around town lying down on either side of Britannia on the tableau wagon.

'That's right, keep it friendly, old fellow,' she crooned as Nero stretched his huge head and started to lick her foot. There was a moment after he was first led up from his cage, when she had touched his fur and smelt that distinctive lion smell and almost panicked. But Levic had been standing just below, smiling encouragement, and she refused to betray any sign of fear to him. So she had returned his smile and the moment passed. Now she felt her old confidence returning and was able to sit back and actually enjoy the parade.

Her attention was caught by the sun glinting off the silver-mounted harness and gleaming from the embossed bridles and saddle-soaped reins. Everything shone. Everything looked perfect. Only show, mind. She realised that all that glistened was not gold, but paper-thin gold leaf; only for show; only to attract the jossers and entice them in to the circus. But what pleased her was the knowledge that they were not being cheated; that, once inside, they would find everything that happened was unquestionably real. Unlike the theatre where all was charade and make-believe, the circus was a focus of reality where performers actually did what they seemed to be doing. Circus artistes never depended on sleight of hand or mirrors or special apparatus to fool the public. There was no place in the circle for magicians or conjurors, only for people dedicated to working their act – that was the essential difference between the theatre and the circus, Levic had explained. Actors in the theatre were there simply to play a part. Artistes were in the circus to work their act.

She was struck by his fervour when he said that. 'We artistes are dedicated to working our act, totally dedicated. It is that dedication which sets us apart from others. I think you understand this, Mirella. That is why I am drawn to you.'

He saw her as a fellow artiste. She was thrilled about that and would do everything she could to prove herself worthy.

'Down! Lie *down*, Billy! Don't do that!' The ram had stirred and was cheerfully butting his head against her leg. Fortunately, on the other side of her, Nero continued imperturbably chewing at his claws.

'Look, look! Come and see. It's the circus!' All along the streets, people stopped in their tracks and stood calling, pointing, chattering excitedly to one another or jostling to get a better view. Older friends or relations were hoisting little ones up on to their shoulders, saying, 'See, that's Britannia, just like she looks on the penny. See the Union Jack on her shield?' But even as they were saying it, their attention was already rippling back to Ajax the elephant walking just behind her, and she was being hailed by another lot of people whooping and calling, 'Hey, look! This one's meant to be Britannia, just like she looks on the penny.'

There was no need for her to wear a performer's expression, she simply couldn't resist smiling as she went over in her mind what had happened yesterday.

Sanger's circus had a trapeze artiste on the bill, but no ropewalker with them at the moment. Levic had helped her rig up a tightrope so that she could continue with her practising and, unbeknown to her, had dropped a hint to Mr Sanger about what she could do. The upshot was that yesterday when she was going through her usual exercises, Sanger had come into the tent to watch her. Had she known he was sitting there, she would probably have fluffed the whole routine, but in happy ignorance she walked and skipped along the rope, tied baskets on her feet and a blindfold on her eyes, just as she had seen Blondin do.

'Levic, I was wondering if I should have a go at . . .' she started to call out, before noticing that he was not alone.

'Come down here, child. I want a word,' George Sanger barked. She had no time to feel anxious. In any case, Mr Sanger was looking, if not exactly

228

pleased, not displeased at least. 'That little turn ain't too bad. Needs a bit more dash and sparkle to bring it to life but it's got something. Yes, it's got something I could see fitting on the bill. We used to have a "Female Blondin" a few years back and the public liked it. Go on, get back up there and go through that little number again, so's I can be sure.'

She repeated the whole performance, conscious this time that every move she made was being scrutinised. When she finished, George Sanger stood tapping the top of his malacca cane against his teeth.

'Hmm,' he growled, 'like I said, it needs a lot more dash and sparkle before it amounts to anything, but I'm willing to give it a go. Come over to the wagon in ten minutes' time and we'll talk turkey.'

And so it was arranged that, as soon as she could get the act ready for public performance – and this meant getting her costume, music and props sorted out – she would be given a slot on the programme.

'Strewth! That was a sharp one,' she muttered as the tableau lurched round a right-hand bend, nearly sending her and the two beasts toppling over the side. 'All right, Nero, settle down. It won't happen again.' She threw a glance over her shoulder in time to catch sight of the grand yellow coach containing Mr George and his brother coming round the corner to bring up the rear of the procession. She was too high up to see Levic, who was riding just behind her tableau on a cream-coloured horse, probably seated back to front or doing a headstand on its saddle.

'Well done, he likes your act,' Levic had said after George Sanger left the ring.

'I wouldn't say that,' she had replied doubtfully. 'It needs lots more "dash and sparkle", that's what he said, and he didn't look terribly impressed after I did it all the second time.'

'Nonsense. I know George Sanger and, take my word for it, he does not put anyone on his programme unless he thinks they are good. Moreover, if he thinks someone is good, then they are good. Believe in yourself, Mirella. It is necessary to believe in yourself if you are to become an artiste.'

Yes, those were Levic's words. Slightly inclining her head in acknowledgement of the cheers as the tableau turned another corner to the right and slowly paraded along a seafront lined with people, Mirella found herself gazing out over the ocean and felt like brandishing her trident and shield in triumph over the waves breaking against the shore.

Believe in herself. Yes, she found it easy to believe in herself when Levic was there to encourage her.

'Now, show me how you'll run back into the circle to take your applause.' She dutifully did as Levic instructed. 'That's right, dance in lightly and blow kisses to the right and to the left. No, no, no. More delicacy, please. You look as if your fingers are attached to your lips with thick elastic.' She tried again, blowing out her kisses as if they were thistledown.

'Better, but still not right. Watch me, Mirella. There, do you see the gesture?' And she watched as Levic appeared to be drawing a fine hair out of his mouth. He repeated the gesture and then waited for her to copy him.

'Yes. Now you have it. Light and delicate. Yes.'

His attention to detail amazed her. And his versatility. There seemed no end to the amount of things he could do and she soon came to realise that, although George Sanger jealously guarded his own authority, he was happy to see Levic acting as unofficial manager in the ring. When other performers had problems or were thinking about making changes in their act, Levic was able to give sound advice because he was usually as proficient as they at the particular trick they had in mind. Full of energy and enthusiasm, he was willing to turn his hand to anything, interweaving his performance with every other act in the show.

Neither were his skills limited to the ring. Last week at Hove, there had been a nasty squall before the circus opened and during the matinée someone spotted a rent in the canvas top. As a result, when the wind started to get up again after the show, Mr Sanger decided that the canvas would have to be dropped, even if it meant losing the evening's performance. Levic, however, refused to make any such concession to the weather. As soon as the canvas was down, he appeared with needle and twine and, heedless of the drizzle, squatted on the muddy ground and sewed up the rent. Then, when this was done, he took a major part in hauling on the ropes and getting the canvas up again. The next performance went ahead on time with Levic as usual keeping the crowd in stitches and holding the whole show together.

Levic brought a fund of demonic energy to his work and never seemed to get tired like other folk. Even when he wasn't physically active in the ring, he would be sitting with a notebook on his knee sketching out the details of some new act. Peering over his shoulder, she would see a succession of outlines unmistakably his. The trail he would take into the ring, the series of expressions on his face – lugubrious, puzzled, hopeful as he addressed the audience and sought their help – all the details carefully worked out. No expression, no movement, no mannerism that was not carefully considered before being decided upon; no misplaced gesture, no superfluous move.

'Goodness, Levic, do you really have to work everything out as carefully as that? Can't you just think up a trick and try it out in the ring, and then vary it once you see how it works out in practice? I mean, everyone knows that acrobats and animal-trainers have to be precise in what they do, but surely clowns don't have to worry so much?'

He looked up at her, at the same time flicking his hair out of his eyes with the end of his pencil.

'Oh, yes. The antics of the clown may look random, it is essential for him to appear happy-go-lucky, but that apparent casualness costs him dear and he has to work very hard to appear artless.'

She loved to hear him talk about his work. Sliding down on to the grass beside him, she asked him what antic he was trying to devise at the moment, and he held out his notepad and started to explain the sketches he had made so far.

As he spoke, he used the pencil as a pointer, holding it in his right hand with the little finger delicately out-stretched. His arm was bare, the tiny hairs surprisingly fair against the sun-tanned skin. His hand and arm moved as he talked, the upper sunburnt area occasion-ally twisting to give a glimpse of clear, pale skin on the under surface; skin so naked and vulnerable, she longed to touch and cosset it. How would he react if she stretched out her fingers and caressed . . .

'So, what do you think? Would the audience under-stand the joke?' Levic's sudden question threw her into confusion.

'I'm sorry, what did you say? I missed that last bit. I was just day-dreaming.'

'I see. So from that I am to deduce how fascinating my conversation must be.'

She glanced up into his face, unable to tell from his tone whether he had taken offence. She saw that his lips were drawn down in an exaggerated grimace, but his brown eyes sparkled with fun as he added: 'Right! Well, you take the lead then, and let us see if I can follow you into less boring channels.'

'You mean you're prepared to talk about something really interesting, such as tightrope walking?' she teased.

'No. I did not go so far as to say that.'

'What, then?'

'Maybe we can think of something interesting that does not require us to talk at all.' Now his eyes seemed to smoulder and scorch into her. Her cheeks reflected the glow and she fell silent, unable to think of anything to say to cover her embarrassment.

Levic stretched out to take her hand and raised it to his lips. She felt the soft warmth of his breath on her skin and longed to throw her arms around his neck and force him to kiss her properly. These weeks spent so close to him had strengthened her feelings for him. She loved Levic and everything about him. She loved the way he spoke, the way he smiled, the way he walked, the way he worked. In the morning, soon after the first shout warned the company that it was time to make a move, she would peep out of the window of her wagon to catch sight of him. And as soon as she saw him, she felt herself being swept away by a tide of happiness.

He might be standing in the grey dawn sipping a mug of tea, or already at work pulling on a rope to ease down a tent or secure a load, checking a coupling, greasing an axle; even, on one celebrated occasion, shoeing a horse which there was no time to take to the blacksmith's. And then, once she was up and about, she found herself rubbing shoulders with him all through the day. Such proximity meant there was no need to sit and dream about him. Indeed, there was no time to sit and dream about anything, even if she had been so minded. The work came first – his work and her work – their separate performances in the circus and their joint commitment to making sure the whole show was a success.

Naturally, the rest of the company soon realised that there was something special between them. There were sniggers and snide remarks, but nothing too blatant – at least in Mirella's hearing – and so she found it easy to take it all in her stride. In fact, she revelled in the fact that people accepted that she was

233

the object of Levic's attention, that he, the great artiste, should consider her worthy of his love. Sometimes, though, she did worry lest things go too far.

I love him and he loves me, and that's all that matters, she told herself when, after a stroll along Brighton beach after the last show of the evening, they had stood, hugging each other close, and kissed. His lips on hers, how could she respond to his warmth except by pouring back her own love unstintingly? They stood, pressing close together.

There was no one else, nothing at all in the world apart from this happiness. Then Levic drew back his head and muttered, 'I want you, I want you,' and his words echoed through her mind and mingled with the sound of the sea sighing against the shingle. 'I want you, I want you,' sighed the sea as it fought for possession of the land, but was inevitably, irresistibly, drawn back into itself.

'No. Not now. We mustn't,' she heard herself say.

'But you do love me?'

'Of course I do.'

'Then soon, Mirella. We must. I cannot bear to be so close and always hold back. I love you so much. You know that, don't you?'

She could feel the cool moonlight falling on her head.

'Yes, yes, Levic. But it would be wrong to . . .' and it was as if she heard her mother's voice, not her own, saying, '. . . you know, come so close before marriage. It wouldn't be right.'

His body stiffened. She felt instinctively that she had said the wrong thing and hastened to repair the damage.

'Not that I'm expecting us to get married. I mean, I know how you hate the thought of being tied down.' She stopped, not sure how to continue.

'I never said that.'

'But it's true. You don't want to be tied down, do you?'

'No, I don't. But that doesn't mean . . . Oh, Mirella,

234

I thought you were different from all the others! I thought you were like me. Not needing to possess people all the time.'

His words were like shingle thrown in her face.

'But I'm not trying to possess you, Levic. It's just that it's so difficult when you're a girl. I mean, you can't just . . . oh, you know what I mean.'

'Yes. I know what you mean,' he sighed. 'And I have no right to make demands on you. But just consider for a moment. When you are up there, on the high rope, are you as cautious about life as now when you stand here on terra firma next to me? And if not, ask yourself why.'

'Yes, I'm still cautious, but I know what I'm doing when I'm on the rope,' she blurted out. 'I can trust myself to do the right thing. But when I'm with you . . . Oh, Levic, I do love you, but I need a bit more time.'

'Of course you do.' He smoothed back her hair and kissed her forehead. 'You need to practise the steps and you need to develop trust. Not in a rope that will only hold you up so long as you tie it tightly to a mast. You must learn to trust yourself and then you will no longer be afraid of the world, or me, letting you down.'

Later, she went over and over these words in her mind, not knowing whether she felt vexed or reassured by them. It was all very well for him to say, "Trust yourself and don't be afraid of the world or me letting you down." Maybe he didn't have so much to lose as her. On the other hand, he had so very much more to give, it seemed churlish of her to begrudge him anything. Besides, in denying him, she was denying herself, because now when she lay in bed at night and remembered that kiss, her body ached with longing for him.

Then she found herself thinking about marriage, a subject she had never given serious thought to before.

Two people coming together to set up home and have children, that was it, wasn't it? Like her parents and her grandparents, was that what she wanted? No, not at all. She just wanted to be with Levic, live with him and share life with him. She was so happy when he was near, it was easy to forget she had ever lived before he came into her life; impossible to imagine how she could bear to live if he left her.

Oh, Levic, I love you and want to be with you, she thought, and it seemed stupid that at this moment he should be lying in his wagon on the other side of the field alone without her. It was so obvious that they belonged together. Still, she would have to be patient and wait for the moment to be right. Maybe the next time he asked . . .

After Brighton, the circus moved on into Kent to open at Tunbridge Wells, then Folkestone, Sheerness, and eventually Rochester where Mirella made her debut on the tightrope. The first evening she appeared the tent was so crowded some of the audience had to sit on the ground – a "straw house", Georgie Sanger called it, rubbing his hands together with glee – but Mirella spared no thought for the crowd. In fact she hardly noticed their presence at all. Her whole attention was focused on her act, and even when she had completed it successfully and acknowledged the applause, the only response that meant anything to her came from Levic.

'Well done, ma petite Blondin,' he whispered, 'that was indeed worthy of your namesake.'

By the end of September they had moved on to Chatham and then Gravesend and arrived at Woolwich where they opened for a short season on the common. She was certainly glad of the rest from travelling.

The last few weeks had been hectic. Long journeys between tobers where they stayed only one or two nights, and her need to fit in all the hours of practice she could manage, meant that, although she continued to enjoy Levic's close company, there had been no opportunity to expand the intimacy established during that late night stroll at Brighton. On the rare occasions when they found themselves alone together, they were both absorbed in perfecting Mirella's tightrope act. And then, on a couple of days when he did have some free time, Levic had dashed off to London to see his agent to discuss business. If it had not been for her practice sessions, she would have gone with him. As it was, she had no time to mope, only time to register anxiety that his future plans might not include her.

Although she would have loved things to go on as they were forever, she knew there would have to be changes soon. Back end of the year was signalling an end to the travelling season. Thinking ahead to the winter, she had sent a letter to Tom suggesting that she might take her tightrope act on the halls and, bearing in mind the engagements he had made at the Aggie and Crystal Palace last year, asking his advice about bookings. It seemed obvious to her that he would not be well enough to play an active part in these new arrangements, but she did not want him to feel she had forgotten all the help he had given her and was now being totally excluded from her life.

'Mirella? May I come in?'

'Yes. Just push the door.'

It was Levic. She had been expecting him to call, because they had a free afternoon and planned to take the ferry across to North Woolwich. The main attraction in the Royal Gardens at the moment was Farini's highwire act and Mirella was keen to see a fellow artiste at work.

'For you,' he said, handing her a posy of mauve daisies mixed with fiery montbretia.

'They're lovely, thank you. I don't know where you manage to find such beautiful flowers.'

'I think of you, and they simply appear. The poets call it sympathetic magic.' He smiled.

'I know what you mean, but unfortunately it doesn't work for me. I was just thinking how nice it would be to go out with a handsome fellow – and then *you* arrived,' she said, keeping a straight face.

'Oh dear, I suppose I asked for that! You have never been susceptible to my sweet talk. But never mind. Today I refuse to be cast down by anything.'

'I thought you were looking very perky. Has something happened?'

'No, not exactly. But something will happen, news of which I have just received in this letter.' He waved a small piece of folded blue paper at her.

'What is it? No, wait a minute. Don't tell me until I've put these lovely flowers in water and poured you a drink.' She reached up to the locker for the bottle of cowslip wine her grandmother had sent, but before she had chance to lift it down, Levic caught her round the waist and spun her round to face him.

'But I think you are going to be interested in my news, because it could concern you. In fact, I shall be very disappointed if it does not.'

'Tell me then. What is it?'

'Ah, that's better. Now I have you interested.'

'Is it to do with your future plans? Something you're going to do when you leave Sanger's?' Her mind was leaping ahead, trying to anticipate. Perhaps he had been offered an engagement at the Agricultural Hall, a place where she could perform too, so that there would be a chance to stay together during the winter months.

'It is indeed,' he said in answer to her question.

'And it might concern me as well?' she faltered, anxious lest her hopes be suddenly dashed.

'Yes, it might very well concern you,' he murmured, his arms still hugging her round the waist.

She looked up into his eyes and found them shining

with excitement. 'Go on, tell me your good news then,' she urged.

'First, my love, a kiss, and then the all-important question I have to ask you.' She responded instinctively, stretching up on her toes so that her face could meet his. Her eyes closed and her cheek nuzzled against his, soft and warm. He turned his head and kissed her cheek. She turned her face until her lips touched his.

Far away in the distance she thought she could hear the sighing of the sea, the tide lapping on the shore, shingle shifting on the beach. And she and Levic were the earth and the sea and the sky, a creation complete in itself. He was drawing her into himself and he was warm and soft and vital.

"Levic," she wanted to say, "I do love you." Instead, she felt herself jump as the wagon door banged open and a man's voice snarled: 'They said I'd find you up here together. And by the look of things, it's just as well I've come when I have.'

Tom, white and shaking with rage, was standing there.

'Hello, Tom,' Levic said quite calmly as he let Mirella draw apart from him. 'It's good to see you out and about again.'

'Yes, I bet it is. I can imagine how glad you are to see me, and I'll thank you to take your paws off my niece and get out of my wagon. There are things I've got to say to Mirella.'

'Look, I know you're thinking the worst but please do not jump to conclusions. Mirella and I . . .'

'You heard me. Get out!' Tom thundered. 'Get out before I fetch a horsewhip to you.'

'Tom, don't. Please, there's no need. Oh, look, Levic, please, you'd better go. Leave us to talk for a minute, will you? I can explain things to Tom.' She felt sick inside. His sudden arrival was such a shock and, worst of all, he still looked so ill, standing there

239

with his poor arm hanging limp and useless at his side. She found his appearance so painful that she had no thought to spare for how Levic would react to being thus summarily dismissed.

'All right. I'll go,' he said briefly. 'In any case, I do not suppose you will be interested in my news now.' She knew he was looking at her but was afraid to meet his gaze. She was looking steadfastly at Tom, willing him to stay calm – as if he were one of the big cats whom only her mind-power could prevent from raging and tearing them all apart.

When eventually she did hear Levic's news, it was not from his own lips but from one of the other artistes. It seemed he was leaving Sanger's as soon as they finished at Woolwich, and he would not be joining them at the Agricultural Hall this winter. In fact he would not be signing any further contracts with them in the forseeable future, because his agent had committed him to a long-term engagement with the Renz circus in Berlin.

His departure left her desolate. She found it impossible to understand how he could just go off like that and leave her. She could never do anything like that to him. Unless he had done something to make her really angry, of course.

Then she began to search her conscience for anything she might have done to upset him. What could it have been? When the answer eventually came it hit her with a sickening jolt. It was not something she had done but the thing she had failed to do that had sent him away. It was obvious when she thought about it. Levic was angry because she had rejected him and by going away he had found the perfect way to punish her.

Chapter Sixteen

Although there were more shows in the Agricultural Hall this Christmas, it felt emptier to Mirella. She stared at the gigantic Christmas tree which formed the usual centrepiece. It looked very much the same as last year's. She gazed around at the various booths: "Tubbs' Beautiful Cosmorama", she read, "faithfully depicting the Great Fire of London, 1666, with the aid of splendid Optical Effects and Lime Lights". Ah, that was a new show. But next to it, Cottrell's Aquatic Entertainment, and then Chittock's Dogs and Monkeys and Professor Ubini's Performing Fleas – she remembered those from the year before. They were built up in the same positions, their proprietors were dressed in the same clothes, and the people hustling round them looked exactly the same.

She raised her eyes to survey the gallery: Read's Cockshies and Self-acting Swings, numerous archery and rifle saloons, May's Original Gingerbread Stall and, at the far end, a cable stretched high across the hall. Her tightrope.

She smiled. Now that was something new, something definitely not here last year. For a moment she felt pleased with herself. So much had happened in the last twelve months – some of it disastrous and horrific, but there had been triumphs too. She had learned to walk on the high rope. She had discovered what it was like to be in love.

Instinctively she peered around for someone, as if expecting to see him in conversation with a fellow showman or in clown costume threading his way through the crowds to get to the corner where not Sanger's but Willie Cooper's Old English Circus was pitched this year. She did not spot him, of course. He was not there. He was in Germany still. And that, she realised, was why in spite of the crowds the Aggie felt so empty to her.

Even now, each morning when she woke, she could hardly cope with the prospect of living through another day without seeing Levic. She still had to give herself little lectures in an effort to come to terms with his absence, arguing that Levic was perfectly at liberty to go where he liked, that he was a free agent – as he had been at pains to keep reminding her. Reminding herself that she was a free agent too. Free to develop her talents and do what she liked. Such thoughts did little to console her, but at least they pointed her towards her work and here she found some distraction from her misery, despite all the difficulties.

To begin with, she had had to cope with Tom's dark mood and try to reach some business agreement with him. For, although keen to keep her independence, she soon realised that she had to have an experienced agent if she was to secure any decent bookings this late in the season. Besides, Tom made it clear that he already regarded himself as her manager and she had not the heart to suggest that she would rather make her own arrangements in future.

Then, while she was doing her utmost to soothe Tom, she grew aware that Levic had taken umbrage and was interpreting her effort to avoid conflict as a sign of weakness rather than a genuine attempt to help her uncle.

'Look, I owe him something,' she had said that last time they met. 'He's always difficult and I don't particularly want to carry on working with him, but I don't see that I have any choice. He's . . . well, he's my responsibility until he's well enough to stand on his own two feet again.'

Levic had raised his eyebrows, his stormy dark eyes staring into hers. His mouth was set, the downturn of his lips emphasised by the droop of his moustache. He said nothing but silently accused her. "You're wrong, wrong, wrong!" his expression was shouting. "You know full well you should not let yourself fall back into Tom's clutches, but you're letting him twist you round his little finger. And after all I've said to you about being your own person."

In one way she knew he was right, but in another she felt that to reject Tom would be to please Levic rather than to act according to her own volition. And that this was what Levic was really after. He was trying to manipulate her to do what *he* wanted.

At this point the battle in her head reached dead-lock. She was so confused about what to do and she needed time to think. But Levic denied her that. He confirmed that he was going to join the circus in Berlin, and within twenty-four hours he had left – without even giving her the satisfaction of knowing how his future plans might have involved her, never asking the "all-important question" he had been about to put before Tom had burst in.

Now, when she thought of the way he left, she felt angry. How could he treat her with such scant consideration and storm off like that if he really loved her? What did she care about his love anyway, if it gave him power to hurt her like this?

No, she knew what she would do. She would concentrate on her work, put all her energies into that. She would become a great tightrope walker, one of the best there had ever been in the world. She could, she knew it. She had the power because she loved being on the rope. Amidst all the turbulence of her personal life, the rope stretched out before her making its unequivocal demands, but demands which she could well meet.

She knew exactly where she was when she stepped on to the rope. True, when she walked outside (which is what she liked to do best) there might be gusts of wind and showers that made the rope more treacherous, but basically it remained the same and she knew how to manage it. Furthermore, she knew that she could step off it at the other end and walk away and the rope would not hold that against her when she returned to walk it again. People were different, always trying to tie you down and snaring you round the ankles when you did not move in the way they wanted.

But they could not touch her when she was on the rope. Nobody could. She was her own master then.

So, it was decided. She would practise and practise until she became a successful artiste in her own right. As successful as Levic was in his. She could do without his interference. She could do without the sort of complications he brought into her life. She could do without him, she told herself. It was just a question of concentrating on her work and she would soon forget him, keeping herself so busy there would be no time to fret about how empty the world seemed now he had gone.

Strangely enough, it had been easier to carry out her resolve during the first few weeks after Levic had left than it was now. There had been so much to do in preparation for the winter season – thinking up new ideas for her act and practising them; writing around to various halls trying to get engagements. And Tom, once he realised that Levic had taken himself out of the picture, could not have been more helpful.

For a start he approached the manager of the Aggie and then built on that success by inserting an advertisement in the notices column of the *Era*: "Mirella the Miraculous Rope-Dancer is engaged with Willie

Cooper's Old English Circus and will open at the Royal Agricultural Hall, Islington, on Boxing Day, December 26th, for a period of six weeks, after which time she will be available for engagements with proprietors of concert halls, public gardens, etc. Opinions of the Press:- Mademoiselle Mirella's agile performances on the rope are astonishing, all feelings of apprehension on the part of the audience being allayed by the neatness and grace of the performer. Apply to Mr Thomas Granger, her sole agent, c/o Royal Agricultural Hall.''

On the strength of that and Tom's old contacts at the Crystal Palace and North Woolwich Gardens, they had quickly secured a decent chain of bookings that stretched right through the winter season and into the summer. All that remained was for Mirella to continue practising so that she could live up to the standard expected of her.

When they discussed the details of her act, Tom was keen to highlight all the elements of risk, playing up any danger to life and limb, even staging a mock fall like the one Blondin included in his show. However, this was something Mirella disliked doing. She wanted people to see something beyond mere danger in her act. She wanted to show them what grace and freedom could be achieved on the rope. Fake excitement did not interest her; she wanted everything she did to be real and natural.

'Look, Mirella, distasteful as it is for you to think about it, your public come every day not just to see you do something very clever while balanced on a rope. If that was all they wanted, you could do the whole act with the rope rigged three feet off the ground. No, my dear. You've got to face it, what really attracts people is the sight of you up there on your high rope holding out the possibility that any moment you might fall and give them something to talk about for the rest of their lives.'

She shivered. Not because she was afraid of what Tom was saying, but because of his tone of voice. Sometimes she had the impression he was testing her to see how confident she really was, even trying to knock that confidence a bit. But there was something else in his voice which disturbed her. He sounded so bitter, as if he had personally paid the price for people's pleasure and would never be able to forgive that fact.

'Mirella!'

She was sure she heard someone calling her. A girl's voice. She spun round to see who it could be.

'Mirella, I've been looking out for you everywhere since I saw your name on the posters. Gone up in the world since we last met, haven't you?'

'Gracious, Lily! This is a surprise. I didn't expect to see you here.'

Lily, dressed in a very full blue skirt, fur-trimmed red jacket and matching bonnet, waved around a furry muff as she spoke.

'No, we didn't come up last year. Pa said he'd seen enough of fairs by the end of the season. But me and Max – you know we're married now, don't you, and travelling with a show of our own? – we thought it would be good to come and look round to see if there are any new ideas worth picking up.'

'And are there?'

'Oh, yes. Richardson's Show has got a good line up this year and the ghost show . . . But, look, before we talk shop, tell me how poor Tom is. I suffered nightmares for days after hearing about his dreadful accident.'

'He's a lot better now, thank you. Won't ever get the use of his arm back, I'm afraid, but it could have been a lot worse. He realises that.'

'Oh, poor Tom. So his days as The Great Kazan are over? That's a pity. I used to enjoy his performances,' she murmured dreamily.

Mirella suppressed the tart comment which came to mind in favour of: 'Yes, Tom was good with the cats. How are they doing, by the way? Did your father find another trainer to take them on?'

'Caesar and Hanno, yes. But Trajan had to be put down because he became too much of a liability. Although, to be honest, when people ask, Pa always points to Caesar as the one who turned on his trainer and mauled him to death.'

'Mauled who to death?'

'The Great Kazan. That's how his legend now ends, anyway.'

'I see. Well, I don't know what Tom will think of that. I've a feeling he won't take too kindly to being written off before his time, so maybe you'd better not mention that part of the story when you see him.'

'All right. Is he around at the moment? I'd like to see him, if he is. You know, just for old time's sake,' Lily said, running a finger along her eyebrow.

'Yes. He's up in the wagon and I'm sure he'll be pleased to see you,' Mirella said with more certainty than she felt.

She led Lily out through the back of the hall into the covered yard where the living-vans were parked.

'Hi, Tom! We've got a visitor,' she called from the top of the steps, and was pleased to see his face light up when he realised who it was.

'Why, if it isn't the lovely Lily! I thought you'd forgotten all about me, my love.'

'No, you know I couldn't do that, not after we used to be such good friends, Tom,' she muttered, her cheeks going pink.

'That's right, we were very good friends, weren't we, once?' Tom said with a new edge in his voice. 'But that was in different times. When I had my full health and strength and before . . . before you got married, Mrs Wombell.'

He stood looking Lily in the eye until her face flared

with embarrassment. Mirella regretted bringing the two of them together again and, in any case, felt she should have done more to warn Lily about Tom's bitter moods. The only thing she could do now was try to steer their conversation into happier channels.

'How about a drink, Lily? Shall I make us all a cup of tea?' she asked brightly. 'Or would you prefer a glass of something?'

'No, really. I won't stop. I only really came to find out how Tom is and . . .' Her voice faltered as she glanced nervously in his direction. 'I'd better go now before Max gets worried wondering where I am.'

'Oh, of course,' Tom agreed, 'we mustn't forget poor old Max, must we, Lily? It wouldn't do for him to be worried about his new bride, would it? So now you've had a good look at your old flame and satisfied yourself that he's quite burnt out as far as you're concerned, you take yourself off.'

'Tom, I didn't mean it to sound like that,' she moaned. 'It's just that I did promise Max that I wouldn't be long and, well, if you want the truth, I expected you to be a bit more friendly.'

'Lily, Lily, if only you knew,' Tom whispered, putting out his good hand to touch her shoulder. For a long moment the two of them stared into each other's eyes. Then Tom said to Mirella, 'Look, isn't there something you should be doing down in the ring – talking with the bandmaster about your music or checking on your rope or something?'

'You mean you two want to be left alone together,' Mirella said, and as Lily made no sign to the contrary, took herself off.

Later, when she returned to get changed for her act, she found Tom sitting alone in the dark. There was a strong smell of whisky in the wagon.

'Has Lily gone then?' she asked simply to break the silence.

'Yes, she's gone. I couldn't get her to stay with me long.'

'Well, it must be difficult for her,' Mirella said lamely. 'I mean, now she's married to Max.'

'That's right. 'xactly what she told me. "Can't do everything I want now I'm married to Max . . ." But the little bitch only said that after I told her I thought the world of her still and tried to put my arms . . . my arm around her.' And to her horror he covered his face with his hand and started to sob.

Forty netless feet above the ground. All those faces staring up at her, blurring into one humming mass in the hazy light. Because of the hundreds of gaslamps, it was stuffy and stiflingly hot up here on the platform, and her hands were slippery with sweat as she stooped to pick up the long pole. But her head felt icy.

Why do people suffer and torture each other so? She had never seen a man cry before. Tom, oh Tom, what on earth could she do to help?

Nothing. Not at this moment. There was nothing she could do for anyone at this moment, no matter how much they needed her. It was a relief to find herself at the end of her rope, having to meet its demands before all else. As far as she was concerned, for the next few moments there might as well be no problems anywhere in the world, for her attention had to be confined to the here and now. All she must think about was getting to the end of this rope without slipping off.

Blank her mind to all other problems then. Close her eyes for a second. Let the everyday world fall away, leaving her alone up here. Alone in the silence of the rope.

Her hands were still sweating. She wiped them one at a time on her gauzy dress. In Ancient Greece ropewalkers always wore white, Levic had told her, because white indicated that they needed the special protection of the gods. She was glad she was wearing white now. She felt in need of protection.

Carefully she stroked the rope with the side of her foot before placing her instep across it, toes pointing outwards. Below, that carpet of people, each shrunk to the size of his own face and that face turned upwards towards her sighing audibly.

Right then. She was on. Gliding out over the abyss. Never mind the heat. Or the people. Just her now. On her own. On her rope. Levic. Levic. If I should fall. It's you I . . . Steady, steady. Pole up slightly on the right. Not too much. Not too much. There. Got it. Steady. Keeping her eye on the marker post fixed at the end of the rope, her haven when walking was done. Smiling. Into the world. It's all right. It's so easy. Up here.

Foot leave rope and swing gently out and back. Walking backwards now. Pause. Other foot out and back. The pole dipping ever so slightly each time to balance her moves. Backward gliding. Her feet finding the rope with little help from her, disciplined enough now to know their path. She still keeping her eye on the marker post watching it slowly recede.

Baskets on her feet next and then the blindfold and sack over her head, but plenty of time, no need to rush. It really wouldn't matter if it took forever. Time did not exist up here on the rope.

She read Cassie's letter over again. It began – in imitation of their father's style – with awkward formality, but as it went on grew to sound more and more like Cassie talking.

Dear Mirella,
I hope this finds you and Tom as it leaves us, as I am pleased to say all are well at present this end. We had a nice Christmas, but missed you

250

because it is very quite here, but then as you know it always is.

All the family send you there love and Ma says tell you to be careful not to put your tightrope to high when you walk on it and get Tom to check it is always tied safely. And she will be glad when you settle down to a nice job and stop being such a daredevil all the time.

Albie does not like going to school and runs home whenever the teacher is not looking. Ma says he orght to know better whats good for him but she carnt do much to stop him getting his own way. Any way shes got her both hands full with looking after Benjie who is still her baby althow nearly five. We carnt get him to stop sucking his thum and he still has a lot of ear-aches wich keep him indoors with Ma. Dad says she spoils him and it dont do any good to mollycoddle a boy because look what happend to his brother who used to be always spoild by his mother when he was a boy. He must have ment our uncle who died but Ma gave him one of her looks and he dident say any more so I dont realy know what he meant.

I get very lonely here because theres nobody my own age to talk to and I miss you, Rella. And you remember how you said maybe I could come and stay with you again some time soon, well I wonder if I can come when you are at the Crystal Palace before Easter. This is what Im realy writing to find out.

I dont know if you know but Grandma is planning to come up then to hear Joe play in one of his concerts but the Captain is not very well and so carnt go with her. So, if it's all right with you, I can travel up with her and then stay on with you after she goes back again.

I know you will be very busy and I wont get in

your way. But I want to see you walk on the tightrope. Pa put that bit of newspaper you sent him with the writing about you in his wesket pocket to keep showing to evrybody. I think he is very proud to have somebody so clever in are family and I wish I was so clever as you as well. Please write back and tell me if it is all right to come and then I can look forward to seeing you soon.

with fondest love from
your loving sister
Cassie

P.S. Please give my love to Tom and I hope he is feeling as good as new once more.

She was delighted with the idea of Cassie coming to stay for a while and, after mentioning it to Tom, wrote back to confirm the arrangements. Her sister's company, enjoyable at any time, would be particularly welcome at Crystal Palace where it might help to keep at bay the ghosts which would haunt the place for Mirella. She had still not received any word from Levic and hardly dared admit to herself her worst fear – that she might never hear from him again.

In these circumstances the thought of going back to the Crystal Palace and being reminded of those times when they had been together in the past was unbearable. That day when they had wandered alone into the Grecian Court, for instance. Standing looking at the pillars of the huge temple and up at the little figures arrayed over its portico, some of them seated, others clutching shields and spears. A feeling of calm settling over her and being able to breathe more easily after being so upset.

Then she remembered why she had been so upset that day and the memory terrified her and sent her running in her mind again into the Hall of the Grecian Court where Levic stood forever at her side speaking about the gods. And she lingered for as long as possible in that tranquillity until another bitter memory drove her out.

At all cost she must avoid entering that hall again.

Still, it would be fun taking Cassie around and showing her the Crystal Fountain and all the other exotic exhibits. A pity it was at the wrong time of the year, but Cassie would love the place and they would make the best of things. They could walk through the grounds to visit all the grottoes and the antediluvian animals and go down to watch little boys sailing their boats on the Great Pond. There would be Joey's concert to look forward to – that would be a novelty for Cassie – and all the other amusements that made the Palace such a popular place for visitors. Yes, it was going to be fun – just so long as she could stop herself remembering that last year, when she was there with Levic.

Now that Tom no longer had the front of the beast wagon to sleep in, he had to make shift the best way he could for accommodation. At the Aggie he had bedded down in a dormitory truck used by several of the hall's casual labourers but came up into the wagon to wash and shave and eat all his meals. At Crystal Palace he had been assigned his own small room in the building to use as bedroom-cum-office. As soon as they arrived, Mirella set about making it look as homely as possible for him – throwing a patchwork quilt over his truckle bed and bringing over some of his clothes, his flask of whisky and a couple of tumblers.

'That's dandy, Mirella,' he said, beaming at her when he saw what she had done. 'You really put yourself out to look after me and I want you to know I appreciate it, even if I don't always say as much.'

'I know you do, Tom. And I want you to know I'm grateful for what you're doing, handling all the

253

bookings and advertising. I don't know how I'd have managed if you hadn't been prepared to take that on.'

'Yes, anyone would agree that you and me make a damn good partnership. And what I can't wait to see is my mother's face when she sees you up there on that high rope going through your stuff, and all the people around her clapping and cheering like mad. Never mind our Joey playing his squeak-box in the back row of some dozy band, that's nothing. And yet to hear her going on about him, you'd have thought he was the only one in our family who'd done anything worth mentioning.'

'I don't think Herr Manns would appreciate you calling his orchestra a band, Tom,' she ventured to say, before changing the subject rather than admitting that she wanted to attend as many classical concerts as she could while she was here.

If she had looked to Cassie for companionship on these occasions, she was disappointed. Having sat through the Saturday concert which their grand-mother Liddy had come especially to hear, Cassie declared to Mirella over breakfast next morning that she had never been so bored in her life.

'Honestly, Rella, how you could sit there so still and kid Gran that you actually like listening to all that stuff, beats me. I suppose you get used to putting on a good performance and fooling people if you work in a circus.'

Mirella smiled. 'I don't know about that, but funnily enough I do like listening to all that stuff. Some of it is so beautiful, it makes me want to cry. I just wish someone would invent a machine so that I could hear it being played any time I liked.'

'Like a hurdy-gurdy, you mean?'

'Yes, something like that, as long as they could get it to sound more like a real orchestra and make it small enough to fit in my wagon so that I could listen to my favourite music before I go to sleep at night and when I'm sitting down quietly on my own during the day. That would be lovely.'

'Oh, Rella, you do have some cranky ideas.'

Cassie had taken to wearing her hair drawn severely back and plaited round her head in a style which made her look older than her fourteen years. She was wearing a blue candy stripe dress with a deep flounce for which the material had been cut on the diagonal and a string of their mother's unfashionable jet beads around her throat. She looked pale and dispirited, not at all the sunny, light-hearted Cassie Mirella remembered of old.

'Well, that's because I'm a cranky person,' she replied. 'And anyway that's what ideas are for, isn't it? To let us explore what we fancy.'

'Don't ask me. I don't get ideas like you do. It takes me all my time to cope with what I'm doing. If I started to have ideas as well, I'd be lost.'

'Oh come on, Cassie, that's not true. You cope with life a lot better than most people.'

'No, I don't, Rella. It might look as if I do, but I don't. I just do what other people want me to do all the time, and that's living their lives really, isn't it, not mine?'

'What do you mean?'

'Well, I'd like to be doing the sort of thing you're doing and not be stuck at home all the time being general dogsbody.'

'Why don't you do what I did then? Leave home and join a travelling show. You can sing and dance. It wouldn't be too difficult to find some outfit to take you on.'

'No, no. I couldn't do that. Ma would have a fit.'

'Yes, I expect she would,' Mirella agreed, imagining how Sadie would grieve if Cassie left home to join a fair. 'But she'd get over it.'

'What, like she did when you left home?' Cassie asked accusingly.

'Well, yes. I know she'd find it harder in your case, but she'd soon come round.'

'I think that shows how little you know Ma,' Cassie said. 'You weren't there. You didn't see how she took on after you left. Nearly went out of her mind, she did. Took a hairbrush and beat it against her head until I thought she was going to knock herself silly. It was ghastly, Rella. One minute she was raving on about you and the next blaming herself for driving you away, moaning like some crazy thing for hours on end until Dad came home and talked sense into her.'

'I had no idea she reacted like that,' Mirella muttered, feeling a pang of remorse. She'd known Sadie would be angry of course, but had not guessed she would suffer any real heartache. 'So what did Dad say?' She found herself longing to hear something to suggest that her father had not just dismissed her as a selfish trouble-maker.

'You know Dad. He just laughed and tried to make light of it. He said, "Well, at least we don't have to look far to see where Mirella gets her waywardness from, Sadie. Remember you weren't much older than her, my love, when you took off from your family to come and set up home with me." '

'Oh dear, I bet she didn't like hearing that.'

'No. She said it was natural for a girl to leave home to get married and she'd have no objection if you'd done that, providing the fellow was respectable of course. But running away to join the fair was your way of deliberately hurting her.'

'But why, for heaven's sake, should she think I'd want to do that?'

'Don't ask me, Rella. She seems to think everything you do is aimed at her in some way, as if you're trying to tell her she's let you down and can't ever do anything right by you. I suppose she just sort of feels rejected.'

'You say Ma feels like that about me,' Mirella said,

hardly knowing whether to laugh or cry, 'but you've got it all wrong, Cassie! It's *me* that's always suffered because I can't do anything right in Ma's eyes. Ever since I can remember I've always managed to upset her somehow. Don't you remember all those rows we had when I was at home?'

'Of course I do. I hated them, especially when they were over nothing at all. Ma would start to nag you about something you were doing and then you'd immediately flare up, and the two of you would go at it hammer and tongs while the rest of us took cover. But, you know, when all is said and done, I think you're the one in the family she cares about most. It's just that she can't find the way to show it, that's all.'

'Good Lord, Cassie, talk about me having cranky ideas, yours take some beating!' Mirella spoke sharply, feeling uncomfortable with this turn in the conversation. 'Still, getting back to what we were saying earlier, if you're so unhappy at home, surely it's up to you to make a move?'

'Yes, well, I would if it was that simple, but it's not. You had Uncle Tom to help you, remember, and that made it a lot easier.' Cassie was sounding quite petulant, as if she thought that when the world was being planned her own interests had been overshadowed by Mirella's and there was no way the balance could ever be redressed.

For a moment Mirella was tempted to go into detail about how these past twelve months had not been a bed of roses for her. Instead, she confined herself to saying, 'I suppose so. But remember, other people's lives seem far easier when viewed from outside than they are from the inside.'

'That's as may be, but I still think some people are born lucky and have more interesting lives than others,' Cassie mumbled. 'Honestly, Rella, sometimes when I'm at home helping Ma with the cooking and cleaning and things, I feel I could die of boredom.'

'Oh dear, I know that feeling, but it's up to you, Cassie. If you're so unhappy with the way things are, then you must change them. You can, if you really want to. But don't think that when you escape from one set of problems, there isn't another lot waiting for you just round the corner. Life's like that. It's what makes it so interesting.'

'Yes, but it's all very well for you to talk. You've made your move. It's not so easy for me.'

Growing irritated by her sister's doleful tone, Mirella started to clear away the breakfast things and announced that she had to fit in some practice on her low rope this morning.

'Feel free to stay here or come and watch, just as you like,' she said, gathering up her special shoes.

'I don't want to stay here on my own. I'll come and watch.'

The wagon had been parked again in that roofless section of the Crystal Palace which had formerly housed the Egyptian Court before it burnt out, and they had to enter the main building to reach the hall where Tom had rigged her practice rope about five feet above the ground. Here Mirella went methodically through her routine while Cassie sat on a stool watching her.

'Does it make it a lot easier, using that pole? It's different from the one you started out with, isn't it? Longer and much heavier,' she said, coming forward to pick it up and balancing it across the palms of her hands. 'And this one dips more. I noticed that when you were walking. It curves like a bow about to shoot an arrow.'

'That's because it's weighted at each end. And that does make it easier, especially on the high rope. Anything that lowers your centre of gravity helps you keep your balance. Try it for yourself.'

'No, I couldn't. Someone might see me,' Cassie said, looking all round.

'No one comes in here. Besides, it wouldn't matter if they did. Come on, there's a mattress here to break your fall, and you can use my shoes if they fit.'

'What about my dress, though? I can't get up on that rope in this.'

'Go back to the wagon and pull out the locker drawer under the bed. You'll find my yellow Turkish costume in it. Put that on.' Cassie still looked doubtful. 'Come on. I'd like to see you have a go. You were quite good when you tried it last year in Woolwich Gardens, I remember.'

'Was I? Do you think so? All right, I wouldn't mind having another go, then,' said Cassie, rushing off to change her clothes.

When she returned, she stood listening while Mirella explained how to fall clear of the pole should she topple and then called out instructions and encouragement while she slowly edged herself on to the rope.

'There you are. You can do it. No, no. Careful! Watch your concentration . . .' Too late. Cassie landed in a heap on the mattress with the pole fortunately bouncing well away from her.

'Oh, shame! You were doing so well, wasn't she, Mirella?'

Mirella spun round when she heard the slurred nasal voice.

'Gracious, Joey! How long have you been standing there watching?'

'Just a couple of minutes.'

'I didn't hear you come in.'

'Good. I didn't want to distract Cassie when I saw what she was up to. I must say, I didn't know we had two female Blondins in the family.'

Cassie flushed. 'Oh, no. Not me. I'm only messing about. I'd never be able to walk up high like Mirella does. I wouldn't have the nerve.'

'I know what you mean,' he agreed. 'I can't believe

259

it when I look up at that rope in the roof of the great hall and think of your sister skipping along it above our heads yesterday afternoon. I think to myself, doing that must take even more courage than arriving late for one of Herr Manns's rehearsals.' Mirella scanned his face in vain for the least sign he was not being serious. 'But what makes it all the more incredible,' Joey continued, 'is that last year in this selfsame building I thought I was watching the only person in the world who could do that sort of thing, and at that time you hadn't even started on your career, had you, Mirella? And now here you are, barely a twelve-month later, treading on Blondin's heels.'

'Not quite, Joey. I haven't managed to walk Niagara Falls yet, or even the Thames.'

'No, but from what Tom says, he's got big plans for you so it's only a matter of time. Seriously, though,' Joey said, glancing behind to make sure no one had come in while they were talking, 'I did want to say how pleased Ma was to find you and Tom working together so well. She was quite worried about him when he was at home all that time convalescing with her. Got himself into these black moods, she said, but coming back and working with you seems to have done him a power of good and she went back to Aldershot this morning with an easier mind.'

Mirella was grateful to hear this. Tom's moods and possessiveness were a continual vexation to her and she was always asking herself whether she should carry on working with him or not. It helped to know that others, especially her grandmother, thought what she was doing was right.

'Did Gran really enjoy watching the tightrope act, though? To be honest, I thought she might sit through it with her eyes shut, like my sweet sister does. Don't you, Cassie?'

From where she sat crouched on the mattress, removing the special soft shoes and putting on her own again, Cassie nodded. 'I can't help it. I always get the jitters and can't bear to look. But not Grandma. She was perched on the edge of her chair all the way through and never took her eyes off you once.'

'Cassie's right,' Joey added. 'I was sitting on the other side of her, and do you know what she said at the end? She said, "I just wish my Jem could have been here today. He'd have been so proud of his granddaughter." '

Mirella's pleasure was short-lived when she caught sight of her sister's look of anguish.

'That makes a change,' she said quickly. 'Most of our family regard me as the black sheep and pray for the day when I start behaving as sensibly as Cassie. Don't they, Tom?' she asked, seeing him now coming into the hall.

'Don't they what? I don't know what you're all talking about, but I'll say "yes" if that's what you want to hear. It's too early in the day to argue.'

'Early for you, perhaps. But some of us, like me, have been up hours. I had to take Mother to the railway station at first light because she didn't want to be away from the Captain longer than necessary. He's pretty poorly again, I gather.'

Two uncles, two nieces, all fairly close together in age, but utterly different in temperament, what an odd foursome we make, Mirella was thinking as she listened to the others chatting away.

'Of course, you know we've got another budding ropewalker in the family now, don't you?' Joey was saying. 'You should have seen Cassie just now, Tom, waltzing along that rope as if it was the Old Kent Road.'

'No, I wasn't,' Cassie said, flushing. 'I can't do it properly. I was only messing about.'

'I wondered why you were all togged up in those clothes. Is she any good at it?' Tom asked, turning to Mirella.

261

'Yes. She's got a good sense of balance, but she hasn't had enough practice to get anywhere with it yet, have you, Cassie?'

'No.'

'Well, you should,' Tom cut in, smiling at her. 'You let Mirella give you a few tips about how it's done. It will help her. There's nothing like teaching someone else to keep an artiste on her own toes. Besides, it will give you an excuse to dress up in that rather fetching outfit.'

Cassie glanced down at the tunic and baggy trousers and grinned. After that she came out each morning and afternoon to practise on the low rope and by the end of her fortnight's stay could walk its length nearly every time without falling off.

The time for Cassie to return home came round far too soon. Her visit had helped all round. For Mirella, so used to being on her own, it was fun to have someone her own age to talk to, although she found it impossible to confide in Cassie anything really close to her heart. It was also good to see Tom cheerful again and putting himself out to make her sister feel welcome.

One evening he took the pair of them out to a local variety saloon where they drank ale and ate a fish supper in a mahogany-panelled hall whilst listening to a lady and gentleman sing a succession of popular ballads. She had lent Cassie her saffron dress to wear for the occasion and helped her curl the front of her hair into an attractive ringlet style. Sitting opposite her at one of the long line of tables, she realised how pretty the effect was and told her so. Tom joined in the praise and Mirella was happy to see her sister flush with pleasure. The trouble was, Tom would keep on paying the same compliments to Cassie until his behaviour grew almost embarrassing. And then, after he had had a few drinks, he started to insult Mirella and seemed to be childishly going out of his way to

262

make her feel jealous of her sister. At first she chided herself for imagining that he would play such stupid games. But as the evening wore on, it became increasingly obvious that he was indeed trying to play one off against the other, although she could not imagine why he should bother to do such a thing.

Fortunately, none of this charade disturbed Cassie who was simply enchanted by everything she saw and heard. She sang her heart out when it came to joining in the choruses, and the next day nearly drove Mirella mad with her incessant renditions of "There's no Love like the First Love" and the refrain from "The Eel Pie Shop".

When their father came up to fetch Cassie home, both girls tried to persuade him to let her stay longer, but he had strict instructions from their mother to resist all such entreaties.

'Maybe she can come up again some other time,' Johnny told Mirella, 'or maybe you, young miss, will one day spare the time to make a visit home.'

Her heart lurched. If only he could have said the words naturally, without that heavy innuendo.

'Yes, well, of course I'll try to come as soon as I've got some spare time, but I know we're terribly booked up for the next few weeks.' The excuse sounded lame even to her.

Johnny looked hopelessly into her eyes and slowly shook his head.

'You know what your mother thinks, don't you? She thinks you've risen so high in the world since you started this tightrope lark that you don't want to lower yourself by sleeping under our roof.'

'Oh, Pa, that's stupid. I'd love to come home on a visit, but you know what things would be like. I'd be bound to say or do something wrong that would set Ma at my throat again, and I couldn't bear another of those awful family rows.'

Johnny sighed.

'But surely it doesn't have to be like that, Mirella? Sadie thinks the world of you. And, although she won't ever admit it, she's proud of what you've done. I think if you two got together now, she'd appreciate you've grown up and you'd find it easier to be friends.'

'I'd really like to think so, Pa. And I'll certainly make a big effort with her next time we meet, I promise. So you tell Ma that I do intend to come home soon and, when I do, I'll rig my rope right over the top of Windsor Castle so that, when I walk across, I shall be putting our family above royalty. Right?'

'Right, my love. That's a deal. But in the meantime, you just take care.' He lowered his head to kiss her before turning to his brother to say, 'And you'll carry on looking after my little girl for me, I know that, won't you, Tom?'

With Cassie gone, Mirella was left with time to brood, and there were times during the day when she found herself flitting around the corridors of the Crystal Palace lost in her imagination. Once, when there were hardly any people about, she crept into the Grecian Court and stood again in front of the temple and statues of the gods remembering how it had felt to be here alone with Levic. Before she left, she stared hard at the statue of Zeus.

'Well, Levic was right about you and your thunderbolts,' she muttered, 'and I'm awake now, damn you.' The god stared back at her impassively. Just like someone else I know, she thought. Now you've made your presence felt, you turn away and take no more notice of the poor devil you disturbed.

Chapter Seventeen

Other performers had warned her about this sort of thing, but she had always vowed it would never happen to her – that experience of suddenly snapping awake and finding yourself in the middle of your act without being fully aware of what you are doing.

Maybe she had become too sure of herself. This long engagement at the Alhambra in Leeds – she had already been performing here for three weeks and had another week to go – meant that she was well used to the position of the low rope on stage, and the other rope stretching up to the balcony, and completely familiar with her routine. But in this job there was no room for complacency. She had to keep her wits about her. One day a few seconds of abstraction might cost her her life.

The fact was, she had been perfectly alert when she started her act. Clearly remembered the band striking up as she skipped on to the stage and the cheers and applause as she took off her cloak and mounted the ladder. Because of limitations on space, her rope was stretched little more than six feet off the ground, so she was hardly in danger of serious injury if she fell, and perhaps this was the clue to her inattention. This kind of stage work presented too little challenge after she had performed in halls like the Aggie and Crystal Palace where her rope was rigged level at a decent height, not six feet but six stories off the ground. At that height she felt herself to be intensely alive and with no inclination to daydream – which was reassuring really, in view of this forthcoming Saturday when she was due to "walk" in the Royal Park as part of the Leeds July Summer Fair festivities. On that occasion the rope would be strung forty feet above the crowd and there would be no safety net, only a tent pitched below to break her fall if she should be careless.

Her nerves tingled as she thought of it. Of course forty feet was nothing compared with Blondin walking four times that height above the raging torrent at Niagara. Sometimes she lay awake at night thinking how marvellous that must have been. Envying him. To walk that high for that distance . . . what joy! All the elements. Water and rock, sun and air – and he in their midst walking his rope, balancing all the forces within himself and in the world. In those moments more than a man, more like a king or a priest.

Watch it, Mirella. You're at it again, daydreaming, she chided herself. And now she saw her growing absentmindedness in a different light, as a reflection of the fact that she spent so much time on her own these days. Well, not completely on her own. There was always Tom, of course. And the people she met in the various hotels and boarding houses where they stayed whilst on these more distant tours. The trouble was, she never stayed anywhere long enough for close friendships to develop and she had always to keep her distance from Tom to prevent him being overfamiliar.

In these circumstances her work on the high rope had become the most important thing in her existence, her lifeline. It filled her imagination day and night like a lover – whereas these trivial stage appearances on a rope only a few feet off the ground were like lads whistling on street corners and she could not take them seriously.

She had never yet slipped off the high rope, but if she did, she had her escape route planned. All would not be lost, as long as she kept her head and did exactly what was necessary. And if an accident happened not through some false move of hers, but because the rope broke? Quite simple then. She would plunge to the earth and nothing could save her.

Which brought up the old question of a safety net, of course. Tom's reasons for not using one when she was first training did not hold good for her professional appearances. In fact, some places refused to let her perform at all until some sort of net was in position. There was no point in arguing when the management was like this and few beyond Tom and Mirella realised that, if she did fall, that net would do little to help, might even cause her greater injury.

She winced when she recalled the first time she had landed in one. It had been in Sanger's circus. There had been a safety net in position under the flying trapeze act and Levic suggested it would be a good idea for her to jump into it just to get used to the experience.

'Understand this, Mirella,' he said, 'that net will only be your friend if you fall into it properly, otherwise it is your enemy in disguise. Its knots will cut you like whiplash if your fall is not carefully gauged.'

'What do I do, then?' she had asked.

'Ball up and try to land on your shoulders, and then quickly roll over. Watch me. I'll show you how to do it.'

She watched him do it several times. It looked easy.

'There. Did you see?' he called eventually, having swung himself down from the side of the net, standing there gasping for breath. 'I took the force of the fall on the muscles of my back. Whatever happens, avoid falling on the base of your skull because that could break your neck.'

After that she had tried her first practice fall and immediately come across an unexpected difficulty. She found it impossible to step off the rope. Her feet stuck to it as if clinging to life itself.

'Right. I'm going to start counting,' Levic shouted up, 'and I want you to jump when I get to three.'

'OK,' she agreed.

'One,' he yelled. 'Two. THREE.'

She had already lifted up her balancing pole ready to cast it to one side as she leapt, but when she heard him shout "THREE", everything inside her froze.

'Mirella, don't just stand there. You've got to jump.'

'I can't, Levic. Not now. Perhaps another time.'

'No, Mirella. Now. It must be now.'

'I can't.'

'You can. Remember what I said about balling up. Now, I shall count to three again and this time, if you do not jump, I shall think you are a coward.'

She scarcely heard what he said until that last word. Coward? Her? She'd soon show him. This time on the count of three, she leapt. And that great spread of knotted rope came up to meet her. And she had curled herself into a ball so that she hit the net shoulders first and rolled over, doing everything right, and yet still the net gouged a lump out of her elbow. And nearly every time afterwards, no matter how carefully she positioned herself as she fell, the net exacted a similar tribute from her poor flesh.

Still, bad as this experience was, at least she had been spared the broken arm or leg (or even neck) that other artistes had suffered after falling in their "safety" nets. And even the tent that was supposed to catch her if necessary on Saturday would be no better than the orthodox net if she encountered that other occupational hazard of a ropewalker – being hit by her pole as she fell.

Mirella smiled as she thought of this possibility. It was a very real danger and no laughing matter, but it would be ironic nevertheless if the gift she had received from Blondin should become the instrument of her downfall. After all, he had been grudging enough about her success.

She smiled again. It really was funny how the two of them eventually became reconciled after the great man had for so long declared his hostility towards her career on the rope.

As a result of the thousands of people who came to see her perform and all the publicity surrounding her act, she received many letters in the post. There were offers of money and jewellery, even a couple of marriage proposals from men she had never met. There was also a message once from some crank who believed she had supernatural powers which would enable her to walk on water and suggesting that he be allowed to make suitable arrangements for such an experiment. So, when towards the end of their stay at the Crystal Palace in March, a letter arrived containing a warning that her life was in peril if she continued with her present type of performance, she read it without taking its contents too seriously.

Dear Mademoiselle Granger,
I am moved to write because I was present in the Crystal Palace on the afternoon of Thursday last for your performance which I found quite charming. When I say that you show the courage of a lion together with the grace of a bird, you will be aware that these words come not lightly from one who, apart from his own not inconsiderable exploits in this sphere, has witnessed the greatest funambules of his day, including the late lamented Madame Saqui.
Mademoiselle, that lady lived to die safely in her bed, but as you must know, she was the exception amongst the flowers of her generation. Where now are young Signor Valerio, Madame Genevieve and Madame Boutelle, Donna Selina and Mademoiselle Irena? I saw

them all, walking as if immortal, but they none of them walk any more. For all of them the rope has been their "Marche à la Mort" and I beseech that you take heed of my warning now and spare yourself a similar fate.

Mademoiselle, I hope you will not take ill this which may be viewed as unwarrantable intrusion on your affairs. I assure you I write with but one motive in mind, and that the protection of an innocent young life which, through no fault intended, might have been influenced by my example to pursue a path most injurious to her safety and well-being. It is only considerations of this sort which force me to write now to beg you to take wiser counsel and give up before it is too late a profession which almost certainly you have embarked upon with insufficient knowledge and experience.

Believe me, Mademoiselle, in expressing the above I act as nothing but your most sincere friend and well-wisher,

J. F. Gravelet.

She was aware of Tom's interest as she sat on the wagon steps reading the letter.

'Who's it from?' he asked as soon as she finished.

'Oh, just some crank as usual.'

'What does he want? I presume it is a "he",' he added, holding out his hand expecting her to pass him the letter.

'He wants me to give up ropewalking because it's so dangerous,' she said, screwing up her eyes in an attempt to make out the signature at the bottom.

'Bloody cheek,' Tom growled. 'Here, let me have a look.'

'It's someone called "Grave let",' she said, for that was how she thought the name would be pronounced. 'I've never heard of him, but he seems to know me.

Seems to think he might even have influenced me to take up ropewalking. Oh dear, another one of those cases. Obviously cracked, poor chap.'

'I think you'd better let me look at it,' Tom said. 'You can never tell where things might lead when you're dealing with someone who's a bit barmy.' So she passed him the letter which he read and immediately screwed up. 'Yes, as I thought, quite barmy. Just forget it.'

And she almost did.

After leaving Crystal Palace and fulfilling a few short engagements in the London area, they had set out to tour part of the midlands with performances being staged at the Surrey Music Hall at Sheffield, the Victoria Music Gallery in Manchester and the Grapes Inn Concert Room at Stockport. Then they journeyed south to Birmingham and it was there, with more than a week to spare before her first engagement, that Mirella saw an advertisement for the Wolverhampton Order of Odd Fellows fête due to be held the following day at the Arboretum Gardens in Worcester. There was to be a grand procession through the city with no less than four military bands, together with the usual archery contests, flower shows, balloon racing and dancing. But it was the festival's main attraction that caught her eye. In the evening Blondin, hero of Niagara, was going to walk a rope six hundred feet long at an altitude of sixty feet amidst a grand display of fireworks.

'Tom, can we go?' she asked, pointing to the notice. 'I'd love to watch Blondin again. It will be really interesting to see how his act looks from the ground and find out what part the crowd likes best.'

Tom needed no further persuading. He went immediately to the railway station to make inquiries about trains and next morning they set out together soon after breakfast.

Neither of them had ever visited Worcester before

and they had planned to spend the morning exploring the city but, it being such a beautiful sunny day, they decided instead to make their way straight to the gardens. Having paid their entrance money, they passed through the imposing wrought-iron gates, admired the two great Russian guns captured during the Crimean War and sauntered along the main drive towards the central fountain. The pleasure grounds were already filling with people despite the fact that there was still a couple of hours to go before the procession of the lodges was due to set out through the streets.

It was odd though, she had a feeling as soon as she entered the place – maybe because she and Tom had so much experience of the particular atmosphere which should prevail on fête days – that something was not right. The paths had been freshly gravelled, pelargoniums bloomed their best, people were in holiday mood, the weather bright and bidding fair to remain so all day – there was nothing obviously wrong. And yet something was not right.

'Look, Tom. There's the rope. What a marvellous site for it.'

Two huge masts had been planted upright in the ground about two hundred yards apart and were held in their places by hawsers or guy-ropes like those used to keep tent-poles steady. Near the top of each mast a hole had been drilled, causing it to look like some gigantic darning needle through which the main rope was threaded before being made fast to a tree. Between the masts the rope stretched beautifully taut and kept steady by dozens of sand bags hanging from it and small side ropes tied to pegs driven in the ground. Just to look at that lovely stretch of naked rope crossing the bright sky made her ache to walk along it.

'Yes. Mind you, that fellow doesn't look too happy. Really got his dander up. I wonder what the trouble is.'

At the foot of the mast nearest to them stood a

huddle of men discussing something. One in particular, red in the face and getting redder by the second, was shaking his head and gesturing up at the rope, looking as if he was about to have apoplexy.

'And do you know how much that lot cost us to rig up?' he yelled, and then lowered his voice so that most of his subsequent words were lost. '. . . a bit bloody late . . . I KNOW it's a genuine case but . . . letting people down . . . my name's going to be mud.'

With the last words his voice had reached screeching point again. Tom pulled a face.

'I think they're having problems. Something wrong with the rope probably. Well, I know how that feels. Still, maybe they can do with a bit of expert advice. Hang on, I'm just going to make myself known.' Before she could tell him that if there were any problems with the rope then Blondin himself would be the one to sort them out, that he prided himself in taking care of all such details personally, Tom had left her and made his way over to the men.

Her eyes returned to the rope and now she noticed the extra ropes and hoist attached to the nearest mast. That was the one he would be mounting and he would not be shinning up – it was too high for that – but sitting on a board which could be hauled up from below by his assistants. She had never had the chance to use anything like that. It must be rather fun, like sitting on a swing, and you'd be able to wave to the spectators as you were borne aloft.

She stood picturing herself being hoisted up to the small platform and then stepping out on to that glorious rope.

'Mirella! Didn't you hear me calling you?' Tom interrupted her reverie, very excited about something. But even when he had finished explaining, she found it hard to believe what he was saying.

'Blondin has called off his performance? Never. He wouldn't do such a thing.'

'Like I said, he's ill and got no choice.'

'Ill? How ill?'

'Not desperately, just a bad attack of lumbago. It's happened once before, evidently. At Plymouth. They had to call his performance off there at the last minute as well.'

'What are they going to do then, Tom? I mean, all these people coming especially to see him.'

The grounds were still filling up and had grown noticeably more crowded since they had arrived.

'No, not 'specially to see him – 'specially to be entertained by someone on the high rope. They won't care if it's not Blondin. In fact, I think they'd be even more excited if it was put about that there was someone – a young girl, preferably, who had never walked this particular rope before and had never walked as high as this before – who was prepared to risk her neck having a go, rather than see a lot of disappointed people have their holiday ruined.'

'Oh, Tom, not me. I couldn't.'

'Too late. I've already offered your services,' he said, fixing her with his stare, 'and I know you won't let me down, will you?'

Although it was not arranged quite as easily as that, there was no time for much discussion. The first performance was scheduled for seven o'clock and before then Tom had to rush back to Birmingham and fetch her stage clothes, her shoes and her own balancing pole. Fortunately Foregate Railway Station was close at hand and he managed to do all this and get back in good time. Meanwhile, she had been driven in a carriage to the hotel where Blondin was staying and led up to speak to the sick man.

He was lying in bed propped up by a mass of cushions and pillows. Even when one had made allowance for the ghastly light filtering through the window-

274

shutters into the room, his face looked very grey and Mirella felt she ought not to be disturbing him. On the other hand the rope hanging in the Arboretum was his own personal property and she could not simply make use of it without his permission.

'Eh bien, so you decide to ignore my letter and continue your way.' He spoke with more of an accent than she remembered. 'But now, look at me! I am in no position to say what you can or cannot do. I who have not the possibility to stand up straight on my two feet and, alas, this morning feel like an old man.'

'*Your* letter?' She thought for a moment he had mistaken her for someone else. But when he started to explain why he had felt driven to warn her about the dangers of their profession, his words brought to mind the letter which had been delivered to her at Crystal Palace.

'I didn't know it was you who wrote that letter,' she exclaimed. 'Why didn't you sign it with your own name?'

'But I did. Jean-Francois Gravelet, that is my proper name.'

'Yes, I realise that, but the letter was from . . .' She tried to picture the signature. 'Oh, so that's how you spell Gravelet. I didn't realise the signature was in French.'

'Mademoiselle, I think it is as well my rope was made in London otherwise you might try walking it this evening upside down,' he sighed.

She tried not to keep him talking long because he was obviously in pain. But as they said goodbye, she knew she was going away with more than the simple permission she sought. He had given her his blessing.

'But I demand you to take great care out there today, ma petite. It would not do for people to say that Blondin's weakness caused a young innocent to fall. Take notice of my agent. He is a good man and I have given him full instructions to assist you in every way.' As she leant over his pillows to offer her face to be kissed, he whispered, 'Bonne chance, ma petite. Bonne chance.'

The odd thing was, when she returned to the Arboretum, it felt like a different place. It looked the same, of course, although very much more crowded. But the atmosphere was different now. She felt completely at home there and happy that she had a job to do, a part to play in making this day special for all these people.

She took no chances during her seven o'clock appearance. It was a strange rope and she treated it with utmost respect. But later on, when she appeared in the dark, her whole performance lit by fireworks, she gave in to the rope's enchantment.

From her perch as she floated upwards she could see the fountain playing white and red and green fire and then, as she stepped on to the rope, there was a great burst of fireworks and she walked in a cloud of smoke and glimmering Bengal lights. The smoke and the smell and the light made her feel like some elemental being lightly touching down on this rope and she danced its length in a dream while the pink and the green light billowed round her. Danced it back and forth. Stepped it blindfolded and yet was still blindly aware of the sparkling stars of light shooting all round her. Stood on her head in the middle of the rope and there was no possibility that she could slip and fall. Not that evening – whilst on Blondin's rope and enchanted by the light.

Next day, back at the hotel in Birmingham, her feet were on the ground but she still felt scarcely human. Tom was in an excellent mood with a fat purse in his pocket and a signed contract for them to make an early return visit to the Arboretum. In the circumstances she was astounded when, whilst gathering up her equipment to take to the theatre, he suddenly started to fume and curse.

'Blast and damnation! Look what that bloody fool of an agent made me do.'

'What?'

'Pick up the wrong bloody pole. This isn't yours. It's much thinner, look. Heavy, though. You feel it.'

He placed it in her palms and she held it out in front of her, testing its balance.

'What wood is this, Tom?' she asked, surprised by its weight.

'I don't know. I was wondering that, myself. But the main thing is, could you use it instead of your own pole? We've got the spare, of course, but I don't fancy charging down to Worcester trying to get the other one back unless it's absolutely necessary. I've got too much else to do today. In any case, there's no guarantee Blondin's gear will still be there. They may well have shipped it back to London by now.'

She stood testing out the slender pole. It was heavier than the one she was used to, but less cumbersome. Something she could adjust to, she thought, and in her mind's eye saw Blondin using this very pole as he walked above Niagara.

'There's no problem, Tom. I'll write to Blondin and tell him what's happened. And as long as he doesn't need this particular pole—' she felt its easy balance in her hands '—I shall be glad to make use of it. It's so beautifully balanced, I think it would keep me upright on the rope even in a storm.'

In a note which arrived some days later, attached to her own mislaid pole, Blondin asked her to keep the one that had belonged to him as a small token of his esteem. It was made of lancewood, he wrote in answer to her query, and it was this which gave it the elasticity she had noticed.

Here in Leeds the theatre stage was small and

prevented her from making use of the slightly longer pole, but there would be no such restrictions on her or it on Saturday afternoon. Then, in the Royal Park, she would be walking on a really high rope in the open air again. And that, in her opinion, was the only sort of tightrope walking worth doing.

Chapter Eighteen

'Ah, this reminds me of the Arboretum,' she sighed appreciatively, sniffing in the scent from the rose borders and surveying the people who were just beginning to emerge after the heavy shower of rain.

'Weather's not so good, though,' Tom growled. 'Hope the crowds pick up in time for your performance.'

'I think they will. A spot of rain won't put them off.'

She continued to glance around her as they walked through the Leeds Royal Park. It was very like the Arboretum: the same fountains, same beds of flowers, same buzz of conversation and ringing shrieks of laughter from (yes, she could almost swear to it) the same people swarming along the paths and across lawns. Occasionally the hubbub gave way to the more melodious sounds of strolling musicians and ballad-singers who attracted a circle of listeners about them, forcing them to linger for a few minutes in defiance of the call of the dance music blaring out from the "Monster Platform" that was the park's centre of attraction.

Earlier in the afternoon she and Tom had wandered through the Smithfield Cattle Market and down through North Street and Briggate to get an idea of what the main pleasure fair was like. But she had soon had enough of the shows and Aunt Sallies and rifle ranges, ''Cheap Johns'', merry-go-rounds and all the other raucous entertainments. Compared with what was happening outside in the streets, the park offered a haven of sobriety in return for its sixpence admission charge.

'Hope the rope hasn't got too wet,' Tom mumbled.

'No, it will be all right. Stop worrying,' she said. 'The rain didn't last long enough to do much damage.'

'You say that, but just look at the mud on my boots. This path's like half-baked Yorkshire pudding.'

'That's because there are so many feet churning it up.'

Even as she spoke the crowd seemed to be growing denser. Children clutching paper cornets of bulls'-eyes or hundreds-and-thousands, young women parading their fancy parasols whilst their male companions dangled damp half-furled umbrellas from their wrists. Amidst so much crowding and confusion it was a relief to arrive at the enclosure where her rope had been set up high above all the noise.

'It's a pity we haven't got one of those seats to hoist me to the top as well as the pole,' she said, as they both set about checking over the equipment and making sure the pole was securely up on the platform, lashed to its side, ready for her use.

'Don't you fret. I've got it in hand and you'll have one for your next outdoor performance, I promise.'

'That's marvellous, Tom. It's not that I mind climbing up, but I do think it actually makes for a better spectacle if I can be hauled aloft like, well . . .'

'Some goddess?' he suggested.

'Well, no. Goddesses come down, don't they? Rather than go up?'

'Yes, but you do that as well. Every time you go up, you have to come down.'

His words sang through her mind as she climbed the rope ladder up to the platform to begin her performance that evening. If you go up, you have to come down. Obvious, really. A simple statement of fact. Why then did the words seem to contain some menace that day?

I'm going up and up, she thought to herself each time she stopped waving to the crowd below and started to climb again. And up and up.

No more waving once she reached the platform. Nothing to distract the crowd from realising how serious the task before her was. Even up here she could sense the solemn mood settling over them as they waited for her to begin. In her white costume which marked her out as in need of special protection, she felt she was about to walk not for herself but for all those people on the ground who would have laughed if you accused them of aspiring to this height. She was walking for them, of course she was. She would not be here walking in the Royal Park if they, all those myriads of faces down there, had not willed her to come and walk up here for them. Their lamb led – no, not led – come very willingly . . .

She unlashed her pole, shifted it from side to side until it lay perfectly balanced in her palms, and stepped on to the rope. Because it had not been possible to tighten the rope completely, it hung in a curve so that her first steps had to be downhill. Below her spread the usual field of faces and a white marquee pitched near the centre where the rope dipped lowest.

Up and up and now going down and down, she was singing to herself, as she slid one foot carefully in front of the other and walked out over space. She soon registered the need to be exceptionally careful today because the rain had made the rope slightly more slippery underfoot than usual. Once across, she paused on the farside platform to acknowledge the applause which came echoing up. She wondered whether to rub a little more rosin under her shoes, but decided this would not help.

Making a great show of her movements, she now

lifted a bandana from the side of the platform and tied it around her eyes and then pulled a sack with holes cut out for her arms over her head and right down to her knees to emphasise that she was completely blindfold. In truth she could see nothing, but at least the sack, by hanging level all round her body, let her know if she strayed from the vertical.

She picked up the pole again, slid her shoe along the rope, found purchase and stepped forward. Alone in the darkness. Everything silent. She was the foot slipping forward, caressing the rope, feeling its strength, assessing its sway; the hands holding the pole, minutely shifting and balancing. She was Mirella the ropewalker inhabiting a world of her own . . . and suddenly the wider world rushed in and overturned it.

Her foot betrayed her trust and slipped as she stepped. She wobbled from one side to the other again and again, fighting to regain her balance. The rope picked up her panic and began to wobble too. Nothing in the world stayed still. The rope was shifting. The pole was tugging her down. She couldn't control the forces ranged against her. They were all pulling her down.

She half dropped, half thrust the pole from her hands. Felt herself slipping. Down. But hands waiting to clutch. Anything. The rope, yes, the rope. Thank God. The rope was between her hands. She was holding on to it. If only she could see, get this bloody thing off her head! But the rope, her friendly rope, would save her. She had it gripped in her hands and she was catching her breath again now. Easy, easy. But get on with it. Your life's in your own hands.

She edged her way along. Swinging her body from side to side so that she could move her right hand along the rope. She couldn't remember what distance she had covered before the accident had happened, but that didn't matter now. She edged her way painfully along in the darkness, feeling for the nearest guy-rope. For God's sake, where was it, that guy-rope?

She couldn't have been this far from one. She felt her arms were being dragged out of their sockets. She wouldn't be able to go much further. Maybe she should just drop and hope she was directly above the tent and that would break her fall.

No. She felt absolutely calm now. She knew what she had to do. Exactly what she had planned for this eventuality. She gripped tight with her left hand and edged her right further along the rope and there it was – the guy-rope that would enable her to slither to safety. She twisted her foot around it and then lowered herself slowly, hand over hand, trying to ignore the pain as skin was scraped off her arms and her shins.

Before her feet touched ground, there were arms seizing her and pulling her from the rope, and voices saying, 'It's all right. We've got you.' She let her body go limp and someone tugged the sack over her head, untied the blindfold and let light flood in. 'It's all right. You're safe now.'

Long minutes elapsed before she could make sense of what had happened to her.

'My pole, it didn't hit anyone when it fell, did it?' She was almost afraid to ask and could not understand why Tom laughed at the question.

'No, your pole didn't hit anyone,' he said eventually. 'It fell fair and square on the marquee like you meant it to do, and it carried on falling, right the way through the bloody thing! Look, you can see the hole it made.'

Sure enough the tent's canvas had been ripped, probably by one of the iron pieces which weighted the ends of the pole. Fortunately the place had been empty at the time so no one was hurt. But the wreckage caused by the pole as it bounced on the ground inside gave a clue as to what would have happened to her if she had dropped rather than climbed down.

Suddenly she felt good about the whole episode. A

tragedy had been averted because she had known what to do and remained calm enough to put her emergency plan into operation. She felt that, like her earlier stagefright, now that she had survived one accident she was better prepared to meet another one. Far from being unnerved, the experience had left her feeling more confident and in no mood to heed Tom's miserable words: 'Well, we got away with it that time, but that doesn't mean to say we'll always be so lucky.'

When the Management at the Agricultural Hall asked if they had anything fresh to offer that winter, it was not difficult for Mirella to decide which new act to include in her programme. That autumn she and Tom had been present when Blondin caused a sensation by riding a bicycle across the high rope at Crystal Palace and this was what everyone now wanted to see.

'Of course it will be a trick bike,' Tom had said, as they travelled to Sydenham by train, 'probably fitted with weights or sideguards to keep it upright. Still, there's nothing to stop us getting the same sort of thing made up if you want. I'll try to get close enough to give it the once over.'

In the event this proved easy, for before the performance the bicycle was put on public display in the Board Room so that people could verify for themselves Blondin's assertion that, except for its slightly grooved wheels, the bicycle was in every respect a facsimile of an ordinary machine which could be ridden as well by road as on the rope. After examining it minutely, Tom memorised the name of its manufacturer: Messrs Gardiner and Mackintosh, engineers of New Cross.

'What do you think?' he asked, after they had watched Blondin, armed with a long balancing pole, ride majestically across the rope.

'To be honest, I'm not that keen. I love the sensation of walking the rope. But, on the other hand, if that's what the public want – and listening to those cheers there can be very little doubt of that – then I'm quite happy to try the same trick. Mind you, I'm not at all sure I'll get the hang of one of those contraptions on the ground, let alone be able to ride it on a rope.'

'You'll manage it all right. You've got two arms and two legs and a good sense of balance. That's all you need.'

Tom himself had never tried riding one of these machines, which is why he left out those other essential ingredients: patience and perseverance. Once on the bicycle, she found she could keep the thing upright without too much difficulty. But getting on and off was a different story. She tried throwing her right leg over the saddle and placing her foot on the treadle fixed to the front wheel, but there was never enough time for her to get really balanced before the left treadle came up and the wretched machine started to run away with her. And then the handles were a problem. Was she supposed to hold them with her hands over them, or under them, or with the ends in her palms? She decided to hold them with her hands over them so that, when she transferred to the rope, it would be easier to grip her pole at the same time.

Fortunately, although she took longer than anticipated to master the machine on the ground, it took her less time to perfect the art of riding it on the rope, and so the new act was ready in time for Christmas.

She was glad that her practice kept her too busy during the run-up period to allow much time for reflection. She had no wish to dwell on the fact that this would be the third Christmas she had spent at the Agricultural Hall, the second anniversary of her meeting with Levic and the second Christmas she had spent without him. It was no good thinking along these lines. He had disappeared from her life and had never even troubled to write her a letter.

At first when no word came she used to worry about him, fearing lest his ship had gone down in the Channel, his train crashed, his coach been waylaid by robbers, or that he had fallen prey to some fever. From time to time, however, reports of the famous Renz circus in Berlin were published in the *Era* and prominent amongst their attractions was mentioned the English clown, Levic. They eulogised his talent – his comic genius, his riding ability, his acrobatic skills. Although she was proud of his success, it hurt to know that his life was so full there was clearly no room in it for her. And the hurt did not go away no matter how much salve in the form of her own work she rubbed into the wound.

To start with her ropewalking had been her lifeline, stretching out to Levic wherever he happened to be, the cord that would one day draw him back to her. He was an artiste. She must be as great an artiste if she was to merit his love. Every time she approached the rope it was with Levic's standard of excellence in mind, as if he were standing there challenging her.

But after a while things began to change. She became absorbed in what she was doing, so completely absorbed that the seemingly impossible happened and she experienced whole stretches of time when she forgot Levic altogether. My work is what's important, she kept telling herself. My work, that's all I'm interested in, all I'm going to think about from now on. Just my work. Constant practice and determination helped her to cross the abyss Levic had left in her life, so that while she was walking her rope she was able to meet thoughts of him head on with her own fierce challenge: 'Look at me, Levic. I don't need you. You wrote me off once, but you won't ever get the chance to do that again, not now that I've achieved so much on my own.'

But unfortunately she could not live all her life up there on the rope, and the ecstasy she experienced when walking high only made coming down to earth again all the more painful. It was in the moments after she had walked among the gods and then returned to the everyday world that her defences were down. In these moments she thought of Levic and ached for him.

Each night, after the show, Tom would try to persuade her to accompany him to a tavern or variety hall. She usually said no, because she disliked the raucous atmosphere and hated being with him when he drank too much and started to become aggressive or, what was worse, give her the glad eye.

'Come on, it's New Year's Eve! You can't sit up in this wagon and mope on New Year's Eve. Everyone's taking out drink and stuff and having a party round the tree.'

'I'm not moping, just thinking about things, Tom. I always like to do that at the beginning of a new year. I mean, 1870. I shall be eighteen next August. It doesn't seem possible.'

'That's what I mean. Come out and stop moping. There's music and dancing. We can have a good time.'

'In a minute then. I'm just going to change into my other dress.'

She might as well go and join in the festivities. After all, the turning of the year was something special, the old year dying to make way for the new. It would be good to welcome in the seventies in style. After all, despite the fact that she was already seventeen there was still lots of time left before she need hang up her bonnet and admit that life had passed her by.

Oh, Mirella, you goose! she laughed, poking a face at herself in the mirror. You don't really feel like that. You're just bored. Riding a bike along a rope sixty feet off the ground isn't enough for you. You want something more to lift your spirits. Who knows? Next year might be the year that something really exciting happens to you. She was glad to see the reflection in the glass brighten at this prospect.

In order to keep its licence the hall had to close no later than eleven o'clock each night, and it was always a relief to the showmen when the doorkeepers locked up after the last stragglers had gone. Although it was good to take money, most of them had been working since ten in the morning and were more than ready for a rest.

Tonight, however, was different. They had all rushed off to their wagons not to grab a bite of supper and then collapse in bed, but to have a quick wash and brush up before fetching out their food for the party. It was twenty minutes to midnight by the time Mirella had changed into her green velvet dress which was so much warmer and emerged from her wagon. She did not immediately join the throng of showpeople gathered by the tree, preferring instead to mount the stairs up to the first gallery and linger for a while in the shadows, surveying the scene.

Most of the lights had been turned off when the Aggie closed and only the centre of the hall was still lit by gas lamps. It was like looking down on a stage set for some elaborate drama which was being enacted by a cast of about a hundred around an enormous Christmas tree and a painted merry-go-round and trestle tables bearing dishes of food and jars of drink. For the moment all attention was fixed on an old gentleman doing a step dance to the accompaniment of the band which usually played for the ghost show.

Behind her the shooting saloons, aunt sallies and swings were all silent and shrouded for the night. She rested her arm on the balcony and tried to make out the tune as it came wafting up into a silence otherwise unbroken except for occasional hollow grunts and the rattling of bars from the menagerie cages lining the sides of the building.

She looked down into the hall, trying to spot Tom

among the crowd, and eventually saw him in conversation with someone in outdoor coat and carrying a cane and hat, having probably just come in from the street. He had his back to her so she could not make out who it was. She glanced at the large clock on the wall opposite her. Ten minutes to midnight. Time she went down to join the throng, except that she felt so reluctant to leave this solitude. She must go, though. Tom would be wondering where she was.

She looked down again. In that moment he happened to catch sight of her and she waved. He did not wave back. She was sure he had seen her but he was refusing to wave back. And then something in his face must have prompted the other fellow to turn and look up and she found herself waving not to Tom but to Levic. Unmistakably, it was Levic standing there in the midst of all those people, here in the Agricultural Hall. Levic was back.

Chapter Nineteen

It did not occur to her to run and greet him. She stood quite still watching him thread his way through the people, make for the stairs and disappear from sight. A dream, then. He had not really been there. It was just her yearning that had conjured him up.

'Mirella! Oh, it is good to see you again.' His arms around her and his face and lips brushing hers were definitely flesh and blood. 'It has been a long time, far too long.'

Still she could not speak. Could only stand, hands in his, looking into his eyes.

'Well, are you not pleased to see me?' he prompted.

'How long have you been back, Levic?' she asked.

'I have just this moment arrived. From Dover I caught the first train to London and then came straight on here. I hoped I should be in time to see your performance tonight, but the train was late.'

Anger buzzed in her head. She wanted to remind him how long he had been away, tell him how desperate she had felt when he left her, ask why he had never written. Instead, she heard herself saying, 'Never mind. You're here now and that's all that matters.'

'That is right, Mirella,' he whispered, lifting her hand to his lips. 'I am here so that we may begin this new year together. Listen.'

From below what had been a murmuring ground-swell suddenly erupted into a rousing cheer mixed with the whirring and clanging of the clock.

'Happy New Year, my darling,' he whispered.

'Yes, Happy New Year, Levic.' She felt so happy.
Levic at her side as if he had never been away.
Looking much the same as ever, black wavy hair
curling over his forehead, moustache and hooked
nose – funny, she had not noticed that before, but it
definitely was slightly hooked – lending him the air
of an aristocrat, she decided.

'Are you going to be here long?' She managed to
stammer out the question.

'What do you mean, here in the Agricultural Hall
or here in London?'

'Here in London. I mean, in this country. Will you
stay here now, or do you have to go back to Berlin?'
As she asked, she looked up into his eyes and saw that
they were smiling the answer.

'No. I am here now and I have no plans to be anywhere else.'

'Thank God.' Her happiness was complete. Following his glance, she raised her eyes to look at her
tightrope faintly glowing as it stretched out from the
upper balcony into the darkness beyond.

'Do you know,' he said, 'the fame of La Petite
Blondin has reached already across the Continent? I
had no idea when I left that you would make such a
success of this ropewalking.'

'Well, I didn't do it on my own. Tom has been a
great help. He has so many ideas, and he has the
contacts and makes the bookings and everything. I
couldn't have got where I have without him.' As she
spoke, she instinctively scanned the crowd below
trying to catch a glimpse of Tom.

'Does he still drink so heavily?'

'Well, yes. He still drinks, but I don't know how
much you would regard as "heavily".'

Tom did not appear to be among the revellers,
many of whom had now formed couples and were

dancing. She wondered where he had gone. It would be nice if he could find someone to dance with but he never tried asking, always protesting that his crippled arm made him an undesirable partner.

'And does he still try completely to possess you?'

'Oh, no. Tom doesn't do that.' She flinched at the implication. 'He only tries to look after me. Remember he's my uncle as well as my manager and . . .'

The words died on her lips as she suddenly became aware that someone was staring at them. In the shadows of the balcony on the further side of the hall, just below where the other end of her tightrope was tied, someone was standing staring at them. Although it was too dark to see him properly, she knew immediately that it was Tom and his presence there in the darkness made her shiver.

The next few weeks were a confusion of joy and wretchedness. Levic had rooms in Holborn where he usually took up residence while resting between engagements. Having been working without a break since leaving for Berlin, he needed the respite. Mirella, however, was unable to enjoy such luxury. She was committed to making her regular appearances at the Agricultural Hall, and so her time was not her own. Nevertheless, much to the annoyance of Tom, she slipped away to meet Levic whenever she could. She did not neglect her practice, nor was she ever late for one of her performances, so she felt there was no justification when Tom complained that she was doing too much gadding about.

'But I've got to have some free time,' she said, 'and so long as my work doesn't suffer I can't see what's wrong with my going out.'

'Come off it, Mirella! You know very well what's wrong. Don't kid me it's right for a young girl like you to go up to that Romeo's rooms on her own at all hours.'

'Not all hours. Mornings are the only time I've got

free at the moment, so I'm only able to see Levic then.'

'Morning, evening, night time, what difference does it make? You and him alone together's not decent, no matter what the time of day.'

'But we're hardly ever alone together. We sit in Mrs Relph's lounge – that's his landlady – and she brings us in some tea and toasted muffins while we chat. And then, sometimes, if the fog's not too bad, we just go out for a walk. I can't see how anyone can take exception to that.'

'No, but you can't see the way it's going,' he snapped. 'He's a smarmy devil. Gets you to eat out of his hand no sooner than he appears, and you too blind or too stupid to see what he's after.'

'Look, Tom, Levic's not after anything. He's just my friend and I like his company.'

'Better than mine,' he snarled.

'I didn't say that. You're my uncle and that's special but, well . . . different from being an ordinary friend. You and I, we work together and I think we usually work together very well, but my life isn't all work and if I choose to have friends whose company I enjoy when I'm not working, then I don't think you have any right to interfere.'

She had said the same sort of thing before, but perhaps not so bluntly. Looking at him now, she half regretted her plain speaking. Tom had gone white in the face, his lips drawn so tight they turned bluish as he hissed, 'No right to interfere when I see you getting thick with a whoremonger like that?'

'I won't stand here to listen to your stupid insults.'

'Yes you will. You'll stand where you are and hear me out,' he roared, grabbing her wrist and dragging her towards him.

'All right. Let go of me then, and let's sit down and talk this over sensibly.' She did not really think much good would come of talking, but figured that was the only way of calming him down.

'I don't know about sensible. It takes two to talk sensible, and the way you've been acting since that bastard turned up, you wouldn't see sense if it crossed the road and punched you on the nose.'

For a moment she was afraid he was going to hit her, but instead he dropped her hand and she tried not to wince as she unobtrusively rubbed her wrist. Whenever Tom started to rant like this, she felt like ending their partnership there and then. But the sight of his maimed arm or the misery in his eyes always prevented her from saying as much.

'Tom,' she said now, trying to keep her voice level, 'I know you don't like Levic but that's no reason to call him such bad names. Besides, you're being unfair to me by suggesting I'd allow myself to be taken advantage of so easily. I keep trying to tell you, Levic and I are just friends, nothing more. We're both too caught up in our work to want any other entanglements.'

He snorted. 'That's the trouble. You're so green you can't see what the bleeder's up to when it's plain as a pikestaff. Levic's got plenty of friends, Mirella. He doesn't run after young girls because he wants to be "friends" with them. Use your sense. He's after a bit more than that.'

'Look, Tom, it's no good going on. I don't want you poisoning my mind against Levic. He's been very kind to me, remember. When you were laid up, it was Levic who helped me get started as a ropewalker, so we both owe him something.'

'That's what he's been telling you, is it? *He* got you started. Never mind everything I've done, it's Levic who got you started on your illustrious career.'

'Tom, I didn't say that.' The words came out mechanically. She should have known it was pointless trying to discuss anything with him while he was in this mood.

'Not in so many words. It's what you think,

though. But let me tell you this, my girl, you were nothing before you came to me. Nothing. I was the one who took you in, made the sacrifices and slaved my guts out to give you the chance to start in this business, so don't imagine I'll give up easy when some whipper-snapper comes along and tries to lure you away from me.'

'Lure me away? Tom, don't be stupid. I love my work too much for anyone to lure me away from it.'

'Maybe. But a rope don't tie you to any particular place, does it? You can fix it up anywhere. In Berlin, Paris, Niagara. And what riles me is that when that joskin goes off on his travels again, he'll want you to go with him and, despite all I've done for you, you'll go.'

'Tom, why must you think so ill of everyone all the time? To hear you talk, you'd think there was no such thing as loyalty and friendship in the world.'

'Yes, you would, wouldn't you?' he said sarcastically. 'But regarding your "friendships", remember this: I'm your manager. I decide who you can associate with. And I'm telling you now, Mirella, keep away from that Levic.'

She shuddered as his pale blue eyes fixed hers in a stare from which she found it hard to withdraw her gaze. At the same time she felt fury that he should try to browbeat her in this way.

'You're going too far, Tom. You've no right to interfere in my personal life like this.'

Still his eyes stared into hers.

'I've got every right,' he said, spitting out the words between clenched teeth. 'And if you defy me, I've got ways of bringing you to heel. I mean, have you stopped to think how your father would react if he knew what dirty tricks you were up to, eh?'

She decided she had had enough and moved quickly away before he could restrain her.

'That's right,' Tom shouted after her, 'run away

from what you don't want to hear, but don't forget what I say. Defy me and I'll bring your father into the picture and we'll see how the situation goes then.'

Everyone felt the effects of the violent storm which hit the area towards the end of that week. Hail beat against the glass-plated roof like a cannonade and every so often the Royal Agricultural Hall was lit by flashes of lightning. None of this worried Mirella. Nor was she perturbed when she heard that some of the glass had been cracked and the hall was going to be shut down for twenty-four hours to enable structural engineers to inspect the damage. In fact she was delighted at the news. Twenty-four hours. A whole day free. A day she could spend with Levic.

Taking her warm green mantle and muff, she slipped away early to avoid the possibility of any scene with Tom and took a hackney cab to Levic's address. Her breath turned into white steam as she spoke to the driver. She agreed with him that it certainly was a "cold old morning", but her heart rejoiced to be out in the pale sunlight.

'Now, where can two artistes who are both temporarily resting from their profession go to find some amusement on this wintry day?'

'I'll tell you where I'd like to go,' she said, watching Levic twine a red muffler round his neck. 'I'd love to visit the Surrey Zoological Gardens at Kennington. Have you ever been?'

'No, that pleasure has so far eluded me, but . . . yes, what a good idea. I know there is a lake there and a lot of the exhibits are under cover, so if it is too cold we can hibernate in the monkey house.'

'Yes, and we can eat lunch there.'

'In the monkey house?'

'No,' she laughed. 'We can ape our betters and eat in their much-advertised Rustic Refectory. And then I was wondering if there might be something on in their concert hall. Joey said they sometimes put on good orchestral concerts there. You know, proper music, not music hall sort of stuff, and I'd love to go to a good concert again.'

'I see you have this whole day worked out.'

'You don't mind, do you? I mean, if there's anything you'd rather do . . .'

'Not at all. To me the Surrey Zoological Gardens and a concert already sound fine, but when I add to them the magic of your company, then they become perfect.'

'Well, one thing's sure,' she grinned. 'I shan't feel the cold today if you keep laying it on that thick.'

It was not the best time of year to see the zoo, but they were happy peering at the eagles in the grotto, the giraffe and other exotic animals. Mirella even enjoyed seeing the collection of big cats. In the afternoon they wandered round the lake and then, in the absence of a suitable programme at the Surrey Hall, journeyed back to the Hanover Square Rooms where they managed to obtain tickets for a wonderful concert given by the Royal Academy of Music.

When, later that evening, they arrived back and stood outside the strangely darkened Agricultural Hall, she tried to persuade Levic to let her go in alone, but he insisted on escorting her safely back to her wagon. He had not quizzed her about her uncle's attitude to today's jaunt and she had said nothing about Tom's threats. So Levic walked, apparently unconcerned, past the rows of living-vans, occasionally calling out a greeting to someone he knew, whilst Mirella peered anxiously around half expecting Tom to appear at any moment brandishing a hammer and screaming abuse.

'I won't invite you in, if you don't mind,' she said when, to her immense relief, she found the wagon quiet and deserted and Tom nowhere in sight. 'Tom would think it improper and I don't want to upset him at the moment.'

'I understand. I only wanted to make sure you reached home safely. I'll bid you goodnight now—' gently he kissed her forehead '—and take my leave. I have enjoyed today, Mirella. It showed me what I have been missing this last year and, with your permission, I shall hope to make up for all the lost time. I love you, you know.' His voice had dropped to a whisper.

'And I love you too,' she whispered back, 'but please, Levic, I must go now. Thank you for a lovely day.'

He left her then and she entered the wagon and prepared herself for bed, grateful that her perfect day with Levic had not been ruined by any outburst from Tom. It did occur to her that she might have to face a further storm on the morrow, but before then there lay before her a whole night of dreams. She was content with that.

She knew. When Tom pussy-footed around her the next day instead of going into a rage, she knew he had another trick up his sleeve.

'So, you defied me and went with that man? After all I said, you went with him,' he snarled. Then, as she braced herself for the storm, he added: 'All right, Mirella. All right,' and stood there smirking.

He's playing a game with me, she thought. Well, I'm too busy to play games, so he must play it on his own. She went off to do her practice, and so busy was she in the next few days that she had almost forgotten the incident by the time the letter came.

Good, something from Pa, she murmured, recognising the writing. I wonder what's been happening at home. She tore open the envelope, but even before starting to read noticed the handwriting inside was shaky. Her father usually wrote in a neat, careful hand, but this was all shaky as if written in a rush – or a rage. She soon found out which.

My Dear Mirella,

For you are my dear daughter no matter how much you have let your father down. I write this because I am not free to come no matter how much I want to fetch you back home here where you belong. You know your mother was against your going your own way in the first place and she has proved right and I was wrong, but then I thought that with my own brother there you would be kept from bad ways. But then you were never one to be guvverned easy so again I was wrong and its no fault of Toms if you have gone astray. Im sure he has done his best by you.
(Oh heavens, Tom, what on earth have you been telling them?)

Mirella, Im pleading with you to come home and give up this wicked life your leading. Your mother and me did are best to bring you up a good girl and it brakes my heart to know you have gone to the bad. But its not to late to make amends and come home to us.

Your mother cried when I read her Toms letter.
(You bastard, Tom. I'll never forgive you for this.)

We have all been very proud of what you done on the titerope and I still carry the bit of paper of it round in my pocket but that dont make up for bad living. I dont care if they give you all the money in the world because the only thing that matters to me and your mother is if your a good girl. Now, its a hard thing my dear but Ive got to say it. I want to know you are going to act better in the future or your mother and me will have done with you.
(She had to read that bit twice and then again for the words to sink in.)

The best thing is for you to come back here and make a fresh start with us to keep an eye on you.

But if you wont have that then Tom is willing to keep you alongside him and help you as always, providing you behave yourself and never let that man play fast with you again.

I think I have said enuff now for you to know how I feel and I hope this will bring you to your senses. If it dont you will have broken your mother's heart and as it is you must know you have brought terrble shame on your family who loved you.

From your shamed but still everloving father,
John Granger.

PS. We have not told Cassie about what your up to and we dont want you to write to her because she is a good girl and it would do her harm to know about these bad things.

She folded the paper quickly and thrust it into her pocket, wishing that she could so easily expunge its contents from her mind.

How could they? How could her father write such hurtful things? Obviously Tom had told them dreadful lies about her, but they should never have believed them without first hearing her side of the story.

Tears were scalding her eyes. She'd never forgive Tom for this: poisoning her family against her and, worse than that, making them all so unhappy for no good reason at all. No, she would never forgive him and she would never again allow him to influence her life. She would rather – yes, she would rather go back and work in a scullery than have anything further to do with such a poisonous creature. She hated him and she would tell him so straight away. After that . . . She did not care what happened after that so long as she never had to associate with him again.

'That man is not just stupid, he is crimina',' Levic declared. 'Deliberately to upset you in that way and

301

then to expect you to pull yourself together enough to walk on a rope sixty feet above the ground – if that is not criminal, then it is insane. And to be honest, I think that is the explanation. Tom is insane and not answerable for his actions. You had no choice but to give him the sack.'

'But his eyes, Levic, when I told him I wouldn't allow him to manage my affairs ever again . . . I thought he was going to leap and tear me apart. His eyes went yellow and so full of hate.' She started to tremble again, her whole body shaking uncontrollably. 'I wouldn't have minded so much if he'd hit me. Bruises disappear in time, but I shall never be able to forget that look he gave me. Why does he hate me so much, Levic? What have I done to make him hate me like that?'

'You have remained you and refused to let him mould you into something he wanted. He does not hate you. He hates his own powerlessness.'

'But to turn my own father against me, Levic,' she sobbed. 'And my mother. And all my family. He must have really hated me to do that.'

'Stop thinking about it, Mirella. There is no point in trying to make sense of the actions of a madman. The main thing is, you have wrenched yourself from his clutches and – you told him you won't be back?' He put the last words in the form of a question.

'Yes. I told him that all right. And he stood there with his lip curled back – you know the way he looks when he's sneering at something – and said, "You'll be back when you've cooled down, because you'll realise how much you need me. Think about it, Mirella. I brought you into this business. I made you what you are. Without me you're nothing." And then he said something disgusting about you, something I can't repeat . . .'

'No need,' Levic interrupted. 'I can guess.'

'And then I walked out. Or rather ran. I had to get away from him and I can't go back, not ever.'

'What about your performance this afternoon? And the rest of your engagement?'

'I can't do it, Levic. I know it's dreadful, but I can't, even though it means letting everyone down. You see, apart from feeling so upset, I couldn't bring myself to set foot on any rope Tom was supposed to have checked. I'd just keep seeing that murderous look he gave me, and . . . and then I couldn't trust myself.'

'All right. That is all I need to hear. You are absolutely right. You must not go near that maniac again, Mirella. I want you to promise me that. Tom is dangerous and you certainly don't need him while I am here to help you. I am very fond of you, you know that, don't you?'

'Yes, Levic, but I don't want you to feel that you have to.'

'Don't worry, I never do anything because I feel I have to. I do only what I want to do and at the moment I want very much to take care of you, so no arguments, please. I am going to seek out my landlady and fix you up a room in this house for the night. You see, everything will be done most properly and there is no need for you to worry any more.'

'Yes, but my father – I don't know what he'd think if I move in here.'

'Yes, you do, and it's time you faced up to the fact.'

'What do you mean? You've met my father, Levic. You know he's not like Tom. He's a really good father, always tried to understand and . . . oh, it's all such a mess! I don't know how I'm ever going to explain things to him. He thinks I've let him down and I wouldn't, not for anything in the world.'

'There you are, you see. That's what you must face up to. I am sure your father is a very good man and most of your family are excellent people, but the fact

303

remains they are your family. They will always try to hold you back.'

'No, you don't understand, Levic. My family aren't like that. They really love me.' She could feel the tears streaming down her face and hated herself for showing such weakness.

'Yes, in their own way I'm sure they do. But the love of one's family comes from the past, Mirella. It represents the clans, the tribes, the old order of things. If you want to be truly yourself you must break these blood ties so that they do not hold you in chains.'

'Break them? You mean, break with my family? But I could never do that, Levic. It would hurt them too much.'

'Ah, you see, that's the hold they have over you. That's what will always stop you from being free. Do you remember when we talked about the bird in the cage and the way people were always trying to possess each other? Well, at the moment your family still imagine that they possess you and that is why there is all this misunderstanding.'

'What should I do then? Should I go home and explain how Tom has been spreading lies about me? Or would it be better to write, do you think?'

'You can go home, or you can write. It doesn't really matter. They will still think what they want to think about you. What really matters is that you care too much about what they think all the time. You shouldn't, you know. You should leave them to their own thoughts and live your life the way you choose.'

'No, Levic. I couldn't do that. I couldn't just ignore my family. I love them too much for that. You hardly knew yours, so you don't understand what it's like.'

'Do you want to go back home to them?'

'No.'

'So write to your father then. Tell him what's been

happening and what you have decided to do. I hope he will be as understanding as you say, but he will be an exceptional father if he is. And remember, no matter what he says, it does not mean that anything you decide to do is wrong. It might be that the pair of you are simply two very different sorts of people living by the light from your own candles and linked, as I have been trying to explain, only by a blood tie.'

What Levic said sounded convincing, although she was not sure she understood the bit about the past and the blood ties. Maybe they would talk about it again when she was feeling less upset and in a mood to follow his reasoning more closely. As it was, his words made her feel slightly less anxious about the outcome of the letter she wrote to her father in which, whilst trying not to be too explicit about Tom's behaviour, she defended herself and explained why she had now taken the decision to dismiss him as her manager and in future would be taking care of her own bookings and living-arrangements.

More than a week passed before she received a reply. During this time she avoided any contact with Tom and continued to live in an attic on the floor above Levic's rooms. It was a cosy retreat but the rent, though modest, was more than she could afford because Tom had always taken charge of her earnings. When she mentioned this to Levic, he assured her that he was only too happy to provide for her needs for the forseeable future.

It was a strange existence. She was so used to working hard – sewing her costumes, practising on the rope, giving performances – that, suddenly to find herself unoccupied was unnerving. She was tearful and felt afraid, altogether unlike her normal self.

'It's the shock,' Levic said. 'You must just take it easy and allow yourself time to recover. But I am sure that, when you have come to terms with what has happened, you will see it is all for the best.'

She wanted to be convinced by his words but it was impossible to believe everything was for the best once her father's second letter arrived. It might have come from a stranger for all the understanding it showed, except that a stranger would not have known how to wound her so deeply. It was cold, angry and to the point. He did not believe her when she said she had done nothing to be ashamed of. All the family were disgusted by her conduct and did not want to hear from her again until she was prepared to mend her ways.

'This can't be happening for the best, Levic. He's so angry, and all over nothing. I'll have to go down there and make them understand that I'm not a fallen woman. Oh, I could murder Tom for causing this upset.'

'What do you mean by a "fallen woman", Mirella?'

She stared at him in astonishment.

'You know what I mean. Someone who has done what she shouldn't.'

Levic was sitting in his armchair smiling quizzically, obviously waiting for her to go on with her explanation, but she was suddenly overcome with embarrassment.

'Done what she shouldn't?' he prompted.

'Oh, you know full well what I mean. Let a man have his way with her,' she said, feeling herself blush.

'And that is something she shouldn't do?'

'No. Well . . . It's obviously something she shouldn't do before she gets married.'

'Obviously?'

'Levic, you don't think it's right for, well . . . that sort of thing to happen before someone gets wed, do you?' She was looking at him sharply now to see if he was teasing. It was hard to imagine how anyone could seriously hold a different view on such a subject.

'I think it could be, yes. When two people love each

other, they should not need a piece of paper to sanc-
tion that love. They should know they are bigger than
rules made by other people. I mean, I don't need a
policeman to make sure I don't take another man's
watch. Why do I need a clergyman to tell me which
woman I may love?'

'But what about children, Levic? If people stopped
getting married and . . . well, lived together as man
and wife . . . there might still be children and that
would be terrible.'

'Would it, Mirella? Would it be so terrible for children to have a father and mother who loved each
other so much they didn't need a document to hold
them together?'

'No, not when you put it like that. But, on the other
hand, I don't see what's wrong with getting married if
you really love someone. I mean, surely you'd want to
promise to be faithful to them all your life.'

'Yes, but there is no need to turn that promise into a
bargain. It seems to me that most marriages are no
more than bargains. You let me love you and in return
I'll make you my legal wife, and that means I shall
have to stay with you for ever even if our love should
die. To me that sort of bargaining makes love sordid.'

'But what would you have people do, if their love
should die, Levic?'

'To be honest, I do not know, Mirella. I just do not
think that chaining people together makes it easy for
love to thrive.'

'But most people are happy to be married,' she
objected.

'Most people are happy to be chained,' he retorted,
'because freedom is uncomfortable. It means living
on the edge and taking nothing for granted. But then,
you know all about that, Mirella. Most people would
never dream of walking on a tightrope.'

'Yes, I see what you mean.' She continued to think
over what he had been saying until something else

occurred to her. 'But as a woman, I find it a lot easier to walk a tightrope than to fall.'

He started to laugh, getting up and coming over to where she was sitting on the other side of the fire, taking her head in his hands and tousling her hair.

'Oh, Mirella, give it time. I do love you so much. Just give it time.'

That night they slept together. Outside the streets were yellow with fog and they had sat in all evening discussing future plans. Levic's agent had fixed up a tour of the provinces due to start in a couple of weeks' time. He would be mostly playing in permanent circus buildings and it should be possible, Levic thought, to secure bookings for Mirella so that she could accompany him and be billed on the same programmes.

'Would you like that? Or do you have any other ideas about what you will do?'

'No, that sounds marvellous. I must get back to work quickly before I lose my nerve. Besides, I need to earn some money.'

'I have told you, that is not important.'

'Yes, it is. You're being very generous, but I need to be independent again. It doesn't feel right to have you paying my bills.'

'Well, think of it this way. I regard it as my contribution to art. Some people buy paintings. Others patronise poets. I like to support pretty rope-dancers. Well, just one in particular, because I am very discerning.'

'If you really mean that, what this particular rope-dancer needs most to support her at the moment is – a rope. Have you thought of that? If I'm to go with you up north, I shall need to buy a new rope as soon as possible and get a couple of poles made up because, much as it grieves me to admit the fact, I don't think Tom will let me have my gear back again.'

'No, and I should not like to think of you going to ask him for it. But that is no problem. Tomorrow we

308

shall visit Messrs Frost Brothers, order a brand new rope, and take care of all those other little details.'

She sighed. 'Levic, you make everything sound so easy.'

'But it is. Where is there a problem? You and I, we shall take the road together soon. We have our work. We have each other. What else is there to worry about?'

He picked up a poker and prodded the fire into brighter life. As soon as he finished, Mirella rose from her chair and knelt on the floor in front of the flames.

'I don't know. I just wish I could make things better with my father. I don't like to think of him so unhappy.'

'Let him go, Mirella. He is prepared to let you go. He said as much in his letter.'

'Yes, he did, didn't he? Said none of the family would have anything more to do with me. Well, I know my mother wrote me off years ago, so that means I'm really out on my own now. But I don't care. I'm used to it. I'm always on my own when I'm walking my rope, and, do you know? I'm always happiest then. That's why I do it.'

She felt herself growing dreamy as she carried on staring into the fire. A log fell, scattering sparks. She felt Levic's hand stroking her hair. She sank back against his chair, resting her head on his knee, but keeping her gaze still fixed on the flames. There was a fiery cavern opening up among the cinders, gleaming amber and gold. The tips of Levic's fingers touched her ear and she arched back her head. He continued gently to stroke her ear whilst in the heart of the fire flames like salamanders crept towards the mouth of the cavern. Levic's face leaned down and his lips sought hers and soon they were kneeling together on the floor and she forgot the fire and became lost in his warmth.

'Mirella, I do love you,' he whispered. 'I've never

309

felt like this about anyone before. Do you love me?'

'Oh, yes.'

'I want you, Mirella. I want you to be mine, my wife, my love.'

'And no bargaining?' she murmured.

'No, no need to bargain. We can get married, if you wish. Anything. I don't mind as long as you love me.'

'I do love you, Levic. I always have and I always will.'

He kissed her, and she was glad when he whispered, 'Don't go to your room tonight. Stay with me.'

Chapter Twenty

Touring round the provincial theatres and circuses with Levic was so different from the wearisome experience she had endured the year before with Tom. She was in love with Levic and being with him cast a golden glow over everything she did. Moreover, they stayed much longer in each place because, once the Management saw how Levic the Clown drew in the crowds, they were reluctant to let him go.

Although she missed the atmosphere of the tenting circus, Mirella was quick to concede that permanent structures had their compensating charms. For instance, they were not so subject to "blowdowns", even if, being built usually of wood, they were prone to destruction by fire. Most of them followed the same design: a single tier of boxes, a pit running round the circle on which the players performed, and a gallery behind the pit, separated from it by a grating, which made those sitting in the "gods" look like the wild beasts in Cross's Menagerie. There was no proper orchestra space, the musicians having to sit in a stage box on either side.

It was a strange feeling to move from one town to another perhaps thirty miles away, and come across another building which on the outside was just like the one they had left behind. As if a fleet of ancient ships had been disbanded and kept beaching up miles inland, some of their hulks to stay for years and years, others to be consumed by fire or simply collapse from bad debts or bad workmanship within a couple of seasons.

They arrived at one of these supposedly permanent buildings in the middle of a performance which was being given in the semi-darkness and slid into the nearest two empty seats.

'It's a good audience for a Tuesday night,' she murmured to Levic, after glancing around. 'It's packed out at the back.'

Levic looked around as well, and then started to chuckle. She did not discover why until the lights went up and she saw that behind them the seats were empty as far back as the walls – which had been painted to resemble a large gallery occupied by a capacity crowd!

'Don't worry, it will be a different story next week. Then this hall will be so crowded, those poor people at the back will be straining themselves off their wall trying to see you properly.'

The tour lasted from February until early summer and during all this time they lived out of portmanteaux and packing cases that were shifted for them from one hotel to another. Only at the very beginning, when they arrived at Cambridge and booked into a hotel for the first time as man and wife, did Mirella have qualms about what she was doing. But no one else looked askance. After all, they were theatrical folk and expected to live in a bohemian way. As Levic the Clown and La Petite Blondin theirs was a fantastical world where the ordinary moral writ did not run.

'Of course, you realise, don't you, that we would be treated very differently if we were living in the days of Good Queen Bess?' Levic told her.

'I suppose so. People were very fond of travelling players then, weren't they?' she said, aware that her knowledge of history was hazy.

'No, I am afraid not. They loathed strangers like us

312

coming into their neighbourhood. They'd have been screaming, "Mother, take in your clothes, the show-folk are coming!" as soon as they got wind we were anywhere near.'

'Well, of course it's still like that if you travel the roads. I've had some very odd remarks from gorgios when I've arrived anywhere in my wagon, and I've heard my mother tell how badly her family were often treated in the past. I suppose people are scared of anyone who's a bit different.'

'That's right. They feel threatened by anyone out of the ordinary.'

'Not us, though. We're respectable, you and I,' she grinned. 'People's washing-lines are quite safe from us.'

'Yes, except that for some people respectability stretches beyond their washing-lines and for them you and I will always be classed among the "ruffians, blasphemers, rogues and vagabonds", Mirella.'

'Good. They sound like excellent company to me.'

Of course she did not mean exactly what she said. Her words were simply an expression of happiness. And she was happy because she was living with Levic. Even if sometimes her mood was clouded by memories of past hurts, she had only to remind herself that she was now living with Levic for those clouds immediately to disperse.

Besides, there was simply no time for brooding. Her own work demanded constant practice. With Levic's help she was perfecting some new acrobatic tricks on the high rope and was almost ready to include a headstand and backward somersault in her act. They had also worked out a comic routine together, similar to the one she had first seen him perform with Blondin at Crystal Palace.

They worked together, lived together, slept together and she loved him. Yet, sometimes, seeing him in the circle, holding the audience in thrall, she had the disturbing impression that he was still a stranger to her. Standing at the back of one of the stage boxes and peering over the heads of the musicians, she would watch as the crowd hung on his every word and gesture, laughed as he lifted an eyebrow, gasped with shock or dismay as he hurtled as if by accident from a trapeze only to be caught by a noose tied round his ankle and swing upside down with his nose a few inches from the floor. The crowd would laugh and cheer as Levic the Clown pulled himself to rights and stumbled into the next antic. Unlike other performers – the equestrians, the strong man, the juggler, the acrobats – he never paused to acknowledge applause. He retained his solemnity throughout and never once wore the performer's smile.

'Levic, why don't you ever smile when you're performing?' she asked him. 'That was almost one of the first things I was taught: always wear the performer's smile when you're in the circle.'

'But you're not a clown.'

'No, but you'd think a clown would smile more than other people, not less.'

'Ah, no. That is not the nature of the clown. Think what it is that is smiling when you are performing. It is not Mirella, is it? It is the art of ropewalking. The art itself is smiling at the image of its own perfection.'

'Only if I manage to do it perfectly.'

'No, it is nothing to do with how well or badly you have just performed. You are the muddy pool in which the art is seeing its own reflection, and it is that reflection that enchants it and makes it smile.'

'So doesn't the art of the clown find itself equally enchanting?' she asked, as Levic stood in front of her looking deadly serious.

'No. Sadly, the art of the clown is always disenchanted with itself. That is its tragedy and why the clown never smiles,' he said so lugubriously that she could no longer tell whether he was being serious, or not. Then, when she thought about it, she did not know whether any of the conversation had been meant seriously, and she had the uncomfortable feeling that part of Levic was still on stage and she no nearer to him than any other person in his audience.

But it was not like that in bed, lying close together, bodies intertwined, mingling warmth with warmth. Levic . . . only Levic then . . . once the clown disappeared.

Levic the Clown, she had come to realise, knew all the answers. He *had* to know all the answers. Life for him was not possible else. He could not see any edge in this world without needing to walk on it. So, if some antic or trick presented itself to his mind, he had to perfect it for performance and all his energies were bent to this end. That is what made him such a wonderful entertainer: he never simply went through a well-worn routine but was always trying something new, or a new way of doing something old, which might push him closer to the edge of perfection.

But at night when they lay together the mask came off and he was different. No longer out on the edge, but back in the centre of the circle. And usually exhausted. Too tired to search out the last smears of greasepaint and rub them off. Collapsing back on to the bed, eyes shut, his body drained. And she would check the fire, put out the lamp and climb in beside him.

'Goodnight, Levic.'

'Goodnight, my love. Come on, let me cuddle you.'

Her head turning towards his, their faces touching. His arm stretching under and around her, pulling her closer. Tips of his fingers stroking her neck and her arm and her breast, gently caressing until she felt herself rising on a tide of longing for him. And he coming to her and satisfying that longing. And at length them both sinking back tired and happy and restored.

*   *   *

315

'Levic, thinking ahead to the summer, I'd like to get a few open air engagements, if I can. I thought of approaching Leeds Royal Park or Aston Park. Or the Arboretum at Worcester – they definitely wanted me back on a return visit and I'd like to do that. What do you think?'

'I'm not sure, Mirella. We are fixed up to travel with Sanger's for the season.'

'I know and I realise that's a full-time commitment for you, but I thought I could fit in the odd weekend engagement elsewhere. It would mean big money and it's what I really want to do, because I need to walk in the sky every so often. That circus tent will get too stifling if I have to work in it all summer.'

'You mean you'll go off on your own to do these weekends?'

'Yes. I'll need someone to help with the gear, of course, but I'll manage the rest on my own if you can't come. Why, what's wrong with that?' She was surprised to see a sudden look of pain cross Levic's face.

'Nothing. Of course you must do what you want and I should be the last person in the world to stop you.'

'All right, then. I'll see what I can get fixed up.'

With the help of Levic's agent, she wrote round to the most likely venues and secured positive results from all but one. The Manager of the Arboretum in Worcester replied that he had already confirmed his booking with Mr Granger who was bringing La Petite Blondin to perform at a special function in the gardens in late September and so he could not understand why the young lady in question was herself approaching him for another engagement this year.

'The swine! You see what this means, Levic? Tom has got himself a job as another ropewalker's manager and is cashing in on my reputation to get her good engagements. Of all the cheek! And I bet he's using my gear as well!'

316

'It happens all the time in this business. Don't worry about it. Just be thankful it is not you who has to put up with his tyranny any more.'

As soon as her anger had cooled, she realised that Levic was right, of course. She felt a sense of relief that Tom had found someone else, hopefully more able than her to cope with his moods. Even, perhaps, able to provide the sort of emotional involvement that as his niece she could never offer.

'I wonder who it is he's got working with him?' she mused. Although she had not set eyes on him since leaving the Agricultural Hall, she heard a rumour that he had gone back to work for a travelling menagerie, believed to be the one now owned by Max and Lily Wombell. 'Surely it's not Lily. She did sometimes do a bit of ropewalking on the parade, but she never showed any inclination to take it up in a big way. Oh dear, I hope it's not Lily. She's always been trouble as far as Tom's concerned.'

This time when they joined up with Sanger's after Easter, they were supplied with their own living-wagon – which was bliss. And there were no snide remarks from the company. Everyone accepted her as Levic's wife.

Once or twice in previous months she and Levic had discussed the question of getting married and more or less decided to do it. At Preston he had returned from the town one day and presented her with a gold ring set with garnets and pearls and, slipping it on to her finger, kissed her and said, 'I want you to marry me soon, my love. It's not right that you don't have your marriage lines. For a woman these things must feel important.'

She had murmured, 'No, not really. I mean, yes, let's get married, if you wish. It will make it legal, but no more binding than it is already as far as I'm concerned.'

317

'Of course that goes for me as well, but I just want you to know that, well . . . after all I said about marriage being irrelevant, I have no objection to it now if it would make you happier.'

'Levic, nothing could make me any happier than I am.'

'Yes, looking at you, I can see you really mean that and it makes me nervous. Supporting another's happiness is a big responsibility.'

'Don't worry. *You* are my happiness, so all you have to do is support yourself. And carry on buying me beautiful rings,' she added as an afterthought.

'Mercenary creature,' he scowled. 'But make sure you wear my ring when you go off on these weekend jaunts you are so busy arranging. I do not want there to be any misunderstanding about your status.'

'You mean I must remember whose possession I am,' she teased.

'That's right,' he said solemnly.

Her first weekend "jaunt" was an engagement to walk a rope suspended forty feet above Aston Park. In the train on her way to Birmingham to prepare for the event, she sat fingering her ring and thinking about Levic.

She could not understand some of his attitudes. One moment he was preaching against marriage and declaring it a travesty of love. The next he was instructing her on how, in his absence, she must comport herself in order not to attract unwanted attentions from licentious gentlemen. Yes, he had actually used those words! Dear Levic. When it came to personal freedom, it seemed that he had one law for himself and quite another for the rest of humanity. Or was it one law for Adam but another for Eve?

Still, it was nice to think he did worry about her. Although it was odd that he seemed more worried about her being pestered by some libertine than by

318

any thought that she could be seriously injured or even killed in a fall. Mind you, he had desperately wanted to come with her this weekend and he probably harboured fears for her physical safety that he chose not to voice. In the circumstances that was understandable. Aston Park had an infamous reputation when it came to Female Blondins. It was the place where, because of a faulty rope, Madame Genevieve had plunged to her death seven years ago and that was why the Park Company was being extra careful now; why in order to get this engagement Mirella had had to contract to use a brand new rope supplied for the occasion and let them provide a safety-net for her as well.

Still, at least she would be walking in the open air again and that was what she yearned to do – so long as no strong winds blew and it did not rain, she thought, remembering that near-disaster at Leeds last year. The thing was, she had to prove to herself that she had not lost her nerve for these big outdoor performances before she committed herself to the Thames Walk in August. That, if she succeeded in doing it, would establish her as one of the foremost performers in the country. But if she failed, there could hardly be a more public disgrace. It would be so well advertised. Thousands would line the banks to watch. If she failed – well, it didn't bear thinking about. She would never be able to look Levic in the face again.

That's stupid, he would be the first to comfort me, she thought, but still she was tormented by a nagging doubt. Levic did put such tremendous store by professional excellence, and hated to let the public down. Sometimes, if she was in a mood to find fault, she felt he was too dedicated to his calling – but then, she could say the same of herself. It was lucky there was no conflict between their professional and personal lives. She wondered what would happen if either of them was ever faced with a choice between the two.

* * *

'I don't like to say it, but the poor creature's husband
was entirely to blame for her death. He was responsible for putting up the rope and he should have
known that if he'd been using it for two years,
hanging it out in all weathers, it could well be rotted
through the middle.'

Mr Banks of the Park Company stopped speaking
and peered at her anxiously. 'But fancy you asking me
about it just now, Ma'am. I'd have thought it was the
last thing you'd want to hear discussed before
embarking on the same sort of exploit yourself.'

'No, it doesn't affect me like that. I know I shan't
fall. But I've always been curious about Madame
Genevieve. She was such a great rope-dancer, and I've
never met anyone before who saw what went wrong
that day.'

She was standing in Aston Park whose Superintendent had just taken her on a tour of inspection so
that she could check the positioning of her rope and
make sure that everything was in place for her appearance the following day. Everything was fine – except
for the Superintendent, who was quite jittery about
the event. Once they got talking it was obvious why.
He had been present on that day when Madame
Genevieve had fallen.

'Well, I'll tell you as I remember it,' he began, as if
repeating a story he had told many times before. 'She
stepped out on to that rope smiling as if she hadn't a
care in the world. She went halfway along and then
she went back and fixed some chains round her ankles
and wrists . . . You don't do that trick, do you?'

Mirella shook her head.

'Well, Madame Genevieve did, and she walked the
whole length of the rope lumbered down with these
chains, and no problem at all. Then next, she ties this
pocket handkerchief over her eyes and pulls a sack
over her head and starts out again. And the crowd

320

were all cheering – it's terrible when you think about it – everyone was cheering that poor woman on, and she hadn't taken more than three or four steps from the platform when she went down—' he snapped his fingers '—just like that.'

'Because the rope had broken,' Mirella prompted, determined to find out as much as she could.

'Yes. The rope gave way all right. One moment she was up there, forty feet high. And the next, lying on the ground crushed and shattered.'

Mirella felt herself shudder. 'She died immediately, then?'

'Yes. The coroner said she probably fainted as soon as the rope gave way, because her face was so serene she couldn't have known what was happening to her.'

She considered that for a moment, from her own experience finding it hard to believe. Then she spoke quickly, in case the Superintendent thought she was scared by what he had said.

'Have no fear. That is not going to happen to me. My agent and I will both be checking that rope and I shall know exactly what I'm doing when I'm up there.'

'Yes, I'm sure you will. Besides, you're obviously not in the same unhappy condition as Madame Genevieve.' He was smiling but his glance had just swept over her body making her feel most uncomfortable.

'What do you mean?'

'When she fell, she was six months gone with child. Which made it a double tragedy. Still, like I said, it was all the fault of the husband for making her use that dodgy rope and letting her walk at all in that condition – if you'll excuse such coarse talk, Ma'am. But then, you did want to hear the whole story.'

She gave two performances the next day: one in the afternoon, and one in the evening accompanied by a spectacular display of fireworks. Despite the sad precedent, maybe because everyone was taking so much care to avoid any further disaster, the whole thing went off without a hitch, and afterwards she felt that the experiment had proved such a success, she was ready to tackle anything, including the walk across the Thames.

Nevertheless, as she sat on the train going home to Levic, her mood was not jubilant. She was haunted by the picture of a woman's body lying crumpled on the ground. Although it was hard to accept that a similar fate might one day lie in store for her, she thought she had come to terms with that possibility. However, what struck fear into her heart now was the image of a poor body lying crumpled on the ground and the realisation that it contained the crushed remains of a tiny child.

Chapter Twenty-One

'There! You must agree, that is a magnificent sight.'
Levic squeezed her arm and she turned her eyes to
gaze again up river.

'Yes. I had no idea it would look so impressive from
this distance.'

In fact, her tightrope stretching across the Thames
from Cremorne to Battersea dominated the horizon,
making her feel strangely remote from everything else
around her. Almost as if she was walking it already.
Which was a pity really, because there was so much
else worthy of attention in this pretty village of
Chelsea.

They had arrived, she and Levic, a couple of days
ago and rented rooms in Cheyne Walk so that they
could be on the spot to check all the equipment when
it arrived at Cremorne. They had witnessed all the
commotion as the huge trestles were being erected and
the cable hauled up and tightened until it looked like
some gigantic empty washing-line strung across the
Thames. But this morning, having seen the last lead-
weighted guy-ropes dropped into place, they had
turned their backs on the scene and wandered down to
the Magpie and Stump for some lunch. After which
they had strolled on towards the Cadogan Pier and
now stood, pausing in the shade of an old pollarded
elm, to glance once more upriver.

It was a fine afternoon, although a little cool for

August, and she was apprehensive about the breeze that was allowing the windmills over the other side of the river to work so well. Still, it's an ill wind that blows no one any good and the millers over there must be pleased, she thought.

'What is that place over there in front of the windmills?' she asked Levic.

'That's Battersea Park,' he replied. 'And you can see Battersea Church in the distance, and just beyond the rope Battersea Bridge.'

'Yes, it's an odd-looking old bridge, isn't it?' she murmured, thinking how when they had crossed its primitive wooden structure yesterday, she had wondered what it would make of the flimsy hempen rival about to appear as its neighbour.

'Are you nervous about tomorrow?' Levic asked.

'No, not really nervous. Excited, I think.'

'You're not worried about this wind?'

'No. It's not a wind. Just a breeze which hopefully will have blown itself out by tomorrow.'

'Well, if it has not, I think we shall postpone your walk.'

'What, and let all the spectators down?' she asked.

'If necessary, yes. Your safety comes first, my love.'

It was reassuring to hear him say it, even though she knew it would take a hurricane to persuade her to give up this big adventure now.

'There's an awful lot of people here today just watching the rope being put up,' she observed. 'Goodness knows how many will come tomorrow to watch the actual walk.'

'Thousands and thousands, to judge by the publicity given to it by the Cremorne Gardens management. Mind you, these folk you see around today are mostly locals. Chelsea is always a bustling sort of place.'

She could well believe that, listening to coalheavers yelling as they loaded up at the wharves and the shouts from the billyboys as they tied up at the draw-dock opposite to unload their bricks and paving stones.

'Oh, look at those poor horses, Levic. Those heavy loads are too much for some of them.'

She flinched as she watched five or six cart-horses above their hocks in water struggling to drag the heavy loads ashore and in constant danger of slipping back into the water and being drowned. She looked up at Levic to see why he was not answering and found that something way beyond the horses had caught his attention.

'Do you see what I see?' he asked.

Her gaze followed his to the horizon beyond the far bank, and she smiled.

Out beyond the windmills in Battersea you could see the heights of Clapham, and beyond that again in the far distance, gleaming in the sunlight on Sydenham Hill, was a glass building.

'Crystal Palace,' she breathed. 'That has to be a good omen, Levic. And just think, I shall have an even better view of it tomorrow when I'm on the rope.'

'I am afraid not, my love. You will have your back to it. You're starting at the Battersea end, remember.'

'Of course I remember. I've got it marked on a map in case I get lost on my way to Cremorne,' she teased. 'But what I might do is turn around in the middle so that I can take in the view behind me.'

'Don't you dare, Mirella. Think of me left on terra firma, please, and do what you have been contracted to do without trying to be too clever.'

'It sounds as if you're getting more nervous than me, Levic.'

'Not nervous, Mirella, just naturally concerned about your safety. I cannot help . . . well, now is not the time to discuss such things, but afterwards maybe, you and I, we will sit quietly and talk about this, yes?'

She agreed without being at all clear what he was asking of her for her attention had wandered upstream again and anchored itself on the slender rope swaying in the breeze high above the river.

The event had been massively advertised with placards announcing that Cremorne Gardens could be reached from all parts of town by omnibus for sixpence or boat for fourpence. The following day thousands took advantage of both forms of transport. Although her walk was not scheduled to start until five o'clock the banks were lined with people hours beforehand and the din was indescribable. Omnibuses and carriages rattling over the cobbles; drivers cussing their horses; street vendors screaming; Italian organ grinders; and the river teeming with small craft, some already safely moored, others still jockeying for position and looking dangerously overloaded with spectators. So much noise that she longed to be miles away, or above it all up there enjoying the silence of her rope.

Fortunately there was less of a breeze blowing today and when she mounted the low platform from which she was to make her start, the prospect was incredibly exciting. She had not been able to rehearse this because it would have been too public and detract from the actual display. But what excited her was not walking above water but walking such a distance without interruption. She had been discussing the prospect with Levic last evening. Filled with a restlessness that forced her outside, they had taken an evening stroll along the river bank. Watching the hay boats with their red sails reflected in the darkening water and Battersea Bridge lit by gas seeming to float in the misty light, Levic had cautioned her against euphoria.

'Sometimes,' he said, 'when you are practising on your rope, you get such a faraway look in your eyes that I fear for you. What you are doing requires total

concentration, Mirella, you cannot afford to
dream up there. For my sake, you must not take risks.
Promise me.'

'There is no conflict, Levic. I do what I do, and you
are always part of that – which is why I love you, and
in a funny sort of way, how I show you my love.'

'Yes, I can understand that,' he muttered, sounding a little impatient. 'When I work too, it is for you
above all others. But when you put yourself in danger,
Mirella – I can't stand that.'

'I put myself in more danger when I fell in love with
you,' she joked. 'Compared with that, rope-dancing
is a walkover.'

She was standing on the low platform now, looking
up at the steep incline of rope which she would have to
mount in order to reach the trestle from which the
rope stretched straight across the middle of the river
to a second trestle before starting its descent to the
bank on the Cremorne side. The crowd fell silent as
she picked up her pole and stood minutely shifting its
weight from hand to hand until she was happy with its
balance. A turn and a wave to the spectators, and an
instinctive glance towards the other river bank where
Levic waited to greet her as she stepped ashore. It did
not matter that she could not see him from this distance. Knowing that he was there waiting for her was
all she cared about.

The feel of the rope pressing into the furrow of her
foot and now she had set out to climb the first section.
The crowd's roar slapping against her head but she,
refusing to be diverted, rising above it, all her attention fixed on that yellow-painted post on top of the
trestle that was her first marker.

Boats below. Something of a comfort, but more of
an intrusion really. She did not need them there. Preferred, when she did glance down, to see the black
water silently swirling below. Most of the time, however, looking neither up nor down but straight ahead,

327

watching the yellow post move slowly to meet her.

Ah, there now. She had reached the first trestle and paused to contemplate the long straight stretch ahead, lining up the rope with the next marker. Then, stepping out again with no need to hurry. There was all the time in the world and she would be there in no time at all, because time did not exist up here on the rope. A glance to the left showed her a row of heads on Battersea Bridge. She smiled. She had swung into her step now, her movements virtually taking on a life of their own. She was floating along the rope, mesmerised by the sighting point. Travelling alone through the universe, being drawn to her proper destination. And there was no need for her to concentrate on keeping her balance or taking the right steps. All that was necessary was to listen inwardly to that certain something inside her which had everything under control.

No, surely she could not already be at the second trestle? She did not want to reach it yet. She was only just beginning to feel in her element; wanted to continue gliding through the sky. She was not ready to go down yet.

She had been prepared for so many things to go wrong. When the Female Blondin made this same crossing nearly ten years ago, one of her guy-ropes came adrift and the main rope began to sway so wildly that the poor woman stood marooned, unable to proceed or retreat, for more than half an hour before ditching her pole and swinging herself down to a rescue boat.

Of course many people maintained that the whole thing had been staged as a publicity stunt and, indeed, when the lady made her second attempt a week later, twice as many spectators were there to applaud her success. However, Mirella heard a very different explanation. Evidently the earlier disaster had been caused by the guy-ropes being cut by some villain out to steal the lead weights. To avoid any repetition of the crime, nightwatchmen had been hired this time to stand guard.

Nevertheless, Mirella was still amazed that nothing else had gone wrong. No rain, no sudden gusts of wind, no backwash from a steamer that might have rocked the rope. And now that she was standing poised on the second trestle, about to start her long descent, she felt almost cheated. Maybe she should turn and go back to the centre and kneel or lie down, do a one-knee balance or a headstand. She really felt she had not done enough to justify the presence of all those people out there watching her. Still, she quickly reminded herself, that was the point of the exercise. Now that they had seen her cross the Thames they would pay to follow her into the Cremorne Gardens where tonight she would walk again and perform all manner of tricks amidst a spectacular firework display.

As far as she was concerned, though, her moments of glory had passed. She had known ecstasy whilst walking that long stretch above the water and selfishly would like to have walked on and on forever. But already it was over. People were calling her. She waved to them. Half turned and waved back to those left behind on the Battersea side, and then began her descent towards Cremorne.

'Levic, I couldn't possibly think of giving up ropewalking! It's my life.'

'And it might cost you your life, think of that.'

'I've thought of that, naturally. But what else would I do if I didn't walk the rope? Singing and dancing and a few acrobatics? I'd find no satisfaction in that.'

'You are not required to do anything, Mirella. I earn more than enough money to keep us both.'

'But it's not the money! I keep trying to explain that to you. It's the excitement, I suppose. I just love doing my work. I'm good at it, and that gives me a sense of satisfaction.'

'Yes, I know you are good at it – which is why you have so many admirers. These chaps who keep sending you flowers and jewellery – it is not respectable for a woman to be the object of such attention.'

'Oh, nonsense, Levic! They mean no harm, and none of them has ever made a nuisance of himself. You know it's all completely innocent.'

'It may be innocent, but it is not necessary. You have a man who is devoted to you. Why do you seek other people's admiration all the time?'

'I don't seek it. I don't even encourage it. Besides, admiration is not dangerous, and this argument started with your worrying about my taking risks. Now it sounds as if you're just jealous.'

Naturally Levic protested that this was ridiculous, that jealousy had never been part of his nature, that he had only her interests at heart. Yet every time he raised the subject – and he had brought it up several times since her walk over the Thames a month ago – she failed to understand his objections to her rope-walking. When they worked her act together in the circus, he took at least as many risks as she did on the high rope. He also clowned his way through a complicated trapeze routine and did equestrian tricks that were dangerous. Outside, too, she had seen him take tremendous risks when pulling the tent down in a storm or confronting ruffians who were causing havoc on the tober.

'Will you give up doing these things because I find them frightening?' she asked.

'Of course not. I am a man. It is different when I take risks.'

She might have accepted this attitude if she had been with child, but since the only life she was putting at risk was her own she felt Levic was not justified in trying to restrict her freedom. And as for the little

330

coterie of admirers which had formed after her Thames Walk, it was ridiculous for Levic to be jealous of any of them. They were simply a set of young toffs who always turned up at her performances and vied with each other in showing their devotion. Apart from invading the ring to present her with the usual flowers and jewellery, one or two of them even turned up armed with their own box of rosin ready to rush forward to anoint her shoes should this be necessary. Their antics were silly but, as she said to Levic, rather charming and quite harmless.

Her last solo engagement of the season was at Malvern in late September and she was pleased when Levic took time off from the circus to accompany her. Originally the organisers had hoped to stage the event on top of the Malvern Hills, but it proved too difficult to stretch the cable from one crest to another. There was also the problem of ensuring that spectators paid to watch the performance, so the venue was transferred to a field at Pickersleigh which could effectively be screened by a canvas wall. According to the poster, admission rates would reflect class. Gentlemen were to be charged one shilling, labourers sixpence, and children threepence.

Arriving at Great Malvern station on a Tuesday, forty-eight hours before the performance was due to take place, Mirella looked up at the hills and regretted the change in venue.

'Look, Levic, wouldn't it have been marvellous to walk up there among the clouds?'

'I am sure we can,' he said, his eyes following her gaze.

'No. On a rope, I mean.'

'That I cannot manage. But those hills in themselves look inviting enough, so if you'll be content to walk on grass like any other mortal, I suggest we climb them together on Friday before going home.'

'Yes. Let's do that.'

After settling themselves into their room at the Foley Arms, they ate lunch and drove to Pickersleigh field where the main masts were already in position about four hundred feet apart. The rope would be put up tomorrow, but she wanted to make sure there were plenty of guy-ropes, pegs and sandbags available.

An enormous crowd was expected despite the rival attraction organised by Tom due to take place at the Arboretum on Saturday. In fact, so many extra trains had been laid on to bring visitors from Worcester and towns on the West Midland and Midland Railways that, to prevent accidents, men were going to be stationed at every curve on the line approaching Malvern to signal any driver whose engine was coming too close to the one in front.

Even though she was told of these arrangements, Mirella was still amazed at the density of the crowd when, at precisely four o'clock on Thursday afternoon, Levic drove her in a carriage and pair to the field. They were greeted by echoing cheers and the Rifle Corps band's rendition of the usual "See the Conquering Hero Comes".

After acknowledging the crowd, she took off her cloak and climbed on to the perch that was to hoist her to the platform seventy feet up. Once there, she was determined not to rush anything. This was her last open air performance this season. She wanted to enjoy it to the full.

It pleased her to think that from up here class was irrelevant and no matter what anyone had paid for admission, they had become just one of those upturned faces seeing the same as everyone else. Also from up here, she could look over the canvas walls and see little groups of people who had gathered on rising ground further afield to catch a free glimpse of the proceedings. She waved gaily to them, before lifting up her eyes to the purple-blue and green hills which seemed to be nudging their way nearer to watch her performance too.

In contrast to her Thames crossing, this time she had to start by walking downhill because it had proved impossible completely to tighten the rope and it hung in a curve. When she was roughly one third of the way along, she stood for some time on one leg, then sat down, and then lay down on her back with her pole across her chest. After standing up again, she danced to the middle of the rope and stood on her head, beating her feet together. Next she lay down on her back apparently to go to sleep and, whilst she lay at ease, placed her pole across the rope beyond her head so that it nearly balanced itself, but remained ready, whenever it seemed about to tip over, to throw her hand behind her head to steady it.

From the ground she would appear to be resting but actually she was preparing herself for the most difficult part of her act. When the moment was right, she leapt into action, caught hold of the pole, flung herself from her back, heels overhead, and landed on her feet on the rope.

A huge roar of applause greeted this trick. Then she ran to the south end of the rope, pulled a sack over her head and went through the blindfold part of her routine. Having lodged her pole in its special niche on the platform, she had a proper rest after this before embarking on the last part of the performance which was more in the nature of a trapeze act really, since she hung from the rope by her hands, then by one hand, pulled herself up, lay across the rope as if swimming, and then swung from her legs.

Now she had finished and was able to swing herself happily down, but her feet were not allowed to touch the ground because as soon as she came within reach more than a dozen pairs of hands seized her and carried her shoulder high to the carriage. Her coterie of admirers was here in force, swooning with admiration, throwing bouquets into her lap, smothering her hands with kisses, preventing the carriage from moving towards the gate.

'Come on, you idiots, let her go. She's given you enough. Can't you see she's tired?' Levic roared. Nobody took any notice.

'I said, leave her alone now. She needs some rest,' he thundered. And he was right. After her exertions, Mirella was almost dazed with exhaustion and desperate to sit down in peace and quiet to recover. However, no matter how tired she felt, she did not want Levic to rescue her in the way he did. Like an angry god, he raised his arm and, heedless of the young men clinging to the carriage, cracked his whip over the horses' backs, startling them into a gallop and driving them furiously back to the hotel.

'You shouldn't have done that back at the field, Levic,' she muttered, sinking down on to the bed. 'Someone might have got hurt.'

'Someone undoubtedly would have got hurt if I had stayed there any longer witnessing their stupid antics,' he glowered, his face distorting into one of his circus caricatures, brows sinking over the eyes and mouth turned down. Suddenly she started to giggle. His face looked so funny and she was so exhausted and so excited and so relieved she could not restrain her merriment – even when she saw that Levic was deadly serious.

'I can't see what you find so amusing,' he snorted.

'It's you, you look so funny,' she managed to gasp before collapsing back on the bed and laughing hysterically, her body bouncing up as Levic threw himself down beside her.

She turned to look at him, but his face came too close for her to read its expression, and she closed her eyes as he kissed her. Her breath soughed away, leaving her empty and utterly languid. She felt as if she had melted into some strange creature not quite body, not quite spirit, not quite senseless nor sensible – a creature innocent of any before or after, existing only now.

'Levic,' she whispered, and the sound gave name to what she was feeling. 'Levic,' she whispered again, but this time the sound drowned in his kisses.

This was different from any time before. He did not murmur his love, did not stroke her hair or caress her breasts or fondle her thighs, but came straight for her. Like a stormy ocean battering into a cave, slapping against its walls, demanding passage. And the walls yielding so that he could press on to find her and she, moved by the urgency of his quest, rising to meet him and being borne away on the tide.

Afterwards, still entwined, they sank into sleep.

'Mirella?' His voice, gentle now, woke her up. 'Mirella, are you all right?'

'Yes.'

'I didn't hurt you, did I?'

'Of course not.' She reached out to kiss him, murmuring, 'I love you.'

'And I love you. Too much,' he added.

'Impossible.'

'No, seriously. I begin to wonder about myself, Mirella. That scene when we drove away from the field – that was ridiculous. I begin to behave not quite rationally where you are concerned.'

She was still in her tired, happy daze and only half listening. It was only later that she wished she had made more effort to understand what he was saying.

'You see,' he continued, 'when you are up there performing on that rope, I am in agony lest you fall, and yet you are so happy doing it, I know I must not ask you to give it up for my sake. I have not the right to impose my will on you, but at the same time seeing you go your own way makes me boil inside.'

'Just don't worry about it. I won't fall, I promise you,' she said easily.

'But it is not simply that either. That bunch of wastrels who hang about you, they make me sick as well. I could murder them when they grab at your hands and you allow them to take liberties.'

'Oh, come now, Levic. Not one of them has ever gone further than kissing my hand. Surely you realise that's all part of show business, and it's silly to take it seriously.' She stretched and yawned, feeling deliciously relaxed.

'Yes, I do realise that, which makes my behaviour all the more intolerable. I have to admit how I feel and take steps to curb my jealousy before it does us both harm.' He seemed to be addressing himself more than her, and in any case she was not troubled by any aspect of their relationship. 'So, more independence on my part, that is what is required. I have been growing too soft with myself, Mirella. But just you watch. I shall be guarding myself against such ignoble passions in the future.'

'Dear me, that doesn't sound much like fun,' she teased.

'I was referring merely to my jealousy,' he replied solemnly. 'As far as my nobler passions are concerned, I shall continue as always to give them full rein . . . So, come here!'

Their plan to climb the hills next morning was shelved in favour of breaking their journey home by stopping at Worcester, and they set off by train from Great Malvern after breakfast.

'There was simply no time to see the town properly last time I was there,' she said, wondering if she dared mention her real reason for making the visit. Levic turned his head and peered at her.

'And, if I pay for your entrance to the Arboretum, you would possibly have no objection to watching the Petite Blondin who is impersonating you there this afternoon?'

'Oh dear, is it that obvious? But do you think it would be a mistake to go, Levic? I mean, I

336

couldn't bear to bump into Tom.'

'I don't think that is a problem. He will be too busy to notice us if we stand in the crowd. And I must confess to being curious myself about the sort of act he has got together, especially as some people think it is you who is performing there today.'

'How do you know?'

'A chap at Malvern asked whether you would be repeating exactly the same programme in Worcester on Saturday and, when I told him you were not going to perform there at all, he looked at me as if I was trying to pull a fast one to get rid of extra tickets.'

'You didn't tell me that.'

'No. I did not want to worry you.'

'Why should it worry me?'

'Don't you see, if someone calling herself "La Petite Blondin" starts going around the country giving inferior performances, that could damage your reputation?'

'I hadn't thought of that, but of course you're right. People would book her under the illusion they were getting me and then, if they were disappointed, they would pass the word around and I'd find it difficult to get engagements.'

'Precisely.'

'Right, that settles it. I definitely want to see Lily, or whoever it is, perform and then I shall know what sort of competition I'm up against.'

It felt odd to enter the great iron gates and stroll past the Crimean guns arm in arm with Levic. So much had changed in her life since she was here last and she found herself prattling on about how it had happened that, having arrived here last year as a spectator (just as she was doing now), she had suddenly found herself stepping into dear Blondin's shoes and lifted, almost literally, to fame.

'Just fancy, the same thing might even happen

337

again. Lily could be struck down with lumbago, and the desperate call for a replacement Petite Blondin go out, and it would just so happen that here in the audience there is such another.'

'And would she go and take Lily's place?' Levic asked.

'Not a chance.'

He squeezed her arm and they ambled on until they reached the edge of the crowd.

'Levic, you won't believe this, but I feel more nervous standing here waiting for someone else to walk that rope than I do before one of my own performances.'

'Now you know how I feel, my darling.'

'I wonder what she'll be like, Levic. She might be much better than me and then I shall have to go away and practise really hard to bring my act up to standard.' Levic of course reassured her, as she knew he would, but as the minutes ticked by she felt herself growing more and more nervous and wishing she had not come. It was a relief when the band struck up with the usual overture and a carriage arrived with the artiste and her manager.

'Look, it's Tom,' she whispered unnecessarily. 'Doesn't he look smart?' She and Levic were standing a long way back in the crowd, so could see little of what was happening on the ground. However, when Tom stood up in the carriage, she had a good view of him in his frockcoat and tophat and found herself instantly recoiling.

'He looks very pleased with himself,' Levic observed.

'Yes,' she agreed, remembering the deliberate air of confidence that he breathed all around him when about to present something risky.

'The little girl doesn't look too happy, though,' Levic said. 'She's putting on a brave face but, if you ask me, she's scared stiff.'

Mirella craned her neck to catch a glimpse of her

rival as she stood up and was formally handed out of her carriage. She had a vision of flaxen hair caught up in a topknot laced with red ribbons, a pink satin cloak, and a pale face from which wide-staring eyes gazed unseeing into hers.

'Oh, no. Not you. It can't be,' she blurted out, clutching at Levic's arm and stammering, 'that's Cassie. But she can't go up there. She's not a rope-walker. We must stop her.'

The next forty minutes were the most painful Mirella had ever known. Watching Cassie take off the satin cloak with a flourish and seat herself on the perch ready to be swung up to the rope.

Her Cassie. Her little sister.

She had not heard from her since their father's letter after Christmas, but she could not imagine how in that short time Cassie could have been properly trained to walk the high rope. It must have been Tom who put on the pressure, wheedling her into doing what he wanted.

''Come on, Cassie, what Mirella can do, you can do better, especially with me here to show you how.''

But why on earth did her parents let her do it? Surely they had more sense.

Suddenly she was aware of the dichotomy in her own attitude. Why was she so shocked to see Cassie doing what she herself did? She knew it was not dangerous if you knew what you were doing and were thoroughly trained. But she also knew there was more to it than that. To be safe, you had to *be* a rope-dancer, not just *do* it. And she knew that she herself was a rope-dancer and Cassie was not.

On the other hand, perhaps it was arrogant to think this way and what she was feeling inside was nothing more than plain jealousy.

Up on the platform Cassie was now waving to the crowd. Mirella shut her eyes.

'Would you rather not watch?' Levic whispered. 'We can easily walk away.'

'No. I must stay. But I feel so frightened for her, Levic.'

'She will be all right. Say what you will, Tom is no fool. He would not risk a performance like this unless he knew Cassie was ready for it.'

'Yes, of course you're right. I just can't believe what I'm seeing. If you'd known Cassie when she was little, you'd understand what I mean. She's such a timid creature, Levic. She'll be going through hell up there, I know it.'

Nothing she saw in the next half hour convinced her otherwise. Cassie did not do anything wrong exactly. She walked carefully along the rope forward and backward. She did the blindfold routine and all the usual tricks in a newcomer's repertoire. The crowd loved her and roared their approval. But there was something in her movements, a certain jerky unsureness – the sort of thing that possibly endeared her to most spectators – which caught at Mirella's throat.

'What do you think, Levic?' she asked, hoping he would dispel her fears.

'It is a good performance. Cassie knows what to do and she has been trained well. But I am afraid you are right. She does not like what she has to do and must all the time fight herself to do it. That could be dangerous.'

Chapter Twenty-Two

Mirella picked up her stocking with the intention of darning the hole in its heel, but soon tossed it back into her mending basket and got up to look out of the window. Cassie was late. Her note had said she would be arriving at about ten this morning and it was already nearly half past.

Still, it did not matter what time she got here, as long as she came. Mirella was surprised to find that she was feeling so nervous and kept reminding herself that it was only Cassie who was coming.

Since seeing her a month ago at the Arboretum, she had not been able to get Cassie out of her mind. To find her performing on the high rope was a shock but, as Levic kept pointing out, Cassie was a free individual and Mirella had no right to interfere in her affairs. But to find her working in partnership with Tom, that was really disturbing. Poor little Cassie! She would have had no idea what she was letting herself in for. Tom's half-crazy moods when he had been drinking, his amorous attentions . . . She shuddered, still unable to bear the memory of that time in Crystal Palace when he had pressed his lips on hers.

By the time she and Levic arrived back in his old rooms in Holborn, she was desperate to contact Cassie and decided to send a letter home with a request for it to be forwarded. Fearing that her father would tear it up if he realised who it was from, she asked Levic to address the envelope. While she settled down to wait for a reply, she had several disappointments. She had been expecting to appear at the Aggie again this winter, but her agent was told that the management had already made arrangements with Mr Granger to bring his Petite Blondin act into the hall over the Christmas period. And after that it came as no surprise when their approach to the Crystal Palace elicited the same response. Nevertheless, the Highbury Barn seemed glad to book her for the period leading up to the festive season and, because she received so many requests from outside London, she instructed her agent to fix up a tour of provincial theatres and circuses similar to the one she had made earlier in the year.

The sound of another horse-bus clattering to a halt outside the house drew her to the window again and this time she was not disappointed. There was Cassie, having been helped down the rear steps, standing looking all about her, and Mirella rushed down to greet her before she had time to feel lost.

'Cassie, it's so good to see you! Come along in. We've got rooms on the second floor, a small apartment Levic has used for years as his London base. Oh, I'm so glad you could come.'

'Is he here now?' Cassie asked nervously.

'No, he had to go out on business this morning, but he wanted me to give you his regards and say he's sorry to have missed you this time.'

'Oh.' That was all Cassie said, but Mirella sensed her relief that the two of them were going to be alone to get over the awkwardness of this first meeting after being so long apart.

'So let me take your cape and bonnet, and you sit down by the fire while I ask Mrs Relph to fetch us up some tea.'

Cassie carefully arranged her pink skirt so that it

would not crease and sank down into Levic's low armchair.

'Hmm, this is nice.'

'Does Tom know you've come here today?' Mirella could not resist asking.

'Oh, yes. He'd be furious if I did anything like this without telling him. And of course,' she added, flushing, 'he wasn't very happy about it.'

'No, I bet he wasn't. Still, I'm really glad you've come.'

'Well, I didn't want to come at first. I was too scared.'

'Scared? What, of meeting me?'

'Yes. Well, no, not exactly. I thought you might be annoyed once you found out I was copying you with the rope-dancing.'

'Silly, I wouldn't be annoyed about that. Mind you, I was a bit surprised.'

'Why?'

'I was surprised you'd want to.'

'Why shouldn't I want to?' Cassie said, her mouth beginning to pout. Mirella realised she was getting off on the wrong foot and tried to backtrack.

'No reason really, but what did Ma and Pa think when you first started?'

Cassie pulled a face.

'They didn't think much of it at all, especially Ma. But Tom brought them round. He said *you'd* never had an accident even though you're far more reckless than me. And he told them I've got exactly the right temperament for it.' She paused, leaving Mirella with the uncomfortable feeling that she was supposed to agree with this statement, then continued, 'Anyway, when it all boiled down, there wasn't much they could do to stop me. I certainly wasn't going to sit at home for the rest of my life, and I didn't fancy going into service again. Besides, Tom told me about all the money you earn and how you have rich gentlemen sending you flowers and jewellery. Do they really, Mirella?'

Inwardly she groaned, but tried to suppress any show of impatience, especially when she saw Cassie's eyes shining like they had on Christmas mornings when she was a little girl.

'Yes, I do get nice flowers and things but that's not a good enough reason for doing it. I wouldn't be prepared to risk my life for a bunch of flowers, no matter who they came from. And I do risk my life, you know, every time I step on to that rope.'

Cassie scowled and her cheeks turned pink.

'Look, I know you're just trying to put me off. Tom warned me that's what you'd do, but you won't succeed so you might as well stop trying.'

'But, Cassie, I'm your sister and I don't want you to get hurt . . .'

'I said there's no point in trying to put me off,' Cassie wailed, brushing tears from her eyes. 'I know why you're doing it. You're afraid of the competition. And, let me tell you, Tom thinks I'm already as good as you at rope-dancing. He says he's never known anyone pick it up so quick and that one day I'll probably be the best there's ever been.'

Mirella sighed. There seemed nothing left to say, but she refused to give up without one last try.

'But do you enjoy working on the high rope?'

'Yes, of course I do. I mean, I don't have to be up there too much. I practise on a low rope and I only do the high stuff for performances and, once I get through those, there's all that cheering and applause. So I reckon it's worth going through a bit of strain if the crowd makes me feel like royalty at the end of it.'

'But there are other things you could do, Cassie. You could dance or sing,' Mirella muttered, conscious that someone had once said the same to her, and therefore not surprised when Cassie replied sarcastically: 'And so could you, Mirella, so why aren't you earning your living by dancing or singing?'

Further discussion was useless. Cassie had clearly taken umbrage. So, once tea and muffins appeared, Mirella changed the subject and tried to talk about the family. There was so much she wanted to know. Were Ma and Pa keeping well? Did they ever mention her name and were they still as angry? Above all, did Cassie think there was any chance they would ever forgive her for going against their will?

She put the questions, but Cassie's answers came with reluctance, her tone implying that Mirella had no right to be asking such things, that she had left the family and so shouldn't now be prying into their business. Despite all her efforts to rekindle their old relationship, Mirella was anguished to find that, when it was time for Cassie to go, their parting was less friendly than their greeting had been.

She was still sitting brooding about the situation when Levic opened the door with a flourish and came in bearing a spray of orange lilies.

'Well, I'm glad you've had a good morning,' she murmured, as he kissed her.

'Yes, I have had an excellent morning,' he agreed, flopping into his easy chair. 'But how did you get on with Cassie?'

'Not too well,' she said before going on to give him a full account.

'I shouldn't worry about it. You've done your best to warn her. What she does now is her own business.'

'But it's not so simple as that. I couldn't bear to see her get hurt as a result of following in my footsteps.'

'Ah, well, that's a situation we may be able to avert.'

'How?' She was curious now, especially as Levic's eyes were gleaming and he was clearly hugging some news. 'Come on, tell me what you have been up to this morning.'

'Well,' he said and then paused, as if to savour the

words before he spoke them, 'can you imagine what the mood will be like in Berlin this Christmas?'

'No. I don't know what it's like at any time.'

He continued as if he had not heard her.

'It's going to be ecstatic. The people went mad last month when their armies defeated Napoleon, and this Christmas they will be celebrating as never before.'

'But the war hasn't finished yet, has it?' It was an idle question. She knew little about what was happening in the world, and anyway her mind at the moment was on other things.

'No, not exactly, but there's only Paris to fall and that can't hold out much longer. The Emperor's been defeated, that is the main thing.'

'Yes, all right. But what has this got to do with me and Cassie?'

'You, my darling, everything. Cassie, not at all.'

'Come on, Levic, what are you trying to tell me?'

He beamed.

'Circus Renz in Berlin are putting on a grand victory gala over Christmas and they have engaged me as one of the chief artistes. It really is a tremendous honour, Mirella, because, as you can imagine, the place is buzzing with patriotic fervour just now and all the other performers are German. I shall be the only foreigner.'

She was silent for a moment as the news sank in.

'You mean you're going to be in Berlin this Christmas? But how long for?'

'Correction. *We* are going to be in Berlin over Christmas and for about two months.'

'But Levic, I can't. I'm going to be at the Barn and after that there's the tour starting.'

'Well, cancel them. This is too good an opportunity to miss. You don't seem to realise what I just said, Mirella. I am going to be the star of Circus Renz this winter. You might at least look a little happy about such news.'

'Levic, of course I'm happy for you, and it's no more than you deserve,' she whispered, going over to kiss him and kneeling down beside his chair, still trying to puzzle out what his news portended. 'But what did you mean when you said this had everything to do with me? Will Renz engage me for the tightrope?'

'Of course not. I thought I made that clear,' he said, sounding impatient. 'They're only taking me on because my act went down so well there last year, but naturally I want you to come with me and there is no need for you to work, so where is the problem?'

She was speechless. He knew very well, after all her disappointments, how relieved she had been to get this Highbury Barn engagement and the tour to follow. At any other time she would love to go to Berlin, but not now when it would mean letting down so many people. Besides it made her bridle to think how Levic could so summarily dismiss the importance of her work when it came to making his own plans.

'Levic,' she asked in a small voice, 'what would you do if I said I couldn't come with you?'

'Don't be stupid, Mirella. Of course you'll come with me.'

'But what would you do if I can't?' she asked, staring into the fire.

She felt the pressure of his hands on her head, forcing her to turn and look him in the face.

'I am going to Berlin this winter, Mirella. There is no doubt in my mind about that. I expect you to come with me. But if you choose not to come, there is nothing I can do to force you.'

'You mean you'd go without me, even though you know my arrangements were made first?'

His eyes blazed and his voice rose in a crescendo. 'Look, Mirella, understand this: I – AM – GOING. What you do is your own affair.'

*   *   *

347

Looking back at that row some weeks later, Mirella found it hard to believe how it had happened. It was so unexpected. One moment she was walking along, her life happily balanced. The next, something had given way and tumbled her to the ground. Levic had left her.

He did not want to be parted from her. She did not want him to go. Nevertheless, he went, leaving her to carry on alone, with the understanding that she would join him as soon as she had finished her run of engagements. But she missed him so much that several times she had started packing a bag to go and join him. What stopped her was pride – both professional and personal. Moreover, as Christmas came and went, to pride was added anger because Levic had not written in reply to the three letters she sent him, and she began to suspect that he was so much a creature of his immediate surroundings that once he was abroad she ceased to exist for him.

Fortunately she had a good team to help her with her equipment, so the practical side of life presented no difficulties. Emotionally, however, she felt crushed and turned as usual to her work for distraction. Every spare minute of the day she spent practising or thinking out new ideas, as a result of which she introduced fresh tricks such as balancing on a chair and performing an elaborate dance routine on the high rope.

Her band of admirers remained faithful, showering her not just with bouquets and brooches, but also with supper invitations. Once or twice, after the show, she allowed herself to be fêted at Verrey's in Regent Street or Cavour's in Leicester Square. It was hard to say she enjoyed these occasions. In some ways it felt good to be out in company, but in other respects these eager young men served only to remind her of Levic and increase her loneliness. She was also always on her guard lest any individual tried to come too close.

Cassie too was a constant source of worry to her. Although they exchanged Christmas greetings in which each mentioned the possibility of seeing the other again soon, they had not actually met up. However, each week in the columns of the *Era* there was some report about Cassie's performances at the Agricultural Hall, including details of the latest tricks she had incorporated into her act. To Mirella's horror it soon became clear that everything she herself did was immediately being copied by her sister. That Tom had gone to the lengths of sitting in the audience, or planting someone else there just for the purpose of spying out her latest trick, made her feel profoundly uncomfortable. But that Cassie, still such a novice, should be prompted to imitate these tricks struck her as criminal folly.

She wished Levic was on hand so that she could discuss the problem with him. Or that there was some member of the family to whom she could talk. After all there must be some other person beside herself who could see what a dangerous situation she and Cassie had drifted into when, every time either of them stepped on to the rope, thoughts of the other dominated their actions.

During her farewell performance at Highbury Barn in mid-February this fear became a reality. She had been practising her most complicated routine so far for this occasion, but when the moment came to step out on to the rope she found herself paralysed by the thought of what Cassie would make of it. How could she do a headstand in the middle of the rope whilst somebody out there was watching and then translating it into a challenge for Cassie? Thinking about it made her so confused that she abandoned half of her prepared programme in favour of something simpler.

'This is no good,' she told herself afterwards. 'I can't allow that sort of thing to happen. I must find a way of sorting it out.'

Another meeting with Cassie was the first idea that came into her head, but she knew that would be

349

useless. Her motives would be misunderstood. Cassie would be bound to accuse her of trying to quell the competition.

She could try talking to Tom. Beard him in his den. See the gleam of triumph in his pale eyes. Hear the same words she had heard from Cassie, but tanged with malice from his tongue. If it would do some good, she was willing to try. However, common sense told her not to waste her time.

Then she thought of Joey. It was almost a year since she had last seen him but he had sent her a friendly letter at Christmas saying that he hoped to see her at Sydenham some time this coming year. It was not clear how much he knew of the rift between her and her family, although she guessed that her grandmother would have told him all about it. She smiled. Dear Gran. She was the one person who had kept in touch over the past year and not condemned. Maybe she should go and ask her advice about Cassie. But no, that would not be fair. It would compromise her position with Johnny and Sadie who might well take offence if they thought Liddy was encouraging their daughter in her sinful ways. Besides, as usual, there was the Captain's health to be considered. He was completely bedridden now, and it was clear from Liddy's last letter that his condition was deteriorating fast and she had her hands full with looking after him.

Joey, then. She had a few days spare before starting her provincial tour. She would go and see Joey at Sydenham before Cassie and Tom arrived for their six weeks' stint and, even if he could not solve anything, she could alert Joey to the difficulties and ask him to keep an eye on Cassie during her stay.

Chapter Twenty-Three

In the distance she could see the black buildings of London pushing their steeples and domes and gilt crosses up through a pall of smoke to touch the wintry sky. Here, walking in the grounds of Crystal Palace, she stared at the dry fountains and the bare, frost-bitten shrubs in the formal gardens and tried to pay attention to what Joey was saying.

'Yes, Herr Manns is still as strict as ever and terrifies everyone at rehearsals,' he said in his indistinct voice. He had grown a moustache and beard which almost completely disguised his harelip, so it was only when he spoke that one was reminded of his impediment.

'Yes, I can imagine that,' she said, trying to work out how to broach the subject most in her mind. She simply must talk about it to someone soon, because it was dragging her down and making her feel ill.

'On the other hand, he can be quite comical in the way he says things,' Joey laughed. 'Take just now, for instance. He said to me: "Ach, Meester Grangeair! You must not blay wiz ze nails: you most blay wiz ze *meat* of your fingers!" '

'What?' Still lost in her own thoughts, she had not been listening properly but, realising that he expected some reaction, she forced herself to smile.

'Don't you understand? Herr Manns didn't really mean "meat", he meant "flesh", the flesh of my

351

finger tips,' Joey went on patiently trying to explain, before suddenly giving up and asking: 'Are you all right, Mirella? You don't look very well, and I think we're going to have a shower. Would you rather go inside?'

'No, it's all right. I'd rather stay out here,' she said quickly. The buildings were too full of painful memories for her – Tom getting drunk and behaving so indecently, and Levic talking to her in the Grecian Court. She did not know which memory hurt more. 'I'm sorry if I'm not good company today, Joey. The fact is, I'm not feeling too well, but the fresh air is doing me good and I'm really happy to see you again.'

They had paused now in front of one of the water temples built like a miniature Crystal Palace and housing a group of stone goddesses shimmering under a silky veil of water.

'How do they get that effect?' she asked.

'The flowing water, you mean? It's spraying down from the dome, look.'

'Yes. I see.' She gazed back at the statues. 'Like perpetual rain. It makes them look beautiful, but cold.'

'That's true, but perhaps they don't mind being cold if it stops them being damaged. Did you notice how some idiots have carved their names all over the other statues in the grounds?'

'Yes, I did. But, if I was a goddess, I think I'd choose to stand in the sun and take my chance of being damaged rather than live under a stream of cold water all my life,' she said, shivering.

'Come on, you're getting too cold,' Joey urged, taking her arm and leading her up the steps as drops of sleet began to fall, 'and that's not good, especially when you're already feeling under the weather. Now, I'm going to insist that you come back to my lodgings to have some luncheon and tell me what's on your mind.'

'Is it that obvious?'

He paused and gave her a sidelong glance.

'As obvious as those goddesses' charms, despite the veils hiding them.'

Joey made it easy for her to talk about her fears. Not all of them, of course. She could not mention the worst aspects of Tom's behaviour towards her when she worked in partnership with him. But she did confide her fears for Cassie's safety on the rope.

'In other words, you think Tom is putting too much pressure on her,' Joey suggested.

'Yes, I do.'

'Did he put too much pressure on you, then?'

'Well, no. Not in that way. But I read in the *Era* what sort of tricks she's performing and I know she hasn't been rope-dancing long enough to do that sort of stuff safely.'

'But you haven't seen her for yourself?'

'Not lately. I saw her last September when she was just starting out and I worried for her even then.'

'Yes, well, that may be the trouble. You saw her when she was a novice and she may have developed very quickly since then. On the other hand, I can understand your worry. You obviously feel responsible for her.'

'That's right. I know my motives may be open to doubt, Joey, but believe me, I really am scared for Cassie.'

'Tell you what, then. Come back here on Wednesday afternoon and we'll both go and watch her opening performance in the Palace. Then, if we agree there's something wrong, I'll have a word with Tom and Cassie and try to sort something out.'

'Would Tom listen to you?'

'If he didn't, I'd go straight to our Johnny and he certainly would.'

'Yes, but I wouldn't want him or my mother to be alarmed without good reason.'

'Right. So, you'll come on Wednesday? You see, to be quite frank, I wouldn't know how to judge for myself, so I need you there to explain what bits of the performance particularly bother you.'

'Thanks, Joey. I'll come, as long as I can avoid meeting Tom. I can see it's a good idea because, as you say, once I watch Cassie on the rope, I might realise my fears are groundless and then we can all sleep easy at night.'

Luckily the sleet slackened into drizzle instead of turning into snow, and by Wednesday there was even some pale sunshine to cheer her journey back to Sydenham. Joey, who had already bought tickets, was waiting for her on the upper terrace and they went in quickly to find a suitable place to stand.

'Ah, Mendelssohn, I think that's meant to be,' Joey murmured as they passed close to the orchestral band struggling to compete with the noise of people still coming in.

'Gracious, they've lowered the rope!' she exclaimed, as she caught sight of Cassie's rope in the central nave fixed not to the very top of the spiral staircase, as was usual in this building, but to iron girders on the second gallery.

'Yes, I asked Tom about that yesterday and he said it was because Cassie had a bit of a fit when she saw how high the rope was being fixed at first, but she calmed down when he agreed to have it lowered. So you see, he does take her feelings into account.'

Mirella groaned. 'Joey, you don't understand. She can be hurt just as much by a fall from forty as from a hundred and forty feet. The fact is, she shouldn't be doing it at all if she's frightened.'

'Yes, I know you're right,' he agreed, as they decided to take up their positions in the first gallery where they had a good view. 'But there's nothing we can do about it at the moment so there's no point in fretting. It must seem strange for you to be in this building as a spectator again,' he added, in an obvious attempt to change the subject.

'Hmm, this time a couple of years ago it would have been me performing here.'

'That's right. I was sitting with Liddy down there on the ground floor watching you. It's a pity you cancelled last year, but you couldn't do anything else after all that trouble with Tom at the Agricultural Hall. He's certainly not an easy person to work with. Never was.'

She had the feeling that he wanted to know more and was too tactful to ask. Just as, after an initial polite inquiry, he had refrained from questioning her about Levic. She was just considering how much to confide in him, when her thoughts were interrupted by a change in the music.

'Ah, that's the overture. We must be about to start,' she remarked.

'Good lord, Mirella,' Joey whispered, screwing up his eyes with pain, 'I can see what frightens you about all this.'

'What do you mean? Cassie hasn't appeared yet.'

'No, but that band! It's enough to make anyone feel desperate.'

She knocked him in the ribs, hissing, 'Come now, no professional jealousy.' And they were laughing together as Cassie made her entrance.

Once she took off her satin cloak, she looked like a small, half-naked bird, her hair tied up in a feathered headress and her body clad in a furry-edged gown with full petticoats over silk fleshings. Mirella and Joey started to clap, only to find that the applause which greeted Cassie was surprisingly muted. Other spectators had noticed how low the rope had been rigged and were clearly disappointed, as evidenced by a man standing alongside them who turned to his companion and complained, 'That rope's never high

355

enough. Last time I came, the girl walked right up there in the roof and she was really good. I think it's a cheek to get people here and then put on a show that could be staged any place else.'

'We oughter ask for some money back, then. After all, if she's only going to walk half as high, we should be entitled to half a refund,' his mate sniggered.

Mirella sat biting her top lip, watching Cassie climb the spiral staircase and emerge on to the second gallery. She remembered herself doing the same thing, but going on up and up again to where the great Handel organ stood. And she remembered what it was like to be up there under a roof arched like a crystal rainbow over the miniature world below, and feeling such exultation that when she stepped out on to the rope the sky above seemed to shout the "Hallelujah Chorus".

Looking at Cassie to see how she felt, she saw on her face a smile as fixed as a death mask. The performer's smile.

'Joey, we've got to stop her,' she said, clutching his arm.

'She's all right, Mirella,' he said. 'It's always worse when you're watching. You just take it easy and enjoy the performance and we'll talk about it afterwards.'

Down below, Tom, having led Cassie into the arena and escorted her to the stairs, now stood mouth slightly open and moving his tongue along his lower lip, gazing up at her. He was the only person, apart from Cassie herself, who could stop this performance. Surely he realised she was not in a fit state to go through with it – after all he used to say to Mirella about the need to have her mind and emotions under control when she stepped on to that rope? How could Cassie be completely under control when she was obviously so frightened?

A deathly hush had fallen over the spectators as,

after wiping her hands with a powdered handkerchief, Cassie picked up the pole which had been
stowed on the balcony and stood balancing it in her
hands. Then, when she stopped jiggling the pole, she
stood stock-still staring at the rope for what seemed
like several minutes.

'Come on, love, d'yer want me to give you a shove?'
The man's voice, closely followed by a chorus of
whistles from the auditorium, had the effect of shocking Cassie out of her trance and causing her to stare
wildly round to see who was shouting.

'Yes, go on someone, give 'er a shove,' another
voice yelled.

Although Cassie was poised about twenty feet
above them, she was close enough for Mirella to see
tears running down her face and she found herself
crying too. And hating all these people for not being
on Cassie's side.

Come on, Cassie. You can do it. I'm with you every
step of the way, she silently urged.

Cassie suddenly jerked into action. Her left foot
stretched out to stroke the rope. She stepped forward
on to it, at the same time swinging her right foot out
and round, and was walking along, her confidence
growing with every step she took.

'Phew,' Joey let out a long sigh. 'If that little scene
was planned, it certainly worked. She's got this audience eating out of her hand now.'

He was right. When she reached the other end,
there was a burst of clapping and Cassie responded
with a beaming smile that dissolved Mirella's fears
and enabled her to settle down to enjoy the rest of the
programme.

Ah, walking backwards next. Not so difficult as it
looks, because you still keep your eye on the mark
post and your body balances easily. Forwards again
and renewed cheers as she arrives back at the platform. Walks out into the middle of the rope and

357

turns. Tricky, this, because the movement forces you really off-balance for a moment, but Cassie manages it all right and now sits down, stretching her left leg along the rope whilst pulling up the other leg and resting her right foot over her left knee, apparently as much at ease as if she were lolling on a park bench. Up again, and a little skipping dance along and back to the centre where she now kneels first on both knees and then on one, stands up, goes down on her left knee with the right one back, and salutes the audience who promptly applaud.

Mirella squeezed Joey's arm.

'You were right,' she whispered, 'Cassie has got better since I saw her at Worcester. She's really good, don't you think?'

'Well, she had me worried at first, but she seems to have got into her stride now. Anyway, you're the expert, and if you say . . .' His words tailed away as a roll of drums announced the next trick.

While they had been talking, Cassie had picked up a hoop which she was now carrying out into the centre of the rope. There she stepped one foot into it after the other, then wriggled it up over her clothes and pushed one arm down through it after the other until she could finally pull it over her head. After that she reversed the process, climbing through the hoop from head to foot, and when with a final flourish she waved it aloft, the crowd roared its approval.

Mirella herself had performed all these feats at one time or another, but not the one which followed where Cassie buckled on a belt from which dangled four chains that she attached to her wrists and ankles before walking the rope. She had seen Blondin do something similar, but had refused to put it into her own repertoire because it looked so ungraceful. Like the basket trick which Cassie attempted next.

Looking at her slowly shuffling along with her feet encased in baskets, Mirella wondered whether she was right to be influenced by such considerations. Tom used to say a little bit of drama was worth a cartful of grace when it came to attracting an audience. But she remembered the look of disgust on Levic's face when she repeated this maxim to him.

'To believe that, Mirella,' he said, 'is to debase our art. There's plenty of drama in nature without us inventing more just for the sake of it. No, our art is all about striving to improve on nature. Using drama as a means, of course, but always employing as much grace and artistry as possible in what we do.'

And she had argued with him. 'But, surely, nature has already produced squirrels and I'll never be more graceful than one of them when it comes to rope walking, so what's the point in trying to compete?'

'And nature has produced a skylark, so why do composers create symphonies?'

'Yes, but . . .' The argument had raged on and no matter how it ended, it left her feeling more alive and eager to tackle something new. Whereas, although what Tom said made more immediate sense, it always sapped her enthusiasm for whatever she was doing.

Levic. Damn! She wished she hadn't started thinking about Levic. Most of the time life was bearable – if she kept him blotted out of her mind. But now here he was again, taking possession of her thoughts, and she found herself desperately longing for him.

Joey clutched her arm. She heard everyone gasp, and found herself pushing her way along the gallery rail towards Cassie almost before realising something was wrong. All her earlier fears counted for nothing, had existed inside her own head. But not what was happening now. This was real. Cassie was in trouble. One moment she had been slowly pushing her feet along in their baskets, the next the rope had suddenly dipped and sagged, giving her such a jolt that she let slip her balancing pole and it went crashing to the ground. Immediately, Cassie started to totter this way and that, flailing her hands in an attempt to regain balance. But it was useless. The rope had built up too much sway. She leant too much to one side and toppled off.

'The rope! Catch hold of it!' Mirella yelled.

It was unlikely that Cassie heard, but instinct gave her the same message and her hands stretched out and grabbed and held on. And there she was, swinging in space, and safe – if she kept her head and worked her way along to the end or even the nearest guy-rope. But for the moment she was doing nothing except swinging in space, opening and shutting her eyes.

Oblivious of all the other spectators leaning over the balcony to lap up this sensational part of the act, Mirella elbowed her way to the spot immediately underneath where the rope was fixed and called, 'Hang on, Cassie. You'll be OK. Just edge your way towards me. It's not far. This way a bit! That's right, that's right. You can do it.'

Cassie had got the idea and started swinging her body from side to side like a pendulum and moving her hands so that she could edge herself along. Down below, Mirella could see Tom and five or six men grabbing the safety blanket and carrying it between them until they were positioned underneath Cassie ready to break her fall should it be necessary. However, she knew Cassie stood a better chance if she could swing herself along to a guy-rope and slide down to the ground.

'That's right, Cassie. To me. Keep on coming,' she urged.

Cassie was staring wild-eyed at her, resting for a moment, but then swinging herself into motion again. Mirella knew how tired her arms must be feeling already, could actually feel the pain in her own muscles with every move Cassie made.

'That's right, Cassie. A little bit more. Nearly there,' she kept repeating.

Then another voice intervened.

'OK, jump now, love. JUMP,' roared Tom from below.

'No, Cassie. Hang on, move towards the guy. You can slide down,' Mirella shouted.

'Jump. JUMP!' Tom was yelling.

'No, Cass. Don't jump. Keep coming towards me.'

Cassie's poor face showed utter bewilderment. She looked down, closed her eyes, drew in her breath and started to swing sidewards again. Then opened her eyes and fixed her gaze on Mirella.

'Yes, Cass. You can do it. Just a few inches more,' she called.

'JUMP!' came the command from below.

Cassie's face contorted and her body seemed to tighten. She gave Mirella a despairing little half-smile.

'NOW!' Tom yelled.

And Cassie shut her eyes and let go.

One moment she was there, edging towards safety, coming nearer to her. The next plunging downwards.

Mirella could do nothing but clutch the rail and watch. It was all over in an instant. Cassie hit the blanket so hard it jerked out of someone's hand and she crashed on to the ground. And lay there like a fledgling fallen out of its nest.

'NO! NO!' Mirella screamed, turning and beginning to run. Dear God, don't let this be happening, please don't let this be happening, she prayed again and again as she knocked people out of her way to get to the stairs.

There must have been chaos all around. She noticed none of it, her mind fixed on that one abiding image of Cassie lying on the ground like a crushed sparrow.

'Cassie? It's me, Rella. You're going to be all right, Cass,' she whispered, kneeling down to touch her face. 'They're fetching a doctor, but you'll be all right.' Then, as she put out her hand to pull the crumpled feathers from her sister's hair, Cassie's eyelids fluttered and she heard her whimper: 'Oh, Rella, he didn't catch me.'

At the same time she grew aware of Tom kneeling on the other side of Cassie moaning over and over again, 'It was this blasted arm that let me down. This bloody, blasted arm.'

Chapter Twenty-Four

The reason Mirella gave for cancelling her provincial tour was that she had to stay near Cassie. This was true – but there was also another reason which she was not prepared to divulge to anyone.

Immediately after the accident Cassie was taken to Sydenham Hospital. There she lay for days, drifting in and out of consciousness while doctors shook their heads over her. During this time Mirella scarcely left her bedside despite the fact that Cassie hardly seemed to know her. Even once she began to recover her mental clarity, Cassie could do little more than sob and beat her head against the pillows, howling at the pain. She knew she had fractured the neck of her thigh bone, but no one dared tell her she would never walk properly again.

Johnny and Sadie came as soon as they heard. Mirella was spooning beef tea into Cassie's mouth when they arrived, and forgetting all former wrongs, she put down the dish and threw her arms around Sadie to kiss her. Although there was an immediate answering warmth, her mother's face tightened once they drew apart again and Mirella was left in no doubt that Sadie had not forgiven her. Johnny, on the other hand, after searching her face in a way that brought tears into the eyes of both of them, hugged her and whispered, 'I'm glad to see you here, my love.'

'Oh, Pa, it's been so awful since Cassie had her

fall,' she whispered. 'She's being ever so brave, but the pain . . . I can't bear to see her in such pain.'

'I know, my love. But she's going to be looked after properly. I don't know how we're going to get the money, but Cassie will have the best doctoring there is, no matter how much it costs.'

Then, leaving Sadie to give Cassie the sort of comfort only a mother can give, Johnny drew Mirella away from the bed so that she could give him a full account of what had happened.

'And our Tom, has he been coming in to see Cassie?' Johnny asked, looking around the infirmary as if expecting to see his brother lurking somewhere.

'Oh, yes. He's been in every day. But he's been terribly shocked by the whole thing, Pa. Keeps blaming himself, and he looks so haggard. I think this accident has hit him harder than when he got mauled himself.'

'And so it bloody well should,' Johnny exploded. Then, making an effort to keep his voice down, 'I hold him to blame for all this. You leaving home the way you did. Cassie – well, she'd have been happy enough if he hadn't filled her head with so much rubbish about the money you were earning.' He glanced over to her bed and quickly away again as if what he saw was too painful to dwell on. 'And now look where it's got her.'

'But accidents happen, Pa. She could have been run over by a horse-bus and suffered worse injury.'

'But she didn't. She fell forty feet from a bloody stupid rope which hadn't been secured properly. So it's no good you defending him. Tom's at fault and I ought to have my brain-box examined for letting him lead you and Cassie into trouble in the first place.'

She thought it wise to change the subject. She felt sorry for Tom and hated hearing him blamed, but in her heart she felt he probably was responsible for the accident. That moment when the rope had slipped

364

causing the sudden jerk that made Cassie drop her balancing pole – she had not questioned Tom, but it seemed pretty obvious that the winch had failed. Probably one of the ratchet teeth had broken. But this was the sort of mechanical weakness one was always on guard against. It should have been picked up by Tom when he checked the equipment before the performance. *If* he had checked the equipment before the performance.

'Still, there's no point in going over the past, Pa. The main thing is, how do we look after Cassie's future? She's bound to be in here another month or so, and all that's got to be paid for. And after that, she's still going to need nursing. I can do that, but . . .'

'No. Your mother's made up her mind that, soon as Cassie's fit to be moved, she'll come home along with us.' As Mirella stiffened at this seeming rebuff, Johnny added, 'Not that we aren't grateful for what you've done, my love. And I can see it's taken its toll by how pale you're looking.'

'Oh, I'm all right, Pa. Just tired. I haven't slept too well since Cassie's accident,' she said quickly.

'Well, we don't want any more problems, so don't let yourself get ill,' Johnny said, tousling her hair. 'I know I've sometimes spoken a bit harsh, my love, but none of that was really meant. Especially when I really come up against it and see one of my little gals maimed. That's hard to take.'

'I know, Pa,' she muttered, blinking to stop further tears. 'But, getting back to Tom, the reason he isn't here is that he's gone to see Grandma Liddy today. It was Joey's idea, because they've both been so worried about where to get the money for Cassie's treatment.'

'You don't mean to say he's gone to ask Mother for money after all she's already done for him?' Johnny demanded. 'Surely he knows she's got enough on her plate looking after the Captain, without being burdened with anything else?'

'Yes, he does,' she said, trying to defend Tom, 'and hopefully it won't be necessary, because the *Era* has started a subscription for Cassie and there's to be a special benefit for her at Crystal Palace. But all that's going to take time, so Tom wants to know if Gran can lend him enough to pay Cassie's expenses in the meantime. He's only trying to help, Pa.'

'Hmm, it's no help if he robs Peter to pay Paul. My poor mother. It's us should be supporting her, not the other way round.'

Nevertheless, Johnny was eventually glad to accept help from Liddy – or rather, the Captain – who, ill though he was, wrote to insist that all Cassie's medical bills be sent to him for payment, so that any money raised by other means could be used to safeguard her future. After all, if the worst happened and she was never able to earn her living again, she might need money some day to keep her out of the workhouse.

Although the subscription list brought in many small donations, more substantial sums were expected from the special benefit which Tom and Mirella now threw themselves into organising. The accident had brought about an immediate reconciliation between them, with neither being prepared to bear a grudge when Cassie's welfare was at stake. Besides, Mirella's heart went out to Tom when she realised how much he was in fact blaming himself for what had happened.

'You see, it was my fault,' he kept saying, 'I should have checked that crab more thoroughly. And I should never have let her go out there feeling so upset that afternoon.'

'Did you upset her then?' Mirella asked.

'No, not badly. Well, you know what I can be like, Mirella,' he confessed, with a shrug of his shoulders and a self-deprecating smile.

'You'd had something to drink?'

'Well, just a little drop, not enough to make me drunk.'

Mirella's stomach turned over when she remembered just what Tom was capable of doing once he'd had a "little drop" of drink.

'Did you touch her?' she demanded.

'No, no. Nothing like that. I just said something that upset her, that's all.'

'So what did you say?' She waited patiently for him to answer.

'I just taunted her a bit with being so scared. Telling her she wasn't a patch on you when it came to ropewalking. I know it sounds wicked, especially now, but I was trying to stir her courage up a bit, that's all.'

Mirella shut her eyes.

'Poor Cass. I knew there was something wrong as soon as she came in. Oh dear, Tom, how could you say something like that? It was wicked.'

'I know, I know. But I didn't dream there was going to be an accident. How could I? But it was my fault,' he started to moan again. 'All my fault, and I'll never forgive myself.'

When Cassie's fracture healed, it left her left leg three inches shorter than the right and virtually useless. She had to get about on crutches. There had been some discussion about whether she should be present as a special guest at the benefit being staged at Crystal Palace, but once Cassie made it clear that she could not bear the thought of ever going into that building again, Johnny came up and took her home a few days beforehand.

It was sad standing outside the hospital, watching her being hauled up into the carriage and forlornly waving goodbye. But Mirella had no time to dwell on the sadness because she had work to do. Since Cassie's accident she had almost entirely neglected her own tightrope practice. Now she needed to brush up her act ready for Cassie's benefit performance.

At first the management of Crystal Palace refused

to stage another high rope act so soon after the disaster, and even Tom thought it might be tempting fate.

But Mirella talked them round. After all, she told the Management Committee, a successful performance was exactly what they needed to restore their reputation. Tom, on the other hand, was convinced once she explained how great an attraction it would be for another Petite Blondin to walk the same rope in the same place to raise money for her crippled sister.

'Yes,' he agreed, 'it would be a great draw. And when you think about it, there's no more risk now than there ever was.'

'Probably less,' she said, thinking about how careful she was when checking her own rope.

'That's right. Less, if you believe what they say, that lightning never strikes in the same place twice.'

The benefit was to be given tomorrow, a Thursday being the only free afternoon available at such short notice. Mirella and Tom had already supervised the rope being rigged one hundred and fifty high, right up near the roof.

'Are you sure you wouldn't be happier with it at fifty feet – where we put Cassie's?' Tom asked.

'No. I'm happier with it up there,' she announced. And thought to herself, at least if I fall from there, I shan't be left crippled. But she was not at all nervous. She had loved walking under the great arched roof of the Crystal Palace before and her need to walk up high again was almost physical. Ideally she would like to have walked on a high rope outside in the open, but it was still too early in the year to arrange such an event.

Just occasionally, especially in the last couple of weeks, she thought to question her own motives and wonder whether she was bent on self-destruction. After all, she had seen what happened to Cassie. And her own life was very bleak at the moment. Still no word from Levic. He had simply abandoned her. And she longed for him, now more than ever before. Yet when she thought of him, a strange weariness came over her; a feeling of being lost. And alone. And desperately lonely.

When she reached this point in her thoughts she inevitably shook herself. Alone? Well, that was the tenor of her life, wasn't it? She had always been alone. The odd one out in her family. Incapable of settling into their friendly mould, no matter how she tried. And she had tried hard, she really had. All through her childhood, trying and dismally failing to find a way to please Sadie. Even when she went to work in the Castle kitchens, she was still trying to please Sadie. But with the best will in the world, she could never fit into that beastly routine. And then Tom . . . there seemed no end to the list of her failures to get on with people. Even Levic.

And yet, she thought, everything had changed when Levic came on the scene. She had felt so different when she was with him. At home, and happy, and – well, so much in love that life and Levic seemed inseparable; one without the other unthinkable. Then he'd upped and left and she'd found herself alone again. With only her work to comfort her.

Still, on the tightrope there was no place for anyone else.

Which is precisely what draws me to being a tightrope walker, she concluded, gazing up at the taut line stretched across the roof and being held steady by more than a dozen pairs of guy-ropes. If I check everything again really thoroughly, I could do a last practice up there just to remind myself what it feels like . . . It was a tempting thought, but one she dismissed almost immediately because it would be breaking the rules to walk up there without someone being on the alert down here in case things went wrong. Besides, she reminded herself, all this is not for my benefit but Cassie's, and nothing else matters at the moment except raising money for Cassie. Nothing else at all, she repeated to herself sternly.

But after tomorrow, whispered a voice in her head, you are going to have to think about other things.

Since the accident, Tom had kept his accommodation in the Crystal Palace whilst offering Mirella the wagon where Cassie formerly slept. She preferred, however, to take a room in the house where Joey lodged and was resting there the next morning before the performance when the landlady tapped on her door.

'I'm sorry to bother you, dear,' she murmured, 'but there's a gentleman called to see you.'

'Did he give you his name?' she asked, trying not to show how annoyed she felt at being disturbed.

'Yes. I told him you wouldn't want any callers at the moment, but he said, "Just tell her it's Levic. I think she'll want to see me."'

'Levic? Did you say it's Levic and he's here now?' she heard herself say as if in a dream.

The woman's "Yes" was echoed by a deeper voice.

'Yes, it is me, Mirella.'

And there, having followed the landlady up the stairs, stood Levic. Levic – his black hair grown longer, almost touching the collar of his coat. Levic, thinner in the face than she remembered, but with his dark eyes glowing into hers. Levic, briefly turning to the landlady, making a slight bow and muttering, 'Please excuse my impropriety, Madam,' and then, without offering the poor woman any further explanation, pushing past her into the room.

In the same instant Mirella was in his arms and they were hugging each other tight. He was kissing her, whispering in her ear: 'Oh, my love, if you only knew how much I've missed you.' Kissing her again and drawing back his head to gaze into her face. 'When I heard about Cassie, I wanted to come straight away, but Renz would not release me until all the celebrations were over. But I came as soon as I could, my love. I was so worried about you.'

'Oh, Levic, why didn't you write? I kept sending you letters and you never wrote back. I thought you must have found someone else.'

'Silly, how could I? There is no one else but you.'

'Then why didn't you write?'

'You know how I hate writing letters, Mirella. I can't make words on paper say what I feel. Written words are so fixed. And what I feel is not fixed, it is changing all the time. Oh, I can't explain. Maybe it is just that I am too lazy to write.'

'But you must have known how unhappy I'd be when you didn't.'

'I know, I know. But please, don't keep talking about all that now. I have come back to be with you, and you are glad to see me, aren't you?'

She frowned. There was something she badly wanted to tell him, but not now. She needed time to get to know him again. It was all very well for him to carry on as if they had never been apart, but she was finding it difficult to adjust to this half-stranger who she was terrified might suddenly disappear again. Seeing him so unexpectedly, he seemed somehow different from the man she had been dreaming about for so long, and she was no longer sure who he really was – her future husband come home where he belonged, or her lover setting aside his ambition to come back to court her? Or was it even possible that Levic was no more than an adventurer whose heart was easily engaged wherever he happened to be, and to whom she meant nothing more than the girl he found beside him at the time? She needed to renew her trust in him again before she told him her news.

'What's wrong, Mirella? You are looking dreadfully pale. You're not ill, are you? Or nervous about this performance they've persuaded you to do?'

'No. There's nothing wrong with me. It's just a shock, having you turn up like this without any warning.'

'I'm sorry. I did not mean to give you a shock, but I had to see you before this afternoon.'

'Why? I mean, why before this afternoon?'

He looked uncomfortable. 'I told you I heard about Cassie.'

'Yes?'

'Well, naturally, it immediately made me worry about you. And then, when I read you were going to perform in this benefit, I could not stand the worry any more and came straight here.'

'Why?' She was beginning to feel stupid. He came straight here because he was worried about what? She found herself staring at him baffled.

'I should have thought that was obvious. I wanted to be sure you knew what you were doing. Rumour has it that Tom was to blame for Cassie's accident and yet here he is a few weeks later organising an exactly similar event and you of all people have let him manipulate you into taking part. I simply don't understand what's going on, Mirella. I don't understand it, and I don't like it.'

'Tom hasn't manipulated me into doing anything, Levic. This performance is altogether my idea to raise money for Cassie. She's had a terrible time, you know, and now she . . .'

He interrupted her. 'But if you needed money, why did you not ask me? There's no need for you to risk your life in order to raise money. And, no matter what you say, you *would* be risking your life, because you are in no fit state to be doing this sort of performance.'

'What do you mean?' she asked, startled.

'I mean you are looking ill. I've never seen you look so pale and peaky. I don't think you're over the shock yet and that is no condition to be walking the rope in.'

'I told you, I'm all right. Anyway, it's too late to change plans even if I wanted to.'

'Nonsense! That's why I am here. I am going to suggest I take your place. I can run through most of my normal routine – do some acrobatics and juggling and music sketches – even a joky bit on the high rope since it's up there.'

'No,' she protested.

'All right, not on the rope if it worries you.'

'No. There's no need for you to be involved at all. It's all organised. I am doing my act because I want to do it.'

'Your pride wants to do it,' Levic snapped. 'Always your pride makes you do these things. Do you remember how you said you wouldn't come to Berlin with me because you had to appear at the Barn? And after that you had a provincial tour arranged that couldn't be put off on my account, and yet it was cancelled at even shorter notice when you had to be with Cassie.'

'That was different, Levic. Cassie needed me.'

He laughed, a dry hollow laugh, and his dark eyes shone with anger.

'Yes, Mirella, and you do like people to need you, don't you? It's not enough that they love you and want you. It's not enough that you love and want them. They have to come crawling to you because they need you and then you'll respond. And do you know why? It's because you rely on another person's need to feed your pride.'

'Levic, please. I can't believe you've come back just to have a row with me. I was so glad to see you. If only you knew how wretched I've been without you. But just at the moment my head is full of what I've got to do this afternoon and I can't think straight with you ranting at me.'

'Oh, Mirella, that's the last thing I want to do. I'm only going on like this because I don't want you up on that rope this afternoon. I don't want you having an accident. I don't want you killed.'

'Levic, do have some faith in me. I know what I'm doing. I'm not stupid. Besides, I'm not going to take any risks because I've got everything to live for now.'

'What do you mean?'

She paused, but this was still not the time to tell him. It would only make his opposition stronger.

'You're back,' she said simply.

'Oh, my love, you're right. We must not quarrel the moment we meet. But I have just come from Crystal Palace where I saw Tom and when he told me you were back in partnership with him, I simply saw red and wanted to put a stop to things before you get hurt.'

'Well, let's talk about it after this afternoon, not now.'

'You're determined to go through with it then?'

'Yes. I'm a tightrope artiste, Levic. I wouldn't dream of calling off a performance once it's arranged. Well, not unless there was some over-whelming reason for doing so, and in this case there isn't.'

'So my wishes count for nothing?'

She shut her eyes and kept them shut while she spoke.

'Your wishes come too late this time, Levic. You weren't here when the decisions were being made.'

'I know. You don't have to keep reminding me. But you know why I went away and you could have come with me. To be in Berlin at the time Bismarck was proclaiming the new German Empire – I wouldn't have missed that for worlds, and you should have been there as well, at my side.'

And in that moment she agreed with him entirely and could not think why she had not been.

'Listen, Mirella,' he continued, 'what I don't want is for you to end up like Madame Saqui.'

374

'Why? I thought she was the one who lived to a ripe old age and died in bed.'

'That is true, but she died alone and people say that because of her pride, she was condemned ever after to wander between earth and sky, knowing no rest. Imagine that, Mirella. An eternity of wandering alone – her only amusement being to walk along a rainbow's edge.'

'Walking along a rainbow sounds wonderful to me, Levic.'

He sighed impatiently.

'I can see it's no good trying to talk sense into you at the moment.'

'Well, I have got a big performance to do in a couple of hours,' she muttered.

'I know, and if I cannot change your mind about doing it, at least I am here to help you prepare. Now, I presume the landlady is going to bring you up some lunch?'

She nodded.

'Right. So meanwhile we shall sit here calmly and you can tell me exactly what you are going to do this afternoon.'

It helped, having that quiet conversation with Levic, putting her feet up on the bed while he sat beside her stroking her hair and gently talking. This was exactly the kind of support she needed at the moment, because she was feeling more tired than she had ever felt in her life.

Looking back on that performance afterwards she could not distinguish dream from reality. The crowds – hundreds and hundreds of round white faces peering up at her from the seats on the ground floor, hundreds more lining the galleries, pointing and waving their brollies and shouting. The band playing the same tunes and providing the same drumrolls and trumpet flourishes where appropriate.

Other artistes going through their routines. Tom, magnificently dressed as impresario, describing Cassie's accident and telling the audience how Mirella had now offered to put her own life at risk in order to raise money for her crippled sister, and how there would be a chance during the performance for them all to show their appreciation of her courage and self-sacrifice by placing further donations in boxes which would be circulating.

All this was real enough. But when the pale sunlight suddenly slipped through the glass roof and changed the rope into a silver thread and looking up she seemed to see in every arched panel the arc of a rainbow – that must have been a dream. Dreamlike, too, the feeling of gliding along that silver thread, leaping and turning and swinging and doing a somersault, and yet her mind perfectly clear and fear nowhere near her. Her rope, her stretch of freedom. She knew its limitations. It separated one point from another invariably. But working within its limitations, and giving it everything she had, allowed her to soar like this into the heavens where there was no separation, but only the one point on the line where she was. At one with all the world, and full of joy.

'Come on, Mirella, back to earth now. That was a wonderful performance you gave this afternoon, but it seems to have left you in a daze. You have hardly eaten any of this splendid supper, nor spoken more than a dozen words since we arrived. Are you sure you are feeling all right?'

Levic had hurried her away after the show even before she had time to hear how much money had been raised for Cassie, but she was glad to get away from the crowds. The weather, as usual at this time of year, turned cold as soon as the light began to fade and so he had brought her back to his rooms in Holborn, lit the fire and asked for some supper to be brought up.

'Yes, I'm fine,' she answered him. 'But I had a strange experience, walking the rope today, almost as if it wasn't me walking but someone else outside my body working me like a puppet. Or . . . no, almost as if I was outside my body and watching it perform like a puppet. It was really strange.'

'You need to eat, my girl. And then you need to sleep. I think you haven't been looking after yourself properly.'

'Levic,' she said, wanting to tell him now.

'Wait a minute, before you say anything more, there is something I must tell you first.'

'What?' she looked at his eager face, wondering whether his news was as important as hers.

'Well, I think we both realise what a mistake it was for you not to come to Berlin with me, and now I have been offered another engagement abroad and I don't want us to make the same mistake again.'

'You're going back to Berlin?' She felt and sounded devastated, but Levic seemed not to notice.

'No, my love. Not Berlin this time. America. A brand new venture. The biggest circus ever assembled in the world and it will travel across the United States by railroad. What do you think of that, Mirella? Will you come with me this time?'

His words, his eagerness, entered her head like a whirlwind sweeping away all her thoughts. America. Some day she would love to go to America, especially with Levic and their child. For that was the momentous news she had to tell him. What she had first suspected at the end of January was now confirmed and she was definitely with child.

'To America? When would we go?' she asked while her mind grappled with this new idea.

'As soon as we can arrange the passage. Probably next week, certainly not much later. Can you be ready by then?'

'I haven't said I'll go yet. You see, there's

something you ought to know. Something that's happened since you went away . . .'

Levic was looking at her thunderstruck.

'No. Don't go on. I think I know what you are going to say and I'm not sure I want to hear it.'

His remark left her almost speechless.

'But . . .'

'No,' he whispered, with his head bowed. 'Think about it, Mirella. I know you like to say exactly what's on your mind, but some things are best left unsaid. I mean,' now he raised his head as if recovering from a blow, 'I certainly don't tell you everything.'

'What do you mean?' she asked, puzzled by this turn in the conversation.

'I mean we said we would not bind each other, so I do not live like a monk either when we are apart.'

'Not like a monk,' she repeated stupidly, struggling to find in his words anything other than the obvious meaning. 'Levic, you're saying there's been someone else while you were away,' she eventually heard herself say.

'Look, all I am saying is: you have obviously had another life while I've been away – at least, I imagine that is what you were trying to tell me.' He stared at her and she saw his expression change from pride to dismay. 'Well,' he added defensively, 'I have never led you to believe any different. As I said, I am not a monk. I have taken no vows. Nor do I ever intend to tie myself to any woman's petticoats, even yours, Mirella. I love you and I want you to come with me to America, but if you won't come, so be it. I shall go on my own but I probably won't stay that way for long.'

'So all those things you said meant nothing? "We don't need an ordinary marriage to hold us together, because we both know the depth of our love." All those things you said, Levic. And the way we felt when we . . . and . . . and . . . Oh, Levic, I thought it was special, that we were both special to each other,

that nothing could ever come between us, and now
. . . and now you just stand there and . . . oh God, I
can't bear it,' she howled, shutting her eyes and
beating her fist against her head to numb the pain.

'Don't, don't do that, for God's sake,' he said,
rushing to grapple with her hand and then hugging
both her arms down by her body to restrain her. 'Oh,
my love, I didn't want to hurt you. It was just I felt
so jealous, and of course you're right, there is something special between you and me, something
wonderful and special that we must never do anything
to spoil.'

He was kissing her hair and her forehead, making
her feel like some fractious child needing to be
soothed. He was good at soothing people when they
were upset. Had probably had plenty of practice.

'Leave me alone,' she whispered so fiercely that
Levic stepped back a pace. 'I don't want you to touch
me again, do you hear? I think what we had *was*
special, but it's ruined now and nothing can mend it.'

'Of course it can be mended,' he murmured, placing
his hand on her arm and trying to draw close to her
again.

Something inside her screamed when she felt his
touch and she hit out uncontrollably, striking him
again and again until he forced her back and she fell
sobbing on the bed.

'But, Mirella, everything would have been all right
and you need never have known any of this if you
hadn't made me think . . .' He sank back into a chair,
covering his face with his hand.

'But you were still unfaithful to me, Levic.
Whether I knew about it or not, that was bound to
ruin everything between us. I don't want to share my
life with someone I can't trust, and I'll never be able
to trust you.'

Suddenly her rage evaporated and she felt completely calm. This was the situation. She could see it

clearly now, like the post at the end of her tightrope. She loved Levic and she would always love him. Her love for him was a markpost in her life, fixed and unalterable. But it was no longer the only one. There was another life beckoning her, a tiny, curled up, innocent life that she already loved more than her own. This life inside her belonged to her alone and she could pour into it all her love without fear of being betrayed.

'Mirella, come with me to America. We can start again and it will all be different, I promise you.'

'No, Levic,' she said.

'But why won't you?'

'Because I can't trust you any more.'

'I don't believe that. I think it's your pride speaking, Mirella. I told you there have been other women, and your pride has been hurt. That's what it is, isn't it?'

'Perhaps.'

'Well, can't you just swallow your pride for the sake of the good times we can have together? After all, you don't want to be like poor Madame Saqui, always wandering between heaven and earth in search of a rainbow, do you?'

'I don't know, Levic,' she spoke dreamily, feeling herself already drifting from him. 'I've never walked along the edge of a rainbow but it sounds more pleasant than being knocked sideways by one of Jove's thunderbolts.'

'I don't understand what you're talking about, Mirella,' he said.

'No, I'm sure that's right,' she agreed sadly.

Chapter Twenty-Five

'But I need the money, Tom.'

'No, you've done enough for Cassie now,' he said. 'That Crystal Palace event worked really well. Even better than I thought it would. It caught the people's imagination, you see, telling them how a young girl like you was prepared to risk her neck to raise money for a crippled sister. Yes, although I do say it myself, that was a stroke of genius and it's really set Cassie on . . . well, if not exactly her feet again . . . it's set her up for the future, if you know what I mean.'

Mirella was glad to see that he had the grace to look a little sheepish when he said this. Tom, who a week ago had been so full of self-reproach that she pitied him, had allowed himself to be easily convinced that he was not to blame for Cassie's accident, and put his remorse behind him.

'But this money won't be for Cassie! It will be for me. I want to earn a lot of money quickly. First I've got this tour of the provinces lined up – the one I was going to do after Christmas. Most of the places have given me new bookings – but that will be finished in May and I want to do something really big then, something that will bring in at least a hundred pounds.'

'Phew, you are getting ambitious! I know that's the sort of fee Blondin commands, but little Blondins don't get paid so much.'

'That's why it's got to be something spectacular. I do need the money, Tom.'

He smiled, one side of his lip curling above his teeth. 'For a trip to America?' he sniffed. 'Planning to follow your boyfriend across the sea, are you?'

'No, I shan't be doing that,' she said, trying to keep her voice steady. She had seen Levic only once since that day two weeks ago when she did the walk at Crystal Palace after which her world had fallen apart. He had come to plead with her to change her mind and go with him to America.

'It is so different when we are together, Mirella,' he said, and even the way he said her name had brought her to the brink of tears. No one but Levic said Mirrell-la in a way that made every syllable sing. 'I never think of going with anyone else then. I want only you. Come with me. Forget the past and come with me. We belong together, you and I. And in the New World . . . just think of it, Mirella, the New World with you and me conquering it by storm. We could, I know we could, if we stay together.'

He had tried to put his arms around her, but her body instinctively stiffened and she heard herself say coldly, 'You conquer what you like, Levic. I'm only interested in putting the pieces back together again once your storm has passed.'

'No, I have no plans to go to America,' she added now for Tom's benefit. 'But I am planning to take a rest from tightrope walking and I want to make enough money to tide myself over.'

'Yes, I can see you need a bit of a holiday. Our Joey was saying the same thing. Quite concerned about you, he is, but he doesn't really understand that what we do is bound to be more taxing than sitting scraping away at a fiddle in a band all day.'

'Orchestra,' she corrected.

'Same thing. Anyway, I take your point about earning some money. My coffers are a bit low as well, so let me give you a proposition. You take me on as your manager again, and in return for my usual percentage I set up a grand spectacle that will line all our pockets. Agreed?'

'As long as you realise it will be just for the one occasion. My tour is already arranged and I can't spare any money from that. And, as I said, after what you call the "grand spectacle" I'm going to be retiring from the scene for a while.'

She thought he looked suspiciously at her for a moment before nodding his head.

'Just the one occasion. That's fine by me. And we'll make it something that will really draw the crowds. A rope tied between two church steeples, for instance. I know that was done in Bolton a few years back, but . . .' His voice tailed away.

'But what? What were you about to say?' she urged.

'Nothing important.'

'But what happened? Who was the artiste? Did it make a good spectacle? Come on, Tom, you can't start to say something and then dry up just like that.' When he still said nothing, she prompted him. 'There was an accident, wasn't there?'

'Yes, if you must know. The chap fell. I don't remember his name, but he wasn't killed, just badly injured.'

She shuddered. And immediately felt a fluttering in her stomach as the little body inside her shook in protest too. She stood absolutely still, listening as if waiting for the unborn child to speak. Although she had felt something like this before, this was the first time she was sure that what she was feeling was the baby stirring. It is true then, she thought. You are there. You are really there, my baby, alive inside me. And she felt a welling up of warmth that made her long to cradle it in her arms.

'Mirella, are you all right? I mean, someone told

me he was badly injured but it may not have been as serious as all that. You know how things get exaggerated.'

She tried to bring her attention back to what Tom was saying, but now the grand spectacle they had been planning seemed unwelcome, even threatening, and she would have abandoned the whole idea had she not needed the money.

'I've got it!' Tom suddenly announced. 'How about another walk across the Thames? Old Baum, the Manager at Cremorne, was more than pleased with how it went off last time. Did the Gardens a lot of good, he said, when I approached him with the idea of Cassie having a go at it. He said yes straight away, but I didn't fix it up because I wasn't sure she'd have the nerve to go through with it, and I didn't fancy having a huge public failure like that on my hands. Still, that wouldn't happen with you, Mirella, so what d'yer say I approach him again and see if he'll offer you enough to have another go in May?'

'Yes, all right.'

'Well, you might try sounding a bit more enthusiastic. I think it's a terrific idea.'

'Yes. I said I'll do it if he offers me enough money,' she said impatiently, aware of another fluttering protest in her womb.

Cambridge and Sheffield, Manchester, Stockport and Nottingham – travelling with a couple of helpers to transport her gear and rig the rope – by the time she finished, all these places had blurred into a kaleidoscope of circus buildings, theatres and music halls. During the course of the tour, Tom sent her details of the arrangements he had made for her Grand Walk across the Thames. However, by the time she received his letter, she had already read all about it in the columns of the *Era*. The Manager of Cremorne Gardens had certainly not stinted on advertisements and for three weeks running now there had been several huge panels, one under the other, each giving details of the event and praising her prowess to the skies. Weather permitting, this Thames Walk was clearly expected to attract larger crowds than ever.

It had been arranged that she would mount the rope from the Battersea side of the river and walk towards Cremorne exactly as she did last time – except that last time Levic had been standing on the bank at Cremorne waiting to greet her.

Walking towards Levic, that is what this tightrope business had always been about as far as she was concerned. Walking towards Levic. Even her earliest attempts had been inspired by the need to impress him, the need to establish herself on some sort of par with him. Always on the rope she had been borne up by the idea that she was walking towards Levic. Always, that is, until now.

It was at Cambridge that she noticed how something in her attitude had changed. Appearing there in one of the funny wooden circus buildings where her rope was rigged about forty feet off the ground, for the first time in her professional life she felt really nervous before a performance. Checked and double-checked the rope, snapped at one of her helpers when he assured her there was no need for her to worry about the condition of the winch, feared she was going to faint when the time came to climb the ladder to her platform and make a start.

This isn't like me, she thought. I must have a chill coming or something. But the chill, if such it was, failed to manifest and the symptoms died away – but only until she reached the next venue and saw the rope being hoisted for her, whereupon the fear returned worse than ever.

Now, you're being stupid. The rope has nothing to do with Levic. Just because he let you down, doesn't mean the rope will do the same, she told herself over and over again. But the words did not dispel her fear,

385

and before long she had to admit to herself what she could never admit to anyone else: that she had lost her nerve.

La Petite Blondin, otherwise known as Mademoiselle Mirella the Miraculous Rope-dancer, heroine of the Thames and Crystal Palace – that was what the posters said. It was unthinkable that such a personage should lose her nerve, especially at a time like this when she had such important engagements ahead of her and needed the money so much. Damn you, Levic, she cursed. I was fine before you came back and wrecked my life. Yet, even as she cursed, she recognised that Levic's betrayal was not the only cause of this dilemma. There was something else that was loosening the bonds of her old enchantment.

It was a lonely business, ropewalking. But she had always loved its solitude. The fact that there was only room for one person on a rope was for her its chief attraction. But in the last few weeks she had been poignantly aware that she was not alone when she stepped on to a high rope, because every time she did so, she saw in her mind's eye the picture of a woman lying crushed on the ground, her body enclosing the tiny form of an unborn child. This vision brought her out in a cold sweat and she vowed, Nothing like that must happen to my child. I won't let it. I mustn't.

It was amazing that no one around her guessed what was happening, except of course that, as strangers, they did not notice the thickening of her figure or the loss of her normal composure. She longed to confide in someone. Several times she thought of writing to Levic to tell him about the situation in the hope of dragging him back to her. But if, even knowing, he did not come, how could she bear the betrayal? And even if her words brought him back, how would he feel when he considered all he had been forced to give up for her sake? No, better to leave things as they were. She felt sure she would be able to manage on her own once she got over the next big hurdle, the walk across the Thames.

She arrived back in London four days before the event and took a room in Battersea, not caring to go back to Cheyne Walk which, besides being more expensive, housed too many memories from last August when she stayed there with Levic. On the morning before the walk she stood on the wooden bridge discussing last minute details with Tom and, gazing at the main rope stretching from one bank to the other, felt her heart sink as if it were weighted as heavy as the guy-ropes which were being dropped into place. It looked so flimsy, that rope, and it was swaying in the breeze because there were not enough stays yet to hold it steady.

'Think of it, all that work being done just for your sake, Mirella,' Tom said, sweeping his hand in an arc which described all the immediate horizon. 'It must make you feel good.'

'I wish it did, Tom, but it makes me feel rather daunted, and I must confess I shall be glad when tomorrow is over.'

'Ah, I want to talk to you about that. I know you said you didn't want to do any more big walks for a while, but Mr Baum has made us an offer I think we're going to find difficult to turn down. He wants to engage you for another four weeks in Cremorne Gardens. What do you think about that?'

'No, Tom. I'm definitely not interested. I just want to get tomorrow over and after that I'm giving up ropewalking for at least six months.'

'Why, Mirella? Why give up now, when your reputation is so high that you can command almost any fee you like? I know you said you needed a rest, but . . .' His gaze suddenly sharpened and she felt herself blushing as his eyes flickered down over her body. 'Humm, so that's it, is it?' he snorted. 'You've got yourself in an interesting condition. You idiot,

Mirella, why on earth didn't you tell me this before? Does your father know about it?'

'No. It's got nothing to do with him,' she retorted, 'or the rest of the family. This is purely my own affair and I shall thank you not to mention it to anyone else.'

'That's ridiculous. You can't keep a thing like this secret for long. How far is it advanced? I mean, how long have you got before you are delivered of your little surprise?' His tone made her wince. Although she had not expected sympathy from him, this contempt was something she found hard to stomach. On the other hand, now was not the moment for them to fall out, even if she could have summoned up enough energy for a row, so she bit back her anger and answered the question quietly.

'I think it will be born early in September.'

'Hmm, so that makes you, let me see,' Tom started counting on his fingers, 'about five or six months gone. Silly girl, you should have told me, and then I'd never have got involved in all this.'

'I'm sorry, but I wanted the money, Tom. Anyway, no one need know that I told you. Or do you think it's too risky and we ought to cancel?'

'Cancel?' he screeched, his face turning white. 'We couldn't possibly cancel now. It's far too late. Don't you realise how much money this little affair's already cost – what with the rope being rigged across the river and all the advertising and special arrangements being made with the boat companies and . . . Good God, Mirella, you must be crazy even to think of such a thing. Don't you realise there are going to be thousands of people assembling out here tomorrow afternoon, some of the nobility and even royalty, I shouldn't wonder, and all to watch you walking your rope across the Thames?'

'Yes, of course I know all that. I did the same thing last year, remember? But I wasn't expecting then and, although I've got no one to blame but myself, I don't think I should ever have taken on this walk in my condition.'

'Well, all that's by the by,' Tom said, grabbing her arm as if to shake his own kind of sense into her. 'You have taken it on, and I don't want you telling anyone else what you just told me about your condition until it's all over, d'yer hear me? Six months gone . . . oh my God, what a bloody idiot you are, Mirella!'

'Take your hand off me,' she hissed, unable to contain her fury now. 'You have no right to tell me what to do or not to do. If I decide this walk is too risky, then I shan't do it and that's that. I'm not going to risk my child just to save your face.'

'Not my face,' Tom said in a wheedling tone, 'it's your reputation I'm worried about, my dear. Anyway, let's stop talking about backing down. We both know it's out of the question, don't we? Besides, there's no need even to think of such a thing, because women walking on the rope in your condition are actually safer than at any other time. Helps them to balance by lowering their centre of gravity, you see. It's a well-known fact.'

She stared at him, before muttering, 'I wonder if anyone told Madame Genevieve that before she walked at Aston Park.'

Tom clearly had no idea what she was talking about.

'She was a ropewalker who died there, Tom, and she killed her baby too.' Her voice broke on the last words.

'For Chrissake, pull yourself together, Mirella. Stop thinking of things like that and concentrate on tomorrow. You start the walk at four o'clock so you'd better be ready at three. You don't have to worry about the gear, I shall be checking all that. But is there anything else we've got to do?'

'The guy-ropes,' she said mechanically. 'Make sure

someone's out watching the guy-ropes overnight in case thieves go after the lead.'

'That's already taken care of. Anything else?'

'Yes. I don't want to do it, Tom. I'm scared,' she whispered.

'Nonsense. You're going to be all right. All you need is a good night's sleep. I think you've got yourself overtired and are working yourself up over nothing, just like your sister did.'

She shut her eyes but could not stop the tears running down her face. Of course, he was right in one respect. She *was* tired, so tired that she was finding it hard to think straight. But his cold response made her remember Levic's concern for her last year. ''For my sake please don't take any risks,'' he kept saying, but she had felt so confident then there did not seem to be any risk in what she was doing. What would he think of me now, she wondered, carrying our child and about to risk its life in this way? He would order me not to do it, I'm sure of that, but I shall have to go through with it because I said I would and I can't let all those people down tomorrow.

'Where are you going?' Tom demanded, as she turned to walk away.

'Back to my room for a lie-down. You're right. I am very tired and probably will feel better after I've had some sleep.'

'Sensible girl. I'll walk back with you.'

'No, thank you, Tom. I'd rather be on my own.' She walked back along Battersea bridge, pausing only to scan the horizon for Crystal Palace, but failing to see it from here.

Straight into bed, but no sleep. The baby moving as restlessly as her thoughts.

There was no reason to think she might fall tomorrow, but if she did? In her mind's eye she saw herself setting out. Standing on the low platform on the Battersea bank, holding in her hands her own special

390

pole – the one she had been given by Blondin at Worcester, recently returned to her by Tom – and starting to walk up the incline to the first trestle in the river. The crowds waving and cheering her on. And would anyone notice that she was in "an interesting condition"? No. Her jacket and wide skirts kept her shape well hidden. There was no need for her to worry about causing a public scandal, so it was not that which had brought on this loss of nerve.

What then? She had lost touch with that inner sense of balance which had always kept her safe. She was no longer the same person who had skipped across the rope last year, because this baby had moved her centre of gravity. (Tom was right about that.) She was no longer drawn to the solitude of her rope. All she wanted now was to safeguard and cherish her child and she couldn't do that if she was walking a rope above the dark swirling water of the Thames.

But I've only got to do it once, and then get through the performance tomorrow evening in the Gardens, and then it's all over, she consoled herself. Surely I can manage that. I've got to. But even as she entertained the thought, her head went cold and a wave of nausea swept through her body and she felt as if her whole being was shouting, "NO!"

'What can I do, what can I do then?' she moaned, swinging her legs over the side of the bed and sitting up as if sitting up would make it easier to ward off despair. 'God, what can I do?' The question sobbed through her again and again without finding an answer. Every time she closed her eyes all she could see was herself slipping off the rope and plunging into the river. When she opened them again, she told herself firmly that nothing like that would happen, but the words carried no conviction. Whichever way she turned, she was trapped.

Unless . . . unless something in the universe came to her assistance. For instance, there could be a huge storm that would prevent the performance taking place. A thunderstorm, like the one that caused Tom's accident at Woolwich, one of Jove's bolts from the blue – why not? Such a thing was quite possible in May. There could be hurricane force winds, or a hailstorm. Whatever it was, she would immediately declare the conditions unsuitable and demand that the walk be postponed. Indefinitely. Oh, the relief! She had found a possible solution, the only one.

When the next day dawned peaceful, warm and sunny, it was clear that Jove was not going to oblige.

She felt ill, and then, worst of all horrors, when she started to dress, she found a small patch of blood on her bedgown. God, how she wished there was a woman she could ask about this. Something must be going wrong. She was sure she shouldn't be losing blood, even this tiny amount, but she didn't know what to do about it beyond what instinct dictated – put her feet up and rest.

She sank back on the bed and thought frantically about what to do. Surely Tom would understand if she sent a messenger and explained. There might even be time for him to get a substitute ropewalker so that they could avoid letting people down. After all, there were precedents. That time when she had stepped in to replace Blondin after he had cancelled at the Arboretum, for instance. But no, that was pure fluke, she had to admit. It would be practically impossible to find a substitute at this late hour. And it was unthinkable to call the whole thing off when thousands of people would soon be assembling along the banks. She had no choice. She would have to go through with it, no matter what the personal cost.

Levic, I wish I knew what you'd say if you were here. I don't want to do anything to risk our child, but I can't see any other way out. You do understand, don't you? she pleaded.

Oh, yes, she could almost hear him say. I understand

392

that your pride will force you to go through with this madness. True daughter of Madame Saqui, I salute you, and wish you well in your wanderings.

No, Levic, it's not pride. It's just that I can't bear to let people down.

Is it, Mirella? Is it just that? she asked herself in Levic's stead.

When, as had been requested, luncheon was brought up to her room, she tried to eat for the baby's sake but could manage no more than a morsel. Three-thirty and the carriage was at the door waiting to drive her through the crowds of spectators to the starting platform. She had no choice but to go.

Tom was looking anxious when she arrived.

'Here we are,' he said, opening the door with a flourish and handing her down, 'your public await you, Mam'selle.' And then he whispered, 'Come on, give them a smile, for goodness' sake. Some of them have been waiting here hours to see you.'

She forced her lips to smile, waved her hand, and then turned to look up at the rope. Despite the calm day, it was swaying slightly.

'Are all the guy-ropes weighted properly?' she asked.

'Of course they are.'

'And the crab? Did you check that the ratchet would hold without slipping?'

'Yes, of course. Do you think I'm an idiot?' he snapped. 'I told you to leave that side of things to me and I've taken care of everything.'

'But I have to be sure, Tom.'

'Look, Mirella, it's too late to start playing games now. There's just ten minutes to go before you start your walk, so I suggest you sit down for a moment and compose yourself. And for God's sake, stop looking so worried.'

She had heard that sometimes people about to die saw all their life flash before them. Something of that

393

sort seemed to be happening to her now as she saw in her mind's eye a dark-haired little girl playing near a wall with Cassie, helping her mother look after Benjie, cleaning out a kitchen grate, running along a river bank, rubbing mustard oil into a lion's fur, screaming as a vicious animal attacked Tom. Then the pictures began to change, the flashes becoming less random, linked by some sort of thread, a rope, along which she was walking between the earth and the sky, her life taking on a direction which led inevitably to Levic. And now here she was sometimes on her rope and sometimes on the ground, living with Levic, working with him and being loved by him, until he drifted away, and she was left alone on a rope which, as she looked ahead, disappeared into a mist rising up from the river so that she could not see whether it stretched any further or no.

These were all just flashes, hardly clear enough to be called pictures, passing through her mind so quickly she was barely aware of what was happening.

But at the end she felt different. She saw her life from a new perspective and was determined that something more should follow. After all, there was a child who had not yet figured and she was damned if she would go into the mist before that child had come properly into the picture.

Battersea church clock began to strike the hour. The band which previously had been playing some nondescript tune, now paused before launching itself into "See the Conquering Hero Comes".

'All right?' asked Tom, stretching out his arm to help her to her feet, 'Here, let me take your cloak. It's four o'clock. Time to start. Are you ready?'

She stood up.

'No,' she said.

'What do you mean "no"?'

'I mean I'm not going to do it.'

'Very funny,' he grinned. 'Come on, let me take your cloak, Mirella.'

'No, Tom. I mean it. I'm very sorry, but I can't go ahead with the walk. I'm ill, and it would be wrong for me to attempt it.'

He darted a quick look round as if to make sure nobody was near enough to overhear what she was saying. Then he turned back to her, his face white with anger.

'Don't mess me about, Mirella. My life's hard enough as it is. Take your cloak off and start walking up that rope. Please. You'll be all right once you start.'

'No, Tom. I'm sorry, but there's no possibility of my doing that today. I've made up my mind.'

'Mirella, I'm pleading with you. It won't hurt you to go up there this one last time. You can't let all these people down now. What on earth could we tell them?'

'Tell them the truth. Tell them that Mademoiselle Mirella is expecting a baby and that not even for the sake of all her loyal public here today will she agree to put that child's life in jeopardy.'

'Oh, very noble,' he hissed. 'But you can't really do this, Mirella. It will cause a public scandal.'

'The public love a scandal, Tom. Next to a tragedy, there's nothing they love more.'

Chapter Twenty-Six

Little Egypt was a couple of acres of what the travellers called "kekkeno mushes puv", or no-man's-ground, about a quarter of a mile from the river on the borders of Wandsworth and Battersea. The land rose steeply to the south where a railway embankment formed its boundary and Mirella could imagine how messy it must look in winter when crammed with horses, tents, caravans and carts. However, on the day that she arrived there that summer the field was smiling with daisies and sorrel and patches of pink bindweed and knotgrass, and it was almost empty, because most families had already taken to the road en route for various fairs or fruit-picking.

She had come there to look at a wagon which she had seen advertised in an old copy of the *Era*. "Living van, 12' × 6', price £20" – that was all it said, and if it had been any good the wagon would certainly have been sold by now, but seeing that the address was just down the road Mirella decided to investigate. After all, she thought, anything must be better than the squalid house she was sharing with such uncongenial people at the moment.

After the fiasco over the Thames Walk she had been unable to face seeing anyone, her family least of all, for she knew full well what they must be thinking about her. Most newspapers had featured the story of how the public's darling had been forced to back down from her famous Thames Walk because of the "interesting condition" she found herself to be in, many going on to suggest that this condition should be deemed "unhappy" rather than "interesting" in view of the fact that it seemed the young woman concerned had never entered the sacred state of matrimony.

Well, having courted the public's acclaim, now she had to bear its disdain. All right, she could see justice in that. And she did not really care what the public thought or felt so long as they left her alone to get on with her life and have her baby in peace. But her parents – especially her mother – she felt desperately sorry for, and wished there was some way she could protect them from this further humiliation.

This thought was nearly her undoing, and she closed her eyes and sobbed. All her life, it seemed, had been leading to this point. She'd been doomed from the start to let her mother down and cause her misery. All those noble ambitions, the things she had done to try to please Sadie and earn her affection! No matter how they had quarrelled, until today she had always clung to the hope that, if only she kept trying, it would all come right in the end and she would somehow find a way to win Sadie's heart. But now that hope was finished. It was impossible to believe that her mother could ever forgive her this disgrace.

She wept until she had no more tears and then, remembering that there would soon be a baby who had none but her in the world to care for it, began to pull herself together and make shift for the future.

With some of the money she had put by she rented an even cheaper room in a back street of Battersea where nobody knew her and she could simply go to bed and rest. Here, after a few days during which there was no recurrence of the bleeding, she felt strong enough to start making plans. The first thing to do was find somewhere better to live and a way of earning some money. She could clean dishes, for example. She had cleaned them before. She could do so again, if it was for the sake of her child. Later on, after the baby was born, she could perhaps get a job in one of the local taverns, serving drinks or even singing. Within reason she would not mind what she did for the sake of her child.

Then she had called upon Little Egypt and found that the people selling the wagon had already moved out, but that did not matter. What was important was that, after tapping on the door of one of the three caravans parked there, she found herself suddenly face to face with someone unexpectedly familiar. A middle-aged woman with friendly blue eyes and tawny-coloured curls straggling out from under a kerchief.

'Yes, my dear, did you want something?' the woman asked, peering down at her over the lower door while at her side the head of a child appeared, trying to peep as well.

'I came about the wagon,' Mirella started to explain. 'But, heavens, I didn't expect to find you here, Phoebe. You don't know who I am, do you?'

'No, should I? Wait a minute, though. You're not Mirella, are you? Dordy me, that's who you are, isn't it? Well, I never. Come along in, my love. This is a nice surprise. How you been keeping?'

For a moment she had misgivings. Having decided to avoid all contact with her family, here she was inadvertently calling on her father's sister whom she had not seen for years. However, Phoebe's warm welcome dispelled her doubts and she was soon sitting down inside explaining her errand and discovering how Phoebe and her family happened to be in the neighbourhood.

'We've come up for some swag,' she said.

'Some what?' Mirella asked.

'Swag. You know, prizes for the stalls. Any

showman will tell you the best place in the country to buy some cheap swag is Houndsditch, so that's where my Joby's gone this morning. He and our boys have driven the cart over there to pick up a load of coconuts and some money-boxes, china and that sort of thing.'

'So you won't be staying here long then?' Mirella asked, disappointed. Meeting up with Phoebe like this had laid bare her loneliness.

'Well, no. I expect we shall be pulling up sticks again before the weekend. We're off to Moulsey Races Fair.'

'Where's that?'

'Near Hampton Court. We open there most years. Didn't your father ever bring you up to see us?'

Mirella shook her head.

'No, I suppose he wouldn't,' Phoebe said. 'Once he settled down, our Johnny turned his back on the fair. So did Sadie. They both became proper flatties – which makes it all the more surprising that you and your sister wanted to take up the business again. How is she, by the way? We heard about that nasty accident at Crystal Palace.'

Mirella passed on to Phoebe all the information she had about Cassie and then had to face the inevitable questions about her own situation. It wasn't so bad, though. Phoebe must have been reading the newspapers, because she showed no surprise when Mirella mentioned her condition. But she obviously was concerned, especially once she realised that Mirella had set her mind against going home and was living on her own.

'And you came here today to see if you could buy a wagon? But, Mirella, where would you park it? Not on here, surely? All sorts of riff-raff use this place. It wouldn't be safe for a young girl like you to live here by yourself.'

'Oh, I'm stronger than I look. In any case, it won't happen, since there's no wagon available anyway.'

She kept her tone light, hoping to disguise the disappointment she felt. Her heart sank at the thought of returning to that filthy house with no prospect of finding any better accommodation that she could afford. At least if she had been able to buy a wagon, she could have scrubbed its interior clean and kept it sweet-smelling like Phoebe's, and perhaps even one day have moved it to more congenial surroundings in the country. She was so sick of this crowded, smoky city.

'Tell you what,' Phoebe said, as if reading her thoughts. 'If you haven't got any ties at the moment, why don't you come and have a little holiday with us? There's a spare bunk in the chavvies' wagon and you could give us a hand on one of the sidestalls to pay for your keep, so you'd be saving yourself a bit of rent money and could make up your mind about where to go before the babby comes.'

She knew that behind Phoebe's last remark was the hope that after a few weeks she might be able to make Mirella see sense and go back home to her parents. For this reason she felt she ought to refuse, except that the offer was so tempting.

'But what would Joby say?'

Phoebe laughed. 'You know my Joby. It's always "the more, the merrier", as far as he's concerned. And it will be nice for the chavvies to have one of their cousins travelling along with us. They've heard so much talk about you.'

'Oh dear.' Instinctively she bowed her head. 'The thing is, Phoebe, I feel so ashamed of myself after not doing that Thames Walk, I can't bear to face anyone who knows who I am.'

Phoebe patted her hair. 'Yes, I can imagine how you must be feeling, Mirella. But much worse things than that have happened to our family, believe me. And we survived.'

'I can't think of anything worse than what I've

done, Phoebe. Tom says he'll never forgive me for making him a public laughing stock and disgracing the family name.'

'Mirella, my love, don't think about it. Whatever you did, it wasn't a hanging matter, was it? Well then, it's not important. And our Tom has almost as much cause to know that as I have.'

Phoebe spoke with a vehemence that surprised Mirella, and she wondered afterwards what lay behind her aunt's strange remark about hanging. Perhaps there would soon be an opportunity to ask, she thought, as she packed up her possessions – for she had accepted Phoebe's invitation to spend a few weeks travelling with them.

Her presence brought their numbers up to eight, for besides Phoebe and Joby, there were their own four children – ten-year-old Billy, twins Annie and Abbie, and baby Meg – as well as Jamie, Phoebe's older son by a previous marriage. Mirella slept in a wagon with the three little girls, while Jamie and Billy slept in a makeshift tent on the ground underneath.

She found plenty of ways to make herself useful and was soon treated like one of the family. This was probably made easier by the fact that she was closely related by blood to both Phoebe and Joby.

'Tell us again how your family are related to ourn,' Abbie begged after she had tried to explain the connection.

'Well,' she repeated carefully, 'my father is called Johnny and he is the brother of your mother, Phoebe.'

'Yes, we know that, but say the next bit again.'

'All right. My mother is called Sadie and she is the sister of your father, Joby. Do you get it? A brother and sister married a sister and brother.'

Abbie still looked doubtful.

'So what does that make you and us?'

'Cousins,' she said.

'Oh,' said Abbie, clearly disappointed, 'I thought we'd be something more special than that. You see, we've got loads of cousins already.'

'Yes, I know,' said Mirella, 'they're the same ones that I've got.' Now Abbie stared at her suspiciously. 'Not all of them, I bet,' she challenged.

'Well, no. You've got some cousins called Cassie, Albie and Ben that I haven't got.'

'Good,' Abbie cried triumphantly. 'I wouldn't want anyone to have exactly the same cousins as us.'

Life with Phoebe's family was more of a rough-and-tumble existence than Mirella had ever experienced before, but it was just what she needed to bring her out of her despondent mood, and it fascinated her to think that this was the sort of life into which both her mother and father had been born.

Johnny had often told her stories of how he and his brother used to make pegs and baskets and sell them in the towns the family passed through on their way to fairs.

"We had to do it, you see, else the family would have starved. That's why I say to you and Cassie, you two young maids don't know you've been born yet, because you've always had bread put in your hands. Isn't that right, Sadie?"

But their mother would look daggers at him, making it clear that as far as she was concerned those days were dead and gone and she did not care to be reminded of them.

'Did you ever travel with my mother's family when you were young, Phoebe? I suppose you must have done, otherwise you'd never have met Joby, would you?'

'Oh dordy, yes. Sadie was my best pal for years, and we was always meeting up at fairs.'

'It's funny, she never talks about the old days. Pa does sometimes, but not Ma. Like you said, she seems to have put it all behind her. Wasn't she ever

403

comfortable in the travelling life? I mean, was she always so deadly serious about everything?'

Phoebe put down her crochet in her lap, and chuckled. 'What, Sadie? You never met anyone more wayward than Sadie when she was a chavvy. Scampe by name, scamp by nature, they used to say, and she led me into some pretty scrapes, I can tell you.'

Mirella pondered on this picture of her mother, so different from the image she'd grown up with. 'When did she change then?' she asked slowly.

Phoebe thought for a moment. 'When she had you, I suppose. She was a wild little thing before that. Drove Aunt Polly mad with all her passions. If she set her heart on something, there was no holding her. That's why her family were half-relieved when she ran off with our Johnny, even though she was so young. But then you and Cassie came on the scene and she settled down into the opposite of what she was before. It was amazing. I'd never have thought Sadie was the motherly sort. But then, having children always changes women. No matter how wild you've been before, you have to settle down a bit when there's chavvies to look after. As I expect you'll find out for yourself one day soon.'

'No,' Mirella declared. 'I'm never going to become like my mother. All she thinks about is keeping the house clean and tidy all the time. I couldn't bear to be like that.'

'There are worse vices, you know,' Phoebe said placidly, turning her attention back to the little coatee she was crocheting for Mirella's child.

It was odd being at Moulsey Races Fair and not being dressed up to parade on one of those platforms from whose dizzy heights she used to look down on the humbler sort of fairfield folk with their swings and roundabouts, coconut shies and gingerbread stalls. This time she stood in front of Joby's "All-a-Penny" booth and diffidently tried to attract customers, for she was beginning to realise what her father had meant when he told her about his early struggles to earn a crust of bread. It was a hard life, there was no doubt about that. But there were compensations.

In the evenings, when the stalls and rides closed down and were shrouded in their tilts, the travellers came together round a fire and talked and sang and danced as if this was what life was really about.

Mirella, too shy about her swollen shape to join in, sat in the shadows and watched as Joby – tubby, stolid, impassive Joby – fetched out his fiddle and played wild, haunting music that set her feet tapping. And the music brought back memories of when she was a little girl and the family gathered for special occasions – she wasn't sure where, but she vaguely remembered her grandfather playing a fiddle like Joby was playing now, or was it her own father who used to play so well? She wasn't quite sure now. But she vividly remembered seeing her grandmother, Liddy, dancing as if life depended on it. And Sadie – yes, that was more recently – Sadie used to dance too. She remembered standing awestruck at the sight of her mother dancing, on her own, coiling her hands seductively in front of her face while her eyes stared as if into some invisible fire, stamping her feet in response to someone else's clapping, and her feet gradually stamping louder and faster as the clapping grew louder and faster until Mirella watching, as now, from the edge of the circle, would find herself sobbing with the excitement of it all.

Watching everyone around her having such a good time, Mirella was suddenly aware how much she missed Levic. Many of these travellers were her kinsfolk and all had made her welcome, but that did not stop her feeling lonely in their midst, and she longed for the birth of her child so that there would be someone to fill the emptiness in her life. It was midsummer and seeing that the baby would most likely be born early in September, she had to make the necessary arrangements soon. Several times Phoebe had talked of Johnny and Sadie, and intimated that Mirella ought to be thinking of going back home, but everything inside her revolted against that prospect. On the other hand, she knew it would be unfair to lumber Joby and Phoebe with any extra burdens. What to do then? She would cling to her original plan. Find a cheap room where she could have her baby and then make shift to keep them both.

Before she could act on this plan, however, there came news through the postal service that upset everybody. It happened on the day they were leaving Moulsey to journey to Walton. At the last minute Phoebe called in at the Post Office and upon inquiry was handed a letter just delivered there from her mother.

My Dear Phoebe,

I hope you and your family are all well, and I was glad to read in your last that you have our little Mirella travelling with you at the moment. I know full well how difficult her life must be but am happy to think she is being given comfort and support by you and dear Joby. If only I had known about her situation earlier I should have encouraged her to come to me.

Dear Phoebe, I have now reached the melancholy part of my letter and there is no way of softening the blow. I have to tell you that my dear Philip passed away at eleven o'clock this morning. I was with him at the last and for me this was a great blessing, although, as you may imagine, his death has left me full of sorrow and nothing can compensate for the loss of such a dear friend and companion.

His funeral service will take place at St

Michael's Church on Friday afternoon. As you know, he was always a modest and unassuming man who disliked any fuss so it will be a simple affair.

Naturally I do not expect many of the family to attend, as I am aware of the difficulties that distance presents. Indeed, not being sure how long you intended to stay in Moulsey, I pen this letter with no certainty that it will actually find you. So, forgive me, my love, if I write no more for the moment. My heart is heavy, but it is a boon at this time to know that, wherever you are, you will share in my sorrow.

Phoebe had perused the letter and then read most of it out loud, pausing every so often to lift up her pinafore to wipe away her tears.

'Oh, Joby, I'll have to go to her,' she wailed at the end. 'Poor Ma. I know it was expected, but it doesn't make it any easier for her. She was very fond of the Captain, you know.'

'I know,' Joby muttered, hugging her to his chest. 'Of course we must go to her. We won't stop at Walton. We'll carry on straight down. Aunt Liddy deserves all the support she can get at a time like this.'

The funeral ceremony may have been simple. Mirella had too little experience to be able to judge such things. The proceedings were very dignified – as suited the Captain's manner of life. But the many people gathered at the graveside – obviously more than Liddy had expected – formed a motley crew.

For a start there were a few local business people and some of his fellow officers from the Rifle Brigade, easily recognisable in their black and green uniforms. Then there were a couple of scholarly-looking gentlemen who kept themelves in the background; possibly solicitors, Mirella thought, remembering how Phoebe and Joby had been hoping that the Captain had made proper provision for Liddy in his will. And then there were many members of Liddy's family – related to the Captain only by marriage (he had no surviving relatives, as far as any of them knew), and there to show their respect for him and to express gratitude for the support he had given her over the dozen years or so since Jem had died.

Jem – Mirella wished she could remember her real grandfather better. He had died when she was six, and all she could recall now was a man with a weather-beaten face and roguish blue eyes who used to pick her up, shake her in the air and tickle her face with his beard as he kissed her; so different from the Captain whom she found it more natural to associate with her grandmother, she thought, looking at Liddy in her mourning clothes, her hair pinned under her widow's cap.

She was talking to the two legal gentlemen – although, now Mirella came to inspect them more closely, neither of them looked sufficiently staid to be a member of that profession. Something fastidious about the way the younger man arranged his neck-cloth and the habit he had of throwing up his hands to emphasize each remark gave him a slightly foreign air; reminded her in fact of Levic. Still, whoever they were, they seemed to have a lot of respect for Liddy, listening carefully and nodding their heads to whatever it was she was saying.

She is good, thought Mirella. I don't think I could do what she is doing at a time like this. I would want to go into a corner and howl my heart out, but not Liddy. She chooses to minister to everybody else's grief before her own, and knows exactly the right words to say to make people feel better. You would never dream, to look at her, that her life had been so full of tragedy.

While thinking this, she unwittingly allowed her

gaze to settle again on the face of the young gentleman who, to her embarrassment, intercepted the stare and smiled back. After acknowledging the gesture, she quickly turned away and went to find Joey who had offered to walk her back to the house where the funeral meats had been laid out.

'Joey, the Captain would have really appreciated that piece of music you played in the church. It was beautiful, and I know Gran loved it.'

'Yes. The Captain was always fond of Bach. That's why I chose that piece. I owe him such a lot, you know. Ma was never able to afford proper lessons for me, so if it hadn't been for the Captain I couldn't have taken up music and God knows what I would have done with my life.'

'Yes, he was such a good man. That's why it's nice to see so many people here today. Phoebe was worried in case there was only your mother and one or two of his military cronies. That's why we came down as soon as we heard.'

'It's certainly a good turn-out, but no more than he deserved. Mind you, most of the folk here, apart from the military, are friends of Liddy rather than the Captain.'

'Yes, I recognised Great-aunt Femi, when I saw her. She looks ancient, doesn't she? A bit like a witch, though I wouldn't want her to hear me saying so,' she whispered, glancing round to make sure the old woman was nowhere near. 'All that weight of gold hanging from her ears. But how did she and all her family get to hear about the Captain dying? None of them can read, can they? Besides, I couldn't imagine Gran writing to let them know, because it wasn't as if he was any blood relation to them.'

'No, Mother wouldn't have told them, but she'd know they'd get to hear all the same. Travellers have their own means of communication. Goodness knows how, but news spreads like fire among them, so that if any one of them gets hurt, very soon they're all feeling the pain.'

'You don't think they just enjoy coming to a good funeral?' she asked mischievously.

'Well, there is that, of course,' Joey agreed. 'You watch Aunt Femi get her teeth stuck into the victuals. Still, that's not what I want to talk to you about. I want to know what your plans are, after this is all over. Are you going back to stay with Phoebe and Joby?'

She groaned, wishing that people would not keep asking her about her plans. If the truth were known, she had no plans, just a vague feeling that things would work out somehow and, if they didn't, then she would cope because there would be no alternative but to go on coping.

'Or will you go back home to your parents?' Joey persisted.

'No,' she muttered. 'I can't do that, so I shall be going back with Phoebe for a while and then I shall find myself a room. I've got money, you know,' she added defensively, thinking of the miserably small amount left in her savings, 'and I intend to find some sort of work after my baby is born.'

Breathless from the effort of walking and talking, she was glad when Joey paused for a moment. They were standing outside the Captain's house, looking up at the wrought-iron balcony and sad windows with all their blinds pulled down.

'This is where you should be when you have your baby, Mirella,' Joey announced.

'Yes,' she agreed lightly. 'It's a lovely house. Anyone would want to live here. What's going to happen to it, do you know?'

'Nothing's going to happen to it, as far as I'm aware. But Mother would find it lonely living here on her own. That's what I meant about you moving in. She would love to have you here, you know.'

'Joey, do you mean this is Grandma's house now?'

'Yes. The Captain left her everything.'

'Oh, Joey, I'm so glad for her. She deserves something like this after the life she's led.'

'Well, yes. But don't say that to her. At the moment she's saying she won't stay here because it will feel too empty now the Captain's gone.'

'Yes, I can understand that,' Mirella said, thinking about Levic.

'That's because you are so like Liddy in many ways,' Joey smiled. 'Which is why I said, "This is where you should come and have your baby." It could all work out so well. Mother needs company and help to run this big house. You need a proper home. Think about it, Mirella, and if she asks you, remember you could be doing her a favour by saying yes.'

At first she hardly dared take his suggestion seriously. After all, Joey spent too little time with his mother really to know her mind, and it was quite likely that Liddy had already decided to sell the house and move to a different part of the country. Furthermore what respectable elderly woman would want an unmarried granddaughter and her child taking up residence with her? No, it was sweet of Joey to want to help, but she must beware of building her hopes on such flimsy foundations.

On the other hand, as she went inside, she couldn't help noticing how lovely everything was and remembering what she had heard as a child – that this house had been designed by the Captain especially for Liddy and her younger children.

'There you are, Mirella. Come on, my dear, let's find you something to eat and a chair to sit down on. You must be tired after all that standing around.' Her grandmother's voice drew her out of the dream she had drifted into as soon as she saw the bowl of marigolds on the sideboard. Flowers so often reminded her of Levic.

'No, I'm fine, Gran. Let me get you something.'

411

'Not yet, my dear. You know, it's given me great pleasure to see you here today. The Captain was so proud after seeing you that time at Crystal Palace. Wouldn't stop talking about it for days. "To think of that little girl performing all those tricks a hundred feet above our heads," he kept saying. "Makes soldiering look like child's play." '

He wouldn't have been so proud of me now, though, Mirella thought, but said, 'I didn't know him very much, you know, but I did know . . . he was special.' She stopped, feeling awkward. How could she say what she really meant when Liddy was standing next to her, so controlled and dignified on the surface, yet obviously grieving underneath. All she could do was take her grandmother's hand and squeeze it to show how she felt.

'Two walking wounded together, eh, Mirella?' Liddy whispered. 'What do you say we join forces then?'

'Join forces?'

'That's right. You move in here to keep an old woman company, and I'll make the baby as many bonnets and bootees as it could ever want.'

'Oh, Gran,' she felt her eyes starting to sting, 'I know you're only trying to help, and I'd love to come here with you, but . . .'

'But what?'

'Do you really know what you'd be taking on? I mean, this is a respectable neighbourhood and there would bound to be gossip. It might spoil everything for you, Gran.'

She looked up sharply, not realising at first that the strange noise she was hearing was Liddy's laughter.

'Oh dear, Mirella,' she said at length, once her chuckling had subsided. 'I didn't think anything could make me laugh today, but in view of the life I've led what you've just said is so comical.'

'No, I mean it, Gran. I know you've had troubles

but you've come through them all now and I don't want to bring further problems into your life. Besides,' she paused, trying to find the right words for what she wanted to say, 'there's the Captain's wishes to be considered. I'm sure he wanted you to enjoy this house in peace and tranquillity and, well, I'm not sure he'd be happy for me to come here and give birth to a child – who will be born out of wedlock,' she added, to reinforce the point.

'No, you underestimate my Philip if you think like that, Mirella. He would be delighted to know his house will become a real family home. In a funny sort of way it makes sense of all the effort he put into creating it. That's what he would say, if he was here, I'm sure.'

After that Mirella stopped trying to think up objections and threw her arms round Liddy.

'Thanks, Gran, and I'll try not to be too much trouble to you, I promise.'

'Trouble? Having a baby in the home again – do you realise what that will mean to me, Mirella? It will mean the future when I was beginning to think only about what's past. My dear, living with me might not be that easy for you, but your child is going to bring new life into this house and that can only be a blessing as far as I'm concerned.'

Chapter Twenty-Seven

She was sitting in the garden of Linden House soaking up the August sunshine. In her lap was some linen she was halfway towards turning into a baby's gown which she occasionally nagged herself to get on with – but for the most part, the day being so warm and she so drowsy, it was more pleasant simply to sit.

Beyond the box hedge at the end of the lawn she could see Liddy wielding scissors and dropping various herbs into a basket. She had not realised before she came to live here what skill her grandmother had in growing and preparing herbs. In fact Liddy had over the years established such a reputation in the locality that there was forever someone knocking at the door to ask for her help in curing their ills, and there were few occasions on which they went away empty-handed. More usually, she was able to make them up some remedy or potion from the plants she grew herself – which, Mirella supposed, was what gave this garden such an air of beneficence.

It was hard to imagine that all this place – the house, the lawn under the lilac trees where she was sitting, the honeysuckle-covered arch being besieged by bees, the shrub borders with their fuchsias and hollyhocks and rose bushes, the golden banks of marigolds and nasturtiums – all this less than twenty years ago had been just open fields.

'When I first came here, this was a meadow,' Liddy

explained to her. 'Look, see down there where the stream is? Well, this bit by the house was all rough pasture like that in those days. And my wagon was parked, not in the orchard where it is now (the orchard hadn't even been planted then) but over there in front of the hedge where we had some shelter. And it made a kushti atchin-tan – there, that's another old gypsy expression for you.'

'Yes. "Kushti" I know that means "nice" – Pa's always using that. But "atchin-tan", what does that mean?'

'Camp-site. It's what Philip suggested calling this house, believe it or not, but I persuaded him that Linden was more in keeping. You see, an atchin-tan for me conjures up a picture of a couple of bender-tents and the family squatting round the yog. Now, do you know what that is?'

'Yes, a fire. Pa still calls it that when he lights one outside.'

This business of quizzing her grandmother about Romany words had begun merely as a game, but the more Mirella heard, the more interested she became in trying to grasp the language. At home it had been a matter of shame when her father forgot himself so far as to utter one of the old words, and Sadie would mutter, "Come on, Johnny, I don't want to hear any of that old talk. We've put all that behind us now." But here, in her grandmother's house, the language took on a richer mantle and Mirella was intrigued by the mysterious lore it seemed to wrap around; fascinated also by the incongruity of Liddy's gracious way of life when set against the background of her apparently wild past.

There were others too who were interested in what Liddy could tell about gypsy customs and language. The two gentlemen whose presence at the Captain's funeral had struck Mirella as odd turned out to be not lawyers but what Liddy called "Romany Ryes", or gypsy gentlemen. Not that they were connected by blood to the travelling people. They were simply students of gypsy customs and language, or, perhaps "students" was too dull a name for these aficionados who made a cult out of finding out as much as possible about the hidden race.

Mirella thought it must be some kind of joke when Liddy first told her about this, but eventually allowed herself to be convinced that the gentlemen concerned did in fact take their research very seriously.

'You see,' Liddy explained, 'they come regularly to visit me because they want to learn to "rakker Romany" and no trueborn gypsy will teach them. And, to be honest, I'm not sure I'm doing the right thing by obliging them. The trouble is, the language has some sort of taboo attached to it, probably because it's been kept secret for so long – and even I, who have no gypsy blood, feel I shouldn't be divulging the words to strangers. What do you think, Mirella? After all, you've got the blood, what does your instinct tell you is right?'

'Good gracious, I've never thought of myself as being more Romany than you, Gran.'

'Well, you are, you know. There's no blood much darker than your mother's people, the Lees and the Scampes, but of course you wouldn't remember your grandparents on that side. It was your grandmother Polly who taught me everything I know about herbs and remedies. A wonderful woman, she was, Mirella.'

'Yes, everybody says that. I wish I'd known her better, but I was only seven or eight when she died, so I don't really remember her that well. And then Grandad Ben died soon after, didn't he? I seem to remember Ma saying they had a double funeral for them.'

'That's right. It was the typhoid epidemic carried them both off, just like it did my poor Jem – the only

417

blessing in their case being that the pair of them were always so very close, neither would have wanted to survive the other.'

'You know, it's funny, Gran, I've never been interested in the family before, but now I'm about to have a child of my own, I want to know all about us – who we are, where we've come from, what is the special legacy I shall be passing on to my child. Does every woman feel like this when they're about to have a baby?'

'Maybe. I can't speak for everyone else, but I certainly felt something like that before each of my children was born.' Liddy's face grew sad, her dark eyes staring into the distance. 'You know, I think life is mysterious for so much of the time, but just occasionally the veil thins and allows us to catch a glimpse of meaning. Well, I think giving birth is always one of those occasions. That's why, no matter what the circumstances, the birth of a child should always be an occasion for joy.'

'I wish you could convince my mother,' Mirella sighed.

'Oh, she'll come round once the baby's born. Trust my Johnny to see to that. Now, getting back to my question, what do you think of my "romany ryes"?'

'Well, I've hardly spoken to them, but they seem to be very civil. What sort of things do they ask you about?'

'Everything you can imagine. They always turn up with a long list of questions: how would I pronounce this word, how would I spell that? You see, they spend their time going round the countryside armed with a notebook and visiting racecourses, fairs, and atchintans – anywhere where they're likely to meet up with travellers – and then they ask them about their families and their forebears and why they eat this and why they won't eat something else. Well,' Liddy began to chuckle, 'that doesn't always go down well in some quarters. Can you imagine the sort of response they'd get from your Great-aunt Femi if they asked her if she always washed her clothes in a separate bowl from her china?'

'Was that what they were asking her about at the funeral, then? I saw them both talking to her.'

'Oh, no. Godfrey and Arthur have learnt to restrain their enthusiasm and proceed a lot more cautiously nowadays. Besides, I warned them about Femi.'

'How did you come to meet them, Gran?'

'Godfrey simply turned up on the doorstep one day after hearing local gossip about this strange woman who used to live in a caravan and dispensed herbal remedies. I think he was quite disappointed to find I had no gypsy blood. Still, we got talking and by the time he left he'd managed to put down several new words in his notebook. So, very soon, he turned up again and this time brought with him young Arthur who, if anything, is even more of a scholar gypsy than his friend. You'll like him, Mirella, he's got a lively mind and a bit of character to go with it.'

'Yes, I can imagine that,' Mirella agreed, calling to mind the fashionably dressed young man who had reminded her of Levic.

'So anyway, before long the two of them were turning up regularly and we've become great friends. It really is remarkable what they have managed to discover about travelling folk that was never guessed at by themselves.'

'What sort of things?'

'Well, all the gypsies I've known have reckoned their families have been on the road since time began but they couldn't tell you where they came from. And yet, these two gorgios have made such a study of their language that they've been able to prove that the tribe originated in India and they've traced the route they must have followed and the countries where they must have stayed on the way.'

419

'They discovered all that from just listening to them talk?' Mirella asked incredulously.

'No, not just listening. Really studying the structure of the language – jotting down all the words and expressions and poring over them as if they were scientific specimens – just like Mr Darwin does. They're so dedicated, the pair of them. That is why, although reluctant at first, I agreed to help them. Can you see any harm in it?'

Mirella took time to consider before answering.

'I suppose it depends on how the gypsies themselves feel about what Godfrey and Arthur are doing. Do they object to these gorgios prying into their lives and treating them like scientific specimens?'

Liddy began to chuckle again. 'If they do, they're more than capable of handling the problem. I'm used to Arthur turning up here flourishing some new word he's been given and then watching him blush when I explain that it means something quite different from what he's been led to believe. On the whole, though, he's made himself quite a favourite. The gypsies call him their "Rye", or "gypsy gentleman", and look on him as their newspaper-cum-notary and letter-writer. You know the sort of thing. "If you see my boy Manfri down Taunton way ask him where his sister Rosie is as I'd like to be hearing from her." And he's very helpful to them like that.'

'There you are then. I don't think you should feel reticent about helping them if that's the case. In fact, what you say makes me look forward to meeting them and having a proper talk about what they're doing. You never know, I might be able to provide them with some words they haven't heard before. I picked up a few choice ones on the circus tober, if I can only remember what they were,' she teased.

'Nark it, my chavvy,' Liddy croaked in a voice that sounded like Femi's, 'you remember whose kin you

420

are and don't go showing me up in front of the fine gentlemen.'

'So you weren't born on the road, but both your parents were gypsies,' he said, his tone full of admiration.

It was overcast today so they were sitting in the conservatory, Mirella in a comfortable cane chair with her feet up on a stool.

'Yes,' she said, 'but I wouldn't have thanked you for pointing that out a few years ago. The house-keeper in the first place I worked made my life a misery because she couldn't stand gypsies.'

'Yes, I've come across people with that extraordinary sort of prejudice, but I feel sorry for them. They obviously don't know what things to value in life, so they must have a very dull existence.'

She looked at Arthur Penarvon as he was speaking. He was a languid young man of about thirty, with grey eyes and sensitive features framed by a shock of dark brown hair waving back from his forehead and a bushy beard. ''The son of a baronet and a gentleman of independent means'', was how Liddy described him by way of answering Mirella's question about how he could afford to spend so much time in pursuit of his studies.

'So how did you come to be interested in gypsies, Mr Penarvon?' she asked.

'Ah, it all began when I was in my second year up at Oxford. Just a chance encounter – or not even that, really. A face at St Giles's Fair. I've often mentioned this to your grandmother. She thinks it may have been one of the Lees or possibly a Lovell. I can't tell you because I didn't even speak to the fellow. All I can remember now is his look. Eyes deep as a man's soul and seeming to promise access to a sort of knowledge that the university had no cognisance of. Oh, I know it sounds fanciful and all too much like that chap

Arnold's poem. It's a damn fine poem, "The Scholar Gypsy", and I'm happy to admit I may have been influenced by it. Nevertheless, I also saw what I saw and I've been trying to make sense of that experience ever since.'

'And do you feel you're getting anywhere?' she asked, finding it very pleasant to listen to Arthur Penarvon talking. Despite his learning, he spoke diffidently, and sometimes so softly that she had difficulty in catching his words.

'Yes. I mean, I'm not sure. What I think I've discovered is that travelling is more important than getting anywhere,' he murmured with an apologetic smile.

'Yes, I think I might know what you mean. I knew someone once,' she said vaguely, 'who thought it better to be a person who hunts and gathers rather than one who farms and builds. Does that make sense to you?'

'Yes, yes,' Arthur Penarvon agreed, nodding his head vigorously and speaking with more animation than she had previously seen on his face. 'I'm sure your friend is right. It's the farmers and builders who tame everything and cramp the human spirit. Not that one should be dogmatic, of course. Everyone has their own path in life, but I think it is so important to leave space for the hunters and gatherers, as you call them, to move about in freedom. And it's vital that we learn from them before it's too late.'

'Learn what?'

'How to be travellers. You know, there's an old poem, Miss Granger, which talks about our life as being no more than the flight of a sparrow through a brightly lit hall. We come from the dark and we disappear again into the dark, and it behoves us not to become too weighed down in the meantime.'

Here he was interrupted by his friend, Godfrey Warrington, who sat peering over his spectacles at them.

422

'Arthur, I can hear you giving your favourite sermon again, but I'm sure Miss Granger doesn't want to hear about flying into the dark on a beautiful afternoon like this. Why don't you ask her instead about the showfolk she used to travel with. Were they connected with the Romanies, Miss Granger?'

She drew in her breath sharply and shook her head. Showfolk considered themselves a breed apart and were so proud of their own traditions that to be lumped with any other people travelling the roads was anathema to them.

'No, not the folks I was with. Mind you, they had their own language and some of the words were the same as you've read me from your notebooks. "Parney", for instance. That's what we always called rain. "Oh dear, looks like King Parney's going to reign today" – that was one of the regular jokes you'd hear on the tober.'

'How interesting. So you've never come across anyone mentioning the "Boro Duvel" in that respect, I suppose?' Godfrey Warrington asked, leaning forward in his chair to hear her answer.

'No. That's a new one for me. Wait a minute, though. "Duvel", that means "God", doesn't it, Gran? I've heard Pa say "Don't do that, for Duveleste" and I supposed he meant something like "for God's sake".'

'Yes,' Liddy said, laying aside the tiny garment she was crocheting, ' "Boro Duvel", that's the "Great God". But why, Godfrey, do you connect such words with rain?'

'Ah,' he sighed contentedly, before launching into one of the scholarly little expositions that delighted him so much. 'I heard it from one of the Lees atched by the river at Walton. He recalled that when he was a chavvy, "Boro Duvel" was often used to refer to "water". And when I asked him why, he came up with something really astounding. "Parney is the

Boro Duvel,'' he said, ''and it's also Vishnu, because it falls from the Boro Duvel.'' Well, what do you think of that? In India, you realise, Vishnu is the god of rain, so one can only conclude that here one was tapping into a deep undercurrent of tradition from the olden times. What do you say, Arthur?'

'Well,' Arthur said, reaching for his notebook, 'I think you *might* be on to something there, Godfrey. Vishnu is one of the Indian gods of rain, certainly, but we must ask ourselves if the word has come directly from the ancient Indian or if there is another possible derivation.' He consulted his notes before resuming. 'You see, I have written down here, ''Vishnu may derive from old gypsy Brshindo and that in turn from Hindu Barish and Sanscrit Varish, so I feel it would be a mistake to conclude that our English gypsy word connects directly with the Hindu god.'' On the other hand, as I say, you may be on to something. I mean it all adds to the weight of evidence. Rather like that time I drew my bow at a venture and asked one of the Hearnes if he knew what ''buddha'' meant, and to my amazement he said immediately, ''Yes, a buddha mush is an old man.'' Just think of that, ''an old man'' he said, not knowing he was giving me the correct Hindustani meaning of the word.'

And as the two men developed their arguments with mounting passion, Mirella stole a glance at Liddy to see how she was reacting to this strange performance, for it seemed to her that the pair had drifted away from the everyday world into a phantastical realm of their own making. Like she did on her tightrope and Levic did on his stage – except that people in the theatre knew when they were putting on a performance, whereas Arthur and Godfrey seemed completely identified with their roles.

Liddy was following the discussion with keen interest although there was a moment when she sensed Mirella's bafflement and turned to raise her eyebrows as if to signal that it was all really a little beyond her as well.

'Ladies, do forgive us,' Godfrey suddenly broke off in the middle of what he was saying, 'we're forgetting our manners. That's the trouble, Arthur and I are inclined to let our enthusiam get the better of us when we meet. Now, let us return to that far more interesting topic with which we started. You were telling us, Miss Granger, about the traditions of the showfolk amongst whom you travelled.'

'Was I?' Mirella asked, searching her mind for anything she might have been able to say on such a subject.

'Oh, yes. I need hardly mention that your grandmother has often regaled us with descriptions of your incredible feats on the tightrope and so we are both great admirers of your prowess, are we not, Arthur? Oh dear, am I being tactless?'

From the corner of her eye she saw the warning glance that Arthur shot in Godfrey's direction and it was this rather than the remark which caused her embarrassment. In fact, although for weeks afterwards she could not bear to remind herself how she had called off that walk across the Thames, she had now come to terms with her public disgrace. Life was too frail and too grand to waste any of it dwelling on past failures. The important thing was that she had acted to protect her baby, and it didn't matter what else happened so long as her child was born safe and sound.

'Mirella, did you hear what Godfrey just said?' Liddy's question called her attention back. She was aware the other three had been talking on about something, vaguely remembered Arthur's voice comparing the showfolks' use of "josser" to denote an outsider with the gypsy word "gorgio", but then her mind had drifted off into its own channels. If the truth were known, this seat she was sitting on was not awfully comfortable. It was making her back ache.

'No, sorry. Were you saying something to me?' She fidgeted again in an effort to get more comfortable, aware that the others were looking at her as if she were someone different. Which was odd because she thought no one else had noticed how far she was from being her normal self today. It was something to do with this heavy sort of dragging feeling in her body and the back-ache which refused to go away no matter how she moved to accommodate it.

'Yes, I think you're right, we should now turn our attention to Romany diminutives,' Arthur was saying as if following up something Godfrey had just said. 'I wonder if you have any contribution to make, Miss Granger? I mean, "chavvy" to denote "child" is universal, but what about "chai" for a girl or "chikno" for a son – have you any thoughts about either of those?'

'A "chai" or a "chikno",' she repeated dreamily. 'A girl or a boy, I don't know.'

'You see, the reason I ask is that the issue is not straightforward. Some would hold that "chavvy" holds within itself the original duality. In other words, "chavo" for "boy" and "chavi" for "girl", but against this is the evidence from Borrow . . .'

Liddy leaned over to murmur: 'Mirella, do you think you ought to go upstairs to lie down? You've turned very pale, my dear.'

Arthur Penarvon, unaware of the interruption, was reading out something about "rakli" also standing for girl, as Mirella nodded her head and started to struggle to her feet.

'By Jove, are you all right? Nothing wrong is there? Here, allow me to give you my arm,' the two gentlemen chorused, as Liddy helped her to find her balance and leave the conservatory with as much grace as she could muster whilst reeling from the first pains of childbirth.

* * *

'Let it in, let it in! Oh please, open the window and let it in before it batters itself to death.' There was a bird trying to get into the room and it kept dashing itself against the glass. Try as she might she could not get to the window and let it in.

Most of the time she knew this was just a dream brought on by fever, but each time she drifted away from the pain she heard the crash of the little body against the lattice and its agony dragged her back to consciousness.

'Oh, Gran, I didn't know it would be like this. How long will it go on for?' She first asked the question after she had already endured the pains for six hours and it did not seem possible that they could get any worse.

'It's your first, my love. The first always takes its time, but it shouldn't last too much longer now. Here, have another sup of this,' Liddy urged, proffering some more of the raspberry leaf tea she had been drinking regularly these past few weeks because it was supposed to help. But the pains went on getting worse, despite the draught of Twilight Sleep that Liddy then gave her. And now she had been writhing on this bed for nearly two days and knew she could not bear much more of it.

Crash. Battering and scratching at the window. 'Let it in, let it in. For God's sake let it in.' Another screech. She couldn't help it. She screeched and screamed. After spending so long trying not to make any noise, twisting the sheet round and round her wrist and then pulling it between her teeth to gag the noise, she screeched and screamed because she had no choice.

'Oh, Gran, I can't, I can't,' she panted.

'It's all right. All right, my love. I'm here. Just hold on. Look, grip my hands and don't try to fight the pain. Go with it when it's happening. It won't be long now. Hold on, Mirella, my love.'

'I can't, I can't stand any more, Gran,' she whimpered. Then she felt Liddy's hand squeezing hers and she opened her eyes and saw the tired hollow face and felt so angry that Liddy too should be suffering like this that she muttered, 'Don't worry. I'm all right really, Gran.' And so she was – until the pain started to tear her apart again.

And then, quite suddenly, after two whole days of travail at the end of which she felt so weak she hardly knew what was happening to her any more, her baby found its way into the world and she was holding it in her arms. A tiny raddled face under a shock of black hair that looked as weary as she felt with the whole business.

'Is he all right? Are you sure?' she asked Liddy.

'Yes. He's perfect. Got the right number of fingers and toes. I've counted,' Liddy smiled. 'So you can hand him back to his great-grandmother now and go off to sleep, my love. You've earned a good rest.'

She slept blissfully. Dreaming now of a light-filled hall with dozens of people in it going about their business. And in their midst sat a king and a queen smiling at a jester dressed in motley who threw somersaults and sang a song whose verses spun out like gossamer to snare the attention of all the assembled company. And it was not long before everyone was captivated by the jester, and she was too – listening to his song as if it were sung for her alone. Until her attention was distracted by a different sound. Looking up high into the roof she saw a little bird flying among the rafters piping its own soft tune. She woke with the music trilling in her ears, and it took a few moments for her to realise that it was her baby and he was crying for milk.

However, as the days went by and the crying persisted, she tended to forget how it could ever have been sweet music to her ears, for that shrill noise separated her from the slumber her body craved.

'Come on, give him to me,' Liddy would urge. 'Let's see if a granny can settle him.' Mirella did not need much coaxing to hand the squalling infant over, especially as it soon became clear that there was something in Liddy's touch which quickly soothed him. But then, she had always had a special way with babies. Everyone in the family said so. Mirella could not have been better placed than here in her grandmother's house, but that did not make it any easier to come to terms with the jealousy which swept over her when she saw her son finding comfort in the hands of someone else.

If her baby had been a girl, she would definitely have called her Lydia, but no such easy solution presented itself for a boy. When she looked at him, her heart lurched because she saw Levic. The same hair, same slightly hooked nose, same merriment in the eyes (when he was not bawling).

'Don't you worry about his crying, that's a sign he's got a lust for life,' Liddy said, having just taken him from Mirella and cradled him in her arms until he was calm again. 'Look, he's happy enough now. So, have you decided on his name yet?'

'No. He looks so much like . . . like Levic, all the other names I've thought of seem too clumsy.'

'Call him Levic, then,' Liddy suggested.

'Oh no, he's not Levic,' Mirella said at once. 'He's got to have his own name, if only I can work out what it is.'

'What about Stephen?' Liddy suddenly suggested. 'Didn't you say that Levic was Hungarian? Well, St Stephen was the first king of Hungary so that would be sort of appropriate.'

'Stephen,' Mirella murmured. 'No, he's not really a Stephen. What is Stephen in Hungarian, do you think?'

'I've no idea. Stefan, perhaps? I've heard of someone called Stefan.'

'Stefan. Oh, yes, that's it! You're Stefan, my love, aren't you?' She held out her hands to take him back and this time he settled contentedly in her arms while she crooned his name.

That evening when Liddy consulted her calendar of saints and discovered that Stefan had actually been born on his own feast day, the name was confirmed as a happy choice.

'Stefan, what would your father make of you, I wonder?' Mirella found herself asking almost every time she looked at her son. 'Oh, Levic, I wish you were here to see him. When he opens his deep eyes and clutches my finger with his tiny hand. He's got such delicate little fingers, Levic, and titchy finger nails and curly eye-lashes, and . . . and everything about him is so perfect that I want you to see him. And, oh Levic, he's so exactly like you I can hardly bear it.'

She kept reminding herself of the oath she had sworn before Stefan was born, that so long as her baby was born healthy and strong, she would consider herself the happiest person in the world. She had meant it. But now that Stefan had been born fine and healthy and she tried to feel nothing but joy, she failed miserably. He was such a demanding baby and she felt so tired all the time. His incessant screaming got on her nerves. She fed him whenever he was hungry, but no sooner had he finished than he was screaming for more so that, to her eternal shame, there were times when she felt like strangling him. He woke her so often through the night that she seemed to have scarcely an hour of unbroken sleep. The result was that she grew so tired that, whenever she thought of Levic, she began to weep for no reason she could explain.

What she would have done without her grandmother she could not imagine. Dosing her with soothing infusions of motherwort and taking Stefan off her hands so that she could catch up on some of that precious sleep, Liddy enabled her gradually to regain her balance. And if, at the end of a few weeks, she felt slightly less possessive of Stefan and more inclined to let Liddy take over the mother role as often as she wished then, she persuaded herself, there was no harm in this since Liddy was such a perfect substitute.

'Mirella, you've never said much about Stefan's father and I don't want to pry, but did he know about the baby before he went away?' Liddy asked one afternoon as the two of them were sitting in the conservatory enjoying the late September sunshine. It was the sort of question Mirella had steeled herself against when she first came to live here, expecting Liddy to bombard her with inquiries about why she and Levic had separated. In fact Liddy seemed to have sensed her reticence and had asked very little until now.

'No, he didn't know,' she said.

'Well, you obviously had your reasons for not telling him,' Liddy suggested. Mirella braced herself for a further question, but Liddy had picked up her crochet and seemed to be giving all her attention to that.

'Yes, I had a good reason. I didn't want him to feel tied to me in any way,' she murmured. 'Well, that was the main reason. He was going to America no matter what I said, so I didn't see any point in telling him. Besides, it's very important that he always feels free to do what he likes.'

'You mean,' Liddy said, without raising her eyes from her work, 'that when he returns, you want to be sure he's coming back to you rather than to his child?'

No, that was not right. It made her sound too petty.

'No, Gran. It's not just that. There were other reasons why I didn't want Levic to know about the baby, reasons that I wouldn't want to talk about.'

The other women. How could she possibly admit to anyone else that Levic had betrayed her, that he had destroyed what had existed between them, that even the birth of their child could never bring them back together in the same way again?

'I see. It's very hard to come to terms with other people's imperfection, isn't it, Mirella?' Liddy spoke quietly.

'No, not really, Gran. I mean, I know I'm not perfect, but . . .'

'But, like your mother, you do have your own very high standards,' Liddy suggested.

'Well, yes. In certain ways. I mean, if someone lets you down . . . I mean, it's important to be able to trust the people you share your life with, isn't it?'

'Yes,' Liddy agreed, 'almost as important as loving them.'

There was silence broken only by the sound of birds in the garden.

'But, Gran, what I'm saying is, you can't really love someone you don't wholly trust, can you?'

'Hmm,' Liddy put down her crochet for a moment and sat, head on one side, as if listening to herself think. 'Personally, my dear, I feel it's more important to trust the love than the loved one. I mean, you don't just choose to love someone, do you? Love is a blessing sometimes showered on the most ill-assorted people, God knows why.'

For a moment Mirella wondered whether Liddy was referring to her own experience and tried to recall what she had heard about her happy-go-lucky, former prize-fighter grandfather. On reflection, however, she dismissed such an idea on the grounds that Liddy was far too sensible ever to have become embroiled with someone as unpredictable, untrustworthy, infuriating and – here was the rub – lovable as Levic.

'You say love's a blessing, Gran, but I think it can be a curse. Especially when you love the wrong person.'

'That may be so, my dear. I don't know your Levic, and even if I did, I doubt I could judge whether he was the right man for you. But what I do know is that one day Stefan will want to know who his father is. And, believe me, it is very important that he finds out in the right way.' Now Liddy spoke with such seriousness that Mirella could no longer doubt that she was speaking from her own experience.

'But that's so far off in the future, Gran, I needn't worry about that just yet surely?'

Liddy sighed.

'No, there's no point in worrying about the future just so long as you do what's right in the present. All I would say to you is, do you think it's right to withhold from Levic the knowledge that he has a child? After all, what he does about that knowledge is up to him but for Stefan's sake it might be best that his father knows about his existence.'

God forgive her, she had never thought about the situation from Stefan's point of view. She had fondly imagined that she could be all in all to him, that he would never need anyone other than herself. Yet even in these first few weeks of his life, she had not been able to cope with him and he'd already come to depend on Liddy as much as on herself for nurture. Apart from that, the more she thought about it, the more she felt that Levic had a right to know about his son and that the only thing that had stopped her telling him before was her pride.

'I think you're right, Gran. Levic should know about Stefan. I shall write him a letter and tell him everything.'

Chapter Twenty-Eight

It was impossible. She had sent the letter only days ago. Yet there was the pony cart at the door and an errand boy announcing that he had a delivery of flowers for Mrs Mirella Granger. After being handed a beautiful bouquet of pink roses, she stood for a moment with eyes closed and pounding heart before ripping open the note which came with them.

> My dear Mrs Granger,
> I take the liberty of sending you these flowers . . .

She got no further. He wouldn't call her "Mrs Granger". He wouldn't write words like these. The flowers were not from Levic. It was a cruel trick. How could someone be so mean? She felt tears welling in her eyes.

'My, what beautiful flowers. Who are they from, Mirella?' Liddy asked, coming in from the garden.

'I don't know,' she replied, quickly pulling herself together and looking down the page for a signature. 'Wait a minute, though. Ah, yes. They're from Arthur Penarvon. Isn't that kind? He's heard about Stefan,' she said, reading on, 'and sends his congratulations and . . . oh dear, seems to think he should have been a little more aware of what was about to transpire (his word!) and begs us both to forgive him and Godfrey for their obtuseness when I was so clearly indisposed . . . fears they must have outstayed their welcome on the portentous occasion of my imminent confinement . . . (Gracious, was that what it was?) . . . but nevertheless is delighted to hear that I have been safely delivered of a . . . Now, what does this say? "Chikno"? What on earth is a "chikno", Gran?'

'Son,' Liddy said with a grin. 'I must say that young man has a striking turn of phrase. What did he write? "Portentous occasion of" . . . what?'

Mirella started to read it out again, but both of them collapsed into laughter before she could finish.

'I ask you – "chikno", Gran! It makes Stefan sound like something I've just hatched.' And the remark sent them off into hysterical laughter again.

'Mind you, we shouldn't really be laughing,' Mirella said between giggles. 'It's most kind of Mr Penarvon to send the roses and he means so well.'

'Yes, you're quite right. He's very considerate of other people's feelings and can always be counted on to do the right thing.'

Summer had drifted into autumn and it was Liddy's fifty-fifth birthday.

'You see, as a great-grandmother I'm no more than lamb dressed as mutton,' she joked, but beneath the remark Mirella sensed Liddy's heaviness of spirit and thought she knew the cause. For the first time in years she had not received any message from Johnny and Sadie. Phoebe had sent her a shawl, and on his last visit Joey had left for her a small package which was now opened and found to contain a brooch made of turquoise and pearls. She had not heard from Tom, but that was only to be expected since he was a notoriously bad correspondent. But the same was not true of Johnny. Mirella knew that her father thought the world of his mother and had never missed sending

436

greetings on her birthday before, and she blamed herself for this estrangement between them.

What made it worse was that she knew Liddy had written to Johnny and Sadie telling them about Stefan and almost certainly trying to find some way of bridging the gulf between them and their errant daughter. The letter had obviously fallen on stony ground. Moreover, Mirella had a nasty suspicion that her parents might even be blaming her grandmother for giving her help.

She racked her brains trying to think of a way to remedy the situation. Maybe if she wrote to Johnny herself . . . but no, she knew nothing she said would do any good.

'Come on, Mirella. We've a job to do today,' Liddy called from the conservatory where she was standing clutching a deep basket.

'What's that?'

'Blackberry-picking.'

'What, on your birthday, Gran?'

'Yes, I always think of getting the blackberries on my birthday because it's coming up to old Michaelmas Day – that's the tenth, you realise – and it's bad luck to pick them after that.'

'Yes, I remember Ma always saying that, but she never explained why,' Mirella said, unhooking a smaller basket and following Liddy out into the garden. They were only going down to the hedgerow separating the vegetable patch from the meadow so there was no need to worry about leaving Stefan.

'Well, the gypsies say that after old Michaelmas the devil spits on any fruit still left on the branches.'

'The devil? That's the "beng" in Romany, isn't it?' she asked. Now that her old energy was coming back, Mirella was faced with her former enemy – restlessness. Apart from feeding, Stefan made few demands on her since Liddy bathed him and Hettie, a servant who came in daily, washed his clothes. So, with time

437

on her hands and threatened by boredom, she decided
to learn about the herbs and remedies that Liddy dispensed to so many callers and even began to take an
interest in the gypsy lore that proved such a fascination to the "ryes".

'That's right. "Beng" is "devil", and "duvel"
stands for "god" in Romany. Now, did your mother
ever tell you that the blackberry is regarded as the
Romanies' special plant?'

'No. She always sent me and Cassie out to pick
plenty for her so that she could make pies and jam and
cordial, but surely everyone does that, not just
gypsies?'

'Ah, yes, but I wasn't referring to the berries so
much as the plant, or to be more precise the leaves.
You see the blackberry is the only plant which carries
true Romany leaves. Look at these. Do you see? Yellow, red and green – those are the Romany colours.
And your grandmother Polly swore by those leaves as
a cure for whitlows, sore fingers, ulcers and suchlike.'

'How did she use them then?'

'Ah, wait a minute. How did it go?' Liddy took
hold of a leaf and stood rubbing her fingers along its
top and then its lower surface, then began to chant:

 ' "The rough side for drawing,
  The smooth side for healing."

Yes, that's what she used to say. You soak a fresh leaf
in hot water for a few minutes, then wrap it round the
sore, placing the rough side next to the skin, and keep
renewing the leaves until all the poison's drawn out.
Then dress the wound with more water-soaked leaves
but this time put the smooth side inward to hasten the
healing.'

'And does it work?'

'Yes, I think so. Our Johnny had a bad whitlow
once that I used blackberry leaves on and it healed up
a treat.' A faraway look came into Liddy's eyes and
the wistfulness in her voice made Mirella wish she had

not mentioned the past. Then, as she tried to think of something cheerful to say, their activity was interrupted by a call from the house.

'Mother! Moth – er! Are you there?'

Liddy turned to Mirella and her face shone.

'It's Johnny,' she said. 'He's come to see us all.'

The next moment Albert and Benjie came whooping down the lawn, followed at a more decorous pace by Johnny, while – Mirella's heart quickened as she saw her – Sadie appeared round the side of the house and stood as if still trying to make up her mind whether it had been a good idea to come.

'Happy birthday, Mother,' Johnny said, seizing Liddy and kissing her. And just as Mirella was deciding that it would be in everyone else's interest if she quickly made herself scarce, her father turned round to her and mumbled, 'Well, my love, we've come a long way to see this new grandson of ours today, so he'd better be up to the mark.'

'Oh, he is, Pa. He is,' she said, reaching up to kiss him. 'And I'm so glad you've come,' she whispered, blinking back her tears. 'And that you've brought Ma.'

She glanced towards the house where her mother stood with a tight expression on her face, clearly not prepared to make any further move towards her. Mirella wanted to run to her. Throw herself into her arms and beg forgiveness. Say or do anything to bring a smile into that face. But she knew Sadie's code of behaviour would not allow anyone to storm their way into her affections, so she curbed her natural impulses. Still, she was determined to do everything she could to bring about harmony, especially as her mother had come here today not just for the sake of Liddy, or for herself, but for Stefan. What would she make of him? wondered Mirella.

'Now, before you boys do anything else, there's the cart to be unpacked and the horse to deal with,'

Johnny was saying. 'Can I leave all that to you, Albert?'

'Yep,' her brother said, jerking his head sideways to flick the hair out of his eyes and grinning shyly. 'Do you want me and Benjie to bring all the stuff into the house, Dad?'

Johnny looked towards Sadie, raising his eyebrows in inquiry. She glanced at Liddy who took the hint and said, 'You're going to stay the night, I hope? There's plenty of bedding and you don't want to do that long drive twice in one day. You will stay, won't you, Sadie?'

'It's all right by me, if that's what Johnny wants,' Sadie muttered.

Johnny nodded his head and quickly signalled the boys to make a start, as if afraid that, given half a chance, Sadie would change her mind.

'Ma,' Mirella murmured, 'will you come up and see the baby now?'

'Hmm, give me a chance to get my cloak off first, won't you?' Sadie said ungraciously.

'Of course. I'm forgetting how tired you must be after that journey. What you need is a cup of tea before anything else.'

'I'm seeing to all that, Mirella,' Liddy called over her shoulder as she disappeared towards the kitchen. 'You just take your mother and father into the sitting-room and make them feel at home.'

She did try. She really did. Took her mother's cloak. Sat her in the most comfortable chair. Racked her brains for something inoffensive to say that would melt the ice between them. Nothing worked. In the end she was reduced to exchanging platitudes with Johnny until it seemed that he could stand the tension no longer and made some excuse about going to fetch his baccy to get up and leave the room.

'Shall I see if your tea's ready?' she asked her mother in desperation.

'No. I haven't come all this way to drink tea,' Sadie grumbled. 'I've come to see this poor little wretch you've seen fit to bring into the world.'

Mirella felt herself bridle but managed to check her temper and say quietly, 'Will you come up and see him then, Ma? He's in my bedroom.'

'I'm not sure. I think I'd better wait for your father.'

'Please come and see him, Ma,' she begged.

'All right, but I think it's a shameful thing you've done, Mirella, and just because we're here today doesn't mean to say . . . Well, all right. Take me up to see him then.' Sadie rose to her feet, straightened her skirt, and followed Mirella upstairs in grim silence.

'There,' Mirella whispered, pushing back the blanket to expose more of Stefan's face to view. He stirred in his sleep, sighing and making sucking movements with his lips. Sadie stared down at him. He turned his head, gave a moaning cry and again began to suck noisily at the empty air. 'It's nearly time for his next feed,' Mirella explained, deciding to pick him up before he started to howl. Still Sadie said nothing. 'Here, could you hold him for a moment for me?' Mirella asked, placing Stefan in her arms and moving towards the window to let in more light. Then, after standing there fussing with the curtains for some moments, she wandered over to a cupboard and purposely kept her back turned while listening to Sadie's voice cooing, 'Hello there, my little one. My, what beautiful big eyes you've got and . . . there, that's right, take your granny's finger. Are you hungry then? Never mind, your mummy's just getting herself ready to give you some milk.'

Sadie's voice was soft and warm as a downy quilt – the same soft warmth which had wrapped itself around Mirella as a child, soothing away her tantrums, keeping her from harm. This was the mother she loved and, yes, the one who loved her.

Sadie, always there to help – if she was asked. Sadie, who expressed her love by criticising and nagging in an effort to find any weakness so that she could bind it up and save her little one from getting hurt. And having to carp and nag because that little one was always too proud to admit she had any weaknesses.

Mirella's eyes filled with tears. This was the scene she could never have imagined: her mother glowing with happiness as she showered love on her grandson and allowed herself to respond to his innocent enchantment. She sat herself down on the low chair she used when feeding him and, when Sadie eventually handed him over, it was with the words: 'He's a lovely boy, Mirella. A real credit to you. Just wait till your father sees him in a minute.'

'Albert, did you bring in that packed pillowcase from the cart?' Sadie demanded, once they were all sitting down after luncheon.

'Yep. It's in the hall. D'yer want it?'

'Yes, please,' she said, smiling and shaking her head at Stefan who was lying in her lap. 'Just a few little things Cassie and I made for him. Not much, I'm afraid, but now I've seen his size I can easily do more.'

'Ma, they're beautiful! Look at this, Gran,' Mirella said, holding up the lacy jacket she had just pulled from the pillowcase, 'and there's mittens and leggings to match. Oh, he's going to be the best-dressed baby in the neighbourhood. But, how is Cassie, Ma? You said she was working, but doing what exactly?' Once the excitement of seeing the rest of her family had died down, she had begun to worry about Cassie and wonder whether there was any sinister reason why she had not come today.

'Making bonnets. Knowing she's got that nice little sum of money behind her, she arranged to be taken on by that big millinery establishment in Windsor with the idea of starting up in business for herself one day.'

'Oh, that sounds splendid. And is she happy doing that sort of work, Ma?'

'Of course she is. Cassie knows that with her leg she's lucky to be employed at all. Besides, making up hats is a perfect occupation for a girl before she's married, so don't you go telling her any different. Not that you'd get far. She's learnt her lesson the hard way, poor Cassie.'

'Yeah, I don't think she's going to want to wander far from home again,' Johnny agreed, lighting up his pipe and stretching out his legs. Then, after Benjie sidled up and whispered something in his ear, he nodded. 'Yes, I'm sure your grandmother won't mind. The boys want to go down to the stream. That's all right, isn't it, Mother?'

'Yes, there's lots of interesting wildlife down there. You never know what you might see, if you go quietly,' Liddy told them. 'It's where your uncle Tom used to spend all his time when he was a lad. By the way,' she added, as Albert and Benjie went out, 'have you heard anything from Tom lately? I haven't had any word since Philip died and, although he's never been the world's best letter-writer, that's a long silence even for Tom.'

Mirella saw the change come over Johnny's face as his brother's name was mentioned. He glowered, his moustache bristling over his pursed lips.

'I know he'd gone back to travel with that Menagerie again,' Liddy continued, seemingly unaware of the raw nerve she had touched, 'Wombell's, wasn't it? But I don't know what he's doing with them – whether it's animal-training or some other act he's got together.'

Johnny started to speak, spluttering with rage.

'No. He's got another act going. Hasn't he, Sadie?'

She nodded her head. 'Yes, he certainly has,' she agreed, staring at Johnny. 'Go on, tell them what it is. Tom came to see us a few weeks back, you see – but, go on, Johnny, you tell them about it.'

Johnny took a long draw on his pipe, blew the smoke out slowly and then began to speak in a calmer voice.

'Well, he turned up at our place one afternoon and Sadie and me were both pleased to see him. I mean, it was bad what happened to Cassie but not altogether his fault, and give a man his due he put himself out to look after her interests properly after the accident happened. Anyway, be all that as it may, as far as I was concerned, the past was bygone. So there's Tom on the doorstep, and I'm thinking he's come to see how Cassie is getting along and that's all to his credit too.'

'Was Cassie at home then?' Mirella asked, trying to work out what Tom could have said or done to upset her father so much.

'No, thank God,' Sadie said. 'She'd already started at the milliner's.'

'Anyway,' Johnny resumed, determined now to finish the story he'd been persuaded to start, 'there's Tom asking to see Cassie and me thinking he's simply concerned about her welfare, but no, it soon becomes clear he's here because he wants something.'

'Wants something?' Liddy echoed.

'Yes, and you're never going to believe what, Mother. By this time he's sitting in our parlour drinking our tea, telling us about this wonderful new act he's working on. No, not savage animals this time. Nor tightrope walking miles above people's heads. Something easy this time – like throwing flaming knives as near as dammit to a human target. Honestly, without a word of a lie, that's what he's doing.'

'But I don't see what he wanted with . . .' Liddy started to say. 'Oh, no. Not Cassie. He surely was never thinking to ask your Cassie . . .'

'That's right. You've hit it. He wanted our Cassie to stand target in his crazy one-armed knife-throwing act.'

Mirella felt like laughing. And crying. Tom with his

mauled arm throwing knives at poor crippled Cassie. How could you do anything but laugh and cry at such an idea?

'But, Pa – Cassie would never have let herself get involved in anything like that again, would she?'

'Not while I'm alive, she won't. "Look, Tom," I said, "our Cassie's training to be a milliner now." And the bugger looks at me and says, "She'll never make money at that. You let her come back on the road with me and I can offer her a much better future." ' Johnny broke off suddenly, looked at Sadie, and they both started grinning like a couple of children.

'So what did you say, Pa?' Mirella prompted.

'Didn't have much chance to say anything. Your mother emptied the milk jug over him and called him more names than you'd think she knew. He got up and I added a few more, and I swear to God, if he hadn't been maimed, I'd have knocked him to Kingdom come, brother or no.'

'Dear, oh dear,' Liddy murmured, shaking her head. 'My poor Tom, when will he ever learn that people aren't objects?'

'Not while he's throwing knives at them,' Mirella observed. 'But fancy you hurling the milk, Ma! I bet that stopped him in his tracks.'

'Yes,' said Sadie, 'and he was lucky it was the jug and not the tea-kittle I had in my hand. Still, it's all over now and after what your father said to him, I don't think he'll try getting any of our family involved in his schemes again.'

'Oh dear,' Liddy said again, and Mirella knew how her grandmother hated there to be any ill-feeling in the family. Fortunately her father realised this too and hastened to set her mind at rest.

'Still, don't you worry, Mother. There was no blood spilt. Only milk. And we didn't spend any time crying over that, either. So although Tom and me didn't part good friends exactly, we haven't become enemies either. We kept it very civil, didn't we, Sadie?'

She ignored his question in favour of leaning over to nuzzle her head against the baby gurgling on her lap.

'Anyway,' Johnny continued, 'trust Tom to fall on his feet again. The Menagerie opened in Windsor last week and – this nearly slayed me – there was his name on the bill! ''The Great Kazan in his Sensational New Knife-throwing Exhibition.'' And one of our blokes went along to see it and said what Tom did was get this young girl to stand up against a board and keep perfectly still while he threw these bloody great knives all round her, getting some of 'em so close they stuck in the gaps between her fingers.'

'Ugh!' Mirella shuddered. 'But how does he manage to hold the knives, Pa?'

'Evidently he settles them in a fan shape in his bad hand and makes the fact that he's maimed add to the drama of the act. And you haven't heard the worst yet. Not content with nearly stabbing the girl, he then sets light to the knives and throws them till she's outlined in flames.'

'Poor girl,' Mirella sighed, realising how easily she might have found herself standing target for Tom at one time. He had such extraordinary powers of persuasion when he wanted something. Still, she hoped she had learnt enough about herself now not to fall so easily under anyone else's influence again. And she had Tom to thank for this hard lesson.

'So who did he find to help him in the act at such short notice?' Liddy was asking.

'Ah, you might well ask,' Johnny said, pulling on his pipe to drag out the suspense.

'He's got a married woman to do it,' Sadie cut in, voicing her disgust. 'Someone you might know, Mirella, seeing you travelled with the same outfit. Her father owns the show – or maybe it's her husband who owns it. They're all part of the same family, anyway.'

'Lily!' Mirella exclaimed.

'Well, I couldn't tell you her name, but whoever she is she ought to have more sense,' Johnny said. 'But there you are, it beats me how Tom always gets others to do his bidding – be they beasts or men.'

Or girls, Mirella thought. She was amazed that Lily would allow herself to become involved with Tom again, yet she wasn't altogether dismayed at the idea. Lily partnering Tom in his act at last. Why not? After all, they had been using each other for a sort of target practice for years now and maybe it was time for their relationship to be pinned down!

Chapter Twenty-Nine

'Are you sure you're warm enough?' Arthur asked, leaning over to tuck the rug more closely round her.

'Yes, I'm fine,' Mirella smiled back at him, but still pulled the hood of her red cloak forward to cover her head more effectively, for they had set out early and it was very cold this morning.

'Mirella, I am most grateful to you for affording me this opportunity,' he added. 'It would otherwise be impossible for me to present myself at such a gathering.'

'Why? You knew Darkie quite well, didn't you?'

Arthur looked embarrassed.

'Could any gorgio get to know Darkie Cooper well?' he asked, biting his top lip.

Mirella laughed. 'I know what you mean. The old devil was a bit daunting, wasn't he?'

Arthur nodded his head, as if being reminded of past skirmishes he preferred to forget.

'Yes,' Mirella went on, 'he and Aunt Femi made a ghastly pair. Still, you shouldn't take anything they said too personally, Arthur. It's just that neither of them were ever prepared to suffer gorgios gladly. They even gave Gran a terrible time when she first took up with my grandfather, you know. You can imagine it, can't you? Femi and Darkie suddenly confronted with the prospect of this little gorgio girl joining their precious clan!'

It had all happened so long ago – more than forty years – and Gran usually finished up laughing when she recalled some of the outlandish things that had happened to her in her youth when Femi and Darkie had been so hostile to her.

'Let me see if I've got the family clear,' Arthur said. 'Your grandfather was Jem Granger and Femi was his younger sister, so Darkie Cooper must have been his brother-in-law.'

'That's right. But the Grangers and Coopers are connected in several other ways, too complicated for me to explain – you know how certain travelling families tend to intermarry a lot – so most of the folk at the funeral today will be related to me in one way or another.'

'Fascinating,' was Arthur's comment before turning his attention back to the horse to negotiate a badly rutted section of the road.

No, not fascinating, just sad, she thought to herself, remembering Liddy's face when the messenger said he had been instructed to let her know that Darkie Cooper had just died over at Blackwater and would be buried the following Tuesday.

'I shall have to go,' Liddy said hoarsely. 'Femi was always so good when Jem and I had troubles, and look how she made the effort to get here for Philip's funeral even though her Darkie was lying so ill back home. Oh dear, she's going to take it hard. They've been together all their lives, those two. Pledged in the cradle, almost.'

'But, Gran, you can't go anywhere in this weather,' Mirella had remonstrated. 'You've just had a week in bed with bronchitis and you're not properly well yet. You'd be asking for trouble. There, see what I mean?' As if to prove her point, Liddy had collapsed in a fit of coughing as soon as she tried to argue.

'Who's going to go if I don't, then? There's Tom gone way up north, and Phoebe down in the West Country. Your father wasn't able to take time off from his work even for my Philip's funeral, and there's no time to get word to Joey even if I knew he was free to go.'

'Well, if I can get Hettie to look after Stefan for the day, I'll go,' Mirella had immediately offered.

'No, I wouldn't want you to go on your own. I'll dose myself up with something tonight and make the effort. I couldn't bear to let Femi down at a time like this.' The following day, however, Liddy had to admit defeat when she could hardly get her breath stepping out into the frosty air.

'Look, Gran,' Mirella pleaded, 'let me go to represent the family at Darkie's funeral. It will give me a chance to meet up with the relatives again, and I can tell Aunt Femi why you're not there. I'd really like to go.'

After that, it had been quickly decided. Hettie, the mother of a fine, bouncing son a week or so older than Stefan, willingly agreed to act as wet-nurse for the day, and even the transport arrangements fell into place once Liddy remembered Arthur Penarvon. In the course of their last discussion he had asked her a lot of questions about gypsy attitudes to death and burial and, as she predicted, leapt at the chance to accompany one of the family to Darkie's funeral.

'Are you sure Aunt Femi won't mind his being there?' Mirella had asked anxiously.

'No. She would if he was a stranger,' Liddy said, 'but he's been over to Blackwater several times since meeting her here, and he's spent hours chatting with poor Darkie, so I think they'll be pleased to see him and take it as a mark of respect that he should appear at the funeral.'

The only other point at issue – the matter of propriety when it came to a bachelor gentleman driving about the countryside with a young unchaperoned woman – was firmly laid aside by Mirella who said that, seeing Mr Penarvon had been generous enough to offer his help, she would consider it churlish to refuse on such grounds. Furthermore, any doubts she may have had were all dissolved by the enjoyable experience of driving beside him along the Hampshire roads in this smart equipage. She could not remember the last time she had gone out in a carriage, and although she had found it difficult to tear herself away from Stefan this morning and continued to fret about his welfare, it was good to be doing something which took her mind off Levic and the anguish of never receiving a reply to her letter.

The camp at Blackwater was packed with people come to pay their last respects to Darkie, for although known throughout his life as an awkward, forbidding sort of character who had made many enemies, all was forgiven now that he had succumbed to their common foe, the mulo-mush. People stood round in quiet groups, talking and occasionally casting glances towards the grey tent set apart from the rest to notice who was coming out and how affected they had been by their sight of the body.

'Will we be allowed to go in there to see him?' Arthur asked, and his words jarred because she was looking round and just beginning to realise that these were her folk and they were in pain and that she had come here today to grieve with them.

'I don't know,' she answered, leaving his side in order to go and find her great-aunt.

'She's up in the wagon, my love. With her sister, Omie,' one of her relations said, pointing to a dark red caravan in the corner of the field. 'You go on up and talk to her. She'll be glad to know you're here.'

But after climbing the steps she thought she must have come to the wrong caravan, for neither of the two old women sitting inside looked anything like Femi. The elder was plump and had a crinkled brown face like one of last year's apples. The other looked like some crazy woman from the woods, her frizzled grey hair hanging loose over her shoulders, her dark brown eyes glassy and staring until there was a flicker of recognition.

'It's little Mirella, isn't it? Come on up, my love. Have you been in to see your Uncle Darkie yet? Don't you be trashed. He looks wonderful peaceful now.'

'Hello, Aunt Femi,' Mirella murmured, feeling suddenly shy. Her great-aunt carried on speaking.

'Yes, he looks handsome again. His face gone back to just how it was when we wed. It got so bloated, you know, near the end when he began to lose hisself. But not now. My Darkie's back to looking really handsome, isn't he, Omie?'

'Yes, they've laid him out nice,' Omie agreed, exposing a pair of toothless gums as she spoke. 'Now tell me who this is again,' she said, peering as if purblind.

'I told you,' Femi said. 'It's Mirella. Our Jem's granddaughter. You know, Johnny's little gal, the one who does the ropewalking. That's right, isn't it, my love?' she turned back to Mirella for confirmation.

'Yes. Well, at least I used to . . .' Femi interrupted her before she could finish.

'And is your grandmother here? She'd know what I'm going through, because she lost our Jem and, God forgive me, I never knowed then how she must have been suffering.'

'And me,' Omie muttered, 'I was widdered young, remember.'

Femi ignored her sister's remark. 'I haven't let nothing bar water pass my lips since the mulo-mush took my Darkie, you know, and I've vowed I won't wash my face, nor comb my hair, nor eat a crumb of the good Lord's bread till he's laid safe in the earth. It's not much, I know, but it's all I can do for him now and I'm trying to do it all the way he'd have liked, 'cos my Darkie was deep in the old customs and he wouldn't rest if any of us transgressed today.'

'So, is Liddy here?' Omie asked.

'No, I'm afraid not,' Mirella said, going on to explain why her grandmother had been unable to come in person but had sent her instead.

'That's all right,' Femi said, clearly disappointed. 'I know Liddy, and she must be proper poorly not to get here today, so you look after her when you get back, d'yer hear me? And you go over now to look at my Darkie, so's you can tell her how nice he looks in his coffin,' she said, her voice faltering and her eyes starting to glaze over again.

'Yes, I'll do that. Oh, and Aunt Femi, Mr Penarvon is here with me. He wanted to come over and pay his last respects to Darkie.'

'Mr Penarvon?' With an effort Femi concentrated on the name for a moment. 'Penarvon? Oh, you mean the gorgio mush who used to come and tickle our ears. I was surprised my Darkie entertained sech nonsense, but there it was. The rye used to turn up with a nice bottle of summat in his pocket and a string of questions as long as his face, and Darkie mused hisself by faking a pile of bosh. Still, the mush usually went away smiling and Darkie's spirits didn't suffer none, so I couldn't see any harm in it.'

'Is it all right if I take him in to see Darkie, then?' she asked tentatively.

'Yes, you take him in, my love. We've nothing to be shamed of over there. He's looking handsome, isn't he, Omie?'

Omie nodded her head. 'Yes. Femi's got him laid out like a king. His watch and chain on his chest and gold sovereigns on his eyes and in his hands. And he's got all his best things with him so's he don't miss 'em where he's going. Yes, she's looked after him all right. She's done him proud.'

'Well, he's always bin a good man to me, so least I can do is make sure he goes off right,' Femi muttered.

After taking her leave of the two women, she paused on the wagon steps to survey the people. Like a dark

454

field splashed with blood, she thought. Everyone was wearing something in red, the colour of mourning – most of the women dressed like herself in red cloaks, while the men had black suits with red waistcoats or neckerchiefs, or had pushed into their lapels one of the little rosettes made of red ribbons being handed out at the gate. And although everyone seemed to be talking, they were keeping their voices low as if reluctant to disturb the hush hanging over the gathering.

'Sarishan, Mirella. How's your grandmother? We heard she's not well.' The same greeting met her at every turn. She answered their inquiries briefly, but no one detained her long once they realised she was with Arthur who, no matter how polite, as a gorgio made them feel ill at ease at a time like this.

'I'm going over to take a last look at Darkie. Aunt Femi asked me to,' she explained, wondering why she sounded apologetic.

'Would it be all right if I came with you?' he asked, with scarcely disguised enthusiasm.

'Yes. Aunt Femi said you can go in to pay your respects if you wish.'

He was obviously delighted to have been granted this privilege and she was glad to have been helpful to him. At the same time there was something about Arthur's attitude which was beginning to disturb her and she felt uncomfortable to be the one taking him into the death tent.

'Oh.' The coffin was resting on three low trestles and inside, his face pillowed in white satin, lay Darkie, the guttering light of the candle burning next to his head causing shadows to dance over his face. She had assumed he would look like the stern old man she remembered, only asleep – like she so often saw Stefan asleep. But he did not. He looked like no one she had ever known – not Darkie, not anyone. He looked only like Darkie's dead body, discarded and left behind. Handsome, yes. She could see what Femi

455

meant. The marble face unlined now and sculpted
back into the family likeness – clear brow and high
cheek bones and sleek moustache framing his firm
mouth. A fine garment – Darkie had always been
meticulous about his clothes – which a man had worn
and now cast off.

'Why do they place the sovereigns over his eyes and
between his fingers like that?'

She winced at the sound of Arthur's voice and,
shaking her head to signify that this was neither the
time nor place to be asking such questions, continued
to dwell on the silent memories coming into her mind
as she gazed at Darkie. His cherished possessions – his
precious cup, his knife and fork and spoon all wrapped
up in a crumb cloth, his violin, even his best set of
harness (yes, he'd like to think they put that in) –
were all tucked into the coffin around him. And she
noticed too the grain and chunk of bread that it was
customary to put in the coffin. And the fact that
Darkie was going to his Maker wearing his best suit
and silver-buckled shoes. He had been a strong character, this Darkie Cooper, and she felt glad to have
known him.

'Kushti sarla, Uncle Darkie!' she whispered, hardly
aware how she came to remember the old farewell.

'What was that you said in there, Mirella?' Arthur
was quick to ask once they were outside again.

'Only goodbye,' she explained.

'Yes, but it sounded like something in Romany,' he
persisted.

'No, it was just goodbye,' she said.

After the hearse arrived, drawn by six red-plumed
black horses, poor Femi was led in to witness the
coffin lid being screwed down, and then a long procession formed to walk to the church. The only
unusual thing in the service which followed was the
tone of the vicar's sermon as he took advantage of the
occasion to inveigh against the evils of drink and

exhort his unfamiliar congregation to find themselves more often within the portals of God's house.

'If that was for Darkie's benefit, I'm afraid he's left it a bit too late,' Mirella murmured to Arthur as they filed out into the graveyard.

'Yes, your people aren't known for their regular church-going, are they? And yet, when it comes to their personal conduct, their sacred taboos and social mores, you couldn't call them immoral, could you? Which is why I'd really like to question one of the elders about their religious beliefs . . .'

She stopped in her tracks and stared up at him with increasing irritation. At home in Aldershot she had found his conversation impressive, but here surrounded by the people he professed to be so interested in everything he said sounded banal.

Darkie was buried as close to the hedgerow as possible. As his coffin was lowered, two of his pals played a dirge on their fiddles while the rest threw down handfuls of earth and coins and, once the hole was filled, watched as Femi poured a jug of mulled ale over the grave. And then it was all over apart from the burning of his vardo.

'I'd love to know why they find it necessary to burn all his stuff like this,' Arthur said, as he and Mirella took their place in the circle gathering round the caravan that had formerly served both Femi and Darkie as home.

'I think it might be just to prevent bad squabbles in the family about who gets what,' she suggested, remembering something Liddy had said about there being a rumpus over some jewellery left to her by Femi's mother years ago.

'There's that, of course, but there's bound to be a more esoteric reason behind such a huge sacrifice. Take Darkie's wagon, for instance. Who in their normal mind would consign that to the ashes unless they feared the dead man might come back to haunt it?'

'Well, I wouldn't mention that to Aunt Femi, if I were you. She'd tell you she doesn't want to get rid of Darkie and she'd welcome him back to haunt his stuff, if that's what he wanted.'

'No, you don't understand, my dear. He wouldn't want to be trammelled by the past. He'd want to be set free as soon as possible. I'm sure that's why they burn all his possessions. So that he isn't held back by them and can thus find repose more easily where he's gone.'

She thought about this as she watched Darkie's bed being torn up and strewn all over the caravan floor, and then the shafts and wheels being thrown in on top of it together with all sorts of other items he had cherished when he was alive. There was a collective sigh as the whole lot was then dowsed with paraffin and a lighted torch tossed inside. Then someone behind her started to argue that something or other was too precious to be sacrificed and that was why the fire was not taking hold. Whereupon one of Darkie's sons hurled a stone through the back window and caused a draught which made the flames roar and soon there was no holding back the destruction.

Mirella stopped thinking about possible significances now. It was enough that this was the tradition and that, mysteriously, the act of standing in a circle and watching Darkie's things go up in flames brought them all into some kind of unity, gave them a heightened sense of sharing in the loss. A mood of acceptance came over the crowd and they stood in silence until the vardo was completely consumed.

'Kushti bok, Uncle Darkie,' she whispered, closing her eyes. 'Good luck on the journey.'

'I'm sorry,' muttered Arthur, having just knocked her with his elbow, and she saw that he had his notebook out and was busy writing. ''Items thrown in fire: bedding, clothes, hat, pair of boots, harness, whip . . .''

'Arthur, what will you do with all that information

you've collected?' she asked, as they were travelling home later that afternoon.

'I might one day turn it into a book,' he announced. 'But not yet, of course. There's so much more I need to find out.'

'And what would be the purpose of writing such a book?'

'Well, how can I explain it to you? By recording as much of the language and customs of your people as I can – before their way of life has been eroded by the so-called progress of this century – I hope to spread a greater understanding of them among our scholars. You see, Mirella,' he continued, his eyes shining with enthusiasm, 'so much is now known about the ancient races of the world and the origin of the human species, and yet here we have these fascinating people in our midst possessing their own language and customs and we allow ourselves to remain ignorant of them. It's a tragedy, because the travelling people have so much of value to teach us if we study them closely.'

'Yes, I'm sure you're right, so why don't you go and live with them? Buy yourself a small caravan and travel . . .' There was no need for her to say any more. She had seen the look of horror cross his face.

'No, no. That would not be appropriate. I go and talk to them and they look on me as one of themselves, you know. Mind you, some of them don't know what to make of it when I go up to them and start to "rokker Romany". Utterly amazed, they are, that a gentleman like me should know their lingo, but that's all part of the fun of it, you see. Still, there'd be no point in travelling with them when I can find out all I want to know by study and observation.'

Dinnilow, she thought, you don't really understand them at all. Nevertheless her irritation dissolved, and she began to feel sorry for Arthur. The life of a romany rye, a gypsy gentleman, must be a lonely one, she thought. Neither gypsy nor gentleman. Like walking a tightrope between two worlds, never committing yourself to either. It was fun walking a tightrope, she knew that. But it was always lonely. Especially when your rope, like Arthur's, seemed to stretch out into nowhere and you walked it simply to keep yourself above other people's heads.

I can't help liking him but he's so different from Levic, she brooded. Arthur's more interested in studying life than living it. And into her head came a picture of the great hall in the ancient poem that he had mentioned and she could see him with his eyeglass peering intently out of the windows, while Levic as a bird was flying through, singing for all he was worth.

She heard the baby wailing the moment the carriage wheels stopped.

'Thank you for driving me to the funeral, Arthur,' she said, 'I don't know how I would have got there otherwise. But you will please excuse me if I dash in. I can hear Stefan crying.'

'Of course. But it is I who should thank you for letting me take you there. For me it afforded an occasion which, although sad, was not entirely devoid of interest with regard to my studies and I look forward . . .'

From the house there still came sounds of the baby howling.

'I'm sorry. I have to go.'

'Of course. But I hope this will prove to be the first of many such occasions – the rest happier in circumstance, naturally – and that you and I, Mirella, will be able to venture forth together . . .'

She did not stop to hear any more but rushed in to find out what was wrong with her baby. By the time she realised her mistake – that it was Hettie's child kicking up a fuss at having to share his mother's precious milk and that Stefan was perfectly happy – it was too late to apologise to Arthur for leaving him so abruptly. He had already gone.

460

Chapter Thirty

A fortnight to go before Christmas and it was hard to admit even to herself how low she was feeling. There was no reason why she should not be content and every reason to be grateful for her present way of life. Stefan, now more than three months old, was thriving, and she adored him. She was very fond of Liddy and continued to profit from her companionship. Neither could she complain of being burdened by domestic worries, since Liddy and Hettie between them took care of most of the household chores. No, she had to admit, life at Linden House could hardly be more agreeable. Yet this eternal restlessness inside her threatened to spoil everything if she did not manage to hold it in check.

It was late afternoon and she was sitting in the drawing-room gazing into the fire trying to decide whether to fetch her cloak and take another turn round the garden or pull herself together and write Cassie that long overdue letter.

'Tell me, Mirella, are you upset because you haven't heard from Levic?' Liddy suddenly asked.

'No. I didn't really expect him to write back.'

'What's troubling you then?'

'Nothing. I'm fine,' she lied.

'I can't believe that. You haven't been yourself for weeks now. Not since Darkie's funeral, when I come to think of it. Did that upset you in any way?'

'No, not the funeral, Gran, although I suppose . . . Well, I was worried about you and your bronchitis at the time, but now you're better and life has settled back to normal and . . . oh, I don't know . . . but there's nothing wrong, truly.'

'You mean you're bored.'

'No, of course not,' she sighed. 'How could I be bored when I've got Stefan to look after and you to talk to. And there's this lovely house, and Christmas just round the corner.'

'Easily, if you look back to last year when you were a star in some London theatre. I realise that life down here must seem very tame in comparison. But all I can say is, be patient, my love. You're still very young – and I'm sure there are a lot of exciting things up ahead of you.'

'It doesn't feel like that, Gran. Since Stefan was born I feel as if my life has slowed down. Not that I regret it, of course. I could never regret having Stefan. He *is* my life now. But it's just that part of me finds it difficult to accept that nothing will ever be the same as it was before he was born.'

'You mean your tightrope walking?' Liddy asked.

She nodded. It was easier to think it was just her work that she missed.

'But there's nothing to prevent you taking that up again, if you really wanted to,' Liddy said.

'No, I couldn't do it again. I think I've lost my nerve.' She looked towards her grandmother, expecting some kind of sympathy as she said this, but was surprised to see her grinning.

'You lose your nerve! That will be the day,' Liddy chuckled. 'No, don't you fool yourself, Mirella. If you wanted to walk a tightrope, you'd walk a tightrope, and nerves wouldn't come into it. So I think you'll have to look a little more deeply than that to discover why you're dispirited.'

Now she felt annoyed, although she didn't know

why. Of course it was just the tightrope walking that she missed. The excitement, the danger, the ecstasy of walking that narrow thread through the sky. The feeling of being alive when she was doing it. Confronting danger. Risking her life to feel alive. How could anyone who had never experienced such excitement begin to understand how dull life was when that stimulus was taken away? It was the dull routine of her present life that was getting her down. It had to be.

But if it was, then Liddy had just given her the answer. She could get up and change her life. Not immediately, of course. But after Christmas. There was Stefan to consider, but she could go back to show business. Walk the rope again, if she wanted to. Go to America, perhaps. Walk across Niagara. Imagine that.

She sighed. Go back to ropewalking, yes, but would that really provide any answer?

She thought back to this time last year. She had been performing at the Highbury Barn over Christmas, that's why she had not gone to Berlin with Levic.

She groaned as she remembered that dreadful row they'd had when he first announced he was going and almost commanded her to go with him. That had happened almost exactly a year ago. And she had insisted that she had commitments that would keep her in England. And of course that was true. But it was also true that her pride had been hurt and that she had reacted out of pique because she had never been able to stand anyone bossing her around. And that had been the beginning of the end of everything between them, her and Levic, because he admitted that almost immediately he had turned to someone else after he left her. And she would never be able to forgive him for that.

Except that there was a sense in which it had not been the end but the beginning of something between them, because already in her womb in early December Stefan had been conceived.

She went to bed that night with these thoughts going

round and round in her head. Her life was becoming a torment. Every night her dreams were so haunted by Levic that, on waking, she reached out her hand expecting to feel his body close beside her. She longed for his arms to encircle her, his hands start to caress, his voice whisper, "Mi-rrell-la, I love you." She wanted him so much. Instead, she touched emptiness. Levic not there, and she might never be with him again. Never again feel his caress, hear him whisper her name, know the ecstasy of coming together and being his.

To remain on earth but never be with Levic again – that she could not bear. She didn't see how she could carry on living without Levic – unless . . . Unless she went back to ropewalking and worked so hard there would be no time left to remember or regret.

But how could she possibly convey this to Liddy after all she had done for her and Stefan? And yet, although it would be hard to tell her grandmother, she felt she had to act quickly before she gave way to despair. What should she do then? Tell Liddy what she had decided. Buy a copy of the *Era* and begin to look for work. And Stefan? She wasn't sure. Take him with her, if possible. It would be difficult, but she would manage somehow. Or maybe leave him here with Liddy until she got on her feet. Her grandmother, she felt sure, would welcome that. And with Hettie as wet-nurse, Stefan would be well looked after. As his mother, she would like to think she was indispensable to his welfare, but the way she had been feeling lately forced her to admit that this was not true.

Her new plan did not make her feel good, but it made life seem possible again. Even after days of castigating herself, acknowledging that Sadie would have been less selfish and made a much better job of being a mother, she still in the end had reluctantly to admit that she had no choice. Had to admit her own limitations and do what she had to do.

After breakfast about one week before Christmas, she was walking back from the newspaper shop with a copy of the *Era* in her hands folded so that she could scrutinise the advertisement columns as she walked. Walking blindly, she nearly tripped when startled by Liddy's voice shouting her name.

'Mirella, Mirella!' With only a light indoors shawl clutched round her shoulders, her grandmother was flying along the road to meet her. Instinctively she started to run as well.

'What is it? What's wrong?' she cried.

'Nothing's wrong. It's just that I wanted to give you this,' Liddy gasped, thrusting an envelope into her hands.

'A letter? For me?' She turned it over in her hands, glancing at the foreign stamp. 'It's from America,' she stammered. 'It must be Levic.'

'I know,' Liddy said. 'That's why I wanted you to see it straight away.'

'Oh, Gran. You shouldn't be out here without your coat. Come on, let's go inside before you catch another chill,' she said hurriedly, squeezing the envelope in her hand as if, after all this time, she would have preferred to make it disappear rather than reveal contents that might disappoint her.

'Aren't you going to read it?' Liddy asked once they were standing in the hall and Mirella had hung up her cloak.

'In a minute. It's funny, I've been waiting for this so long that now I can hardly bear to open it in case Levic has nothing meaningful to say to me any more. Can you understand that, Gran?'

'Yes, I know what you mean, Mirella. I spent two whole years longing and dreading for news from the Crimea when my son Jemmy was fighting there in the war, so I know how you feel.'

'Do you mind, then, if I take it upstairs and . . .'

'No, of course not. It's only natural you want to

read it on your own. So you run along to your room. But don't forget, I'm here if you want me. And if you don't want to talk about it afterwards, then that's fine. We'll say no more about the matter.'

Her hands were shaking by the time she got to her room. This is stupid, she thought, I don't really care what he's got to say anyway. It's just the shock of suddenly hearing from him after all this time, that's what it is. To give herself a little further respite, she went over to Stefan's crib and stood for a moment looking down at him. Apparently aware of her presence, he opened his eyes – enormous dark eyes full of Levic's intensity and her own restlessness, she thought – until he spluttered and gurgled at some joke that was all his own.

'What are you laughing at, you little rascal?' she murmured, chucking him under the chin until he rolled his head from side to side with pleasure. 'Don't you realise I've got a letter here from your daddy which I'm about to open so that I can find out what he thinks about you?' Stefan continued to roll his head from side to side, all the while keeping his gaze fixed on her as if defying any attempt to take her attention away from him. 'No, it's no use, Steffi, I can't put it off any longer. I must open it and see what he says.'

She sank down in a chair next to the window, turning her back to Stefan as if to shield him from anything that could be construed as rejection by his father.

My darling Mirella,
No doubt this letter from me will come as an unwelcome intrusion into your life after all this time and I apologise if this is so. Yet I feel impelled to write.
My darling, for that is how I still think of you, Mirella – the only true love of my life – I realise it may be Christmas before this falls into your

hand and I want to wish you the happiest of festive seasons despite the fact that for me it marks a most melancholy anniversary. You may have forgotten, but it is almost exactly one year since I made that fatal decision which changed the course of our lives in a way I have never ceased to regret.

(*Come on, Levic, why so stilted? What do you think about Steffi? Are you horrified? Or glad? Please be a little bit glad. Her eyes scanned down the page, but in the absence of any obvious reference to 'baby' or 'Stefan', she returned to read on more carefully.*)

Well, I know it is no use regretting what cannot be changed, but I want you to know, Mirella, that for the first time in my life I do have regrets. I regret parting from you to go to Berlin. I regret what happened there, because it lost to me the only person I have ever truly loved.

Oh, my darling, if only you could find it in your heart to give me another chance, I swear to you things would be different. You and I together again, Mirella – think of it, my love, travelling the world together just as we always planned.

Which brings me to the point where I want to convey to you some idea of what life is like here in this vast new country – except that I doubt I have the skill with a pen to do it justice.

(*But our baby, Levic! Why aren't you mentioning the baby? She skimmed again to the end of his letter.*)

. . . Well, my darling, I must draw to a close despite the fact that now I am writing to you I would go on forever if I thought I could paint a picture of life over here that you would find irresistible. For it offers so much that is wonderfully exciting, and indeed for me falls short of perfection in one respect only – the lack of your dear presence . . .

(*She skipped again*)

. . . in any case, I write this with painful lack of certainty that it will reach its proper destination. As you see, I address it to your parents' house in the hope that, if it does not find you there, they will forward it to wherever you are . . .

(*But I put Liddy's address clearly on my letter and told you . . . Oh, no! Levic, I see now. My letter never reached you. You don't know about Stefan. You don't know about anything that's happened, Levic. Oh, God!*)

She started to cry. It was all so stupid and unfair. She had written and told him weeks, no months, more than three whole months, ago – and waited and waited for the reply which never came, thinking that he didn't care, that he didn't want to acknowledge the child, had found someone else – any reason to explain the long cruel silence. But that her letter had never reached him – she had not really considered that possibility. Even though now, when she read over the itinerary of his American tour – the sheer amount of travelling he had accomplished in the last few months and the outlandish places he had visited – it was obvious how easily a letter could go astray.

And now at last he had written, and she longed to pack a bag and grab Steffi and go to him. But she couldn't. He still didn't know about the baby and she had no idea how he would react when he found out. And what was worse, he was so very far away. Over three thousand miles. Three thousand miles away – when this letter saying he loved her made her want to fall into his arms. Oh, Levic!

She sat in the chair and sobbed for a long time. It was all so impossible. She took up his letter again. Read the bit about America. Read the last paragraphs again. His present engagement was due to last over Christmas and then for a further six weeks. After that he was free of commitments for a while and (wait a moment, she hadn't really taken this part in when she read it before) . . . and he intended to come back to England for a spell and hoped that, if she was agreeable, they might meet up again.

Six weeks after Christmas. That would take them into February. Plus the journey time, of course. But to think that then she would see him again! And he would see Stefan. In two months' time. She sighed. Two months. It felt like a lifetime.

Liddy was at work in the kitchen when she went downstairs. Wearing a coarse hessian apron and sitting on a high stool at a table covered with newspapers to keep it clean, she was in the midst of polishing her silver ready for the luncheon party arranged for the following day; nothing elaborate, just a modest affair to welcome Joey home when he arrived back from Sydenham for the Christmas holiday. His former music-teacher had been invited, as well as Godfrey and Arthur and, having sent Hettie into town to buy one or two delicacies, Liddy had taken it upon herself to make sure the cutlery was presentable.

'Oh, Gran, why didn't you say you were doing this? Let me fetch an apron and then I can help.'

'That would be nice. I must confess this isn't one of my favourite jobs,' Liddy said, making a grimace.

Mirella expected to be asked about Levic's letter, but no question came until, trying to keep her voice steady, she opened the subject herself.

'Levic never got my letter, Gran. He's written to me – and it's a lovely letter – but he didn't get mine so he still doesn't know about Stefan. And the thing is, I know I should immediately write back, but he's still on the move and I can't be sure he'd get my next letter either.' She stopped, aware of the mounting hysteria in her voice.

'But he's written, that's the main thing,' Liddy said calmly. 'Does he mention coming back to England at all?'

'Yes,' Mirella said, now with her apron on and sitting down at the other side of the table ready to help. 'Once he finishes his present tour – which should be about February time – he's coming back then.'

'There you are. That's not long to wait, and it gives you something to look forward to over Christmas.'

Mirella picked up a cloth and pulled a pile of forks towards her.

'You don't think I should write again, then?' she said, beginning to apply some paste.

'Yes, write to him if you've got an address. It can't do any harm.'

She thought about that as she continued to rub on the paste. His letter was so full of love and regret and hope, it made her want to forget all their past differences and start again. But could it possibly be as simple as that? Had Levic really changed?

She called to mind his description of life in America – the acclaim he had received when he appeared in the Hippotheatron building in New York, the pride he felt when he was presented to President Grant, the excitement of travelling west by railroad, covering more than a hundred miles a night to reach the next city by dawn and then sitting down to eat breakfast with two hundred fellow artistes who made up what must be one of the greatest shows on earth.

Through all his words shone the ardour of ambition and commitment. He loved his work and he wanted her to come and share in it. Conditions, especially when they were travelling, were rather primitive, he explained, but the management was friendly and he knew they would take her into the company – *if* he could persuade her to apply.

"Yes, write to him. It can't do any harm," Liddy had said. But it could. It could. Telling him about the baby now might spoil everything. Levic had established himself in America, but the sort of life he led left no room for a child. If she wrote and told him about Stefan, he would almost certainly be horrified and regret having contacted her again. February would come and go, and he would not return to England and she might never see him again. And she couldn't bear the thought of that.

'Mirella, do you mind if I say something?' Liddy's quiet voice interrupted her thoughts.

'No, not at all.'

'Well, there's really no need to be so thorough with those forks. I shall be rubbing them over again with a washleather in a minute anyway.'

'I'm sorry,' she said mechanically.

'No, there's no need to apologise. I'm sure you're doing it right. But look, this is a quick way I've found to remove the paste from between the prongs.'

Mirella watched as Liddy picked up a fork, stabbed it into an old linen cloth and jerked it up and down several times.

'Gran!' she exclaimed with mock horror, 'you're not supposed to do it like that.'

'I know,' Liddy agreed, looking guilty, 'I know I shouldn't really, but it saves so much time.'

'Right. Well, I'll do it your way then,' Mirella said, feeling her spirits beginning to lift.

This would be the first time Joey had set eyes on his great-nephew so, wanting Stefan to look his best, she dressed him in the gown and bonnet Sadie had made.

'There, you'd steal anyone's heart now,' she murmured, placing him back in his crib while she got herself ready to welcome the visitors. Red dress or green? she wondered, before deciding on the green because red reminded her of mourning cloaks and she was determined not to be despondent today.

After all, it was clear that Levic still thought of her

471

with affection. That made her happy. She had decided she would write again to tell him about Stefan. And in case such news influenced him against coming back, she would continue to look for work after Christmas. Possibly as a rope-dancer.

Last night she had a dream in which she was walking above the trees while crowds of tiny people below stood watching her. There she was, skipping effortlessly along with her balancing pole in her hands until – horror! – glancing down, she saw she had made a mistake. It wasn't a balancing pole in her hands. It was Stefan. She had brought Stefan up on to the rope and was trying to walk along holding him. But whereas she had found it easy to walk along the rope before, now that she was aware of his presence she was too terrified to make a move. As she stood paralysed, it started to rain and she knew she had to get Stefan to safety before the rope grew too slippery. She forced herself to step forward again, and found she could manage even with a baby in her arms. She glided along easily and even had time to glance up and notice that the sun was out and shining through the rain to form a rainbow up ahead.

She was woken as usual by the sound of Stefan crying for his feed but could not forget the sight of that rainbow. All morning the mood of the dream stayed with her. She even found herself humming a carol as she brushed her hair, fixed it back with a comb, and patted it in place. She was in the midst of putting in her second pearl earring when she heard the front doorbell being pulled and Hettie going to answer it.

Joey, she thought, because it was still too early for the other guests. She went to Stefan, who was making restless noises in his crib, and took him up into her arms, excited at the thought of showing him off to Joey. She listened again to the noises downstairs and after recognising Joey's nasal voice, realised he had not arrived on his own but had another gentleman with him.

Her heart sank and she started to tremble. Not Tom, surely. Please, not Tom. That would spoil everything today. Still clutching Stefan, she stole to the top of the stairs to see who it was.

Sure enough, down in the hall stood two men in greatcoats. And even though both had their backs to her, she recognised that one was Joey in the act of embracing his mother who had just come out to greet him. Then he started talking – obviously introducing the other fellow and explaining why he was there. He had met him at the railway station and they'd shared a cab, she heard him say.

Thank God it wasn't Tom. This man was at least a couple of inches taller than him, and thinner. Besides, there was something altogether more stylish in the way he dressed, she thought, staring at the back of the light drab greatcoat. Suddenly she froze. She could see only his back and the top of his head with its wavy black hair, yet this was enough to put her in mind of – yes, Levic. And once she had that idea, she seemed to be hearing his name and his voice and to grow more and more convinced that it was he – while at the same time knowing that it was impossible for him to be here.

Then, with these thoughts whirling around in her mind, she began to take in something of what was being said by that precise, musical voice echoing up from the hall.

'Her letter, you see, must have been following me all across the continent . . . received it the same day I sent mine . . . you can imagine how I felt . . . a son . . . so I dropped everything, broke my contract and came immediately. I had to see her.'

It sounds like Levic, but I mustn't think he's really here because in a moment I'm bound to wake up and find out I've been dreaming, she warned herself.

All of a sudden, though, the people down in the hall

473

turned with one accord and stood gaping up at her. Liddy and Joey and – Levic. Yes, Levic, it really was Levic in the flesh! And he was gazing up at her as she stood here holding Stefan in her arms.

'Mirella,' he murmured, moving towards the stairs.

And she stepped towards him. Without a thought, stepped straight into space and found herself falling, slipping and falling, twisting her body as she fell, trying to protect Stefan.

And continuing to fall as if forever. Aware of shouts and someone rushing up towards her, but more aware of this strange sensation of floating through the air as if in a dream – without fear, because she knew someone was there to catch her.

There was a thump as her body collided with his, then a gasp. It took a moment for her to realise that she had just fallen down half a flight of stairs and, still clutching Stefan, landed safely in Levic's arms.